Honor & Evie

ML, Summer '08

Susannah Bates was born in Suffolk in 1970. While reading English at Durham University, she co-wrote her first play, *Smoke*, for the Edinburgh Fringe, where it was nominated for the *Guardian* Student Theatre Award. She then went on to study law in London and qualified as a solicitor in 1997. She practised law in the City until she gave it up to become a full-time writer. Her first novel, *Charmed Lives*, was published in 2001 and selected for the WHSmith Fresh Talent promotion. She is now married with a son and living in London. *Honor and Evie* is her third novel.

Also available by Susannah Bates

Charmed Lives
All About Laura

Honor & Evie

Susannah Bates

C̄

Century · London

Published by Century in 2007

1 3 5 7 9 10 8 6 4 2

First published in the United Kingdom by Arrow Books 2007
Random House, 20 Vauxhall Bridge Road,
London, SW1V 2SA

www.randomhouse.co.uk

Addresses for companies within The Random House Group Limited
can be found at: www.randomhouse.co.uk/offices.htm

The Random House Group Limited Reg. No. 954009

A CIP catalogue record for this book is available from the British Library

ISBN 9781846052682

The Random House Group Limited makes every effort to ensure that the
papers used in its books are made from trees that have been legally sourced
from well-managed and credibly certified forests. Our paper procurement
policy can be found at: www.randomhouse.co.uk/paper.htm

Typeset by SX Composing DTP, Rayleigh, Essex
Printed and bound in Australia by
Griffin Press

For Robin

Acknowledgements

Thanks to the following for the help they have given me in the research and writing of this book: Oliver and Annabel Bates; Charlie Bicknell; Charlotte Bush; Ellie Clarke; Philip Cranworth; John-John Crichton; Charlotte Eagar; Fergus Gilroy; Justin Gowers; Charlie Gurdon; Robert Hardman; Rose Horne; Gail Lynch; George Meyrick; Annabel Sebag Montefiore; Anthony Newman; Claire Panta; Alison Rae; David Rennie; Emma Rose; Andrew Scott; Anna Simpson; Alison Thomas and Clare de Vries.

In particular, thanks to Kate Elton and Justine Taylor – my editors at Random House – and to my agent, Clare Alexander, without whose expertise, inspiration and good judgement this novel would never have been written.

But most of all, thanks to my husband and my parents. I feel fortunate to have had such considered involvement and support for my work from the people I am closest to; fortunate that they are brave enough to tell me when they think I am going wrong as much as encourage me when they think I'm doing well. I hope that the time and effort they have given to this book and its writer have been justified, and that they know how deeply they are valued.

PART I

Chapter One

Honor's Cabinet

After they leave Earls Court, the tube trains on the District Line heading out to stations with grassy names – Parsons Green, Southfields, Wimbledon – come up from underground. They rise to daylight and the backs of people's houses; to an expressionless face at a window; to droopy lines of washing, flaky woodwork, the closed tidiness of some lawns, the neglected blur of others; to an open rattle on the track. The succession of snapshots is still punctuated by the odd dark dash of tunnel – a sudden muffle – but never for very long. The wheels roll faster. The stations spread out. Doors open to gusts on the platform and fading advertisements. Carriages get emptier. The trains head west and south over a river that in terms of class and house prices, as much as land and water, still maps a wavering line.

Evie Langton lived with her parents on the cheaper side of the line. That's not to say there weren't parts of Putney – even then, in the late eighties – every bit as prestigious as Kensington and Chelsea. Some of the houses, particularly the large Georgian ones over-

3

looking the water or the whitewashed villas further east with their sprawling gardens and iron gates, had a hushed elegance that certain Londoners – Londoners who cared more for space and river breezes than postcode snobbery or having haute couturiers on their doorstep – actively preferred.

But that was not the Putney the Langtons inhabited. And while they counted themselves lucky to be living in the row of terraced houses that made up Morland Road, it could hardly be described as glamorous. Flanked by industrial warehouses on one side and a railway line on the other, it had not inspired decades of planning authorities to care too much about protecting the original soft brick from angry fists of concrete that had sprung up in the gaps. Cigarette ends lay in the gutter. The gothic church at the very far end, with its stained orange sign – 'Jesus Lives!' – seemed on rainy days rather to imply the opposite. And Evie, at nineteen, was starting to notice something more than water in the liquid boundary that separated her from Honor, her cousin and her friend, who lived in casual splendour on the other side of the river.

Until that year it hadn't mattered where they lived, so long as it was close. It hadn't mattered that one of them was richer. And Honor's father had been more than happy to keep it that way – blur the line – pay for his niece's boarding school education, include her in their family holidays, fund her air fares, her ski hire, her sailing tuition . . . William Montfort liked being generous. It wasn't his sister's fault that she'd fallen for an artist with more charm than money. They'd all fallen for him. With his scruffy trousers, weathered hands and total indifference to wealth and status, Giles Langton had exactly the qualities the Montforts most

4

liked. They had been thrilled when Rachel had married him.

Of course, there were times when the man could be exasperating. No, he wouldn't be wanting any farmhouse on the Favenham estate, they were really very happy in Putney. And no, he and Rachel weren't up for a skiing holiday that year – knees playing up. In any case, he had a mural to finish in Wales. But while Giles could always find an excuse when it came to accepting things for himself or for his wife, with Evie it was different; particularly, Evie's schooling. And when William offered to pay for Evie to board with Honor at some smart establishment just outside Bath, Giles had no difficulty in accepting. Any doubts he might have had about the other things – the holidays and restaurants, the sudden shopping trips – any qualms he had about spoiling his daughter or raising her expectations were invariably countered by Rachel.

'Darling, it's a chance in a lifetime . . .'

'You want her to give it back?'

'But all her friends are going . . .'

'Oh Giles, do be sensible. She's got to have something to wear.'

Looking at them now – squashed together on the far side of a kitchen table that had seen better days – Giles hoped he'd made the right decision. At the time it had seemed so simple. How kind of William. How lucky they were that Evie should have the same start in life as Honor.

But what Giles had failed to consider, back then, was the extreme proximity of the two girls' lives, and the kind of effect it might have on his daughter. Perhaps it was latent sexism on his part. A decade ago, one little eight-year-old girl had seemed pretty much like

5

another. He'd have sat with them as he was doing now, but then they were just a couple of kids: giggling, tiresome, frequently silly . . . entirely interchangeable. He paid very little attention to children in those days. Rachel and Xandra, William's wife, would talk at length about their daughters' varying characteristics, but to Giles such motherly talk was impossible to take seriously.

Somewhere in the back of his mind, he must have imagined Evie and Honor leaving school as similar as they'd been – to him – as little girls: same schools, same holidays, same friends, shared grandparents. At no point did he foresee the effect the two girls would have on each other; or how, more particularly, the subtle differences that had existed in them as children would lead them into the polar opposites they now were.

He couldn't say when it was that he'd started to notice it happening. But the more time they spent in one another's company, the more extreme those poles became, until it was impossible to say whether Evie liked wearing black because she was naturally rebellious, naturally rougher – or because Honor was so fond of cream and white. Impossible to say whether Evie was sullen and awkward because of something inherent – or simply because Honor was so light, so cheerful, so poised and polite, so sunny and attentive, so perfectly at ease.

There they sat now, with their backs to him, bending forward over a large package that sat on the floor. There was Honor: her hair held back in a butterfly clip, the line of her jaw completely visible, completely smooth. Her spine was very straight, in spite of the bending. She leant from her hips, reaching forward with careful fingers, picking neatly at the sellotape, easing the paper off.

And there was Evie – hunched forward, radiating impatience: 'Just *tear* it, Honor.' Giles couldn't see her face. These days he rarely did, so quick was she with that shield of hair. But in her own way she was just as transparent as her cousin. Giles could tell Evie's thoughts from the interested tilt of her shoulder, the angle of her elbow at the edge of the table, the tight curve of her knee as she held it in with her other hand. He saw the bitten nails.

'. . . Oh, for God's sake . . .' And before Rachel could stop her, Evie had sprung forward and ripped away the wrappings.

One rough yank was all it took. Through the gash in the paper a small pair of door handles were visible. A curving panel. A pretty set of legs. And – lifting the rest of the paper aside – Honor revealed her birthday present from them all. It was a little cupboard in plain greyish wood.

'Oh my goodness . . .'

'Happy birthday,' said Rachel, refilling Giles's teacup.

'How lovely! How—'

'Lovely?' said Evie, looking at her father with a raised eyebrow.

Ignoring her, Giles turned to Honor. 'I thought I could paint it for you,' he explained, coming round to the girls' side of the table. 'You know, like that ottoman I did for Charles's twenty-first. I thought you might like some say in what you wanted me to put on it – which is why it looks a little—'

'Plain?'

'No, Evie! No.' Honor spun round. 'Really, not at all,

7

Uncle Giles! It's wonderful! It's very kind of you.' She kissed him. '*Thank* you. I love it. Love it already – and that's before you've done a thing. I'll take it to Oxford with me in October and have it right by my bed and . . .'

Giles smiled. 'Well, perhaps you should wait and see how it turns out. You might find that you prefer it plain. But I've got some photographs of other things upstairs, if you need any ideas. I thought perhaps you'd like some scenes from Suffolk, and maybe Switzerland – and even London, if you want. Your mother seemed to think that a few reminders of all your achievements at school might be nice. She mentioned a tennis trophy you won at some tournament in Frinton, which would look great in the centre here, if you . . .'

Honor looked uncomfortable.

'Or I could do a pair of crossed racquets, if you'd prefer something a little less showy? Or . . . or your oboe? I'd need to borrow it to see how the reed works, but it would look great along this panel, here – or perhaps along the bottom?'

'And what about her Laser dinghy?' said Evie, amused. 'You can't miss that out. And her pony, with all those rosettes she won? And you'd better not forget the Deportment Cup, Dad. Aunt Xa would never forgive you for that. Or her costume from playing Nancy in the school play . . . oh, and her head girl's badge! And—'

'Evie—'

'In fact, are you sure the cupboard's big enough?' Evie managed, before Honor took the string of sellotape she'd been toying with and slapped it over her cousin's mouth – smothering her laughter and holding it there until sounds of muffled submission convinced her to let go.

Giles met Rachel's eye across the kitchen – both smiling, both conscious that if anyone knew how to control their daughter and steer her into more civilised behaviour then it was Honor.

But it was a strange sort of friendship. With her taste for the offbeat and her dislike of the conventional, Evie should by rights have loathed her glossy cousin. Instead, and with a healthy dose of teasing, she adored Honor – expressing that love in the perverse, passionate, loyal, partisan, personal, excluding, wilful, possessive, furious way that came to her most naturally. Honor was her best friend. Evie didn't really believe in any other kind of friendship. It was all or nothing. Anything in between seemed somehow suspicious – or false.

And Honor returned the loyalty. Evie wasn't an easy friend. She was moody and critical, quick to take offence. Most people turned away at the first sign of trouble. But Honor – with deeper reserves of patience – seemed to understand her cousin's moods. She rode out the storms and stuck by Evie, nobly taking the blame for her cousin's misdemeanours when they were younger and always insisting that Evie be included in whatever game she and her friends were playing: hopscotch, kick-the-can, spin-the-bottle . . . no matter that the others found her difficult and odd.

Not that it was gratitude that bound Evie to Honor. No, it was more an understanding that – past vast gardens of cultivated niceness – Honor still had some raw ground. There were wilder places beyond the walls that Evie would seek out from time to time. She knew how to provoke Honor into gagging her with sellotape. She knew that Honor wasn't quite as swept and mown and perfect as she seemed. Admittedly, it was harder to get through these days. Honor was ordered; her desires well clipped. When she was with her own family, or out with her blander crowd of friends, her particular blend of manners and charm was as baffling and artificial – and pointlessly circuitous – as an Elizabethan maze. It was only here in Putney – here, where Honor was safe and accepted no matter how silly or strange her views; or out alone, just the two of them, with Honor having drunk rather too much . . . only then would she become the person Evie loved. Only then would she be real – and admit to petty irritations, naughty thoughts, random ideas, irrational leanings.

Sometimes, if Evie was really lucky, she might even get Honor to swear. She'd nearly tipped her over just now – why, she was within inches of telling Evie to fuck off and stop winding her up about the little cabinet. If Giles and Rachel hadn't been there too, Evie was *sure* she'd have said it . . .

And that was the Honor she recognised and loved: the one that could still say 'fuck' and smother her in sellotape. But it made Evie sad that Honor didn't like that side of herself; sad, that all Honor's efforts seemed geared in the other direction . . . and later that evening, she said as much.

Honor kicked off her shoes and smiled. 'You sound like Abe,' she said, leaning against the wall of Evie's bedroom and taking the cigarette Evie offered.

It was nearly eight o'clock. Tea had been cleared and Rachel was downstairs, cooking supper. Giles was in

10

his studio, making notes from the ideas they'd had about the little cupboard. Honor should have been driving home – back across the river to her parents' house in Kensington. She'd done what she came to do. She'd had tea, opened her present, discussed her options, and now it was time for her to leave. Tonight, of all nights, she needed to be early. Instead, she couldn't drag herself away from the warmth of Evie's little bedroom, and the subject of her new boyfriend.

'. . . I can't wait for you to meet him.'

'He'll be there tomorrow night, won't he?'

'Of course.' Honor put the cigarette to her lips and inhaled. 'In fact, I've placed you next to him – so you can both spend all dinner plotting how to corrupt me. I assure you he has plenty of ideas . . .'

Evie grinned. She liked the sound of Abram Wyatt. With the kind of parties Honor's mother insisted she attend, and the kind of people Honor was mixing with these days, Evie had half expected her to fall into dating someone 'suitable', someone who worked in the City, or studied law at Cambridge, or – or something truly dreadful (and truly interesting, to someone of Xandra Montfort's ambitions) like land management.

Instead, Honor had found herself an actor – fresh out of drama school with one major TV series already under his belt and a full-length feature on the way; an actor, what's more, who seemed as keen as Evie was to steer Honor away from Kensington and deb dances . . . into the underground bars of Soho and the cafés of Earls Court. He sounded great.

But in spite of all the things that she and Abram Wyatt were meant to like in each other, and in spite of the fact that he'd been going out with Honor for almost three months, Evie had yet to meet him. Her A-level

11

retakes were imminent and her thoughts too full of last year's disaster. She'd spent those precious revision weeks on the train back and forth to London to see her boyfriend at the time, an Irish barman whose wild hair and persuasive accent had seemed so much more important than lifeless revision notes and mock exam papers . . . only to find that he'd disappeared one day with her entire tape collection and all she had was an E and two Us to show for it. After that experience, Evie had decided to get serious. She knew she'd never get to Oxford or Cambridge, but realised now that she wanted the student life. She didn't want to get left behind. 'Then make it happen,' Honor had said. 'Don't go out. Put in the hours.'

And Evie had taken her advice. She'd quit partying. There was no drinking. No staying out late. No lying in. No distractions – Irish or otherwise – whatsoever. And while the rest of her old classmates were taking gap years in India and Africa, or hanging out in London taking cooking courses, driving lessons, and going to parties, Evie settled into a different life – travelling daily on the Underground to an unfashionable tutorial college off Russell Square, and studying in her local library at weekends.

Tomorrow night was to be her first break from this routine. Tomorrow night, she was making an exception . . . for Honor was having a party. A huge dance, hosted by her parents, to celebrate what should have been Honor's eighteenth birthday but was in fact her nineteenth – no way her mother would have permitted such frivolities last year when Honor had *her* A-levels to take; no way she was letting anything get between her brilliant daughter and her brilliant career. ('And frankly, darling, there's nothing wrong with people thinking you're a year younger than you really are. Never too early to start. I promise you, you'll thank me for it later').

Privately, Giles and Rachel thought Honor's career had nothing to do with it. Far more likely that Xandra wanted nothing – not even exam revision – to spoil her daughter's debut. No matter that it was 1989, that debutantes were a thing of the past and girls of a certain background had stopped being presented at court over three decades ago. No matter that the Queen herself had rejected the ritual as meaningless and dated. There was still a little man at *Tatler* magazine who'd kept the vestiges of it alive, maintaining exclusive little lists for the daughters of women who still minded about that sort of thing . . .

Xandra loved this little man with his little lists – to her they weren't so little – and Honor's preparation for this party was every bit as important as her A-level revision. She had to look radiant and relaxed. She needed to spend time at the gym, and time in the salon – not the library – if she wanted to attract the right sort of attention. Better, in short, to wait a year. Do the exams. Do the party. Do each thing properly. Don't even think of mixing them.

Evie did not have such luxuries at her disposal – not that either she or her parents minded. After three months' slog, they all felt she'd earned a break. It wasn't long until the exams started, just another fortnight. Between now and then, there was only Honor's party . . . and Evie, full of well-earned pride at her sustained levels of abstinence, was looking forward to it every bit as much as Honor was.

Her only regret was that, unlike her cousin, she'd have no boyfriend in tow. But perhaps that was no bad thing, after the Irish distraction. Besides, knowing the kind of men she usually went for – and the dodgy views of her aunt – she probably wouldn't have been allowed to bring him even if he *had* existed. No, this time she'd just have to resign herself to the not-entirely-unappealing prospect of getting to know Abe Wyatt.

'Honor?' Rachel was shouting up the stairs.

'Shit,' said Honor, dropping her cigarette in Evie's little ashtray as she noticed the time.

Evie grinned. 'Need your beauty sleep?'

'It'll take more than sleep, don't you think?' said Honor, smiling back as she hurriedly retied her hair into its butterfly clip and reached for her shoes. Evie watched her from the door, thinking that on anybody else such modesty would have rung hollow. With all that grooming and all that poise, Honor's beauty was blatant. Head-turning. And it was only because her mother was so fussy, always on at Honor to –

'– do something with that hair, darling. Please. You look about twelve.'

or –

'Are you sure that shirt really suits you? One needs very good arms indeed, you know, to carry off a style like that . . .'

It was only because Xandra picked her daughter to pieces so frequently that Honor's view of herself was so low – and her modesty genuine.

Rachel met them on the landing. 'Your mother just rang,' she said to Honor, trying not to look conspiratorial. 'I told her you were on your way.'

'Oh God, I'm sorry . . .'

Rachel kissed her. 'It's fine. It was lovely to see you – and we can't wait for tomorrow night. We . . . Giles?'

She rapped hard on the studio door. 'Giles, darling – Honor's leaving.'

Giles emerged, taking off his glasses. He stood in the hall with the rest of them, while Honor collected her keys and bag and thanked them for her wonderful present.

'Don't be silly.'

'I hope you like it.'

'And if there isn't enough room, I'm sure he could decorate the inside as well – couldn't you Dad?'

'Evie. Will you *stop!*'

'. . . Oh, and gilding! It wouldn't be *your* cupboard, Honor, without a good lick of—'

'Good *night*,' said Honor, with an unconvincing look of reprimand. 'I'll see you all tomorrow.'

The door swung to behind her. And as Honor went out into the cool of the street, Rachel and Evie turned to go down to the kitchen, with Evie still laughing and joking about the cupboard as she followed her mother down the stairs.

'I'm serious! I think he should make the whole thing gold. Top to bottom, inside and out. It would sum up Honor's life about as perfectly as—'

'Don't you think it would look a little vulgar?'

Evie's chuckle drifted up the stairs. 'That would serve old Xandra right.'

'*Aunt* Xandra, darling.'

Giles ran the bolts across the door and trudged down behind them, his step heavy on the old boarding.

'You could still put gold on the inside, Dad, couldn't you?' Evie prattled on as she took handfuls of knives and forks from the drawer and started laying the table for supper. 'Oh, go on – just on the inside!'

But Giles wasn't responding. He took three wine

15

glasses from the cupboard in the corner and, unsmiling, placed them on the table.

'Dad?'

'What.'

Suddenly conscious that her mood was out of step with her parents', Evie's voice grew quieter. 'What is it?'

'I think gold leaf's quite expensive,' said Rachel. She stood facing the stove, easing dry spaghetti into a large saucepan of bubbling water, her back to the room. 'Especially on the inside where no one gets to see it. I'm sure that's what your father meant, darling. He–'

'It's also fucking inappropriate.'

'Giles.'

'No!' cried Giles. 'No, I'm sorry. We've got quite enough lies on the outside of that thing without starting on the inside as well. Jesus. If we're talking about the inside of poor Honor's cupboard I can think of a good few things more suitable than—'

'Oh, for heaven's sake.' Throwing the empty spaghetti packet into the bin, Rachel turned to him. 'It's not supposed to be a masterpiece. People won't analyse your precious cupboard in centuries to come. It – it's not meant to have hidden truths. It's just a pretty bedside cabinet with a few—'

'Hidden truths?' said Evie, slowly.

Giles and Rachel looked at each other again, across the kitchen table. This time neither smiled. Neither spoke a word. Rachel's face wore a look of weary reproach. Giles's was angrily defensive. And Evie, her eyes darting hurriedly from one parent to the other, saw only that she'd stumbled on some sort of secret. Something to do with Honor's cupboard. Something—

'What truths?' she asked.

16

Rachel sighed as she turned back to the stove, stirring the spaghetti with a large spoon. 'Well, go on then,' she said. 'You may as well tell her, don't you think? You've already blurted out half of it . . .'

'*Me*?'

'I don't see what advantage there is to holding anything back now.'

'Half of what? Hold what back? What?'

Giles looked over his daughter's shoulder. He was waiting for Rachel to turn round again – waiting to read her expression – but Rachel was fixed on the cooking.

'Dad, please. What's going on?'

Giles looked back at Evie with an expression so serious she barely recognised him.

'What's happened?' she begged.

Giles placed both his hands on her shoulders. 'If I tell you this, Evie, you have to promise me you'll keep it to yourself.'

'Oh, I promise.'

Giles leant in to her face and met her eye. 'Not even tell Honor?'

'Not even . . .' Evie looked away. She and Honor never kept secrets from each other.

'Well you won't need to hold it in for long,' said Rachel, reading Evie's thoughts. 'And you'll be doing Honor no favours if you do blurt it out, believe me. There'll be more than enough for the poor girl to worry about after the weekend without having her party ruined by thoughts of whether there's any truth in it, and – and what her mother will do when she discovers—'

'Discovers *what*, Mum? For God's sake, I—'

'Promise you'll keep it to yourself,' said Giles firmly, 'and we'll tell you.'

17

So Evie promised and over dinner she learnt that, for the past three years, Honor's father had been having an affair – and that the woman in question, who happened also to be an old friend of Rachel's, was now threatening to go public.

William Montfort wasn't famous. Yes, he had a title. And – yes – he'd been extremely successful in his property dealings. He was grand and rich and sociable, but his private life would hardly have been worthy of media interest were it not for the circumstances surrounding his decision, back in the mid-sixties, to marry Xandra Villiers, the sometime model and girl-about-town with the snub nose and waif-like figure that had so matched the look of the moment.

Xandra Villiers had attracted a certain amount of press interest back then, mainly on account of the other men she'd dated. A big-name photographer, a rock star, a smooth TV presenter to whom she was rumoured to have been engaged, before suddenly and surprisingly, announcing that she was to marry a baronet from Suffolk. Sir William Montfort wasn't anything like as glamorous as Xandra's previous boyfriends. But for some reason his old-fashioned credentials – his title, his lifestyle, his place in the social establishment – meant a great deal to a girl whose background was considered shaky, and whose real name – Sandra Batch – had been quickly dropped on signing with her first modelling agency.

William had been mesmerised by her. Bored by the girls on offer – girls he'd known since childhood, or girls just like them . . . all with the same interests, same schools, same friends in common – he'd longed for someone different; someone with no 'background' to speak of. Someone more like Xandra who, for all the seductive modern glamour of her world, had always secretly longed to be an aristocrat.

And so, on a bright weekend at the end of April 1965, Sandra Batch became Lady Montfort. And instead of jetting off to Marrakesh, or San Francisco, and smoking something strange in the cool shade of a palm tree while admiring his wife's spectacular braless body underneath something floaty and vaguely see-through . . . William had to resign himself to the very way of life he'd hoped to avoid. Back on the shooting scene, dragged out to white-tie parties, hauled off to Ascot to sweat under his top hat, while Xandra swapped her Ossie Clark dresses for Hardy Amies and took to wearing pearls.

They still managed to hold it together. With houses to decorate and parties to throw, and a whirl of pretty engagements to honour – not to mention the arrival of children – Lady Montfort barely noticed her husband's disappointment. She considered his lack of interest in things like Ascot mere affectation. And William didn't bother to correct her. In time, the lure of Marrakesh waned. Floaty clothes weren't fashionable in the eighties. And William learnt that it was easier to go along with his wife's social schedule, easier to get his kicks from the challenges of his property business . . . and from finding other diversions behind that impeccably tailored back. And only now – with a silver wedding behind them and the dark clouds of retirement not far beyond – only now was the whole structure starting to crumble. For William had been philandering—

Evie choked on her spaghetti. 'Philandering?' she spluttered. *'Uncle William?'*

19

Reaching to pick a lump of candlewax from the table, Giles bent his chin to hide an involuntary smile. It was serious, this turn of events. Of course it was. With four children to consider, the destructive potential of a desperate mistress was terrifying: the bitterness and damage . . . not funny, not funny at all. But, oh, if William could only see her face! The awful surprise of an eighteen-year-old – that a paunchy man of fifty-eight would even get an *opportunity* to have an affair.

'I suppose he thought he could get away with it,' said Rachel later on as they got into bed. 'God knows enough people do these days.'

Giles looked up from setting his alarm clock. 'Do they?' he asked innocently.

Rachel grinned. 'Or so I'm given to understand,' she said, jumping in beside him and pressing close for warmth, 'from the shocking gossip you pick up at those Decorative Arts Fairs, my love . . .'

Chuckling, Giles put the clock back into position, turned off the light, and settled close round his wife's body, as close as he could get, not minding that she was cold. It was his favourite moment of the day.

'It's just that most of them don't get caught,' she said into the darkness. 'Or their lovers have better manners. Or at least they don't have the rotten luck to pick a mistress as—'

'Brazen?'

'Or maybe just desperate. From what I remember of Diana Miller, she was always slightly chippy . . . even at school. Always looking through my pencil case and wanting to borrow stuff . . . minding terribly if I said she couldn't. My heart did sink when he told me who

20

it was. And – and I know it was only some old houseboat she wanted, but you know what William's like: once he's set his mind on something, or if he feels someone's forcing his hand . . .' Giles kept a tactful silence. '. . . she probably took more offence than he intended. Probably thought he was leaving her. Although how Diana could think that it would ever be acceptable to – to go so far as speaking to the press . . . putting poor William through—'

'Poor *William*?'

Rachel sighed. 'I'm not saying he's blameless, Giles. But I do think that he might have been lured in by a false sense that Diana was one of us; that she . . . I mean, the fact that I actually knew her . . . I know I haven't seen her for years, and I know she's not part of our lives any more, but – but it wouldn't surprise me if he'd thought the connection would protect him somehow. And I can't help thinking that if it wasn't for me . . .'

Giles closed his eyes, unwilling to counter her so very late in the evening. It was almost midnight. Rachel wasn't thinking straight any more; didn't know what she was saying. No point making an issue of it now. Yet the line she was taking – this sympathy for her brother; this exaggerated sense of her own responsibility for the mess that William was in, just because she, Rachel, had once known the woman – had a depressing familiarity.

So while Giles didn't try to stop her from talking in that way – knowing that, sooner or later, sleep would drag her off; that letting her ramble into the night was a far more effective way of dropping the subject than any direct confrontation – he couldn't help but feel that the reprieve was only temporary.

21

It wasn't just William and Xandra. Somewhere overhead there was a change of direction in the winds that blew about Giles and Rachel's marriage too. An old threat was returning. For twenty-five years Giles had quietly and deliberately steered them both away from the complications of Rachel's family and background: doggedly refusing endless offers of holidays and houses and the like in a desperate attempt to establish some distance from all that Montfort wealth and status . . . determined to put a fair stretch of water between themselves and any sense of obligation towards Rachel's brother and his ways. But what good were these high principles if Rachel still felt compelled to drop everything in William's favour the second he clicked his fingers? What on earth had been the point? How could poor Giles hope to keep some sort of independence when Rachel herself seemed so keen to relinquish it all to her brother?

Giles didn't like it. But lying there, it seemed to him that he had no choice but to turn about, submit to the changed conditions, and hope that the weather would improve. And as sleep tore at Rachel's sentences – her words disintegrating, until all that was left was the ebb and flow of her breathing as she rested in his arms – Giles remained uneasily awake.

Chapter Two

Honor's Party

Only Xandra, thought Rachel wearily as Giles drove round the back streets of Mayfair in search of a parking slot. His dinner jacket exuded a musty smell, absorbed from years in the debris at the back of their hanging cupboard. His dress shirt pinched at the neck. And as they were sucked back into Park Lane for the third time, his mouth tightened visibly and his knuckles turned pale. Rachel watched him, full of wretchedness that she was somehow to blame for this; that, yet again, it was her family – or, at the very least, her sister-in-law – causing him distress.

For only Xandra would have chosen to do things this way: at the Wellesley Hotel, with hundreds of people and stiff gilded invitations that guests had to bring 'for security purposes'. Only Xandra would feel comfortable with a full formal dinner – blow the cost, blow the ostentation, blow the inconvenience – followed by dancing and, no doubt, any press photographers she could muster. Such a performance. Such a show. Such a terrible lot of bother.

It wasn't for herself that Rachel minded. She rather

liked dressing up. And even Evie – awkward, irritable Evie – seemed quite excited. Oblivious to the tension in the front of the car, she was now leaning along the back seat, looking out at other guests tripping in twos and threes along the pavement, self-conscious in their dinner jackets, their satin heels and flowing hems, the wind blowing at their hair as they hurried round towards the ballroom entrance of the hotel.

No, it was poor old Giles – struggling into a parking slot, decked out in clothes he loathed, to face an evening with people who'd make him feel a failure, and nothing to look forward to but the moment when Rachel would meet his eye and nod – poor Giles would have given anything to drop his wife and daughter at the door and escape, back across the river.

'We won't stay late,' Rachel said, unclipping her seat belt and giving her face a final check in the mirror under the sun-visor.

Giles opened his car door and stepped into the street.

'I promise,' she went on, raising her voice so he could still hear her talking from inside. 'We can leave after dinner if you like. Just slip away – they'll never notice. And – and Evie, darling, you think you could get a lift with Honor? Or there's always a cab if you're desperate. But you must promise me you won't take the night bus in that dress . . .'

'Has she got enough money?'

'Oh masses,' said Evie, clambering out of the car.

'Masses?' said Giles.

She gave him her sudden grin. 'Yeah – thought I'd book a room if it gets late. You don't mind, do you?'

Giles grunted. But the sight of his daughter on the pavement – all blown about, her dark hair whipping

24

across her face as she slammed the car door and walked towards him, smiling – made it impossible for him to remain ill-tempered. Evie's black skirts billowed with layer upon layer of asymmetrical flounces – flounces that might have looked frilly and girlish on someone else, but when subverted by heavy eye make-up, a tightly laced bodice and spiky ankle boots, the effect was really more Spanish gypsy than Sloane Street princess – and considerably sexier.

And while Rachel thought she'd been brilliantly diplomatic to find something that would satisfy the tastes of both daughter and sister-in-law, Giles couldn't help thinking that his wife's styling skills extended to something more than tact. Left to her own devices, Evie persistently obscured what looks she had. Years of unflattering clothes and awkward bearing had, Giles realised, eroded his view of her. But here, now, in clothes that Rachel had found – in heels that made her walk differently, and shapes that pulled at the right places – it was almost worth the nightmare of his own evening dress if it meant he could enjoy his daughter in hers.

There were lots of people milling around the steps of the Wellesley Hotel, clutching invitations that would get them past security staff. Some had stopped to greet each other, smiling through the blast, clutching at their skirts and hair, while others hurried straight up into the shelter, where a couple of photographers were waiting.

'Oh God,' murmured Rachel, tucking her hand round Giles's arm and dipping her head as they went in.

She needn't have bothered. The photographers were far more interested in Honor, who was standing just inside the doorway, posing dutifully between two of her mother's more important friends . . . while Xandra stood nearby – glancing intermittently at a list of names and chatting to the man on her right. Discreetly they looked up – searching through the arriving guests. '. . . I know,' Xandra was saying. 'It's a shame. He's probably still at the embassy. Those things always do drag on. But we've done pretty well, don't you think? We . . .' Looking up: 'Thank you, Marina. Of course. We'll see you inside . . .' And then, returning once more to the man at her side, '. . . So that's the Etheringtons. And Peregrine? Was he . . .? Good. And I saw they got Prince Josef, and . . .' spotting Rachel suddenly: 'Oh, Rachel! ...Rachel?'

But by the time Xandra reached the other side of the foyer, Rachel and Giles had disappeared and only Evie remained, looking rather strange, in Xandra's opinion, with those funny leather bracelets tied round her wrists, and two studs in her left ear lobe. Nonetheless, with compulsive insincerity, Xandra began complimenting a suspicious Evie on her 'unique style' . . . only to be interrupted by Honor rushing forward.

'Evie! Evie!' she cried, kissing her excitedly as Xandra drifted off in search of bigger fish. 'Oh Evie, you look amazing!'

Only Evie wasn't listening. She was staring at Honor's necklace: a twisting set of diamonds – some the size of fingernails – that sat against her collarbone. Noticing the direction of Evie's stare, Honor rolled her eyes.

'Obscene, aren't they.'

'Obscene,' said Evie, safe in the knowledge that nothing could be further from the truth. For while Honor's diamonds were the entire focus of her look, the rest was a masterclass in grown-up discretion: a sheath dress of navy satin, with slim bare arms and her hair pulled back. It was all very chic and simple. To Evie, it was too simple – almost as if something were missing – but the overall effect was undeniably impressive.

'I feel as if I should curtsy,' she said.

Honor smiled, pulled her closer and confessed that someone just had, for real. One of the hotel staff.

'*No.*'

'It's true!' Honor pulled back, laughing. 'I promise! She must have mistaken me for one of the—'

She was leaning in again, and Evie leant in too, finding it impossible to ignore the giant camera pointed in their direction. The man holding it waved another group aside. Would – ah, smiles! – would they mind? Just for a second? Lovely! One more? *Lovely*! And in the flash of that second, Evie felt what it was like to be her cousin: the dazzle of professional attention, a bigger lens, a brighter bulb. And then out came the pad of paper – 'And how do you spell that? L-A-N . . . G-T-O-N? And is that "Miss", or . . .? Is that right?'

The man thrust his notepad under Evie's nose, and she looked at her name written there, in wonky capitals. Yes, it was fine. 'Thank you, miss. And now' – turning from her, looking round at the revolving door – 'who else?'

Pleasantly disoriented, Evie looked round for Honor and found she'd lost her to the attentions of a red-faced friend of her father's.

'Of course not,' she was saying in an entirely different voice from the one she used with Evie. 'Don't be silly. We're thrilled that you could come.'

There was her pretty hand, warm and reassuring on

the arm of his smoking jacket as she listened to his spluttered compliments. There was her smile. And there: the deflecting murmurs, the swift change of subject . . .

'And you remember my cousin Evie, don't you? She . . .' But it was too late. 'How odd.' Honor looked round. 'She was here a moment ago.'

The man said something that Evie couldn't hear.

'Oh, yes,' said Honor, smiling at him again. 'Of course. You are brilliant. I'd never have thought of that. And she . . . Goodness, it's a crush in here . . .'

From the shadowy fronds of a large flower arrangement, Evie watched them move away, back into the heart of the party. It never failed to amaze her how Honor could give so much more than the minimum to the dull, or the crass, or the downright selfish. Why did Honor waste her time like that? Why didn't she show more discernment? It wasn't as if she was blind to faults in others. If anything she was quicker, more observant, than Evie. But still she persisted in being nice.

'Oh I know,' she'd said, uneasily the other night, when Evie had called Rupert Sykes a dreary sloane, and questioned Honor's judgement in inviting him to her party. '. . . but when I think of the time I got stranded in Berkeley Square just before Christmas and he helped me find a cab, and came with me – all the way back to Launceston Villas – and made sure I had my keys with me. He was so sweet . . .'

'But he fancies you, Honor! It's blatant self-interest!'

And although it was a compliment, Honor still hated being told that sort of thing – hated the responsibility of being told that someone she thought of as a friend might have different feelings for her.

'Why can't you accept that sometimes people are just

28

nice?' she'd say. 'That they're not always motivated by self-interest? That they might genuinely want to help?'

And when Evie pointed out that someone like Rupert *genuinely wanting to help* a girl like Honor tended to coincide, absolutely, with self-interest, Honor closed off. 'All I'm saying is that if you persist in seeing the worst in people, that's exactly what you'll get from them.'

'And if you're naïve enough to ignore it, Honor, you're in for a nasty shock.'

Evie emerged from her floral hiding-place, free and unrepentant. If Honor chose to waste her party being charming to eager red-faced men, that was Honor's problem. Evie had better things to do. No doubt Honor would be rescued at some point, or find some tactful way to offload the old man on to some other unsuspecting guest (probably thinking she was doing them a favour). Things always had a way of working out for Honor. And sure enough, within seconds, Xandra was hurrying past, smoothly determined.

'Honor?' she called out, briskly. 'I'm sorry, Richard. Could I grab her for a moment? Darling, the Dudleys have arrived . . .'

For a moment Evie watched them. And as she watched they were joined by William and all three moved off to greet the Dudleys. With so much beaming and laughing, so much warmth and affection, it seemed extraordinary to think that somewhere behind her uncle's party face – hidden from everyone, even his wife – a nightmare was unfolding. Perhaps even now Diana Miller's story was whirring out in black and white, copy after copy after copy, rattling inexorably on and down and round and through some vast printing labyrinth, like rows of falling dominoes.

29

By the weekend, the pretty structure of that outwardly perfect marriage would be flattened.

Yet for now, tonight, the balance held. And as someone who found it hard to conceal the smallest anxiety, Evie felt unsettled by such smiling self-control. Helping herself to a long cool glass of champagne from one of the many trays on offer, she turned from the scene at the doorway and made her way into the ballroom.

Because she shared Honor's family life as well as her social life, there were lots of people Evie knew: aunts and uncles, long-lost cousins, girls she knew from school, boys she'd been with on skiing holidays, or teenage discos, friends of Honor's older brother Charles – who couldn't be there tonight because of the job he had in San Francisco. It should have been fun. They all talked to her, all smiled, all asked her how she was . . .

'I'm fine,' she said again, and again. 'I'm fine.'

But she wasn't. Having spent the last three months looking forward to this party, Evie now realised the very person she'd imagined enjoying it with – Honor – had other obligations. In some ways Evie had been expecting this. She knew that it would be only *cultivated* Honor on show tonight; that she should consider herself lucky to have seduced from her those small irreverent remarks about the diamonds. But Evie was less prepared for all the other claims to Honor's attention. It had not occurred to Evie, until now, how little relevance she'd have tonight. So far as the hosts were concerned, evenings like this weren't meant to be spent with close friends. They were about catching up with people they hadn't seen for months – and probably with good reason. And while the other guests had the maturity and self-control to play along, Evie couldn't do it.

'I'm fine ...' This time to Rupert Sykes – whose parents lived near Honor's in the country, who'd known them both as children, and who was now at agricultural college – as he bent with the ritual and lightly kissed her cheek. '. . . I'm fine, Rupert. How are you?'

'I'm very well.'

Both paused; then Evie remembered it was her turn.

'And how's Cirencester?' she said, as if reading from a script.

'Brilliant. Got a house now, share it with a couple of mates: James Hinton – know him?'

Evie nodded.

'And Rappy, of course,' he said smiling, as if Rappy was an asset. 'You know, you really must come and stay with us, Evie – when your exams are over, maybe? Rappy's always on at me to get girls to visit us. You should have seen him last week ...'

But Evie was rather less impressed than Rupert by the things Rappy did. She tried, and failed, to hide it – which only made things worse: Rupert simply worked harder, reached further, in the wrong direction. He didn't understand that tales of Rappy's exploits – how he'd drunk so much one night he'd broken the loo seat in two – were unlikely to get Evie on the first train down from Paddington. She didn't want to know what kind of condition Rappy was in when Rupert had found him the following morning. She didn't want to know what kind of car one of the others drove, or how they'd nearly crashed it last weekend ...

'How riveting,' she said at last, unable to cleanse her words of irony.

31

Rupert's smile vanished. 'I'm sorry,' he said. 'I—'

'Why are you apologising?'

Holding back his fringe, Rupert glanced around the room. 'I – I'm not sure, Evie. You seemed a bit cross. I thought perhaps I'd—'

'Cross?'

In the silence that followed, Evie drained her glass – and Rupert grabbed his chance. 'Let me bring you another,' he said. 'Champagne, was it?'

Evie gave him the empty glass – the token permission for him to go and not come back to her – and Rupert gladly took it. The people closest shifted round and Rupert was gone, swallowed into the closing gap between the back of someone's dinner jacket and someone else's bare shoulder. Evie was alone again, surrounded by 500 party voices – individually civilised, collectively monstrous – rising in a tidal wave of small talk, thundering over her head, sloshing into her face once more.

'Hello Evie. How are you?'

It was Victoria Morris, Honor's friend. The one who'd had the nose job. Evie looked at the new one. 'I'm fine. You?'

'Really well! God, it's bliss not having to be at school, don't you think? No more rules, no more teachers,' Victoria took a drag from her cigarette, 'and no more exams! Oh. God. The relief . . .'

Evie took another glass of champagne from a passing tray. 'So you're enjoying that secretarial course then, are you?'

'Loving it. Everyone's so nice. We come and go as we like, and it's not like it matters if we fail. Not when most of us are off to uni in October and have no *intention* of actually using the skills . . . It's really just an excuse to party! I'm just so glad I didn't go travelling this year – aren't you? Just think of all the fun we'd have missed!'

'Just think.'

'What was that?'

Evie yawned. 'Oh – it doesn't matter.'

'No, say it,' Victoria insisted, her voice growing tight.

And there was something so petty about her tone, so ticklingly confrontational – like a fly buzzing round her face – that Evie was unable to resist taking a swat.

'Well,' she said, still smiling, 'since you ask, I must say I can think of better uses for a gap year than typing lessons and parties.'

'Like retakes?'

'And nose jobs.'

Victoria gave a sharp gasp.

'On the other hand,' Evie swatted on, 'I can see it wouldn't be much fun arriving at university with the great honker you had at school, so maybe it wasn't such a waste of time.'

'At least I'm *going* to university.'

'Oh, I don't know. Call me vain, but I think I'd rather have my own nose.'

Victoria bit her lip. 'You know, Evie, I can't think why anybody bothers. I was trying to be nice. I – I saw you standing all by yourself and I . . . well, I can now see exactly why that was.'

Evie held an unrepentant stare. And Victoria, livid, turned on her heel. But it was hard for her to make the kind of exit she had in mind – the room was just too crowded – and it was a good minute before she was able to squeeze past the group on their left.

33

Caught between feelings of exhilaration and shame – eyes flashing, blood pulsing – Evie's brain crowded with muttered phrases of self-justification. Trying to be nice, my ass! You weren't trying to be nice. You just wanted a good old gloat. 'Oh, look at all the parties I'm going to, and all the fun I'm having, and – la-di-dah – isn't my life perfect?' Well I'm sorry, Victoria, but you asked for it. You . . . What was I supposed to do? Take it like a lamb? Let you walk all over me like you're some sort of—

'Phew!' a voice suddenly said behind her. 'Wouldn't want to get on the wrong side of *you*.'

Evie spun round – and there, two feet away, was Abram Wyatt. They might never have met, but she'd heard too much about him in the last few months not to know instinctively that this was Honor's boyfriend. It would have been hard for her to identify him from the single episode of *Cavaliers and Roundheads* that Honor had made her watch – where the moustachioed Royalist he'd played seemed very different from the clean-cut man that stood before her now – but Evie could still tell. From the marketable design of his shaving-ad face, from the distinctive proportions of his actor's body – with its bigger head and surprising lack of height – to the smiling look of recognition, the lack of criticism in his eye . . . It couldn't have been anyone else.

Slowly, she grinned back. 'Well if you do get on my wrong side, Abe, at least you'll know about it.'

An hour later, in accordance with Honor's seating plan for dinner, Evie and Abe were rapt in conversation, swapping views on everything and anything that came to mind: from the pros and cons of plastic surgery to

Honor's dodgy taste in friends; from what they thought about the other guests' dress sense to the delicate question of when, if ever, one should lie about that sort of thing . . .

'Oh, definitely!' said Abe, laughing. 'What possible advantage is there in telling someone they look terrible?'

Evie could think of plenty. '. . . but why say anything at all? You don't have to go out of your way to lie. I mean, take Aunt Xandra . . .'

'Ah.'

'In the foyer just now, telling me that she *loved* my dress, and what *marvellous* style I had . . . And I just thought: Shut *up*. I already know what you really think. Stop *pretending* that you—'

'I expect she knew exactly what she was doing,' said Abe, with feeling.

Evie looked at him.

'She's no fool – that aunt of yours. I suspect it was her way of letting you know precisely what she thought, while apparently giving you a compliment. She does it to me all the time – "Oh, I do think it's wonderful you're an actor, Abram. Just fascinating! We simply must come and see you in your next thing . . . we'll all be so proud!" And the maddening thing is that one can't fight back, or even accuse her of being—'

'—the snide old bitch she really is. Oh God, Abe. What amateurs we are.'

Abe chuckled. He'd twisted sideways so that he was facing her, with one elbow flung across the back of his chair and a wine glass dangling from his fingers. Evie had his full attention – she'd had it all through dinner while the poor girl on his other side had nothing but

35

the shadow of his shoulders – and it made her feel alive. Here, at last, was a comrade. Here was someone whose eyes lit up at indiscretion – the naughtier the better; someone who, when Evie pointed out an ex of hers sauntering past their table, simply murmured, 'Fucker.'

He gave Evie the delicious impression that he was unconditionally on her side. He wasn't interested in the other point of view, didn't try to rise above whatever petty squabble she told him about, or set himself up as an impartial judge. Her enemy was his enemy.

'But if it makes you feel any better,' he continued, still on the subject of Xandra, 'I don't believe – not for one moment – that your aunt's *oh-so-perfect* life is anything near as perfect as she'd like everyone else to think.'

Evie's eyes grew wide and Abe smiled, swilling the remains of his wine around the bottom of his glass.

'Strictly between ourselves . . .' he said –

'Of course.'

'. . . I think that *darling William* might be having an affair.'

Evie felt her heart beating.

'And if Lady Montfort doesn't already know about it,' he went on, 'I can't believe it'll take long. Not with those sharp eyes of hers.'

Evie swallowed. 'But how—'

'I saw them.'

'*What*?'

Abe grinned. 'I saw him with her. She wasn't bad looking, in a brassy sort of way. Not a patch on Lady Montfort in terms of elegance and so on, but – but that's even more insulting, don't you think?'

36

Evie's brain was spinning. 'What happened?' she mumbled. 'When . . .?'

'About a week ago . . . ten days . . . something like that. And then I saw them *again*! The day before yesterday! They' he leant forward to whisper in her ear, 'they meet for lunch in the romantic ambience of an Angus Steakhouse just outside my agent's office. I saw him going in there the first time and Jesus I was surprised . . . So surprised, I thought I might have made a mistake . . . I mean, Sir William Montfort, of all people, sitting on one of those plush banquettes? How likely is *that*? So I followed the old sod inside and – and got the hell out again when I saw who he was with!'

'But what made you think that she—'

'The fact that he was kissing her?' said Abe, laughing. 'The fact that he looked happy? The fact, frankly, that it was an Angus Steakhouse. I mean, why else would anyone go there?'

Evie giggled in spite of herself. Dinner was over, she'd had a bit to drink and – when mixed with the lure of Abe's conversation – strange things were happening to her judgement. Diana Miller, and the threat she posed to William and Xandra's marriage . . . It was starting to seem more like a gossipy joke than a blow to Honor's happiness. Faced with the temptation to tell Abe something that would really make him sit up – to take his ace piece of gossip and trump it with everything she knew about her uncle's lover going to the press that very week, and how they were on the brink of the whole thing exploding – Evie realised she was much too close for comfort. She was almost relieved when their conversation was interrupted by the sudden arrival of Honor at their table – bending forward between them, close enough to smell her scent.

37

'Oh, you two are dreadful. I was watching you all through dinner: you talked only to each other! And – and *look*!' Laughing, she indicated the empty chairs on either side.

'Rude people,' Abe remarked, pulling up the chair on his left so that Honor could sit on it. 'Poor old Evie, left with only me to talk to. I tell you, Honor, she's been the model of politeness . . .'

Amused, Evie glanced at Abe, expecting to meet his eye and share the sense of a narrow escape.

But Abe wasn't looking in her direction. He'd turned to Honor on his other side, and was holding her hand, leaning towards her, asking about her dinner. Was she okay? Had she enjoyed it? Was . . . Abe shifted further round so that he was facing Honor properly. Was her godfather a total nightmare?

'Oh, he was fine. Especially once we'd got him his precious glass of whisky. Even asked me to dance.'

'God.'

'But the poor man was completely out of breath after only a couple of moves. And he was clearly desperate to get back to the malt. So I decided to put him out of his misery and – and now here I am . . .'

As Honor finished speaking the band – who'd been playing since dinner – switched to a sultrier number: one with a salsa beat. Abe got to his feet, still holding Honor's hand.

'Poor darling. Would you dance with me instead?'

Evie could see his face, reflecting the flashing green disco lights as he made his request. She was startled by the change in his expression. He seemed so different: shy, concerned, almost deferential. And then she realised that Honor had not moved from her chair. She wasn't even looking back at Abe. Instead, her concern was for Evie, and whether it was fair to abandon her friend at an empty table.

'Oh, heavens – go!' said Evie, shooing at them with her hands. 'Go! Go! Go!'

She watched them cross on to the dance floor. She saw them slip into the Latin rhythm of the music – easily and happily; swinging their hips and smiling at each other – and felt a stab of jealousy. But whether it was Abe she wanted to possess, or Honor's ability to inspire the kind of devotion she'd glimpsed in that sea-green flash of light across his face, or simply the companionship that he and Honor shared . . . Evie couldn't tell.

It didn't help that he was forbidden. There was a part of her that twitched at 'PRIVATE – NO ENTRY' signs. It was the part that smoked at school and wandered out of bounds; the part that preferred to gatecrash than receive an invitation. Evie loved what she couldn't have. But it wasn't as if Abe was anything special: he'd made her laugh, but so did her father. And okay, he was easy-looking – but Evie had no taste for the mainstream. Whatever it was – boys, books, movies, clothes – she tended to the offbeat; the slightly damaged, second-hand, charity-shop option. Her friendship with Honor was the single exception to this rule, and that wasn't about to change.

So she resolved instead to count herself lucky that Honor's new boyfriend was someone she liked so much; someone who'd encourage Honor in the right direction. Abe was an asset, she told herself. He'd be good for her friendship with Honor – and that, after all, was what mattered.

But still Evie was lonely. She tried to distract herself with the party: seeking out the few guests she did like,

smiling and chatting with them, even dancing –
although Honor's fourteen-year-old brother was
hardly her dream man and the contrast simply
highlighted what was lacking. Nevertheless, it was
easier to dance than talk. Ben might only have been
fourteen, he might have had a few more inches to
grow, but he certainly knew how to dance. The music
was old-fashioned – to suit the taste of Xa and
William's generation really far more than Honor's –
but Evie didn't mind. She liked Elvis. And Ben (who
must have had lessons) was flinging her around with
the full force of his adolescent vigour.

And if it wasn't for the band stopping to wish
Honor happy birthday – getting everyone to sing
along in unison – they might have danced on to the
end of the night. Both were fit enough, and neither
had any inclination to talk to anyone else. But as the
party stood and sang – to a reluctant-looking Honor,
smiling on the stage – Evie's head grew calm. The
room became still again: just tiny spots of light from
gently spinning disco balls drifting across a mass of
guests.

She sang to Honor, her cousin and her friend. She
stood with all those other people – some of whom had
never met Honor, and some who thought of themselves as close, though none so close as Evie – and felt
very distant from her. She thought of Diana Miller, of
everything that lay in store, and found that she had
tears in her eyes. Not tears that would roll down her
cheeks, just a slight watery blur – cleared with a blink,
checked with a swallow, a quick glance away from the
sight of Honor on the stage, away from the thing that
had moved her, and into the eyes of a man she'd never
met before.

He was sitting at one of the tables at the edge of the dance floor, not gazing (with everyone else) at the birthday girl, but looking instead at Evie. And for a couple of seconds, nothing happened. Evie didn't bother to smile – she didn't feel like being polite – and neither did he. Then, turning her eyes back to the stage, Evie sang on with the others to the end of Honor's 'Happy Birthday'.

And that should have been it. With his slim build, pale skin and mousy hair, the man by the dance floor was hardly remarkable. He could have been any of the hundreds of milder-looking men at the party that night. Ordinarily Evie would not have given him a second thought . . . save that he hadn't smiled, and still seemed so very interested in her. She continued to feel his attention: it was on her like a light.

Unable to stop herself, she looked at him again – and this time he smiled. Evie smiled back. She held her ground while, all around her, people were moving. Honor was coming down from the stage, the lights were changing, the drummer was clicking his sticks – 'One, two, three . . . *Let's twist again . . .*'

'Come on!' said Ben, grabbing her hand.

'. . . *like we did last summer . . .*'

But Evie pulled away.

'Oh, Evie. You can't! I love this song. Just—'

'Look, Ben,' she said, pointing to where his younger sister sat alone in her sugar-pink dress, her eyes gently closing, 'look, there's Nina – all by herself. Why don't you get her to dance with you?'

'But—'

'Or Honor? I'm sorry, Ben. I – I'll catch you later . . .'

Evie slipped away through the dancing couples. She was convinced that the other man would follow her, and she was absolutely right. But it wasn't until she reached the stairs that she felt a hand on hers, catching it to the banister.

'Don't tell me you're leaving . . .'

Evie turned. She glanced down at their hands, at their fingers overlapping . . .

'I'm sorry,' he said, letting go. 'I just . . . didn't want you to escape, without . . .' He broke off, laughing – but the laugh was awkward. It burst in his throat. His eyes swerved, as if embarrassed. He fell silent. The clumsiness of it gave Evie an unfamiliar sense of power.

'I don't usually do this,' he explained. 'Don't, you know, hunt down strange girls at parties, pin them down and ask them for a drink. I just . . .'

Slowly Evie smiled. He wouldn't have been her first choice. Not her second or third, either. But she liked it that he was a stranger: there was something random about his approach, some sense of adventure. And she liked it that he'd noticed her, and had bothered at all – however jerkily – to pursue her. He made her feel interesting and attractive. And that, right now, was food enough.

At the top of the stairs, and round to the right, was a bar that overlooked the dance floor. Evie settled on a stool – high up, with her back to the rows of bottles – spreading her Spanish flounces and looking out while her new friend leant in the opposite direction and ordered their drinks. His name, she discovered, was Matthew. He was twenty-four. He lived in Kilburn . . .

'And what do you do?' said Evie.

Matthew opened his mouth, closed it again, and then said, 'What do you think I do?'

42

Evie looked for clues, but there wasn't much to go on. The black tie and dinner jacket gave nothing away – nothing, at least, to her untutored eye. Aunt Xa would probably have found something in the number of buttons on his cuff, the style of his collar, the cut of his leg, but to Evie it was just a blank canvas. She was stuck with the pale face, the floppy hair, the clever eyes . . . and while the Kings Road voice – scruffy Old Etonian – told her something of his background, she was still no closer to guessing his career. He was probably still a student, or perhaps a teacher, or . . . Her eyes lit up with mischief.

'You're an accountant.'

He gave her an indignant look

'A bank clerk?'

No reply.

'Loss adjustor? Chartered surveyor? . . . Estate agent?' Grinning at him now, Evie ran the gamut of unsexy jobs, punctuating them with alternate guffaws and glances, to check when she might have gone too far. But Matthew was laughing, too. In the end he admitted to working in a sewage plant, and Evie laughed so much that the champagne bubbled out of her nose.

'Oh God.' Still giggling: 'God, Matthew, it's going everywhere! Pass me one of those napkins, would you?'

Matthew passed her a handful of napkins, took the empty glass from her hand, and watched, laughing, as she dabbed herself down. 'That was elegant,' he said.

'That was rude.'

'Not half as rude as you saying I looked like an accountant.'

She finished dabbing at the spilled champagne and

handed back the clump of damp napkins. Chuckling, he took them, and was about to return her glass when he saw that it was empty. 'You want another?'

Evie nodded, smiling. And as drinks were replaced and the minutes ticked by, the pair of them settled into conversation, with Matthew generally asking the questions and Evie happy to answer them. He was fun to talk to, mainly because he steered the conversation inexorably back to her, and what she – Evie – thought. And, flattered, she was happy to oblige – letting him lead the conversation into whatever part of her life he liked. Happy to answer his questions about boarding school or day school – which did she think was better? And what about family life? What did she think about parenting? Was it good to be strict? Would she want to be a parent, herself? Did she think it was important to get married? Or—

'Why, Matthew! Are you offering?'

'No,' he said, comfortably. 'But only because I'm not such a great fan of marriage.'

'You're not?'

'Can you think of a happy one?'

'I can think of lots of happy ones! My parents', for a start—'

'You're sure of that?'

Evie gave him a sharp glance.

'People can be pretty crafty when it comes to giving impressions, especially where marriages are concerned. Nobody wants anyone to know they're unhappily married, not until they've made the decision to separate, and it's my guess there are millions of marriages like that. Millions of them – inwardly miserable, outwardly perfect – my own parents included, I'm sad to say. I had no idea, no idea

44

at all, that my father was having affairs. Not until . . .'

He broke off, conscious that Evie had gone very quiet.

'Oh God, Evie. I'm not saying that your parents' marriage is a sham! I . . . Jesus. I haven't even met them! I don't know what the deal is – I'm sure they're very happy. I just—'

'It's okay,' she said, toying with the rim of one of her flounces. 'Really. I'm just thinking about what you're saying . . . about marriages not being what they seem. And I hate to say this, Matthew, but I'm actually thinking you might be right.'

'Me? Right?' He was laughing.

'I'm serious. Only the other day I was told that my . . .' She stopped herself. '. . . a man, that is – about my parents' age, happily married and so on – it all seems perfect . . . having an affair. Just like you're saying. And this one's all about to get really nasty because the other woman – the mistress, I suppose you'd call her – is on the verge of bloody telling everybody! All because he won't go on holiday with her, or jump when she clicks her fingers or whatever it is. I probably shouldn't be saying anything now, but . . .'

Matthew smiled. 'I think your secret's safe, Evie – you haven't even said their names!'

Evie smiled back. 'Well, anyway, this couple – they've been married for twenty-three years or something, they've got four kids; everyone thinks they're this perfect family – and it's weird, Matthew, seeing him – the father – putting on such a show. And nobody knows. Just me, my parents, and – and Honor's boyfriend's smelt a rat, but he's got no idea what's really—'

'Honor's boyfriend?'

Evie looked back, appalled.

'What are you . . .?' He leant closer. 'Are we talking about the Montforts here?'

'No.'

He didn't seem convinced.

'No, Matthew! Really. It's . . .'

But she couldn't think of anyone quickly enough – not anyone convincing. Who else could it possibly be?

'Evie.' His voice was soft and soothing. 'It's okay.'

'But I promised them! I promised them I'd—'

'You promised them you'd keep it secret?'

She looked at him miserably.

'Well then, we'll do just that. At least, I will. I won't tell anybody, Evie. I promise. And believe me, I'm really very good at keeping secrets.' He smiled at her, 'I'm a pro. So,' growing serious again, 'so please, Evie. Please? Come on, let's have another glass of champagne and – and just forget we ever had that conversation . . .'

And because he seemed so nice and seemed to understand her anxiety – because, on a more practical level, the damage had already been done – Evie went along with his suggestion. They had more champagne and tried to change the subject. But as both of them were unable to think of anything else, the conversation slipped gradually back to the subject of infidelity, to what had happened to Matthew when his parents had split up, to how Evie might be able to comfort Honor when the news broke.

And when the party finally ended, it seemed he'd become quite a friend. Okay, so he didn't fit her idea of a lover. His hair was too tidy. His world – what little she knew of it – too similar to her own: too safe, too conventional, too ordinary. But that didn't mean she didn't like him. She wasn't so narrow-minded to write him off just because of those things. And when he asked for her telephone number, she gave it – and he, in turn, put a business card in her bag.

'We could go for a drink or something,' he said as they parted on the pavement outside the hotel. The wind had dropped and the air was still. Honor and Abe were waiting a few yards down the street.

'Yeah. That'd be nice.'

'And . . .' He smiled at her. '. . . and good luck with the—'

'Thanks.' Evie smiled back for a moment. And then, as he set off into the night, she turned to the waiting car. Honor was inside, but the car door was open and Abe was out on the pavement, smoking a cigarette.

'Ready?' he said.

Evie nodded.

Putting the cigarette into his mouth, Abe held the door for her – and then squashed in close behind, pulling the door shut. The car moved slowly out into Park Lane, heading south.

'So . . .' said Abe, tossing his cigarette end out of the window and closing it – so that everything outside seemed to fade. It was just the three of them enclosed in the car together. 'So, Evie. Who were you canoodling with just now?'

Evie grinned.

'Naughty girl. I saw you both, up there by the bar!'

Honor turned to her cousin. 'What's this?'

'Nothing.'

Abe and Honor looked at each other over Evie, sitting between them.

'It *was*!' Evie insisted, laughing. 'We just had a couple of drinks – that's all. It was hardly canood—'

47

'Who's we?'

Evie sighed. 'Well, me – obviously – and he was called Matthew . . . Fletcher? Forrester? Something like that . . .' Honor continued to look puzzled. '. . . lives in Kilburn if that's any help. But—'

'*Kilburn*?'

'Yes, Honor. Kilburn. What's so wrong with that?'

Abe coughed. 'I don't imagine Honor knows anyone living in Kilburn . . .'

'You think he gatecrashed, then?'

Honor smiled at the hope in Evie's voice. 'Unlikely. The security was pretty tight. Mum even had the place checked over by policemen and dogs before everyone arrived. And then there were all those uniformed guys at the door, and a whole lot more in cars outside.' She shook her head. 'Poor Mum. All that effort for a Foreign Secretary who doesn't even bother to turn up . . .'

'And instead we get the mysterious Matthew,' said Abe, lighting another cigarette. 'So what's he do?'

'No idea,' said Evie, happily. 'No idea at all.'

'Oh come on, sweetheart, don't give me that! I saw him hand you his card . . .'

And Evie, remembering the way they'd joked about Matthew's job – remembering also that she'd never got the truth from him – began to feel more curious. She opened the bag on her lap and took out Matthew's card, holding it to the window so that she could see the text.

'He's a journalist.' She began putting the card with its precious telephone numbers safely back into her bag.

'. . . which makes sense, I suppose. He seemed quite bright, and . . . Hey!'

48

She reached but it was too late. Abe had snatched the card from her fingers, and while Evie's bag and contents fell to the floor of the cab, while she scrabbled for them in the dark, he examined it more closely.

Then he laughed. 'Well I hope you didn't tell him anything significant,' he said, flipping the card back and forth, over his thumb.

'Why should that—'

'He wasn't a guest tonight, sweetheart. He was working.'

'Working?' said Honor.

Abe showed her the card, 'See there? He's the bloke from the *Morning Post*.'

Chapter Three

The Morning After

Rachel Langton never got up late. Even after evenings like last night she was up at seven, having her bath, preparing for the day. Giles, on the other hand, would grab any excuse for a lie-in. He loved being in bed. If it weren't for a sense that it would irritate Rachel, he'd gladly lie there all day, every day, drifting gently in and out of sleep.

But the idea of Rachel being irritated by this – or, God forbid, depressed – was far worse than the moment of getting out of bed. And so, unable to bear the idea of doing anything that would provoke her, or cause her to despise him, or make her think he wasn't trying, Giles would make a point of getting up too. When he thought about the state of their household accounts – comparing the small but regular income they received from Rachel's limited inheritance with the embarrassingly tiny sums of money he brought in from his work . . . guilt alone propelled him from the duvet.

Today, however, he hesitated – in amongst the pillows – wondering if good behaviour from last night would entitle him to extra time . . . and if so, how much? One hour? Two? He did have things to do – like writing back to those very kind American cousins of Rachel's with quotes for a couple of murals in New Hampshire, and starting work on Honor's little cabinet – but nothing urgent, nothing—

'Giles?'

Giles opened an eye.

'Darling.' Rachel pulled back the curtains, the sudden light and rattling of the rings along the pole startling him awake. 'I'm sorry to wake you, but it's almost eight and we really do need to talk about Diana.'

'Almost eight?' Giles wriggled up the bed a fraction, trying to show willing. '. . . Diana . . . of course . . .'

Rachel sat on the bed, bright as a bird. Even the way she was sitting suggested a degree of focus and energy he couldn't hope to match, sprawled as he was in the crumpled sheets.

'We need to decide what I'm going to say,' she went on with humiliating patience. 'William's calling at ten – remember? – and while, of course, I don't want to commit myself to going all the way up to Edinburgh if you're absolutely dead against it, I do think we should at least talk about the—'

'Oh yes. I'm sorry, darling. Of course . . .'

It was coming back to him: last night's conversation in the car on the way home, with Rachel full of the latest news about her brother and his mistress. According to William – and contrary to what they'd all been led to believe – Diana Miller had not yet spoken to the press. She was still threatening to do it, still talking about meetings with some journalist that were yet to be confirmed. But William was hopeful that she

51

might now be persuaded to change her mind . . . and his sister, it seemed, was the one to do it.

'You're just good at this sort of thing,' William mumbled in her ear as they'd danced together after dinner. 'She likes you, Rach. She respects you.'

'Oh honestly, William. We're hardly—'

'I'm serious. She's always going on about how much she admired you at school, how you were the only one that was nice to her, and I . . .' He swallowed, and Rachel saw to her horror that he was close to tears.

'William?'

'You – you see,' he stumbled on, with hands on her shoulders that were clinging more than guiding, 'it's not that I don't love her any more. On the contrary, I was really happy with the way we were – the arrangement we had. And I just don't see why she can't accept what's there, instead of pushing for every damn thing she can get.'

Frowning, Rachel steered him into a quieter part of the floor. 'I didn't realise,' she'd murmured. 'I thought it was just about some barge, William. Some houseboat in Woodbridge she wanted to buy . . .'

'And you think I should let her?'

Rachel was silent.

'You think it's okay to have her hanging around on our doorstep?'

'I—'

'Ten miles is too close, Rachel. Even if it *is* only for the odd weekend, she – she'd be turning up whenever she liked – bumping into Xandra in the chemist . . .'

'No, of course. I do see that wouldn't be ideal.'

'We can go to Paris, or Rome, or – or wherever she likes! And I've got no problem going up to see her in Edinburgh. I just—'

'Sure, William. I understand.'

'Then why the hell can't Diana?'

Rachel stopped dancing, pulled back from her brother and looked him in the eye. 'Because Diana's lonely,' she said. 'She's up in Edinburgh all by herself. She might have a serious career and, no doubt, a beautiful flat, and a great figure and – and a riveting love life . . . and she's making a pile of money – but it's not enough. She wants more. More of *you*, William . . .'

'Well, she certainly won't be getting it by talking to the press,' he muttered.

Rachel sighed. 'You really think she'll do it?'

William looked at the party going on around them, at all the dancing and laughing and drinking, under the coloured lights. 'I don't know,' he said wearily. 'I thought she would. Thought she already had, to be honest – which is why I was so foul to her yesterday and said those awful things. But when she rang this afternoon – sounding so miserable, Rachel, and so . . . But the more I tried to talk to her, and say that I didn't mean it, and – and that I was just trying to protect my family . . . it just seemed to make her angry again . . .'

'And that's when you thought of me?'

William nodded. 'I just can't seem to say the right thing at the moment. But I do think that you . . . that you might be able to explain to her that I love her, I really do, I want it to work – I know she'll believe it if she hears it from you – but she has to understand how important it is that I keep the two worlds separate.'

So Rachel agreed to do it. She wasn't entirely happy with the idea of getting involved. It seemed to suggest that she somehow approved. But the alternative, the possibility that William would say something tactless and send Diana running to the papers, simply wasn't

53

worth the risk. There wasn't time to make a plan now, but if he called in the morning, any time after ten . . .

'And we'll take it from there. Okay?'

'Okay,' said William, giving her arm a grateful squeeze.

Giles thought it was a terrible idea. 'You really think that one telephone call from you will make any difference?' he said to her as they drove back across the river.

'I don't know, darling. I—'

'Come on, Rachel. If the woman's as lonely and desperate as you seem to think she is – and I'm sorry, but I have to say that anyone toying with the idea of doing a kiss-and-tell has got to be slightly deranged – then how's she going to feel when your call ends and she puts down the receiver . . . and there she is again in her sad empty flat with her sad empty life and her meals-for-one in the fridge?'

The image sank – real and convincing – into Rachel's mind. 'Oh God. You think I should go up and see her, then? Spend a few days—'

'Fuck no. I think you should stay well out of it.'

'But—'

'No, Rachel. Absolutely not.'

Rachel was silent, and as Giles parked the car in Morland Road he began to feel bad for snapping. He followed her up the steps, taking the keys from his pocket. 'Let's speak about it in the morning,' he added in a kinder voice, rubbing her shoulder as he unlocked the door. 'I'm just tired, sweetheart – too tired to talk about it now . . .'

But now here it was: the morning. And Giles still

wasn't happy. Rachel's interest in her brother's plight still annoyed the hell out of him, yet he had no idea – no idea at all – how he was going to convince her that William wasn't the priority.

'Let me get up,' he gabbled, hurrying into the bathroom. 'I won't be long, I promise. We can talk about it over breakfast.'

Two hours later Giles had finished his breakfast and was leaning back against the fridge, a cup of coffee in his hands, while he watched Rachel unload the washing machine. He saw the sheets they'd had on their bed last week – a wet rope of greyish watercolour-white, twisted round the various pastel colours of his shirts – pulled like innards from the drum.

The kitchen was quiet after the climax of that final spin – a spin that had drowned out their voices with its frenzy and had made Giles think, again, of money. It wouldn't have been like that if they'd gone for the more expensive brand that Rachel had wanted. He wouldn't have had to stop mid-sentence. He could have made his point . . . although, being a point he could tell she'd anticipated, Giles rather questioned the wisdom of making it at all. They both knew what the outcome would be. Perhaps it was better that the machine took over. It expressed his irritation perfectly.

'. . . I'm not planning to be there for ever,' said Rachel, pulling out a final pillowcase and slamming the porthole door. 'It would only be a couple of days – a week, maximum – just until the heat dies down. I'm sure William could find a way to be with her by the weekend . . . and I will make sure you're not neglected, sweetheart. I promise there'll be enough food, and clean clothes and things.' She smiled. 'You'll hardly miss me at all!'

She stood with the bright blue laundry basket in her arms, looking at him over its load.

And Giles, defeated, lowered his eyes and drank his coffee. He couldn't deny that William was in trouble, but why involve Rachel? Okay, there was the raw threat of Diana going public, and Giles did sympathise – up to a point. But if William was selfish enough to embark upon a double life, he should bloody well be prepared to clear up his own mess when – inevitably – the whole thing blew. Not run like a child to his big sister. Rachel had her own life, here with Giles in Putney. Why would she want to disrupt all that with sudden detours to Edinburgh – especially with Evie so close to her exams? She was needed here at home.

But what was the point in saying any of this when it was all too clear that she'd made up her mind? Right now – to Rachel – her brother's need was paramount. It was greater than Giles's, even Evie's. And Giles was still silent – still floored by the way that, in articulating such thoughts, he would be the one to appear mean-spirited and selfish while William would emerge as simply 'human' – when the telephone started ringing.

Quickly – before Rachel had a chance to drop the washing – he crossed the kitchen and picked up the receiver.

'Hello? . . . Ah, William! Wonderful party last night! Thank you! We were both so impressed by the—'

There was a long silence while Giles listened, biting his lip, and Rachel hovered as close as she dared. 'Yes,' he said at last. 'Yes, she did mention something along those lines, although . . .' Giles glanced momentarily at his wife – and then, quite unable to resist the expression in her large brown eyes, gave in. 'No, of course she doesn't mind. In fact, she's just here, William. I'll pass you over.'

By midday the Edinburgh plan was fixed. After a brief conversation with William, Rachel spent half an hour – half an hour, Giles couldn't help noticing, at their expense – speaking gently and patiently to Diana in her office.

'No, of course I don't think that, Diana. If I did, I certainly wouldn't be coming all the way up to see you . . . No. But it doesn't mean that I'm— No, Diana, it's not like that. I'm just desperately sorry for – for everyone, really. And I'd no idea that you were so— No, of course. But not *everything*, surely. I heard that your career— But William told me about some beautiful flat you've bought in Drummond Place, and – and about that project you did in Leith that won a whole lot of design awards? That sounded incredible! And all down to your— sure. Sure, I understand. But— Okay, perhaps I don't entirely, but I can see that you're— Oh, Diana, please don't cry. I promise it isn't as bad as it seems. You – you're just at a bad point right now, and of course it seems like the end of the world, but it really isn't. And when I'm there with you, I'll— No, I *will* be on the six o'clock— tonight, that's right. It gets in at ten thirty . . . No, I promise I will . . .'

Giles couldn't listen. He went into the garden. And it was only when the call had ended and he could see Evie back inside, helping herself to something from the fridge and talking to Rachel – presumably about last night – that he felt calm enough to go in again.

'Ah!' he said, closing the door. 'Here she is! Crawling out of the woodwork . . .' Evie sat at the table, unsmiling. 'Hungover, sweetheart?'

'No, Dad. I'm just tired. Is there any bacon left?'

'I can cook you some more,' Rachel took a packet from the fridge. 'And eggs, too?'

Evie declined the eggs; she felt sick enough as it was. Ever since Abe had pointed out to her the implications of Matthew Forrester's career, she'd felt like this – with a crawling sensation in her gut, as if some strange sea creature with long tentacles had found a way in. It had lurched and squelched when, at the foot of the steps to Launceston Villas, she'd waved goodbye to Honor. It had grown quiet, but ominous, as she'd continued her journey on with Abe – dropping him at his flat on the Fulham-Chelsea border – then clutched horribly when, back in Putney, she'd paid the cab driver and found herself alone once more – climbing the steps to the sleeping house. And it had still been there at five in the morning – thoroughly embedded like a tropical worm – as she'd lain awake, listening to the birds.

Her first instinct had been to ring him. Ask him, plead with him, beg him not to do it. William was hardly newsworthy on his own. And while Xandra still appeared in gossip columns, it wasn't often, and rarely as the main item. There had to be more important things for Matthew Forrester to write about than some ageing model and the indiscretions of her stuffy old baronet of a husband. And yes, okay, occasionally some magazine would run a feature on beautiful women from the sixties and seventies but it was usually people like Twiggy and the late Talitha Getty. The other girls, girls like Penelope Tree or – or Xandra Villiers, were hardly top billing. A couple of years ago, Xandra had let *Tatler* come down to see them in Suffolk – taking soft shots of her against the light, drifting round her rose garden as if she'd dug and planted the thing herself – but it was only as part of a much larger feature on posh families in East Anglia.

No. It was fine. Matthew wouldn't be interested – not, at least, from a professional point of view; not for a major broadsheet like the *Morning Post*. Evie was only flattering herself and her family, in thinking there was something newsworthy in the things she'd blabbed. And perhaps, if she rang him tomorrow, Matthew could reassure her – and everything could go back to normal, to how it had been yesterday when she'd still kept her word.

But, seductive though the idea was, Evie knew it couldn't be true. There was simply no escaping the fact that Matthew had been working. He hadn't come for fun and flirting. He'd come to do a job . . . and, boy, had she helped him! What good would it do for her to ring him now? She'd probably only make things worse. Give him more to write about.

Her father had once said that the media was like quicksand. Those that struggled and thrashed about were the ones most likely to sink. You had to know what you were doing – or wait for a friend with a cool head – to stand any chance of survival. And Evie, in this case, had no one to turn to. With a new surge of hatred for Matthew, she realised it was the first time in her life that she wouldn't be able to confide in Honor. And as for her parents . . . The crawling sensation returned. Evie wriggled and twisted, catching her leg in the sheets. After the trouble she'd caused with her retakes, after all the disappointments she'd thrust upon Giles and Rachel . . . how could she possibly do this to them now?

No – Evie had sighed heavily, thrown off her sheets,

and turned on to her back – no, she was alone. She couldn't trust herself to handle the kind of call she wanted to make. If she was stupid enough to have done this in the first place, how could she be sure she wouldn't do it again? Her only option was to spread her arms, lie very still, and hope. But sleep still eluded her. And it wasn't until she heard her parents getting up, and became strangely lulled by the sound of their bath running, the creak of the pipes, the hum of the extractor fan, the distant murmurs of the *Today* programme . . . that she finally drifted off.

But the telephone soon woke her. And what with the smell of Giles's bacon and some half-formed fear of who it might be on the other end of the line, Evie was wide awake once more – and this time she got up.

Her parents were full of chatter. Had Evie enjoyed herself? What was Honor's boyfriend like? And who had she danced with . . . *apart* from Ben? And – and had she seen the Etheringtons? They'd been asking after her. And nice Rupert Sykes? And what about her dress? Was she happy with it? Everybody had been saying how lovely she'd looked. Even Xandra. 'And the cab wasn't too expensive, was it?'

Evie shrugged. 'I left the change in the hall.'

Rachel put the bacon on to a plate, and handed it to Evie – who began making a sandwich, with lots of butter and tomato ketchup.

'Oh, and Evie darling?' Rachel's voice became serious. 'Uncle William rang. Just before you came down. He . . .' She hesitated. '. . . he seems to think there's a chance that that affair of his won't reach the papers after all . . .' Evie looked up. 'Apparently Diana Miller hasn't given any interviews – not yet, that is. She's only been threatening to do it, and there's a chance she'll agree to stay completely quiet so long as it's handled sensitively – which would be wonderful, don't you think?'

Silence.

'Not even Xandra need know. But Diana will need quite a lot of convincing and persuading and I . . .' Rachel sighed. 'The thing is, Evie, Diana's actually a sort of friend of mine, and William seems to think that it might be a good idea for me to be with her for a few days – she lives up in Edinburgh – just to be certain that she . . . you know, doesn't change her mind, or do anything stupid . . .'

'Sounds sensible.'

Rachel swallowed. 'I – I just hope you don't feel I'm letting you down, sweetheart. The timing couldn't be worse. But it'll only be until next weekend, I promise. I will be back in time for your exams . . .'

Evie passed her the bottle of tomato ketchup and half a slice of toast. 'It's fine, Mum. Stay as long as you like. Makes no difference to me.'

Rachel couldn't resist looking at Giles.

With her head bent, Evie munched at her sandwich, oblivious to the problems of her parents as she continued to dwell on her own. The anxiety in her stomach was momentarily quelled by the process of eating – the bacon definitely helped – but this latest news about Diana Miller, and the fact that the only story about the affair might be the one that Evie herself had leaked . . . It was simply too awful to contemplate.

And the prospect of having to speak to Honor filled Evie with dread. It would have to happen at some point that day: the ritual post-mortem that followed every party they attended together; doubly expected after it being Honor's own. She'd want to know what

Evie thought of the band, the food, the other guests – including Abe, of course. And no doubt she'd want to grill her about Matthew; whether she fancied him, whether she expected him to call, what she'd do if he did . . . All of this would be up for discussion, and Evie just wasn't sure she could handle the deception – not to mention the guilt. All their lives, Honor had been there for Evie, always on her side, always loyal, always discreet, no matter how difficult things were for Evie. Now, finally, here had been a chance for Evie to repay her – and instead she'd gone and blabbed the lot to a gossip columnist.

In the end it was Honor who made the call. And Giles – delighted that the expense of their daughters' gossip would be borne, this time, by William – was more than happy to disturb Evie from her bedroom revision. 'It's Honor,' he said, poking his head round the door. Evie closed her eyes. 'She only wants to talk about the party, sweetheart.'

'I know, Dad. I just . . .'

Surprised, Giles looked at his watch. 'And I'm sure you could do with a break, couldn't you? You've been up here for hours.'

Sighing, Evie put down her pen. He was right – in a way. Having covered three pages in as many hours, she was hardly fit for productive work. And it wasn't as if she could avoid this conversation altogether . . . she just wished it could have been different.

Chapter Four

Abe

On days when he wasn't working, Abe Wyatt found it hard to know what to do with himself. The current project – a feature-length movie based on a novel about an Englishman fighting in the Spanish Civil War – required nothing more from him for a month or so; which was not enough time to find anything else, and yet too much time just to sit around. Abe found it unsettling.

Up until last week, he'd had the exhilaration of cabs arriving at dawn to take him to the studios, and late returns. He'd been working like a dog and now those scenes were in the bag, with nothing more (for his character, at least) until the switch to Spain. He was free to do what he liked . . . and that morning, he lay in clear bathwater with his toes curled round the far end of his luxury tub, half listening to the radio while he reread an interview he'd done with the *Sunday Times Magazine* back in March to promote *Cavaliers and Roundheads*. He examined the pictures with a strange expression on his face.

'What Next for Abram Wyatt?' said the headline. What next indeed, beyond *Spanish Boots*? The offers were there – he and his agent would be discussing them in detail that afternoon – and he was going to have to make some choices: London or LA? Bare boards or celluloid? Art House or Commercial? Adjani or Basinger?

Abe threw the magazine aside. It hadn't got to that stage, of course, but he knew now that such dreams were no longer impossible. Something was happening, something real – extra-real, now that he'd seen it in magazine newsprint – so real it made his head spin.

But although it was real it was also undeserved and at some half-acknowledged level Abe knew this. It wasn't talent that had got him here. It wasn't clever manipulation, or hard slog, or patience, or courage. It was luck. And while that was part of his charm – the slightly surprised look on Abe's face was fast becoming his signature look – it could all vanish tomorrow, and Abe didn't like to think too much about that side of things. He preferred not to ask too many questions, not to look over his shoulder or down at his feet, in case the tiny ledge he'd reached – and the widening drop below – proved too daunting.

And so, to keep himself from looking down, Abe sought out distractions. There had been a time when he'd liked to sit in silence or gaze out of the window. Now a perpetual chatter filled his life – from the radio, or the television, or his agent in the car – someone, somewhere, always talking. With magazines and newspapers and scripts to read, and trainers at the gym, or plugged to his Walkman, Abe was forever occupied in the business of looking out, not in. And for moments when the outside failed to deliver, when boredom or fear became insistent, Abe got high.

Last night, for instance: Honor's birthday, stiff

parents, lots of people he didn't know; or, worse, people he did know, but hadn't seen since school – all so tricky, so awkward – so he'd had a couple of lines of charlie. So what? He'd needed something to get him through the evening, hadn't he? Something to make him scintillate, keep him alive . . .

Listening to traffic reports he didn't need, Abe got out of the bath. Naked, he stood at the basin and began to shave – concentrating on observing his chin at highly detailed angles, sweeping over every last patch of stubble, getting it perfect but still managing to avoid the stand-back confrontation with his face as a whole, his face as him. It was fine to look at the pictures in the magazine: Abe the commodity, no problem there. But the sight of his own reflection, the sight of Abe the man, wasn't such an easy ride. He preferred to grab a towel, wipe it roughly over that face – up, down, drop – and return to the mirrorless bedroom.

Once he was out in the street, however – sunglasses on, costume perfect – Abe began to relax. It was already mid-morning. Not long now until the lunch meeting with his agent. And in the meantime he could go to the café for a couple of hours and be studiously ignored by polite South Kensington Londoners who knew better than to intrude on his privacy; he could order a large cappuccino from the waitress, settle in a corner, flick through his newspapers . . . and play at not-acting for anyone willing to play along at not-watching.

Abe's agent was a calm woman in her fifties whose tidy English looks sat at odds with her Joan Collins *femme-du-monde* transatlantic accent. It was, of course, precisely this combination of safety and glamour that Karen Rossetti was aiming for – a combination that pressed all the buttons for drama students with an eye on the big time. They wanted thrills but they wanted security too, and Rossetti got it right. She knew what she was doing. Having spotted Abe's potential at drama school – his looks and energy being far more useful to her than mere talent – she'd lost no time in persuading him to sign.

'You want someone who'll look out for your interests,' she'd told him, opening her handbag, 'someone who really understands your worth. You're too good to sit around at the bottom of some over-inflated agent's list. You want to be part of a small, select, highly focused stable of next-generation actors. You want to be represented by someone who has the time and the connections to sell you personally – get a buzz going. Now, there are a number of people out there who can do that for you. I'm one of them. Roger Bateman's another. Lyndsay March is pretty good – I don't know how things'll be now she's got another baby on the way, but . . . Well anyway, here's my card.'

Abe took it.

'You go check out the other guys – you do your homework – and when you've made up your mind, you just give me a call.'

Abe told her he'd already made up his mind. He wanted her. He knew he wanted her.

Karen closed the handbag with a smile.

Now, ten months later, she was delighted with Abe's progress. It wasn't going to be a long career. It needed a bang to make it worth her while, and that was exactly what they'd got. The BBC costume drama hadn't had the best reviews, but the publicity had been great. Abe's photograph had been on the cover of all the TV and radio listings and now was the time to sell him big.

66

Wearing a fresh coat of lipstick and smelling of soap, Karen greeted him in the lobby of the agency and whisked him straight back out again, past an empty Angus Steakhouse to the air-conditioned London-Italian restaurant on the corner, with starched white tablecloths and breadsticks. The generous spacing of the tables gave them privacy, and there was enough room for her to open the file she'd brought – 'Move further round, darling,' she said, angling the papers so that Abe could see them too, 'and take a look at this.'

Three feature films – two in LA – a television project, three commercials, and a West End show . . . each one with character descriptions and dates already written in.

'Of course, some of those haven't been finalised,' said Karen, waving a breadstick over the dates, scattering crumbs. Then leaning closer, crunching loudly, she ran down the list. 'They're doing castings next week for that, and that one as well. I've got all the scripts back at the office. These Ferenezi guys are brilliant – you saw *My Brother*, didn't you? Exactly. This new one isn't as funny, but there's a perfect part and they're desperate to meet you . . . it'll involve going out to LA for a while, but that's no bad thing – and you could probably combine it with seeing that lot' – she tapped the page with the end of her breadstick – 'who were also keen, although I've never really trusted Marti Price. Rumours are they're still waiting for funding. But if it's true they've signed Nina Richards then it might be just too tempting . . . And see here? You won't be able to do it at the same time as *that*; and of course *that one*'ll clash with Spain but I don't imagine you'd be interested in . . . well, anyway. There you are, darling. You take a good long look at it while

67

I get on with the important stuff . . .' Putting the breadstick down, she picked up one of the menus. 'White wine okay with you?'

Abe stared at the list as the wine was ordered and poured out, stared at his own name in serious black-ink capitals at the top of the page beside the Rossetti Agency details – and was filled with an unfamiliar urge to giggle like a girl. Any one of these parts would have been enough for him. 'I'll take the lot!' he wanted to shout.

But as their lunch progressed and Karen ran through the options in more detail, Abe quickly realised which projects he most wanted. And while her explanations seemed objective enough – while she spoke reverentially of the artistic value of getting involved in serious theatre; and, sensibly, of the attractions of television, soaps in particular, and the stability such work could provide – it still seemed to him that she was simply going through the motions. 'Yeah, yeah,' said the voice in his brain as his eye wandered back to the list, to the big-screen items with their big-shot names . . . the powerful production companies . . . the A-list actors . . . already, he was there with them, treading the red-carpet road to Hollywood, his name in tubes of neon.

Twitching with impatience, he waited for Karen to finish her ravioli – she seemed to be taking for ever – and move on from discussing his theatre and television options. Jesus. It wasn't as if he'd chosen acting for the love of greasepaint and soliloquies and hard dark boards. He was no bloody thespian – everyone knew that – and small-screen stability was hardly glamorous.

But Karen – observing his every flicker – knew exactly what she was doing. And it wasn't until they'd ordered coffee that she pulled the list a fraction in her direction and turned at last to the feature films. Her tone remained calm and measured. There was nothing star-struck about the way she discussed the bigger names, the higher fees, the sexier locations, the LA life . . .

'Of course the only way to do it properly is to be there on the ground.'

'That's not a problem. I'm completely up for—'

'I'm talking living there, Abe.' Karen unwrapped a chocolate. 'A lot of these people are just too busy and, frankly, too important to hang around for a day or so while you get yourself on a flight. I know it sounds harsh, sweetie, but at your level there's far too much competition to risk handling things from London . . . God – the amount of wasted potential we've had through our doors – and before you know it, someone else is wearing your clothes, driving your car, collecting your award . . .' She met his eye. 'What I'm trying to say, Abe, is if you want the Hollywood dream – and you've got to *really* want it—'

'I do.'

'Then it's going to come at a price.' Abe nodded. 'And the first thing you should know is that LA isn't everyone's cup of tea.' Karen's pale fingers squashed the thin gold wrapping into a minuscule ball and dropped it into the scoop of her teaspoon. 'Don't get me wrong – it's great if you're at the top of the heap. You're right there where the action is. You've got a beautiful house in the best part of town. You've got cooks and drivers and gardeners and restaurants giving you their best tables. The whole world treats you like a god. But for most people it isn't like that, as I'm quite sure you know.'

'Absolutely, Karen. I—'

'Your life will be pretty ordinary. Lonely, even. Not so much from lack of company, perhaps, but the whole value system in that place can get to you . . . even if you're a success. It takes a certain sort of person, Abe, to handle that kind of lifestyle. A certain sort of ambition – a willingness to make sacrifices . . .'

Abe smiled at her. 'I'm willing.'

But Karen did not smile back. 'You have to understand there's no guarantee in any of this,' she said. 'You could go out there with contracts signed and schedules set up, and still find that the whole movie is pulled. You might be the most beautiful, talented kid on the block – and still never get that break. All around you there'll be people with faster cars and better bodies and stronger contacts . . . You won't see your family for months. And unless your girlfriend is some sort of saint – or prepared to come out with you – you can absolutely forget that side of things . . .'

'I understand.'

'You do?' She was looking at him hard. And Abe, fired up by a sense that this was some sort of test, that all he had to do was show a bit of conviction, was all for getting top marks. Of course at some stage he'd have to think about his life here in England: his flat, his friends, his parents out in Sussex – and what the hell he was going to do about poor old Honor – but those were all things that could be sorted out later. Yes of course he loved them, of course he'd miss them, but if it came down to choosing between his life as it stood and this golden ticket . . .

'Just say when you think I should go,' he said simply. 'I could get out there next week, if you like. There's nothing more on *Spanish Boots* until July, so I've certainly got the time. We could have those meetings with Ferenezi and Price . . . you would come too, wouldn't you?'

Karen smiled. 'It may be a little short notice, Abe. I'm not entirely sure how my diary's looking, but that shouldn't stop you from going. We are linked to an extremely good agency out there – which in any case would be a much better arrangement from your point of view. They'll know exactly what's going on, who's serious, who's pissing about, and – and who else you should see. In fact, I might even speak to Gemma today about getting a few more casting directors to see you if there's time.'

'Great!' said Abe, excited. 'That's great! And assuming you think it's worth my while, Karen, I could even stay out a bit longer, find somewhere to live, and be ready to move permanently when things finish in Spain . . .'

Karen took her credit card back from the waiter and bent to sign the slip. Worth his while? Who knew? Abe's chances were slim – but then again, whose weren't? Karen had pointed out the risks, she'd given that project list a fair assessment, and still he wanted the dream. How could she now ask him to turn his back on it when maybe – just maybe – some starry luck would come his way?

'Fantastic,' she said, scribbling her name across the paper slip and handing it back to the waiter with the same measured smile. 'That's really fantastic, Abe. I'm thrilled. If you've got a moment to come back to the office, I'll give you those scripts and put in a call to Joe Ferenezi's secretary – she should be at her desk by now – so that we can get a meeting in the diary, and then Janice can book your flight . . .'

Abe followed her out of the restaurant, quite certain that the whole room was watching him.

71

Chapter Five

Off the Hook?

As good as her word, Rachel caught the six o'clock train from King's Cross to Edinburgh. Giles took her to the station. For all his disapproval, he still wanted to be with her. Still wanted to help her in with her suitcase, buy her a ticket, make sure she had a seat – the place was full of people with determined expressions – and wave her off from the platform. Instead, all he could do was heave the suitcase on to a trolley, give her a rushed kiss and hurry back to the car before he got a parking ticket.

Turning to wave, all he saw was Rachel's back – handbag slipping from her shoulder, hair a little tangled from where it had brushed against the head-rest in the car, pushing a rickety trolley through the wide glass doors, into the heart of the station.

Giles returned to a quiet house. He and Evie weren't used to being alone together and it became clear, very quickly, how much Rachel initiated in terms of conver-sation. With her, there was always something more to say. She was always planning and worrying and wanting to know what they thought about things – and it had made them slack. They took their cues from her, and not always gratefully. Giles hated being asked what he was thinking. A hunted look would cross his face and he'd either come up with something corny about how beautiful she was looking – which tended to shut her up – or else something unspeakably dreary about the car. And Evie, with her monosyllabic answers, was almost impossible to draw out. Her default mood was critical silence. And while Giles's was more reflective, neither of them were prepared to take responsibility and actually 'make' conversation.

They sat at the kitchen table, eating chicken kiev, boiled potatoes and frozen peas.

'Mm,' said Giles. 'This is good.'

'Mm,' said Evie, reaching for the pepper.

After a very long minute: 'So did you get any work done, then?'

'Some.'

'Oh, good.'

'Not much, though.'

Giles shrugged. 'It was a late night.'

'Yeah.'

'I'm sure tomorrow will be better.'

'Yeah.'

And after another long minute of chewing, Evie said there was a film just started on ITV – a good one, apparently, with Mel Gibson and a lot of other actors Giles had never heard of.

'But that's great!' he cried, picking up his plate. 'Why didn't you say so before?'

They abandoned the kitchen table in a flurry of relief and headed for the sitting-room sofa. Giles didn't care that the film was every bit as superficial as he'd thought it would be. He and Evie sat in comfort that was both physical and mental – and the television filled the gap left by Rachel. When the telephone rang at ten o'clock, Giles had almost forgotten he'd even been expecting her to call.

'I'll get that, shall I?'

'Mm,' came the distracted reply.

Giles took the call in the kitchen – and was surprised to find a young man's voice at the end of the line: apologising for the lateness of the call and asking, very politely, if Evie Langton was in.

'Oh. Oh – yes,' said Giles, trying to sound normal. 'Yes, of course. Who shall I say . . .?'

'Matthew Forrester. We met last night at her cousin's party.'

Giles came back up the stairs, carrying the portable telephone. Covering the receiver with his hand, he stood in the doorway with a teasing expression.

'It's *Matthew*. Says he met you last night at—'

But Evie wasn't smiling back, and it was clear from her behaviour – from the hurried way she'd dropped the remote control and was waving both hands in front of her face – clear, that the call wasn't welcome.

'You sure?'

Evie nodded vigorously.

And so, somewhat reluctantly, Giles returned to the voice at the end of the line. 'I'm sorry, Matthew. She must have gone out . . . Yes, of course. Let me just get a pen, and . . . and it's Matthew – Forrester, you say? Great. Okay, then, I'll see that she gets it.'

Giles put down the receiver and turned back to Evie – who was staring at the screen with rather too much concentration. He put the note with Matthew's number on the arm of her chair. 'Here you are, then.'

'Thanks.'

The note lay untouched where Giles had put it, then slipped off and fluttered to the ground. He hesitated for a moment – it seemed he was going to say something – and then the moment passed.

'So what's been happening?' he said, settling back in his chair. 'Are any of them dead yet?'

Evie had no idea how the film ended. She stared at the screen unseeingly while a chill crept through her. Somewhere in the back of her mind she must still have believed that her instincts would prove right, that Matthew Forrester could be trusted after all, and nothing of what she'd told him would ever go to press. Helped along by the distractions of the day – the call to Honor, her mother's departure, the strange supper she'd had with her father, the Mel Gibson movie – Evie had somehow been able to put the initial dread at a distance. But now, once more, it was right up close, so close she couldn't even see the television for it.

Evie was no fool. She knew what journalists were like: how they could stalk people, and doorstep them, and do God-knows-what in pursuit of a story. And there was her father, grinning away in his comfy chair, thinking she was avoiding some kind of admirer . . . Oh Lord, if only he knew.

And over that weekend, her anxiety only grew worse. It fell into a disquieting rhythm – up close one minute, distant the next – with the repetitions growing ever more frequent. There were still times when she felt entirely normal. She'd be at her desk with her head in her hands, furiously memorising a Chaucer quotation; or clipping her toenails in the bathroom; or scrubbing the remains of fish fingers from a baking

75

tray . . . and suddenly it would hit her. The mist would come down. And poor Evie would find herself staring at the knots in the wooden surface of her desk; or halting mid-clip with her foot against the bathroom stool, or staring at the kitchen tiles while soap suds dribbled down the tray.

But none of that compared with how it felt speaking to Honor on the telephone.

The first call hadn't been so bad. Evie had no problems saying how much she'd liked meeting Abe, and chattering on about the party: what had worked, what hadn't, who'd been looking good, and analysing Victoria Morris's new nose . . .

Honor tried to sound reproachful: 'Abe told me what you said to her, Evie. He— '

'Well, I hope he also remembered to tell you what *she* said to *me*. Stupid cow. Banging on about her boring gap year – spending Daddy's money like it's some sort of achievement and then showing off about whatever second rate university it is she's going to; thinking she's every bit as clever and glamorous as you, when we all know that that's about as believable as . . . I swear to you she deserved it, Honor . . .'

Silently, Honor bit over a smile.

'Although, rather annoyingly, I did think the new one looked miles better. Sticks in my throat to say it, but—'

'Oh I agree! I thought she was looking really pretty—'

'For a change. And in a few years' time some poor sod'll marry her and then wonder why he's got a brood of kids that look like elephants . . .'

Oh, yes. It was easy to hide behind the gossip and the bitching – just so long as Honor didn't ask any difficult questions. And it was only now when they talked again on Sunday night and Evie let slip that her mother was away for the week . . .

'That's nice,' said Honor, yawning. 'Where's she gone?'

Evie froze. 'I'm not sure. Some friend of hers, I think. Not anyone I've ever met, but—'

'How mysterious.'

'Not really . . . not . . .' Evie's brain was spinning. 'Just a bit inconvenient, to be honest. It means poor Dad has to do all the cooking while—'

'Your father – *cooking*?'

'He doesn't mind. In fact, he's quite good. And with all that revision I've still got to do, it's not really sensible right now for me to do it, so he—'

'Good for Giles! Can't see Dad making much more than a cup of coffee in the kitchen, and even then he'd probably sulk about it . . .'

. . . only at those times did Evie feel the ice split and crack beneath her feet. Of course she'd always find her balance again. The moment would pass, along with other little moments – like when, a little later, Honor spoke with mild apprehension about press coverage of the party . . .

'I hope they're not too rude. Didn't realise we had the newspapers there as well as the magazines.' She sighed. 'It's typical Mum. Happy to complain about it, but still can't quite resist all that attention and flattery, and no doubt she'll still be courting it in her eighties. But at some point it's got to backfire, don't you think?'

'I don't know.'

'They can't go on being complimentary for ever.'

'I'm sure it'll be fine . . .'

Or when Honor asked about Matthew . . .

77

'Who?'

Honor laughed. 'You know very well *who*, Evie Langton! The guy you were with when we left – the journalist.'

'Yes . . .'

'Well go on then! Has he rung yet?'

'God, no. Wanker. Sometimes I wonder why anyone bothers to ask for my number when it's clear they're never going to use the thing. I expect they always call *you* back, but—'

'No they don't!'

'Only because you've got Abe,' said Evie, quickly latching on to the new subject. 'So, do you think you really will go out and see him in Spain, then?'

But it was still torture – all the lying, the subterfuge, even just simply staying quiet – engaging in that slip-by-slip dishonesty she so despised in others.

And by Monday Evie could bear it no longer. Grabbing her purse from the windowsill, she slipped out past her father hard at work in his studio, and headed for the newsagent.

The shop was airless and empty. Usually, Evie only went in there for cigarettes and Smash Hits magazine, and it took a while for her to find the *Morning Post* in amongst the other newspapers – spread, at floor level, along the narrow length of the shop.

'And twenty Marlboro Lights,' she said, giving the man a fiver.

Not bothering to check her change, Evie left the shop with the newspaper under her arm. She stuffed the cigarettes into her bag along with the coins – just dropping them in at random, not looking for her purse – and hurried on to a place where the pavement was broader, where there was room to stop and lean against a shop window and begin her search. She'd planned to have a cigarette at the same time, maybe even go to a café, but in the end her curiosity proved too powerful. She didn't even make it to the top of the hill. Everything she wanted to know was inside this small rolled-up column of paper and the urge to look was overwhelming.

There was nothing on the cover, thank God, and she opened the first page: news, news . . . stuff about the government, stuff about China . . . Fergie looking awful, Cindy Crawford looking great, but . . . no . . . no . . .

Evie turned the pages – unsure, exactly, of what it was that she was looking for. The broadsheet was unwieldy in her inexperienced hands and began to come apart. The sport section fell to the ground with a couple of flyers, and Evie bent to pick them up – losing her grip on the rest of the paper.

'Fuck,' she said, sounding like her father.

Shuffling it back together, she searched on; squatting on the pavement with the pages spread in front of her.

It took ten minutes for Evie to realise that there was nothing there. Ten minutes of squatting forward, losing all sensation in her calves, for her to find the relevant column. It wasn't like a magazine diary. There were no pictures. Just five small paragraphs in a box down the side of the page: Bob Geldof and some parking fine; the Archbishop of Canterbury's latest gaff; something leaked about an unnamed Westminster councillor; two rock stars battling it out for the same Belgravia property; and then – Evie nearly lost her balance –

Honor Montfort, daughter of Xandra Villiers and property magnate Sir William Montfort, celebrated her eighteenth birthday in style at the Wellesley House Hotel last week, along with the cream of London's political and social elite . . . including sexy sixties songstress Trixie Lascelles, whose talents were not aired that night. Whether Trixie is happy with her agent's explanation for this – 'Ms Lascelles never mixes business with pleasure' – is not entirely clear. But it does explain why the pleasure-seeking Montforts chose up-and-coming band Indigo to entertain their guests. Time for a new agent, Trixie?

Evie pulled the paper together and stood up, grinning. She'd met Trixie Lascelles a couple of times at Favenham and, on both occasions, Trixie had ruined the evening by crooning at the piano. Reading Matthew's piece for a second time, Evie couldn't help finding it funny – naughty Matthew, bad Matthew – until it occurred to her that she wasn't exactly immune herself. She wasn't off the hook. There was nothing to stop the bastard from turning on her tomorrow.

And so on Tuesday morning, feeling rather less amused by the piece on poor old Trixie, Evie trod the same path to the newsagent. This time she didn't bother with the cigarettes. Didn't even bother to buy the paper; just turned to the diary page and hungrily read the paragraphs . . .

Nothing.

She put the paper back.

'Excuse me?' said the man at the till, but Evie didn't hear him. She walked out with a frown.

On Wednesday, however – when the result was still a blank – Evie's thoughts took a different turn. Flicking back through that day's paper, she began to ask herself if she'd been a little hasty in assuming the worst from Matthew. She began to wonder if, in fact, he was really

80

being rather decent – not printing the story. It was surely losing value every day. If he left it much longer, it wouldn't be news at all.

'We're not a library. Either buy it, love, or—'

'Okay, okay.' Evie put the newspaper under her arm, found some change in her pocket and placed it on the counter. 'I'm sorry.'

Back in her room Evie sat on the bed and, taking her wastepaper basket up on to her lap, removed all the torn-up little bits of Matthew's *Morning Post* business card from its depths. Thank God for her mother's absence. Emptying bins was hardly top of Giles's list of priorities – he didn't even know which day the rubbishmen came – and Evie was in luck: all the bits were there.

She took them downstairs, laid them out on the kitchen table – carefully arranging them so that it was possible to decipher the number at the bottom – and picked up the telephone . . . only to find herself sitting there five minutes later, finger still hovering over the handset while she wondered what on earth she could say to Matthew that wouldn't make her sound silly or downright paranoid. It was just too messy and embarrassing. And the more Evie thought about it, the more inclined she was simply to put the telephone back down and lose the torn-up card – scatter it in amongst the slimy crusts and carrot skins that lurked at the bottom of the kitchen bin, make it safely irretrievable. Forget he'd ever given it to her.

And when Rachel returned to London two days later – having succeeded in her mission to persuade William's mistress into thinking that the last thing she'd wanted was to destroy the poor man; that it had

81

never been her intention to hurt his family, or cause any kind of distress; that of course she'd never been serious about going to the tabloids: what kind of a bunny boiler did Rachel think she was? – Evie knew she'd made the right decision. What possible advantage could be gained from putting herself through the humiliation of calling Matthew, only to say that there'd be no kiss-and-tell after all? Every time Evie thought of what had happened, the shame made her skin crawl: her disloyalty – gossiping about Honor's parents to a complete stranger; her rudeness – not bothering to return Matthew's call when his intentions must have had nothing to do with the story; her arrogance – thinking that the story had any value; her stupidity – in not even being able to get the facts straight in the first place; and finally, her cowardice – in the way she was quite unable to confess what she'd done, and in her resolve to keep the whole cheek-burning episode buried, along with a torn-up business card, in the putrid darkness of a kitchen bin.

'So it's all over, then?' said Giles, in the dark of their bedroom.

For a moment Rachel did not reply, and he was beginning to wonder if she was already asleep when she spoke back, heavy and sad. 'I suppose so. In a way. William told me he was going to catch the seven o'clock flight, so he must be with her now . . . which will certainly mean that Diana's happy. And if we want Xandra and the children to be safe, and the family to stay together, and the press well clear . . . then I guess that Diana getting exactly what she wants is the only guarantee of it right now. But' – sighing – 'but you can't really say that it's "over", can you? Not when she and William are right this minute having the kind of reconciliation it's probably best not to think too much about. Not when . . .'

Giles placed his hand on her arm. 'At least she didn't blab, Rach.'

'I'm starting to wonder if she was ever going to. Seems to me it was just some stupid tiff . . .'

'That's not how it sounded last week, sweetheart. And – and imagine how you'd be feeling now if they hadn't been crying wolf, if she really was on the verge of going public.'

'But *you* didn't think I should go, did you? *You* knew from the start that it was a mistake for me to get involved.'

'I might not have been right.'

'But you were, Giles. And the worst thing is, they now think – probably quite understandably – that I'm on their side. Thought I'd be *pleased* when he rang to say he'd bought that stupid houseboat for her after all and making illicit plans – right in front of me – for her to come down and see it when Xandra isn't around . . .'

'Oh God.'

'Diana was so ecstatic she had to stop him mid-sentence so that she could share the news with me. Even suggested I come with them to help choose furniture . . .'

Silently, Giles stroked his wife's hair – wishing there was something he could say beyond 'I told you so'; wishing he'd been wrong; wishing, more particularly, that Diana Miller had gone to the sodding newspapers after all and that – for once in his life – William Montfort had got what he deserved.

'I mean, it's not that I can't sympathise,' Rachel went on, with a sudden change of tack. 'Poor Diana –

struggling at school because she came from a different background; struggling in her twenties trying to earn the money that everybody else was given by their parents . . . and never getting the right invitations to the right parties; never fancying the men that fancied her, yet all the time trying so so hard to get it right. Joining tennis clubs, going on blind dates, and having her hair done every week – and I have to say she was looking amazing, even with her eyes all puffy – but still always on the outside; always denied the kind of relationship that everyone else seems to have as a matter of course, the One True Tove—'

'Oh for God's sake.'

'I'm serious, Giles. And then a man like William walks into her life – sitting nonchalantly in the boardroom of an Edinburgh solicitor's while they thrash out the details of some property agreement – twizzling a pencil between his fingers and catching her eye across the table . . . and then she remembers who he is, and reminds him about her connection with me . . . and before you know it, they're having an affair . . . you can see how it happened—'

'You certainly can.'

'So – so why do I feel so contaminated?'

Giles sighed. 'Because you're on the other side, my love. Because you're a married woman. Because however much you feel sorry for people like Diana, however much you want to make life better for her, it's not always possible. Especially not when it's your own brother's family she's threatening to destroy.'

PART II

Chapter Six

Between Shifts

It wasn't a restaurant Honor knew. She must have walked past the place a thousand times – her hairdresser was only a couple of blocks beyond, and there was a juice bar on the corner she sometimes stopped in – but still Brasserie Beach had never caught her eye. It was an ordinary diner, an Anglo-American-Franco-Italian-anything-goes type of place, with wicker chairs and plastic plants and posters of movie stars on the walls. The waitresses wore a predictable uniform of shirts and ties and short black skirts – and bored expressions. The background music was easy guitar. And walking through the doors on a sleepy September afternoon, Honor was surprised by how full it seemed to be – and by how much of it there was, stretching out into a garden at the back.

'Table for one, madam?'

Honor smiled at the woman behind the desk – a slim Indian, with shining hair and beautiful teeth. 'I'm sorry,' she said. 'I'm really just here to meet Evie. Evie Langton? She said she'd be having a break around four, so I . . . Well, I do see I'm a little bit early, but I was hoping . . .'

'Fine,' said the woman, her mask of welcome falling away as she returned to sorting through a pile of laminated menus. 'You can wait over there if you like. She shouldn't be much longer.'

Honor slid on to one of the seats of a badly-lit booth to the left of the bar – one that was still littered with the previous occupants' coffee cups and dirty napkins and torn pink sugar-sachets. She took a menu from the clip by the wall, but had yet to find anything on it she liked by the time Evie appeared looking pale and stressed – pulling off her tie as she slipped into the seat opposite; releasing her hair from its regulation ponytail.

'Sorry about that.'

'Don't be silly.' Honor kissed her. 'I was early.'

'There's been some fuck-up over the shifts – which means I've now only got half an hour before the next one starts. But if you don't mind staying here and watching me munch my way through a plate of spaghetti . . .'

'Of course I don't! I just wanted to see you.'

At this, Evie smiled. 'Yeah,' she said, fiddling around in her money belt and pulling out a packet of cigarettes. 'So go on then – how was it?'

Honor hesitated, unsure how best to handle this conversation she knew they'd have to have. It was just so incredibly unfair. Here she was, tanned and glowing from having spent most of July and August in Spain, where she'd joined Abe on location, sunned herself beside a series of swimming pools and then been swept away with the cast and crew on a succession of glamorous wrap and post-wrap parties, and one rather decadent boat trip. And there was Evie;

88

pale and drawn from having spent the best part of those same months earning a pittance at Brasserie Beach and getting over the shock of failing her retakes.

Clearly, she should play it down. Although in truth that would hardly be a problem. On the contrary, Honor's challenge would be in not complaining about her lot – not when Evie's must have been so much worse. It seemed so ungrateful to say that her time in Spain had been far from happy: that for much of the time she'd been bored and lonely – probably would have got through her entire first-year reading list if only she'd had the books at her disposal – and that when Abe had got back in the evenings, his main desire had been to join the rest of the crew in the bar . . . drinking, sometimes snorting, themselves into oblivion.

Yes, the scene had been glamorous. And, yes, they'd been surrounded by beautiful and successful people – especially towards the end, when the whole project decamped to the cool blue coast – but it wasn't for Honor. There was nothing gentle about it. Nothing kind, or even particularly polite – unless you were prepared to pay for it, or were sufficiently high up the ladder – and then, of course, it was only oil and obsequiousness and blatant self-interest. Good manners didn't come into it. Instead, ambition had crackled in the air. Wannabe actresses and models had seduced their way past night-club security guards and hotel staff, all making a beeline for the big shots on the project, the director and the producers, the starring actors, and – increasingly – Abe, who hardly objected to the fuss they made over him. So far as Honor knew, he hadn't strayed – but it had been a constant worry. And the longer she stayed, the more depressing it became. She didn't want to fight for Abe's attention. It wasn't her style: she didn't do the rat race, the hard world where only the fittest survived.

Even the glamour of smart hotels and rented villas left a bad taste in her mouth. She began to resent the hired life: the professional smiles, the miniature bottles, the hairdryers fixed to the bathroom wall, and the beautiful linen sheets and towels that had been on someone else's bed the night before, and wrapped round someone else's body . . . And the more personalised the service was – turned-down beds, little chocolates on the pillow, the concierge remembering her name – the more distasteful Honor found it. *All yours, darling* it seemed to say, but only for the afternoon, or night, or week, or whenever it was you paid the bill and moved on. It was all – very slightly – prostituted . . . down to the sand between her toes.

'It was fine,' she said at last. 'Abe did well. They were pleased with his dailies, or his rushes, or whatever it is they call them. And it was wonderful to be out there in the sun. I didn't join him on set much – there isn't a great deal to do and there's a lot of hanging around, even if you're actually in the scene, so I'm afraid I did spend rather a lot of time by the pool . . .'

'Poor you,' said Evie, lighting her cigarette.

'No! No, it was great. I was just a bit . . . lazy, I suppose. Probably didn't make the most of the social life on offer, but it was lovely to be with Abe. And heavenly to lie in the shade – quietly reading and dozing and letting the world go by.'

Evie looked at her cousin, fretting and squirming on the other side of the booth, and felt a surge of affection. 'Well I'm glad,' she said with a sudden smile. 'If anyone deserves it, it's you. All that work you did at school, all that work you're going to have to do at

90

Oxford next year . . . I'm glad you could let yourself be lazy – for once in your overdiligent life!'

Honor felt embarrassed. 'So what about you?' she said, changing the subject. 'What's your plan of action?'

Evie glanced at her watch. 'My plan of action,' she echoed, distractedly, checking round over her shoulder to see who else was in the restaurant, 'my plan of action . . . is to get some food before Samira gets on my case again. I . . . Carla?'

Evie was on her feet, approaching a plain girl in the same uniform – the same black skirt and tie and rolled-up white shirt-sleeves – but worn with none of Evie's rakishness.

'You couldn't go down and ask Gary to do me some of that linguine, could you? Thanks Carl. And a Diet Coke?'

But by the time the food arrived she hardly had a moment to eat it. The same slim woman who'd greeted Honor at the desk had returned from whatever it was she'd gone off to do with the menus, and was back behind the desk, talking to a supplier on the telephone. Her gaze hung impatiently over their little booth, and the clock hands ticked round to the half-hour mark.

'I'd better go,' said Evie, hurriedly scraping her hair back into its ponytail and snapping the band in place. 'We've got a load of deliveries at the back that still need sorting.' She leant a little closer. 'And I certainly don't want to give that bitch the satisfaction of telling me to—'

'Evie?'

'Yes, Samira. I'm just—'

'I really think those lettuces should come in now. It's

91

not good for them to sit out there in the yard – not in this sun. And anyway, your—'

'I'm there.' Evie pulled her tie up and got to her feet. 'I'm sorry, Honor. I'll call tomorrow when I— *Yes, I'm coming!*'

And she was gone, taking with her all the debris from their table: the coffee cups and glasses the previous customers had left, along with her own plate and glass, and the overloaded ashtray, the scrunched-up paper napkins and sodden sugar sachets that Honor had pushed to one side . . . all smartly gathered together and balanced in Evie's hands as she hurried down the stairs to the kitchen.

Honor watched her go. She saw the little black skirt, the money belt, the dancing ponytail, the white shirt with 'Brasserie Beach' printed brightly on the back – identical to those of the other waitresses busying around at the back of the restaurant laying out fresh tables for dinner that night, folding napkins, sorting through candles. And there was something about the uniforms – even with top buttons undone and ties loosened and the skirts pulled crazily short – something that seemed, to Honor, degrading. Like being back at school. Except so much worse – for Evie had no plans. Unlike most of the other girls, she wasn't waitressing 'to fill in' or make a bit of vacation money or fund a travel dream. This was her life.

Honor picked up her bag – it was one she'd bought in a Spanish market, with fading straw and a bright pink lining. Not bothering to acknowledge Evie's manager – so pettily superior at the desk, in her crisp trouser-suit and her black hair hanging free – Honor walked out through the glass doors of the restaurant. She returned to the bustle of Kensington High Street, full of wretchedness for her friend – heaving crates of iceberg lettuces out of the sun with 'Brasserie Beach' in curly branded letters across her bending back.

At one in the morning the late shift was over. Unhooking her leather jacket from a kitchen peg, Evie didn't bother to put it on – she was still too hot from clearing up. Instead, she slung it over her arm and, with Samira long gone and no one to object, left the restaurant by the front entrance.

He was waiting by his car, reading a newspaper in the orange street light – but looked up the moment she emerged.

'Hello sexy . . .'

Evie grinned. She knew he liked her uniform. He liked the tie and the little black skirt. He liked the clunking money belt. He even liked the ponytail and the logo on her back. 'Take me home,' she said, kissing him sleepily.

Matthew kissed her back. And then – gently relieving her of the jacket, and the black nylon backpack she persisted in carrying everywhere – he guided her into his little blue Renault and took her north to Kilburn.

Chapter Seven

Matthew and Abe

Now they were together, it seemed to Evie that going out with Matthew was just about the easiest thing she had ever done. Those early days – the lengths she'd taken to avoid him back in May and the feeling of dread his name had inspired the night she'd refused to take his call – it all seemed very distant somehow, and not entirely real. Some other world, with other people walking around in it.

Eyes closed, she sat back in the passenger seat as the little Renault sped left down a deserted Portobello Road and out, under the railway line, towards the cottages of Kilburn Lane . . . and felt, again, a surge of gratitude towards whomever or whatever had brought Matthew Forrester into Brasserie Beach that hot night back in August.

Nothing had been going her way. It had been her first week in the job, her first Friday night, and – still wretched from the recent news about her A-level results – the last thing Evie had needed was a party of ten hungry men in her section of the restaurant. Sulkily, she'd stood with a pile of menus, waiting for them to take their seats – hating them for being so late, hating the fact that most of them were already drunk, and above all hating Samira for passing them off on to her when Carla's section was virtually empty and infinitely easier to serve.

'. . . Just a waste of everyone's time,' a fat large-chinned man was saying to his neighbour and anyone else who'd listen. 'The place is overregulated as it is. The last thing we need is . . . *Bugger*. The thing's wonky. It . . . Waitress? Oi, waitress!'

Evie looked at him.

'Do something about this table, can't you? And a few beers wouldn't go amiss . . . a Budweiser for me, and . . . What about you, Dave? You want a Bud?'

'I'm sorry. We don't do Budweiser,' said Evie, on her knees – stuffing napkins under the table leg by his foot, 'We've got Stella, and Michelob.'

'Anything else?'

Evie closed her eyes. 'You want me to check?'

'If you don't mind. And could you bring us a couple of jugs of water while you're at it? And a packet of Silk Cut. And—'

'Cigarettes are down by the toilets, sir. There's a machine on the right at the bottom of the stairs.'

'Come on, love. Can't you get them for us? I'll give you the cash, if that—'

'I'm sorry.' Evie stood up, her face flushed from bending. 'You'll have to get them for yourself. So it's two jugs of tap water, and how many beers?'

And that was when she saw him: on the other side of the table, deep in conversation with a German-looking man with very short hair. Both were looking at a slip of paper, but something about the moment – a sense of being scrutinised, perhaps, as Evie double-checked; or maybe it was simply her voice, asking for their drinks' order – something made Matthew look back at her. His surprise swiftly turning to amusement as he registered who she was.

'We'll order the beers when you tell us what you've got, love,' said the man with the large chin, leering at her legs.

'Hm?'

'I said *we'll order the beers when you tell us what you've got!*' He was shouting now. 'Bloody hell. We've got a right one tonight, lads! She—'

'So you don't want Stella or Michelob, then?'

'What I want is a Bud.'

Evie pulled at the hem of her skirt. 'But we don't have Budweiser, sir. I told you that. It's—'

'Don't have Budweiser . . . won't get me cigarettes . . . What kind of a joint is this?'

Evie stood silently.

'I'm talking to you, sweetheart,' said the man, suddenly getting to his feet. The chair made an ugly scrape across the floor. 'Or are you too stupid to understand what I'm saying? Jesus, waitresses . . .' he turned to the rest of his party, making sure they were all listening. 'Most don't speak a sodding word of English, and the ones that do have an IQ of three. And then,' swinging back to Evie, 'and then you have the *cheek* to expect a tip?'

'Is there a problem?' said Samira, suddenly appearing from behind Evie's shoulder.

'No – no, Samira. He—'

'I'd just like a beer and a packet of cigarettes. Is that so much to ask?'

Samira gave him a charming smile. 'Absolutely not, sir. What kind of beer would you like? We've got Stella

96

Artois and Michelob, and a new one called Garten-
burg, which is a rather unusual brew from Belgium
that's particularly good with the steamed mussels, if
you were thinking of—'

'Great.' The man sat down again. 'I'll have that.'

'And a packet of cigarettes, you say?'

'That's right. Silk Cut, if it's not too much trouble.'

'Evie . . . would you?'

Evie stared at her. They were never encouraged to
do this for customers, especially at the busier times
when they were barely able to keep up with the orders.

Samira returned the stare with a patronising smile.
'You just pay for it out of your belt, Evie,' she said, very
slowly, as if agreeing with the man's assessment of her
IQ, 'and add it to the bill. It's not so difficult.'

'But—'

'Now?'

Head lowered, Evie did as she was told – with the
man laughing behind her as she turned to go
downstairs.

And she was still fiddling around in her money belt
for the right change for the cigarette machine when, to
her horror, Matthew came wandering down the stairs.

'Evie?'

'Hang on a minute.'

Matthew waited while the coins clunked into the
machine and Evie pressed the button for Silk Cut.
Slowly, the machine churned round and one shiny
white-and-purple packet fell out into the bucket at the
bottom. Evie picked it out and turned, reluctantly.
'Yes?'

'It's Matthew – remember? Matthew Forrester? We
met at—'

'I remember.'

97

'I was just – just wanting to say hello, I guess. Wondering how you were . . .'

'Oh, I'm wonderful. Can't you tell?'

Matthew bit his lip. 'Yes, I'm sorry about that. I don't actually know the guy. He's some City friend of—'

'And you think that makes it all right?'

Silence.

'Honestly,' she snapped. 'How fucking rude can you get?'

Matthew's eyebrows rose a little. 'Not returning calls?' he said. 'That ranks pretty high on my list. Cutting a man dead? Making him feel like a nerd? That's not very nice.'

'What did you expect?'

'Well Evie, I'd have hoped that—'

'Come on. You weren't exactly straight with me that night. You never told me what you were really doing at Honor's party. You let me gabble on, believing—'

'Yes, yes, all right,' Matthew muttered as voices he recognised – voices from his table – approached the top of the stairs and before Evie quite realised what was happening, he'd thrust her backwards through a pair of swing doors and out, past the sizzling and bickering of the kitchen staff, into the open yard. 'Okay then,' he said, releasing her arms as suddenly as he'd gripped them. 'Go on.'

Evie wasn't used to being pushed around. While part of her wanted angrily to push him back, another part was stirred by what had just happened. She liked his quick reaction, his physical decisiveness – hadn't expected it, somehow. Not from someone brainy. And the way he'd handled her – that hard straightforward grasp – suddenly Evie found she didn't care to go back to the restaurant just yet. So what if Big-Chin had to wait a few more minutes for his fags? So what if Samira had to send out a search party? So what if she was sacked?

It was cool and dark out in the yard, lit only by flat white stripes that fell from the kitchen windows. Unwrapping Big-Chin's cigarettes, Evie offered them to Matthew – who refused – and reached into her money belt for a box of Brasserie Beach matches.

'Well, that's it, really,' she said, lighting one. 'I'm sorry I didn't trust you, Matthew. But if you lie to people then you can't expect them to—'

'Lie?'

The flare of the match illuminated her face – and his. For a second their eyes met. 'You lied about your job,' she said.

'No, Evie. That's not true. I didn't tell you what it was, but we both know that's not the same as—'

'I seem to remember you telling me you worked in a sewage plant.'

'Yes,' he said, mouth twitching, 'and I remember you being so convinced by that one that you spat champagne all over your dress . . .'

Mulishly, she looked at him.

'Just because you're feeling guilty that you were a little indiscreet, don't take it out on me! I might have a duty to tell people I'm a journalist when I'm actually working . . . but at that stage of the evening, I most definitely wasn't. All I did was listen to you, and keep my trap shut – which, when you recall that the so-called story never even came out, was probably the right thing to do, no? You should be *thanking* me, not—'

'Then why the big secret? Why couldn't you tell me what job you did? If it was really so irrelevant, then—'

'Why do you think?'

99

Evie didn't catch the undercurrent in his voice. 'I don't know,' she muttered, dragging on the last of her cigarette. 'I'm not a fucking mind-reader . . .'

Smiling, Matthew looked at her – standing there so crossly in her uniform. He looked at the way she was leaning against the wall; at the slanting hem of her little black skirt and the nonchalant tie – knotted halfway down her front; and the wonderful line of her mouth as she took the cigarette away and blew a jet of smoke into the night . . . and found himself wondering why he hadn't tried a little harder back in May.

'Okay,' he said. 'I'll spell it out: I love my job. I'm still not quite in the area I'd like to be in, and – and in any case I'm sure there'll always be problems, whatever journalism I do . . . but I wouldn't change it for the world.'

Evie took a final drag on the cigarette, and dropped it to the concrete. 'Then all the more reason to tell people about it,' she said, stamping out a spray of orange sparks. 'Wouldn't you say?'

'Not when people despise me for it. You only have to look at the way you yourself reacted when you bothered to read my card to see what I'm saying . . . and believe me, you're not the only one. The minute people – and it's invariably the most attractive people, the ones I'd like to know better – the minute they find out I work for a newspaper diary – even one like the *Post* – they cut me out. They think, as you yourself thought, that I'll use them. They think they have to watch everything they say. They close up. They're very careful. I never get to hear what they really think. I don't get close to them at all . . .' He waited for her to look at him again. '. . . So you see, that's why I didn't tell you.'

With his eyes fully accustomed to the dark – using what he could from the kitchen light – Matthew watched for Evie's reaction. Her mouth was free now, and slightly open. Her eyes gleamed beneath the irregular weight of her fringe. And then, very slowly, she smiled – showing a childish row of bright white teeth that, for all the orthodontistry she'd endured, still had more character than perfection.

'You wanted to get to know me better?'

'You could put it like that.'

Matthew read the message in her smile: green lights all the way. He watched her reach for another cigarette from the packet in her hand. He watched her – she was still smiling – as she checked to see she had the right end and put it into her mouth. He watched her reach for the box of matches, take one out and scratch. The flare lit her skin . . . her neck, her chin, the side of her face. And in that moment's glow, he noticed how smooth and pale and soft it was, under the line of her jaw. His blood began to rise. Whipping the cigarette from Evie's fingers and holding it, smouldering, with his arm stretched out behind him, Matthew pressed her against the wall. Ignoring her reaction – it was one of laughing outrage – he made for that very part of her, that perfect scoop where neck became face, the place that still contained the remains of yesterday's scent – the place a predator would choose when going for the kill – closed his eyes and kissed it.

The laughing stopped. It seemed for a moment that she was purring – her throat was resonating under his lips – and then she shifted slightly so that, instead of her neck, he was kissing her smoky mouth. Smoky lips, smoky tongue, and sharp white teeth that were a little hard to predict . . . It might have been a turn-off, but not

101

for Matthew Forrester. He liked the wildcat in her. The—

'Evie?'

'Fuck.'

'Evie, are you out there?'

'Fuck, Matthew. What the hell do I – ?'

Smoothly, Matthew stepped into the light. 'Zhorry,' he said, sounding suddenly much drunker than before. 'Wasz jus . . . looking for zhe gents.' He stumbled over a loose crate. 'Waz told downsztairs, but . . .'

'Christ.' Samira shrank back to the safety of the kitchen. 'Deal with this idiot, would you, Gary?'

Evie waited in the shadows until the voices faded and the yard was silent again. Then she crept back in to the cigarette machine, bought Big-Chin a fresh packet and returned to her duties upstairs – with a swing in her step and a spark in her smile because she knew that Matthew was watching her, and that he liked what he saw.

She was certain he'd still be there at the end of her shift and she was absolutely right – that shift and many others, all through August and into September. He began by taking her to a bar in the Fulham Road that stayed open late, and then on to Putney where he'd leave her at the door. But that soon changed, and it wasn't long before she was going back with him instead, back to the privacy of his little flat in Kilburn, where there would be no fear of interruption and no need for explanations.

Giles and Rachel knew what she was doing, and were at heart relieved. Of course they worried about her. Rachel in particular –

'I hope she's being sensible . . .

But darling, don't you think we should at least find out his name? . . .

102

He sounded rather nice – I wonder what he does for a living . . .'

– but Giles stood firm. The important thing was to see their daughter happy again and to know that, just because she was still living at home, Evie wasn't being denied the adult lifestyle that, as a student, would have been hers without question.

But while Evie had no desire to tell her parents about Matthew, with Honor it was different. She longed to share the news with her friend – particularly when Honor came back from Spain and was there in London, only minutes away. Evie was hardly a natural secret-keeper, certainy not where Honor was concerned. And it was only the sense that Honor wouldn't approve – the sense that, for all his intelligence and charm, a journalist like Matthew would always be something of a pariah to someone in Honor's position – that held Evie's tongue at bay.

Abe, too, was back in London. With the filming in Spain now complete, he had no more work lined up until the move to LA, which had been set for the end of the year. And while this posed no major financial problems (indeed, Karen Rossetti was delighted with the state of Abe's account, confident there'd be sufficient royalties coming in from international repeats of *Cavaliers and Roundheads* to keep everyone happy for some time), he still rather longed for something to fill his days and distract him from the question of when to tell Honor the whole truth about LA.

At this stage – with nothing definite in the pipeline – it just seemed better not to trouble her with the prospect of a more permanent move. And now that she'd started her first year at Oxford, it wasn't as if she'd miss him.

Not properly. Sure, she'd called every night from her college telephone – was even planning to be back with him in London this weekend – but it wasn't the same as having her around all the time. And if she was prepared to put *him* on ice for *her* career, then surely . . .

She might not welcome the idea but Abe was certain she'd understand. The brief trip he'd made at the end of May – to meet the producers and casting directors his agent had lined up – had been a success . . . at least it was according to Karen. Joe Ferenezi had loved him. Marti Price had loved him. And while the only definite job he'd come away with was a cameo part in *Florida Coast* – one of Marti's TV shows – Karen still thought it was a result. They wouldn't be casting for the new Ferenezi until January, so she wasn't disappointed by the lack of anything concrete on that front.

'And they're making the right noises, darling,' she was now telling him as they sat in her office. 'That's what really matters.'

Abe nodded uneasily.

'I know it's difficult, sweetie, but you've got to be patient. It's what this business is all about. All *anyone* can do is be ready to go when they call, and – and you're in by far the best position to do that if you're actually living there.'

'I know, Karen. I'm just—'

'It's the right decision.'

'You think so?'

Karen smiled right into him – bright and firm and certain. 'I know so,' she said. 'And it's not as if Price and Ferenezi are your only options. I've got three scripts through from the guys at GoldMax, and another one from Larry Chase . . . all with possibles for you. The only thing we need to decide right now is the best time to move out permanently. You could go now, but as you've only got a few days on *Florida Coast*, my advice would be to stay in a hotel, perhaps combine it with meeting Larry – who'll simply love you, by the way – and then go properly some time after Christmas . . .'

Abe left her office at four, laden down with scripts and flattery – her smooth drawl in his ears. He got a cab home to the increasingly familiar sight of a silver Mercedes parked on the far side of the street. He couldn't see Phil's face behind the sheet of light on the slanting windscreen, but he recognised the hand that dangled from the window, the tapping fingers, the running engine, the twitchiness of a wild animal momentarily exposed.

Paying the cab driver with the last of his cash, Abe realised he had none left for Phil, who wasn't in the market for cheques. And Phil – getting out of his car, slamming the door with some eloquence – had the look of a man whose patience was wearing thin. Still, Abe decided to risk it. Phil had waited. He clearly wanted the business. And Abe, for sure, wanted the drugs. He'd get the guy inside, get sorted. Then go and get the cash for him.

'Yeah, I know, man. I'm sorry.' He unlocked the front door and stood aside to let Phil in. 'You go on. I'll follow you up.'

Grabbing a bunch of letters from his slot in the rack, Abe put them in his mouth, lifted his scripts again and climbed the stairs to the first floor. With some difficulty, he leant against the dark wall on the landing, freed a hand for his keys again – to let Phil into the sitting room – and followed him in: spitting out the letters, putting down the scripts.

105

'I – I'm really sorry, man,' he added, switching on the radio to relieve the silence. 'No cabs anywhere, and the traffic was shit – must be some kind of event on at Earls Court.'

Phil sat on the sofa. His look was monochrome: pale and narrow – steel-tough sixties – with a fitted poloneck, and slim knees in tailored trousers, touching the edge of a glass designer coffee table that Abe had bought at great expense from Harrods back in June. Phil never said much. And while Abe floundered on, wondering if this was simply the usual Phil-style silence, or whether Phil was actually pissed-off, Phil's hardened washed-out eyes circled the room, finally resting on Abe – who withered.

'So how much did you want?'

'How much have you got?'

Leaning forwards over the coffee table, Phil took a folded paper packet from the inside pocket of his coat, and another, and another, and placed them on the glass table top. 'Depends what you're looking for,' he said.

Abe fingered the first packet.

'Want to try it?'

Abe tried all three – rubbing a little of the powder round his gums like Phil did, but unable to spot the difference. 'Yeah, man. That's good . . .'

Phil looked at him.

'But you say that's the purest – right?'

Phil didn't even bother to nod. He began refolding the other two packets, leaving the third for Abe to consider. 'That'll cost you eighty,' he said. 'Should be more, but—'

'Eighty?'

'A gram.'

106

'That's expensive.'

Phil shook his head. 'That's a good price.' He sat back. 'That's good stuff you've got there, Abe, and I know where I can get more.'

Abe frowned. 'I'm sorry. I must have misunderstood something. Last time you sold me a half for . . .'

Phil took the packet from him. 'Yeah, well. I can sell you a half for fifty if you want, but—'

'*Fifty*?'

'You want it brought to your door, mate, you gonna have to pay. You said you wanted more this time.'

'I do, Phil. Of course I do. But . . .'

Phil cracked his knuckles.

'Shouldn't it be more like sixty? Seventy . . .?'

Phil put the packet away.

'Phil?'

Phil got up and walked towards the door.

'Okay, okay, man – listen . . .'

But Phil had already started down the stairs. 'It's eighty for the good stuff,' he called back, 'seventy-five for the rest. Take it or leave it – but don't dick me around . . .' He was muttering now, head bent, as he sprang down the last three steps and made for the outside door. 'And don't get me off my ass if you're not fucking serious. I've got a shitload of better things to do with my time—'

Abe caught him at the bottom. 'I'll take it,' he said, breathless. 'I'll take it, Phil. Eighty for the good stuff – no more questions – just need to get some cash.' Still talking, he leant against the front door. 'I got my cards, just here – see? And the bank's round the corner, up at the end on the right – no distance at all. We—'

But as he spoke, there was a rattling from outside and the door began to shake. Someone was trying to get in – and it was only when Abe stood aside that he realised it was Honor. Honor, with a suitcase and the spare set of keys he'd given her when they'd said goodbye last week.

'Hello,' she said, looking from Abe to Phil to Abe again.

They looked back at her – neat and poised against the light. Abe sensed something uneasy about her smile, but it was too vague, too subtle, next to the thought of all that cocaine in Phil's pocket – edging away from him, through the door.

'Honor, this is my friend Phil. Phil – Honor. Listen darling, we've just got to go out for moment to – to get something for Phil, and then I'll be back . . . You'll be okay?'

'I'll be fine,' she said.

'Great.' He smiled – 'See you in a minute,' – and closed the door.

Honor stood with her suitcase in the dark hall. She heard them walking down the steps. 'Sorry about that . . .' Abe was saying, and now he was laughing at something the other guy was saying, something she couldn't make out.

She climbed the stairs. She knew what they were doing. She didn't need to be streetwise to know what kind of business Abe's 'friend' was in. What surprised her was how much she minded. It wasn't as if she didn't know about this side of Abe's life. He hadn't tried to hide anything. But face-to-face with that other man – the absence of light in his eyes, the flat voice and yellow smile – it rocked her. There it was: Abe's other side, embodied in that shell. And in that moment, what had been simply theoretical – easy to ignore, easy to defend – was suddenly and insurmountably vile.

She entered Abe's flat – Abe's world: the toppling piles of scripts; the dance music radio station, racketing on; unopened letters on the floor; unbottled smells from the bathroom, sandalwood shower gel and minty toothpaste, jarring with the hour – she stepped through it, her step soundless on the carpet. She switched off the radio, shut the bathroom door, put the scripts and letters on his desk and opened a window – wide.

She sat on the sofa in the same place that Phil had occupied, sank back and shut her eyes. She thought he'd be glad she was early. She'd tried ringing from the college, and again from a service station – to say that her last lecture had been cancelled and that she was on her way – but there had been no answer. She'd assumed Abe was still out with his agent, but no. Oh, no. He'd been sitting here all along, with that efficient-looking dealer and his nasty smile, stocking up on coke supplies to the beat of Soul II Soul, while somewhere far away a telephone was ringing . . .

Ten minutes later, Abe was back – striding into the room, heading straight for the radio.

'Stupid machine would only give me fifty. Had to find a bureau de change that would take my credit card.' He tossed his keys on the sofa and sat down. 'But now it's done. Now I can concentrate completely on you.' He kissed her. 'Everything okay?'

Honor hesitated.

'Too many Freshers' parties?'

'Mm.'

'You – you're not freaked out about this, are you?' he said, reaching in his pocket for the tiny roll of paper – no longer than a matchstick, no wider than a pen – that had cost him so much money.

109

Honor looked at it. 'No,' she said slowly. 'No, Abe. I just—'

'Just what?'

She looked away. 'That guy . . .'

'What – Phil?' Abe laughed. '*Phil*? Oh, darling, darling . . . you don't need to worry about Phil! Might look dodgy and charge me the earth, but this coke really is first class, and he . . . Listen to me sweetheart. I found him through Karen. And if anyone knows about who to go to for this kind of stuff then it's—'

'Karen – your agent?'

Abe nodded. 'Met him at one of her client parties. He used to be an actor, but then the work dried up and now he's selling drugs.' He grinned at Honor from under his sexy slice of hair. 'So you see, you mustn't be too hard on him, darling. It could happen to any of us.'

'You wouldn't do it, though.'

Abe shrugged. 'I don't know,' he said. 'This kind of work isn't guaranteed. None of us really knows – who sinks and who floats, and how we handle it, especially if we're not particularly talented – can't say what kind of things we'd consider if push came to—'

'You're saying you'd deal drugs?'

'I'm saying never say never, Honor – like I don't know if I'd squeal under torture, and I don't know if I'd trample over women and children to survive some mass disaster.' Abe looked at her – aware, suddenly, that he'd raised his voice and wishing that he hadn't. 'Maybe I'd do the right thing,' he added, with a hopeful smile that he couldn't quite sustain. It felt self-righteous, and he cancelled it out with a laugh and a foolish expression. 'But I do have a nasty feeling I wouldn't . . .'

And so, with sad detachment, did she. There had

been a few short weeks in London – weeks when they were both back from Spain, but before she'd gone up to Oxford – when it had seemed to Honor that things were almost back to normal. Abe had been calmer, more sensitive . . . easier to love. And it had been possible for Honor to convince herself that the difficulties in Spain – the drugs, the partying, the restlessness – were some isolated aberration.

But she'd been wrong. And later on that October afternoon, lying with him, Honor found she couldn't rid herself of the idea that what she'd taken for the real Abe was only a surface impression; that the 'isolated aberration' she'd seen in Spain was nothing of the sort; that, inside that splendid body-costume she thought she'd come to love, was a wiry skinhead peddling coke. He looked like a hero – he could play the part – but that was all it was.

So when, the following Sunday, Abe told her about his plans to move out to LA, Honor felt little more than a sprinkling of relief. She left for Oxford with a lighter heart and a more affectionate kiss for him than she would otherwise have given – for it was easy to show she cared when there was an end in sight.

Chapter Eight

Oxford

With her first term at Oxford drawing to a close, Honor decided to hold a party in her rooms. As a first-year student, she'd been allocated one of the nicest sets in her college and she was determined to make the most of it. It wouldn't be a big party. Just the few friends that she and her room-mate had made so far, plus anyone willing to make the journey from London.

'You can crash on the floor,' she said to Evie. 'It's not strictly allowed, but everyone does it. I've got a sleeping bag you can borrow, and there are cushions everywhere.'

Evie said she'd love to come. Love to see Oxford, stay the night, meet Honor's new friends . . . There was just one small favour she wanted to ask.

'Yes?'

Would Honor mind very much if she brought someone with her?

'"Someone"?'

'He's very nice, Honor. He wouldn't—'

'*He?*' Honor gasped, laughing. 'My God, Evie – have you got something you want to tell me?'

Taking a long deep breath, Evie told Honor that she and Matthew – yes, the Matthew she'd met at Honor's party; the Matthew who lived in Kilburn and, yes, yes, writes for the *Morning Post* . . . Well, they bumped into each other again, back in August . . . He happened to be in the restaurant with a crowd of friends, and she—

'August?'

'That's right. And – and that was it, really. We started seeing each other straight away. It's been amazing, Honor. He's just about the nicest, sexiest, kindest, funniest, most interesting . . .' She was smiling as she thought of him. Honor could hear it in her voice. '. . . *So* beats the socks off Danny sodding Milligan . . .'

'And you've waited until now to tell me about it?'

Evie was silent for a moment. And then said, rather more quietly, 'I was worried you'd hate him. I thought, what with him being a journalist and the way Abe was talking in the car, it just seemed simpler to—'

'What's Abe got to do with anything?'

'He is your boyfriend, Honor. And he may even have a point, I suppose. But—'

'Just because Abe's funny about journalists, that doesn't mean I am. I think the guy sounds wonderful. Who cares what he does for a living?'

'But what about your parents? Your whole—'

'My parents . . . my boyfriend . . . *they* might have a problem. But I absolutely do not. I'd love to meet Matthew. I think he sounds great. And' – smiling now – 'if you don't bring him this weekend, Evie, I'll take it extremely personally . . .'

And so, at eight o'clock that Friday evening, Evie and Matthew crossed through the tourist barriers that divided Honor's college from the rest of Oxford. Street sounds fading with every step, they passed into a stiller world – and for a moment Evie felt what it must be like to be an undergraduate. Guided by Matthew, who himself had been at Oxford just a few years earlier and knew the way to Honor's building without having to ask, she walked along the flagstone paths, past real students who looked back at them both and assumed that she was clever; that she belonged there too.

As Matthew had suspected, they didn't need to know the number of the staircase, or the room, to tell which Honor's were. It was clear just from looking at the building. The curtains had not been closed and, through telltale rectangles of steamy yellow light from a set of rooms on the first floor, there were definite signs of partying. As they approached, someone lanky reached up and opened a window, flooding the neoclassical stillness with laughter and tinny music. And there was something about the moment – the party on the first floor, the grey shadow below; the easy gesture of the man opening Honor's window, the familiarity he had with its mechanism, the casual way he took a cigarette from his mouth and turned back to the party, while Evie and Matthew stood below, on the other side of the cool stone wall – something about it sapped her of confidence. Who would they know in that light, laughing room? Who would want to talk to them? Here – on the outside – was where she felt comfortable. Here was where she belonged: just her and Matthew, together, alone.

The music was too loud for anyone to hear a door opening, and only Abe – helping himself to a cocktail from the table by the door – was in a position to greet them. He put his glass down with a grin. 'Evie –'

114

'Abe!' she cried, delighted. 'I thought you were in LA!'

Abe shook his head. 'Not until tomorrow,' he replied, kissing her. 'Crack of dawn, unfortunately – and only for a few days. Then back for Christmas, and out for good in January. It's a bit of a marathon, to be honest.'

'But exciting!' She smiled at him. 'I bet you can't wait . . . Now Abe, this is—'

'Oh, I know exactly who *this* is.' Abe threw a knowing glance in Matthew's direction. 'I've been getting all the gossip from Honor . . .'

'God,' said Matthew. 'I hope it wasn't too awful.'

'Nothing to worry about. No worse than the gossip you peddle, at any rate . . . Now would either of you like a Moscow Mule?'

Radiating false innocence, Abe turned back to the drinks table while Evie's cheeks flashed scarlet. And she was still searching for a response when she felt Matthew's hand on her shoulder – and turned to see him quietly shake his head.

'Let it go,' he mouthed.

'It's ginger ale, lime juice, vodka,' Abe was saying as he poured out each ingredient in turn. 'Revolting, I know. But trust me – it's better than the wine . . .'

Matthew stood there with a blank expression. Having been a diarist for nearly three years, he knew better than to rise to jibes – but it didn't stop him from minding. Because for every person he met who considered his job rather glamorous (and why shouldn't they? He was writing for a living, he was surrounded by intelligence and wit, he was wining and dining some of the most interesting people in London) for every look of envy, there would be another look of suspicion. Mostly it came from people of his parents' generation, people who didn't understand that journalism had far more status these days, and that – perhaps worryingly – it tended to attract people of a far higher calibre than politics or the army ever would. But there were still a few who'd been taught from a very young age to mistrust any form of publicity, or who'd had some sort of negative experience, or – like Abe – knew someone who had . . . a few people his own age who treated the job with disdain, and Matthew minded. He'd never set out to 'peddle gossip' – far less be a diary editor – but it was, for the moment, his job. And while he wasn't planning to stay in it for long – while he and his colleagues, his friends, his boss, his family . . . all knew it was simply a stepping stone to an infinitely more serious career – it was still, right now, with all its nasty connotations and social difficulties, what he did.

Matthew had always been precociously clever. At school he'd been a year younger than his contemporaries. He'd then gone straight to Oxford, worked extremely hard, and come out with a first. But although his background was privileged and his education private, Matthew had never embraced that side of university life. He found the decadent Oxford dining clubs like the Bullingdon and the Assassins off-putting, even depressing. He knew the people who belonged to those clubs – even quite liked some of them – but the sight of them all together, drunk and showing off, made him cringe. And while he knew most of them by name and had no problem with them, one to one, he steered a different course socially, and was drawn instead to a more serious sort of person.

These people were probably no brighter than the cross-dressing fishnet-stockinged revellers of the Piers Gaveston Society, but their tastes coincided with Matthew's. They liked spending time in the library. They liked to discuss events in the Middle East, and question the merits of a two-tier education system. On vacations, they'd either get jobs that combined money and CV points, or they'd load up their rucksacks and head for the Third World – while the Piers Gavestons grabbed weekends in Cannes and St Moritz, or strolled along the King's Road, fiddling with their hair.

But while Matthew rejected them, he continued to observe them – and in many ways, his current job gave vent to this very particular kind of interest. He was of them, yet detached. He was curious but unimpressed. And while his capsule pieces had the requisite starstruck air, there was a streak of irony in his reporting for those who chose to see it.

At twenty-four, Matthew Forrester was still much too young to be a gossip column editor. Not so long ago, the appointment would have been unthinkable. In the days before Mrs Thatcher, journalists trod a prescribed path of apprenticeship – it suited the unions to work it that way – and upstarts like Forrester would have been kept in their place. They'd have spent their twenties learning the ropes on local papers, before perhaps graduating to drearier stories on the nationals. Only the truly dedicated, and middle-aged, reached the giddy position of section editor. Since Thatcher, however – and since the activities of Rupert Murdoch and the exodus to Wapping – the unions no longer had the ability to control the whims of their editors. It was 1989. And if Tim Fleming wished to promote a twenty-four-year-old to editor of the diary section of his flourishing broadsheet then no one, not even the unions, could stand in his way.

But it hadn't made Matthew popular. He already had a team of resentful underlings who were older than him. And it was only because he was so bright, so clearly someone to keep and nurture, that Fleming had stuck his neck out and offered him the job. Sure, Matthew's contacts were good . . . but so were those of countless graduates, and it was his particular brand of useable intelligence – fearsome brainpower *on the ground*, not stuck up in an ivory tower – that made him stand out. Fleming didn't want to lose him. By the time he was thirty-five, Matthew Forrester's name alone would sell copies. He'd be their man in Washington or running the political desk. But he needed experience. He still had things to learn – things about how the paper was run – and making him diary editor was the perfect solution. That way he could attend the daily editorial conferences and be drawn into the heart of the paper . . . yet his daily work remained light and safe – as if he was only playing at the role, not doing it for real. He could make his mistakes in the paddling pool of social London as opposed to dodging bullets on the Gaza Strip.

And Evie, knowing much of this – knowing how Matthew hated the gossip he peddled; knowing, too, how decently he'd behaved over her own indiscretions about William and Xandra; and how prestigious his position at the paper really was, and what it meant for his future; how it deserved respect, not condemnation – Evie longed to come to his defence.

But Matthew had silenced her, and she had no choice but to defer – listening, tight-lipped, as Abe finished mixing drinks, chattering all the while. And as

118

Abe chattered Evie began to realise he wasn't quite himself. Still looked the same: still screen-sexy, with that dominant presence he always seemed to carry about with him, that way of taking up far more space than his five foot ten seemed to justify. But there was something strange tonight about his eyes; something in the way he hopped from subject to subject – fleetingly intense – she was glad when they could take their drinks and move away from him.

But with Honor nowhere to be seen, and no one else familiar, it wasn't long before the lost feelings that Evie had had outside returned. For while Matthew had no problem striking up conversations with virtual strangers, instantly discovering something in common with them – something to do with Oxford, or journalism, or some philosopher they'd both studied – Evie struggled to connect. Too often, when people found out that she wasn't at the university and wasn't even living in Oxford, they'd find some reason to move on.

So Evie stood alone with a diminishing Moscow Mule – too cross with Abe to return to him; too proud to run and interrupt Matthew, who was now deep in conversation with a tall, malnourished-looking man. What did she care if there was no one to talk to?

She leant against the fireplace, with the rest of the party eddying around her.

'. . . I may not have a first in my Descartes essay,' someone said, coming close for a moment to flick cigarette ash into the fire. It was the same lanky boy she'd seen from outside the building. 'But I'm still not convinced his position has anything to do with it.' He turned away, back to the group he was with. 'Nobody's disputing that the animals suffer, Philippa, they just . . . No, I don't agree. I'd say it's more a question of priority than the nature of humanity . . .'

Evie didn't understand a word, but there was more than enough in the nonchalant drawl, in the expensive trousers and the affected way he was smoking for her to figure out what kind of person he was – or wanted to be: someone who had everything and saw no reason not to flaunt it. And instead of finding it sad – instead of recognising that the boy's need to show off signified, if anything, some deeper insecurity – Evie was intimidated. And it was with great relief that she saw a door open in the far corner of the room and Honor coming through – carrying a half-case cardboard box of wine – followed by a girl with kinky red hair and very dark eyebrows, also carrying a box.

'Then we'll have to get someone to go out for more,' the girl was saying. 'This'll never get us through the night. Not when the Oriel lot get here as well.'

'Evie!' cried Honor, suddenly noticing her. 'Oh, Evie!' She put down the box. 'How lovely! You . . . Jessica?' Turning, smiling broadly: 'Jessica, this is my cousin Evie. Evie, this is Jessica – my room-mate.'

The two girls smiled.

'It's so good to finally meet you,' said Jessica, minutes later, as the three of them got to their knees and started breaking into the boxes. 'Honor's been telling me . . . You're a waitress, right?'

Evie nodded.

'In London?'

Evie nodded again. 'It's not permanent or anything. I've only just—'

'But it must be nice, being paid to do your work,' Jessica went on, grappling with heavily stapled cardboard. 'Unlike us poor students. We call ourselves clever, yet we spend some of the most valuable years of

120

our lives getting plastered! You know, the more I think about it, the more convinced I am that it's people like you who—'

'People like me?'

Jessica looked up, her arm resting for a moment on the top of her box. 'My sister's just the same. I mean, why waste time on a second-rate degree when you can get a perfectly good job without one?'

Evie looked back, at the intelligent eyes beneath the strong dark brows; and then round at Honor – who seemed to think that Jessica was being kind – and longed for something smart to say . . . but nothing came to mind. Stupidly, silently, she knelt there – until Jessica returned to her fight with the cardboard and Honor went off for a pair of scissors. After three months at Brasserie Beach, Evie could have shown them a swift neat way to do it by hand – but that was hardly something to brag about.

And in the end, Evie felt she had no choice but to return to Abe – who, like her, was spending much of the evening on his own. Unlike Evie, however, this state of affairs seemed to be very much Abe's own choice. It might have been the drugs he'd taken – certainly, that would have helped – but Evie felt it more probable that Abe genuinely didn't care; not when he was off to LA in the morning. With horizons that glamorous, what did he care for student parties in England?

He looked very comfortable, raising his glass as she drew near and making room on the sofa.

'Having fun?'

Evie sank on to the sofa. 'Laugh a minute. How about you?'

Abe leant forward with a bottle of champagne – whipped out from its hiding-place in the wastepaper basket to his left – and peered at Evie's glass. 'You'd better down that, sweetheart.'

'All of it?'

'I'm not mixing vintage Billecart with whatever hogwash you've got in there.'

'Hogwash I believe you made yourself . . .'

Abe chuckled. 'Well of course if you think you'd *prefer* it to this then I'm certainly not about to—'

Evie turned to the open window behind them, tossed her hogwash through it and held out an empty glass.

'My, my,' he murmured, filling it up. 'You clearly went to finishing school . . .'

Evie sat back, drank the champagne and let him entertain her with a running commentary on everyone else in the room. Whatever it was he'd taken that night, it was certainly loosening his tongue. To begin with, she found it quite funny.

'. . . You think he's out of deodorant? Jesus' – chuckling – 'look at it! Halfway down his arm . . . And what do you make of the blonde?'

'The blonde?' said Evie, sitting forward for a better look.

'Talking to Damp Pits. Perhaps you can't see her? She—'

'Oh yes! Yes, I can. At least I think I can. She's—'

'That's right. The one trying to look sultry and intellectual all at once; the one with the glasses and the skirt up to her – I have to admit – surprisingly neat derrière. Guess Damp Pits must have something going for him after all – money, probably. Although why he couldn't spare two ninety-nine for a spot of Right Guard . . .'

'Maybe she likes the natural smell,' said Evie, giggling.

'And the nice clammy sensation she'll get a little later when she strokes his manly torso?'

But it was rather less amusing when Abe got bored of the couple in the corner and turned his attention to Matthew, who'd left the tall, malnourished-looking man, and was now talking to Honor.

'Ah, yes . . . still gossiping for money?'

Evie's smile vanished. 'That's *not*—'

'I'm sorry, sweetheart. I know he's the man of the moment, I know you think the sun shines out of his jacksie, but honestly. Bloody people. We had them pestering us every day in Spain – hanging around in the bushes with those enormous cameras, gatecrashing the wrap party, mobbing poor Mike Grafton at the airport. They really are the pits, Evie. I'm surprised you—'

'But Matthew's not paparazzi! He's not even—'

'I don't care. I hate them all.'

'Even when they advance your career?'

Abe rolled his eyes. 'So that's what he tells you he's doing, then?'

'Hardly,' said Evie, losing patience. 'I think he'd say he has rather more interesting things to write about than the state of your career.'

But Abe wasn't listening. He was transfixed by the sight of Matthew and Honor trying to talk above the thumping music coming from a speaker at their feet. Matthew was standing by the food table, eating a sausage as he strained to hear what Honor was saying. For a second, he leant forward – so that she could repeat it into his ear; and then he straightened up again – still munching, still watching her steadily and smiling.

123

'Just can't trust them,' Abe was muttering. 'Can't trust them for a second. And if they're not stitching you up, they're dreaming about fucking your girlfriend.'

Evie turned to see if he was joking, but there was nothing jovial – nothing light – in the way Abe knocked back the remains of his champagne and continued watching Matthew and Honor.

'Abe . . . Come on . . . He's hardly—'

'Look at him.'

'He's *talking* to her, not—'

'Look at the body language! Look at his face!'

Evie looked, but all she saw was two people having a conversation. Yes, Matthew seemed interested in what Honor was saying – but why shouldn't he be? Evie was pleased to see him making an effort. Pleased to see that two of the people she loved best in the world – people she feared would never see eye-to-eye – were actually getting on.

And then Honor glanced round and saw them watching her. Amused, she turned to Matthew – pointing back to where Abe and Evie were sitting – and the two of them came forward.

'There you are!' Honor said.

She perched on the edge of the sofa, next to Abe, while Matthew pulled up another chair. 'We were just wondering where you'd got to,' he said, smiling at Evie and ruffling her hair. 'We—'

'Were you?' said Abe.

Matthew turned to Abe, surprised.

'Seems to me you were more than happy talking to Honor.'

The four of them were silent for a moment, with Abe looking round belligerently while the others turned away, picking at a fingernail, fiddling with a sleeve, or simply looking at the floor.

Contrary to Evie's expectations, she and Matthew were not to sleep on the sitting-room floor that night, or even on the sofa. Jessica – whose persistence with a an oarsman from Oriel was finally getting results – had agreed to let them use her room, and Honor had made it look wonderful. There were flowers by the bed, new soap in the basin, and smooth fresh sheets on the bed.

'Well, this is rather better than floorboards . . .' said Matthew cheerfully hopping into bed and curling himself around Evie's body in a way that was so warm and comfortable it made her glad that the bed was single. He pulled at the string above their heads, turning off the light.

'You all right?'

Evie nodded.

And then, more thoughtfully, into the darkness: 'You sure? You seemed a bit lost at one point. I thought perhaps you—'

'Really Matthew, I enjoyed it.'

He held her closer. 'I'm glad,' he said. 'Not sure I could say the same, though – to be perfectly honest. I mean, of course I liked your cousin. And that tutor of hers was all right. But some of her friends . . .'

'Abe, you mean?'

Matthew hesitated. 'Even without Abe, they were pretty appalling – didn't you think? Being a class snob is one thing. And being an intellectual snob – that's not much better. But both together? And that *embarrassing* conversation about Kant and Descartes . . . Did you catch any of it?'

'Not really. I wasn't—'

'Christ, it was bad. Everyone pretending to know it all when they're clearly as ignorant as the rest of us; terrified that someone'll realise they're not Einstein, and much too insecure to say anything they haven't already read in some God-awful textbook. It was just so contrived, and I – I suppose I couldn't help seeing it through your eyes, Evie, and wondering what you thought . . .'

Silence.

'You do realise it's all show, don't you?'

Evie sighed. '"Show" or not', she muttered, 'it's got to be better than discussions about who's doing what shift and how many bottles of ketchup to—'

But while she was talking, he began moving around – reaching up, patting at the wall by their heads . . . and the light was on again. She broke off, blinking.

'The only skill these people have,' said Matthew, looking down with kind determination while the short string from the bedside light, with its plastic bead, swung madly above them, 'and me, I suppose – is a trick of passing exams. Sure, we can remember what happened in 1815 and who invented penicillin – and yes, we can worm our way into places like Oxford and Cambridge – but what's so special about that? It doesn't make us interesting or original or particularly likely to make something of our lives.'

'Unlike barmen and waitresses, then?'

Matthew closed his eyes. 'All I'm saying, Evie, is that you're every bit as interesting and bright as the people who were here tonight. You have nothing to feel small about. Nothing to hide. And if anyone made you feel that way, they were wrong. All right?'

'All right,' she said, smiling at him; pulling at the little string, pulling them back into the night . . . and

126

Matthew went with it. He knew she still minded desperately that she wasn't at university, that she was 'only' a waitress. But he felt, too, that she understood what it was he was trying to say, and that – for her – it was enough. He could feel it in the free way she was kissing his face – reminding him of other, simpler, ways of shaking out anxiety; reminding him of that thing he loved most about her: that glorious ability to put a stop to the whirligig of thinking and chattering, and just be together in the dark.

They both slept deeply that night and long into the morning. Slept on while a strip of lazy winter sun fell through a gap in Jessica's curtains and advanced in fractions across the room. It moved like a spotlight, giving each little object five seconds of life. It slid over the enamel of the basin, catching the curved chrome of the taps and flashing through the fine glass circle at the mouth of an empty tumbler. Then it dipped to the floor, brushing the rim of a neglected shoe – one of Matthew's, tossed carelessly aside as he'd undressed – illuminating the battered underside that wasn't meant to be seen . . . and climbed on, up again, bending at the curve of the mattress; crinkling and wrinkling with the disturbance of bedding – until, finally, it touched one of Evie's smudged eyelids.

She woke to sensations of light and warmth, to a kind of weightlessness. Mellowed and softened by the protective flesh of her closed eyelids, the sunlight seemed entirely benign and for a moment she lay in that hazy, yellow-pink world – happy to be in the present, with the morning sun on her skin. And then the strip of light moved on – flatter now, across the super-smooth white of their borrowed pillows – leaving her face in the shade. Evie opened her eyes. She

127

took in her surroundings, linking them to things remembered and catching once more the line of her conscious life: the unfamiliar pattern of the curtains – Jessica's curtains – and a nagging sense of inferiority, not entirely gone; her clothes a little crumpled on the chair, and Matthew's arm, heavy and safe, across her body.

Lying there, looking again at the smart soap that Honor had put out for them in the basin, at the pretty flowers, and the suspiciously luxurious spare sheets on their bed, Evie found herself wondering about Honor's student life, and if it was entirely normal. Weren't real students meant to be poor and driven? Weren't they supposed to dress in charity-shop clothes, eat baked beans, drink beer and inhabit bedsits?

With one sitting room and two berth-like bedrooms attached and a communal bathroom at the top of the general staircase, Honor's living quarters might have qualified – technically – as a bedsit, but the panelled walls and eighteenth-century carvings were surely cheating. And while Honor had said that her rooms were beautiful and marvelled at the college's history, Evie couldn't help suspecting that, deep down, her cousin had not been able to handle the economy loo-paper, sunken armchairs and shallow mattresses of college life. One had only to look at the way Honor's space had been furnished – at the set of four Parisian-looking chairs, at the indigo cushions on the sofas and the slim-smart lamps on the polished desks with matching olive-and-plum silk shades . . . All had Xandra's unmistakable stamp.

And then, of course, there was the little cabinet from Giles – discreetly positioned between the sitting-room windows, supporting a small glass hurricane lamp and a couple of over-employed ashtrays. That weekend was the first time Evie had seen the finished article, and she couldn't help smiling at the result. For in the end, Honor had simply matched it to the colour scheme that her mother had chosen for the rest of the room – almost over-tasteful – in greys and whites and lilacs, with a couple of traditional-looking garlands painted on to the doors.

And maybe it was the same with Honor's friends. Maybe there was something irresistibly familiar and safe about such people. Remembering the way Honor had been the night before – mixing happily with her guests, including that vile boy with the floppy hair, smiling and listening while he gave her the full force of his opinion – Evie realised there had been something in Honor's expression that reminded her of the one she'd worn for the red-faced man at her London party; something oddly passive. It made Evie think that Honor hadn't really chosen any of these people to be her friends. Somehow, she'd let them choose her.

Honor was working at her desk when, shortly before midday, Evie and Matthew emerged. Abe was already gone – a taxi had come for him at seven – and the whole place was tidy again: glasses had been washed and cleared away; ashtrays emptied; surfaces wiped. She'd even had time to sweep the floor and pull the furniture back into place. Windows had been left open all night, and what was left of the smell of smoke had been chased away by the fresher one of coffee and buttery toast.

'God, that smells delicious,' said Evie, heaving her suitcase on to one of the sofas and coming over to Honor's desk.

Honor smiled. 'You want some?'

'Mm . . .' Distractedly, Evie picked up one of Honor's books. She glanced at the cover: *Thucydides – The History of the Peloponnesian War* . . . and put it quickly back. 'Love some. But – but Matthew was thinking – there's some pub he knows, some place a few miles out of Oxford – further down the river. It's got old wooden beams and open fires and apparently it does great chips. He thought we might all go there for lunch, if you were up for it.'

'Fantastic.'

'But we have to leave now, he says – if we want to get a table.'

Half an hour later, they were there – settling along a scruffy bench at a table by the fire, picking up menus and choosing drinks. Matthew was still a little way behind them. Seeing that there was nowhere close to park the car – and determined not to lose another second – he'd dropped Evie and Honor at the door with strict instructions about which table to go for and how he liked his Bloody Mary . . . and said he'd be there just as soon as he could. And so, with Honor to herself for a moment, Evie decided to ask a little more about the situation with Abe.

Honor sat back, fingers toying with the menu as she considered her reply. 'Well, I suppose you could say that's it.'

'It?'

'He's off to LA. I'm staying here.'

'But you'll see him at Christmas, won't you?'

Honor shook her head. 'He'll hardly be here,' she said. 'The flight gets in on Christmas Eve – so he's going straight down to Sussex to be with his parents – and then he really has to go straight back out again. To get settled in, I imagine, before filming starts.'

Evie leant forward anxiously. 'And you're not upset by that?'

'Not remotely. In fact, I think it's great.' Honor's expression grew cooler. 'You saw the way he was last night.'

'But last night was—'

'Last night was typical, Evie. The drinking and the drugs and – and all the stupid things he says . . . He was just like that in Spain. Even in London. *Particularly* in London, to be honest.' Honor sighed. 'It simply wasn't working – for either of us. And it's so much nicer, so much more civilised, to let it go like this: no rows, no falling out, no . . .' she hesitated, '. . . no unnecessary harshness. I'm sure he's every bit as relieved as I am that it's happened this way! I can't tell you how amicable it's been . . .'

It sounded surreal to Evie – the whole concept of 'amicable'. She couldn't imagine a relationship ending like that, with a closed lid and a tidy bow. How did you go from loving someone passionately to casually waving them off at the airport, to another country, and other friends, and other women's arms and lips – with no hint of anger, no feelings of rejection, no torn wreckage to mend? Of course she was glad to see Honor smiling. And yes, she could see that, as a couple, Abe and Honor were not perhaps as well suited as they'd seemed to be at the beginning of the year. No doubt it was for the best that the relationship should end. But there was still something odd about the manner of its ending; the way that Honor was now dropping the subject – as if they'd been talking about some coat she'd decided to throw away – and turning instead to the all-important task of catching the waiter's eye.

131

They were ordering drinks when Matthew came in – blood hot, skin cold, from walking in the winter air – and it was Honor he saw first: extending an arm with *plié* grace as she pointed out something on Evie's menu and asked the waiter a question. Her body language was so distinctive – so fluid, so easily upright – it was as if she was suspended from the ceiling, not fixed to the floor with the rest of them. But while it wasn't stiff, it was still formal – even a little dated, like his grandmother's would have been. Matthew wasn't entirely sure he liked it.

He wasn't even sure he liked Honor.

Before her party, back in May, Matthew had yawned his way through the obligatory articles in *Tatler*. Idly, he'd examined the pictures to see if the Montfort girl really was as beautiful as the magazines said – and had had to agree that, in a distant, snooty sort of way, Honor was exactly the sort of girl he fancied and despised in equal measure. Back then, she'd represented the very worst aspects of the work he did. But whilst Matthew might have had no problem dismissing the split-second two-dimensional images of Honor on his desk – or the equally two-dimensional impression she'd made on him as she'd stood illuminated by the flashbulbs at her Wellesley Hotel party . . . things were rather more complicated talking to her in the candlelit flesh of a student party. It wasn't that his original feelings were gone, exactly. Honor Montfort was still a spoiled debutante; she still annoyed the hell out of him – and the faux-Brideshead crowd he'd met last night absolutely confirmed his suspicions. For while she could not have been nicer to Matthew, or more welcoming – taking immense trouble to ask him about himself when she had all her own friends to consider, and listening attentively to his replies – her very politeness held him at a distance. And it was distancing that, like members' enclosures and VIP lounges, drew lifeblood from teasing proximity to those less fortunate; distancing that provoked, in Matthew, a degree of republican wrath he'd not felt since graduation.

In short, she bothered him. Last night, with those ludicrous people partying around them, and Abe's rudeness, and Evie's inferiority complex to contend with, last night there had been enough distractions for Matthew to be able to block, superficially at least, the effect Honor was having on him. But today it was impossible. He couldn't dismiss her from his thoughts. And, much to his discomfort – before he'd even reached the table – Matthew knew which cousin it was, sitting there, that interested him most. Honor's manners, her conversation, her clothes, her circumstances, even the way she moved – that formal body language – were all about privacy . . . and there was a part of Matthew that, while hating it, simultaneously craved admittance. For all its pepped-up crassness, Abe's observation the previous night had not been entirely off the mark.

'Well I hope we got the right table,' said Evie, happily making room on the corner bench.

Matthew sat down. He put his car keys and newspaper on the table and shoved them, very slightly, in Honor's direction. Then he leant over the table, thrust forward his elbows and picked up Evie's hand. 'It's perfect.'

'And I ordered your Bloody Mary. You didn't want horseradish, did you? Honor was certain you wouldn't want it, but I—'

133

'Was she, now?'

Smiling, he glanced at Honor, who glanced back without thinking . . . and exposed herself to something that Giles and Rachel had been dreading for most of Evie's life: a whisper of difficulty in the friendship that, whether through the clamour of affection, chance deflection or deliberate parental muffling, had always been too faint for either girl to hear. For Evie, that was still the case. But for Honor, in that moment – in that imperceptible synchronicity of eyes, a fluttering line of lids and lashes that linked her thoughts to Matthew's – the whispering was fully audible.

No matter that she irritated him. No matter that he'd once found her cold and arrogant. No matter that she was the exact type of overprivileged daddy's girl that Matthew so enjoyed despising – it was still Honor he'd first noticed when he walked in just now. It was Honor, not Evie, who darkened his pupils . . . and Honor herself had seen it.

In spite of himself, it was Honor he chose. It was Honor they all chose: always Honor, always first. Overpowerful, overblessed . . . and the thought gave her no joy. With other men it hadn't mattered because Evie hadn't cared. But this man was different. This was someone Evie actually liked, and her happiness lay like a butterfly in the palm of Honor's hand – was perhaps already being damaged, simply by her presence. What had just happened was as damning as if Matthew had passed Honor a love note and she'd accepted it. Already she was guilty.

'But she was right, wasn't she?'

Matthew looked at Evie with blank eyes.

'About the horseradish?'

Matthew reconnected with a grin. 'Absolutely,' he

said. 'I'm sure it'll be perfect! Now, pass me that menu, would you, sweetheart? I'm ravenous . . .'

When he looked at Honor again, she was sitting very still: with her back straight, her head bent, and the car keys and newspaper, untouched, before her.

Evie loved that lunch. Loved having them both there: Honor opposite and Matthew right beside her – Matthew at his best, laughing and being charming to Honor; pulling off his jumper as the fire grew hotter, his cheeks becoming pinker, his eyes getting brighter as his Bloody Mary arrived . . . It was hard not to lean on him, inhale the traces of soap on his skin, and feel his warmth through their clothes, hard not to behave as if it was just the two of them there alone, as they'd been alone last night.

He was much better at it than she was. He could press a finger to her thigh and run it gently upwards while elaborating on the finer points of work patterns at Oxford and how Honor might make the most of her time there. He could lean back with one arm round Evie's shoulder, extend the other for a pair of sugar cubes to toss like dice into his coffee, and still cut questions through Honor's account of her first term, still give the impression he was listening.

For Evie, such gestures – a finger on her thigh, an arm round her shoulder – stopped her in her tracks. Laughing, she'd have to ask for help to regain her train of thought. She'd have to pretend that it was alcohol, not desire, making her muddled and incompetent. It was impossible – quite beyond her – to think about anything else with Matthew's finger burning a trail of promise through the denim surface of her leg.

*

135

'. . . Quite,' said Honor the following week, in answer to Evie's question.

'Quite?'

Her first term was over, and she was back in London – looking out of the kitchen window with the telephone clasped to her ear. The Launceston Villas garden had been clipped to mathematical perfection. The edges of the frost-green lawn were sharp and ruler-straight, the holly trees on the flagstoned terrace, exactly spherical. Low box hedges rimmed the borders with uncompromising strictness. The winter sun sent diagonal slants from tree trunks and the edge of a neighbouring roof, so that even the light seemed to conspire with the cool science of Xandra's plan. The irises of Honor's eyes were silver from the reflected brightness of it all.

'He just seemed a little . . .'

'What?' said Evie, bristling. 'Seemed a little what?'

Honor closed her eyes. There was nothing in all that horticultural precision that could help with this particular tangle. How could she tell Evie what she really thought – that Matthew didn't seem to be in love with Evie at all, that he'd spent the entire weekend trying to catch Honor's eye; that fingers on thighs and arms round shoulders didn't mean that his brain was engaged? Touching wasn't enough in Honor's book. Matthew should have involved Evie in his conversation. He should have wanted to know what Evie thought, where Evie would like to go travelling next summer. Instead, his curiosity had been all about Honor – and she despised him for it. But how could she say so to Evie? How could she tell her dearest friend that her main source of doubt about this man Evie liked was his very particular interest in *her*, Honor.

How vain and arrogant would that sound? How crushing.

Yet nor could Honor lie. She couldn't mislead Evie – not when Matthew was already succeeding at that so brilliantly. What kind of friend would let the poor girl gallop on, so joyful and oblivious, with no word of warning of the drop that lay ahead?

'Careless,' she said at last. 'I thought he was careless.'

'Did you,' said Evie, without a hint of question.

'I'm sure he didn't mean to be. It was probably just the way he had to rush back to London after lunch, leaving you to take the—'

'He couldn't stay any longer, Honor. He had work to do – as you know. And anyway, it was my suggestion he go back early! I thought you wanted more time to talk about Abe – just the two of us. He left early to be considerate! Not because he didn't care.'

Again Honor pondered. 'I meant careless with you, Evie. Careless about you, somehow, or . . .'

Evie laughed. 'Well you don't need to worry about that.'

'Good. I'm glad.'

'He's being wonderful to me.'

'Then that's great!' said Honor brightly. 'And you could see how nice he was about Oxford – so interesting about all those societies, and how to avoid the hordes of braying Sloanes. Sloanes just like me I expect—'

'He wasn't saying that *you* were—'

'Oh I know. And to be honest, Evie, he's right. I should make more of an effort to meet different people with different interests – it is a real opportunity . . . The stuff he said was useful; really interesting.'

'So you liked him!'

A cloud passed over the Kensington sun. Honor looked out at the greyer greens and the cold stone lines of the terrace.

'Yes,' she said, defeated. 'Yes, I did.'

Disappointed, Evie put down the telephone. Automatically, she began gathering together her purse and travel pass, stuffing them into her black nylon backpack along with a fresh Brasserie Beach shirt for that afternoon's shift – but her mind was still a few steps behind, still with Honor and the conversation they'd just had. Honor hadn't needed to spell it out just now for Evie to tell that she had doubts. There were things that Honor couldn't hide, no matter how tactful her words: from the merest alteration in the pitch of her voice, and that way she had of hesitating. Evie knew her too well.

It wasn't entirely surprising. As Matthew had pointed out back in August, on that hot first night at Brasserie Beach, being a diarist had its drawbacks. Certain people – some, admittedly, with more justification than others – were instinctively cautious around him. And, for now, that was an accepted part of his life. It was something he'd considered long and hard, and decided he could live with. Occasionally things got nasty but, to Matthew, that was a price worth paying.

Evie understood all this, but still she wished her cousin had been less prejudiced. If only Honor knew the truth: that Matthew had had it in his power last May to make life infinitely harder for her family; and that he'd chosen not to. Then, surely, she would not have been so quick to dismiss him. But while Evie knew that she'd never be able to tell Honor what had really happened – the fact of William's affair, the threat of his mistress going public, and the part that Evie had played by recklessly telling everything to a man she'd only just met – she was still desperate for Honor to see the real Matthew. It wouldn't take much. Another weekend, perhaps, or maybe an evening together in London . . . just a few more opportunities for Matthew to show Honor the kind of man he really was.

Chapter Nine

A Weekend Invitation

In the end, however, it was almost Easter before Matthew and Honor met again. In spite of Evie's best efforts to organise something – dinners, lunches, weekends, all regretfully turned down: too much work, prior commitments, sudden obligations to dine with great-aunts and gnarled tutors that Evie had never heard of – they succeeded in avoiding each other for nearly four months. And it was only by stealth that she finally made it happen.

Evie and her parents often went to stay with the Montforts in March. With the shooting season over, and the garden bursting into flower, it was the perfect time for William and Xandra to have 'non-sporting' friends to stay at Favenham, and the Langtons fell absolutely into that category.

Giles and Evie sat over their breakfast as Rachel took the call.

'William, we'd love to. We . . .' flicking through her diary, '. . . no. It's completely free. I should run it by Giles and Evie just in case either of them has made other plans. Evie may have trouble getting time off from her restaurant, I suppose . . . but I'm sure there won't be a problem. We'd love to see you all – and the garden, and the daffodils, and dear old Mrs Marsden . . .'

A resigned look crossed Giles's face as, picking up his coffee cup, he took another sip. Evie, on the other hand, was every bit as delighted as her mother. Yes it could sometimes be tricky to take weekends off from waitressing, but the March rota hadn't been drawn up yet. There was plenty of time for her to give Samira notice.

'They're not asking anyone else, are they?'

'I don't think so, darling. They don't usually. Charles had a girlfriend there one year – remember? But other than that it's always been just us . . .'

'Just us' sounded perfect. Okay, so Matthew hadn't been invited. But given the fact that Evie still hadn't even got round to introducing him to her parents, that was only to be expected. And it certainly didn't stop her from thinking she could bring him too. Uninvited guests were always pitching up at Favenham. With four children – two of them still in their teens – William and Xandra were used to stretching numbers at the last minute; and Evie, in many ways, was still an honorary child of theirs. They often allowed her the kind of extra liberties that would normally be restricted to their own. And there was hardly a shortage of bedrooms, or chairs to pull up round the dining-room table. With no other guests to worry about, and no real formalities to observe, what difference could one extra person make? After six or seven months of being with Matthew, Evie was more than ready to introduce him to the rest of her family – and if she could combine that with getting him to see Honor again, so much the better. All it needed was careful handling.

Asking him first if he was free that weekend (without saying what it entailed); making sure she spoke to him about it well in advance (so that there was no chance he'd have anything else planned); and then saying that he'd been specially invited, that it would be incredibly rude of him – not to mention embarrassing for her – if he declined, Evie pestered and badgered and shamelessly manipulated poor Matthew into accepting something he hadn't even been invited to.

'But what about the Diary thing?' he said finally. 'Aren't they worried—'

'They don't know about it.'

Matthew closed his eyes.

'Oh come on, Matthew. Please? Can't you simply handle it the way you did with me? Gloss over it, get round it – lie, joke, prevaricate, it doesn't really matter. I know, and you know, that you won't take advantage – you've already proved that you won't—'

'But Honor knows me!'

'Okay, so I'll tell her to keep her trap shut.'

Matthew sighed. He knew it would be a mistake. Not so much because of the impression Honor had made on him back at Oxford before Christmas, an impression he didn't doubt he could handle, if indeed it remained at all; but because of what he did for a living, and the knowledge that – if Honor's parents had any idea what it was – he would not have been invited. Everything sensible and decent compelled him to resist. But Evie's determination, combined with a strange impulse to put his feelings for Honor to the test, made him waver. And the idea of actually staying at a house like Favenham and chatting to Xandra Villiers about the Rolling Stones over a glass of wine . . . The journalist in him was, just a little bit, curious . . .

'Speak to Honor,' he said at last. 'If she's comfortable with it – and if you're comfortable with it – then I'll come.'

Evie promised she would. No need to tell him that she wasn't planning to do it straight away; that if she waited until a couple of days before they were due to leave, not only would Honor have no way out of the weekend herself, she'd also have no choice but to accept that Matthew was coming, especially if her parents were okay with the idea. And so, on the Thursday before they were due to leave, Evie broached the subject with her mother.

'I do understand it's a bit last-minute, Mum, but he's not doing anything this weekend and I just know how much he'd love it if he could come down with us too . . .'

Rachel's beam said it all. Thrilled at the prospect of finally meeting the person who was making her daughter so happy, thrilled that their relationship had got to this stage, she was struck by an unfamiliar urge to whoop like an Indian squaw and jump around the kitchen. Of course he must come! William and Xandra wouldn't have a problem—

'Leave it with me, sweetheart,' she said – reining in her excitement and restricting herself to a heartfelt kiss on Evie's cheek.

But when later that morning Rachel called Xandra at the London number, she did not get quite the response she had been expecting.

'What, *this* weekend?' said Xandra.

'I know it's supposed to be a family party but she really is keen to bring him, Xa, and we were just hoping that you'd . . .'

143

There was a long silence. And then, again: 'What, *this* weekend? In Suffolk?'

Frowning, Rachel checked the calendar above the telephone. There it was – in her own handwriting – and a brisk line from Friday to Sunday: *Favenham – weekend*. 'The 13th?' she said, haltingly. 'I – I'm sure William said the 13th. We did discuss other dates, but it was the only one we could all do—'

'Well I wish he'd taken the trouble to tell me about it.'

'Oh God . . .'

'– damn him.'

Rachel swallowed.

'*Damn* him!' Xandra said again, indignation increasing its grip on her. 'How dare he expect me to do these country weekends of his properly, and entertain his friends and family – which, I have to say, I've done without a word of thanks for the entire shooting season – if he doesn't even let me know what the arrangements are?'

'I'm so sorry, Xandra. I'd no idea—'

'I mean,' – getting more hysterical by the second – 'I can't *do* this weekend! I simply *can't*! We've got the Warburgs coming to dinner, and Max Jameson with his new girlfriend . . . I *can't* – just – cancel it.'

'Then let's cancel Suffolk,' said Rachel. 'I'll call William, shall I? He's already at Favenham, I imagine —'

'Well he's certainly not here.'

'Okay, Xa. I'll call him there. I'll tell him we're not coming, and then with any luck he can come to London for your dinner party and it'll be as if nothing was wrong.'

But Xandra was way past being mollified. '. . . wretched *wretched* man. I *told* him last week that this party was happening. I *told* him to make sure we had enough champagne and get the Sèvres sent up from Suffolk . . . we even talked about whether it was wise to have Max's girlfriend when he's not strictly divorced yet, and – and he said nothing! *Nothing!*'

'I'll talk to him now,' said Rachel, increasingly alarmed by Xandra's tone. It sounded as if there was more to this than a simple clash of diaries. She wondered how much time they spent together these days, if at all . . . and what had happened with Diana Miller's houseboat. 'Give me five minutes, Xandra – I'll call you right back.'

But when she spoke to William, he was equally intransigent.

'But William—'

'Oh sure. She might well want to put her la-di-da friends – none of whom I believe I've even met – above her family, but if she thinks I'm prepared to join her in that decision, she's got another think coming. She wants to have her blasted dinner party? Fine. Let her have it. But I'm damned if I'm cancelling my own sister. How dare she?'

'We really don't mind rearranging, if that—'

'Well I do. And it's not just you I'd have to rearrange, Rachel. We've got poor Lavinia Beaumaris coming for lunch on Saturday, and I'm certainly not cancelling her – not with all the troubles *she's* been through recently . . .'

'So you'll handle the weekend alone then, will you?'

William was silent.

'You'll tell Lillian what to cook for your lunch party, and get the right ingredients in for her? You'll decide which beds to make up and what flowers to put out and which napkins to use and what towels we'll all need, and make sure there's enough lavatory paper and – and water bottles by the beds and the right newspapers and so on?'

Still he said nothing.

'. . . it's not as easy as it looks.'

'No of course.'

'So unless you're expecting me to come down today and do it all for you—'

'Oh Rachel – would you really?'

And instead of laughing at her brother's audacity and telling him to sort out his own mess, Rachel found herself seduced by William's tone of premature gratitude. It pressed at some long-forgotten maternal button, and made her shrink from disappointing him. Upstairs, she could hear the familiar creak of the studio door and Giles's feet on the landing . . . coming down for lunch, humming as he went.

Rachel glanced at the kitchen clock. 'All right,' she said in a quick low voice. 'I'll be on the six o'clock train.'

'Oh *darling* Rachel—'

'And in the meantime, you call Xandra and apologise.'

'Apolo—'

'That's my condition. You make sure she has everything she needs to give her dinner party. She was talking about you sorting out the champagne, and – and something about the Sèvres, I think?'

William laughed. 'She doesn't need the bloody Sèvres! There's more than enough—'

'Just do it, William.'

*

Giles sat on the bed, watching Rachel kneel on the floor, packing her old suitcase.

146

'It's not me I'm annoyed for,' he said wearily. 'It's you.'

'But darling . . .' putting in her favourite pair of shoes, Rachel looked up at him affectionately. 'I *want* to go. Of course, I'd love it if you came early too . . .' Giles had to turn away. '. . . but as you're never particularly comfortable at Favenham . . .'

'What do you mean? I love Favenham. I'm very comfortable there. I just—'

'You know what I'm saying.'

Giles picked up a hairbrush. 'There's nothing unusual about a man not wanting to drop everything for his in-laws,' he muttered, running its bristles through his fingers before passing it to her to put into the case.

'Yes,' she replied calmly, 'and that's exactly why I think I should do this alone.'

'Why do it at all?'

Rachel closed the lid of the case. 'Because William needs me,' she said, snapping it shut – first one side, then the other. 'It wasn't easy for him to ask.'

Giles snorted.

'And in any case, I like going home.'

And there it was: the root of the problem. Giles put his head in his hands. *But this is your home!* he wanted to cry. *This is where you belong. You – you've been here with me for twenty-five years, and I . . . Oh, my darling, what more can I do? How can I hope to compete with a place like Favenham?* All the old feelings were stumbling through his brain once more . . . but he was cut off from giving voice to them by the sudden ringing of the telephone.

Rachel picked it up. 'Yes, of course,' she said, looking at her watch. 'There's some stew in the freezer I can bring. That should be fine for just the two of us . . .

But you don't mind *cooked* onions, do you, William? I know you don't like those nasty red ones in salads, but' – sighing now – 'there really aren't very many in there. I can always pick them out. And if you could ask Lillian to leave out some vegetables, then we're— I don't know. Whatever's around. Potatoes, maybe? And something green? She'll know what to get. And you've got enough for breakfast, haven't you? Great. Then tomorrow morning we can both go to— Okay, then, *I'll* go to Sainsbury's first thing, and all you need to worry about is getting the Sèvres packed up in time for the courier . . .'

Ten minutes later she was gone, wheeling her suitcase down Morland Road in the direction of Putney East Tube station. And Giles, watching from the window, found himself wishing he'd taken her by car after all – or at least insisted she take a cab. She was too old, he felt, to be struggling on to the Underground with a heavy suitcase. Too old to be jumping to her brother's every whim.

It wasn't until quite late the following day that Giles, Evie and Matthew left for Suffolk. This was mainly on account of Matthew's work commitments, although Giles was in no great hurry to get to Favenham either. His desire to be with Rachel again was equalled – perhaps even exceeded – by his reluctance to be under Montfort roofs once more.

Matthew could tell Giles wasn't happy from the moment they shook hands.

'That all?' Giles said, throwing Matthew's suitcase into the back of a rusty Volvo.

'Yes. Yes I wasn't sure quite how much room you'd have, Mr Langton, so I—'

148

'Right.' Giles slammed the boot. 'Now where's that daughter of mine?'

'I think she said she was—'

'Honestly. I don't see how we're going to be there by eight if she keeps running back inside. She . . . Evie!' Giles reached inside the car and tooted on the horn.

And his bad mood barely improved for the duration of the journey. It was there in the uneven rhythm of his driving, which meant Matthew had to hold on to the ceiling handle to stop himself from flying down the length of the back seat; and it was there again in the deep, restless sighs that Giles exhaled from time to time.

'What's wrong with you?' said Evie finally.

'Me?'

'I thought you were looking forward to seeing Mum.'

Grimly Giles checked his rear-view mirror and shifted lanes to overtake a lorry. The Volvo strained and whined and the car behind them had to brake. The driver flashed at them and honked. Just below the whirring and churning of the car, Matthew was sure he heard Giles muttering, 'Arsehole.' And it was only when they'd passed the lorry, and had been passed in turn by the car behind, that Evie got her reply.

'I am.'

'Then—'

'But your mother is not the only component of this weekend, Evie. And frankly I can think of better things to be doing right now than driving the pair of you down to Suffolk.'

'Oh.' Evie turned to Matthew and pulled a face. 'Sorry I asked.'

Matthew smiled back at her – but he didn't feel smiley inside. He felt sick. And while his queasiness might have been caused by Giles's driving, it was not helped by the possibility that he – Matthew – was one of the less favourable components Giles had just referred to. Telling himself it was paranoia, Matthew kept his eye on the fading horizon. He'd been invited. He was a bona fide guest. And, yes, there'd clearly been some sort of mix-up – with Lady Montfort not being there after all and Evie's mother having to step in at the last minute – but that was hardly Matthew's fault. He'd done nothing wrong. Nothing, that is, except—

'So Matthew,' said Giles who, catching the sarcasm of Evie's apology, was now trying to make an effort. 'Evie tells me you're a writer.'

Matthew swallowed. 'Well really more of a hack, I'd say. Of course one day I'd love to write a book, but—'

'What kind of book?'

'Oh, I don't know. A biography, maybe. Or a travelogue? I've always been fascinated by the Middle East, but then so is everybody else. I'd need a really good angle . . .'

'You must be in a better position than most.'

'You think so?'

Giles indicated left off the dual carriageway, in the direction of Favenham. Only twelve more miles now. 'I don't read the papers much these days, I have to confess. It's all too depressing. But aren't they sending journalists like you off out there all the time? Tehran, Beirut . . . always in the news – you must have reams of first-hand material.'

'Uh . . . not exactly.'

'Oh?'

'I mean, not yet.' Matthew laughed nervously. 'I – I still have quite a bit to learn.'

150

'Oh sure,' said Giles, wondering if Matthew was really a journalist at all. He sounded pretty vague – not even able to say what kind of writer he was, or what he'd want to write about. No doubt he was freelance. He'd probably written two or three measly articles since leaving university, yet here he was telling Evie he was a writer . . .

Matthew squirmed in the back of the car. He felt Evie's hand reach round behind her seat. In the darkness, she squeezed clumsily at his knee.

Half an hour later they were carrying their suitcases into a low-lit panelled hall. For all his earlier irritability, Giles now seemed quite excited. He strode across the stone floor – past tapestries and spindly chairs, past a deep, blackened fireplace fully ablaze, and a chaotic arrangement of flowers from the garden that could have only been done by Rachel – calling out, 'Hello! Hello!'

'We're in here,' replied a deeper voice from behind an open door on the far right. 'Just leave your things in the hall and come and have a drink.'

Evie followed the voice, turning in the doorway to make sure that Matthew was close behind.

'You okay?' she asked him.

Matthew looked at her, at the skewed hair and the heavy eye make-up. To some, the urban clothes she wore – the black denim jacket and the kohled-up eyes – might have seemed intimidating. But to Matthew, nodding in reply, there was something reassuring about the street cred she projected. He understood it.

What he found intimidating was Honor – dressed in a brown suede miniskirt, skimpy cashmere and preppy flats – sitting calmly on the sofa with her slim

151

legs crossed. She stood up to greet them with the same physical grace he'd noticed the last time they'd met, back in December at Oxford, when the three of them had lunched at the Boathouse pub. When she came close, she smelt of bath essence and champagne. 'Matthew' – kissing him – 'how lovely to see you.'

He didn't believe her. And as they stood there chatting, with Honor's politeness impenetrable as ever – asking how the journey had been, making sure he had something to drink, taking him over to meet her father – Matthew knew that he'd been right to spend the last four months avoiding her. Nothing had changed. If anything it was worse. The effect she was having on him, from the smallest hesitation in her speech and the way she was playing with the piping on the back of the sofa, to the limited way she was meeting his eye, he . . . Jesus. He'd only been there five minutes and already her every tiny gesture had the resonance of thunder. Matthew was amazed that anyone could do that to him, far less a safe, controlled, pampered girl like Honor Montfort. He found he could hardly speak for the impact of it all and the terrible pressure to behave as if everything was normal.

He was glad when she left him talking with her father and went over to see if Evie or Giles needed a drink – glad to be able to breathe a little more freely and get a grip of himself – but it wasn't long before he was looking at her again.

And Honor, alerted by some sixth sense that she was being watched, glanced over her shoulder and caught him. Quickly, angrily, she turned away – standing at the sofa with her back once again to the room as she picked up a bottle of champagne and poured some carefully into Giles's empty glass.

At nine, Rachel led them in to dinner. Giles watched, noticing the easy way she fell into the role. Whatever she'd done about dinner – whether she'd cooked it herself or got Lillian to help – it would all be under control. She'd be thinking about the table plan, and whether she should make any last-minute adjustments. Upstairs, it would be just the same. Curtains would have been drawn and covers turned back. There'd be flowers on everybody's dressing tables and water by their beds. Everything would have been thought through.

Oh, she did it well. She might have spent the best years of her life trying not to be her mother . . . but the genes were winning, and it made Giles sad that all he could offer her was Putney. You should have married a house like Favenham, he thought – walking to the place she'd allocated him for dinner, halfway down the far side of the table. You should have found yourself an ambassador or an MP, or perhaps another William . . . someone whose life, or job, depended on a wife with talents for this kind of stuff; someone who'd allow you to fulfil your potential. Not some flaky artist.

And as she continued to direct each person to their chair, Giles realised where Rachel was planning to place herself. In truth, where else would she go? – except at the far end directly opposite her brother, as if they were the ones who were married, as if Favenham were their show and Giles the awkward spare man.

Honor watched her too: taking the place of her mother. Unlike Xandra's weekends – even the so-called informal ones – this felt unusually comfortable. Rachel seemed much more at ease: not hurrying to make sure

153

the smokers each had ashtrays, but happy just to let them flick ash into the fire; not fidgeting with the curtains so that they hung 'just so'; not watching the clock obsessively or bothering to ring the little bell that Xandra loved using when each course was finished – even for the smallest occasion. Honor wondered if there was anyone in the kitchen at all that night. Perhaps Rachel had done the whole thing herself and given Lillian a night off? It was impossible to say.

But even though she knew her aunt had been wonderful – stepping in at the last minute and working all day so both her parents could have their way – Honor still rather wished that William had turned to her, his daughter, instead. Yes, it would have been difficult with the dissertation she was struggling to finish that week, and it would have meant staying here in Suffolk for the whole weekend instead of rushing back to London halfway through . . . for while Xandra had never planned to include her children in the smart dinner party she was giving at Launceston Villas and hadn't even bothered to mention it to them – which was why Honor was as much in the dark about the clash of dates as her parents were – those plans, it seemed, had changed. Xandra now needed Honor. She had to go. But there was something slightly shaming about someone outside their immediate family, even someone as close as Rachel, coming to their rescue. Of course Honor was grateful for the chance it gave her to show she wasn't taking sides – grateful to be able to dash down to Favenham for the first part of the weekend, and then back to her mother for the second – but she still felt it had come at a price.

She didn't like the fact that Matthew Forrester was

seeing this crack in their family arrangements. She worried what conclusions he might draw, especially as her father looked so happy at the other end of the table.

'. . . And would I have to tip you?' he was asking Evie as, laughing, he filled her glass with wine.

'Absolutely.'

William rolled his eyes. 'Okay. And tell me, Evie: what's the tipping rate these days? I always thought it should be ten per cent, but recently I've been to places where they—'

'*Ten* per cent?'

'Is that too much?'

Evie gave him a stern look. 'It's twelve and a half,' she said. '*Minimum.*'

'I'm expected to calculate that?'

'You're expected to round it up.'

'I see . . .'

William smiled at his niece – rather admiring the feisty way she was prepared to fight for her extra two and a half per cent. To him, it seemed a pity to see that kind of attitude wasted on small-fry tips at Brasserie Beach. 'And what about other jobs, Evie?'

'Other jobs?'

'Well you're clearly not going to want to be a waitress for the rest of your life, and I just wondered what you—'

'What's wrong with waitressing?'

William hesitated.

'Are you saying it's inferior?'

Her voice had become loud enough for Giles and Honor – sitting at the opposite side of the table – to drop the conversation they were having and listen.

Unruffled, William cut into his duck breast. 'Of

course it is,' he replied. 'For you, at any rate. And . . . and all I'm saying, Evie, is that I think you could do something better with your life.'

'Like?'

'Like property, for instance.'

'What would I know about property?'

'Not very much, I imagine – at the moment. But if you were interested, and wanted to learn a bit more about it; if you wanted me to find you a dogsbody job at an estate agent, or – I don't know – get you some sort of work experience on the Vauxhall Project, perhaps . . .?'

'And what would they pay me?'

'Nothing, probably. But—'

'*Nothing*?'

'But the experience you'd get would be invaluable, Evie. It—'

'As a dogsbody? Making tea? I think I'd rather be a waitress – thanks all the same, Uncle William.'

'But Evie, you have to think long term about things like this! Surely you can see that if you spend a few months of unpaid work somewhere half decent, you'll stand a much better chance of making something of your life, instead of—'

'Instead of what, Uncle William?'

Again William hesitated – sure of his point, but unwilling to be any ruder than he had already been about where poor Evie was working. He was aware, too, that the whole table was now looking at them; that his answer needed care. And then – somewhat to his relief – the telephone rang.

'I'm sorry,' he muttered, putting down his napkin. 'I really have to take that one.'

Leaving his food half eaten, William made his way

out to the nearest telephone – the one in the kitchen – closing the doors behind him.

Giles knew that William was right. Of course, Evie should be aiming higher than waiting tables; of course she was better than that. He also knew that William was trying to pay her a compliment; that his offer to help her sounded genuine, and kind. Serious work experience would make a real difference to Evie's CV. But for all that, part of Giles still loved his darling daughter for spurning the man's offer – wildly and splendidly. It was what he always longed to do himself, but so often lacked the courage.

Happily, he stood up. And with that familiar change of mood which made him switch suddenly from an attitude of closed preoccupation – when it was hard to get him even to reply to the simplest question – to a free desire to be helpful and co-operative, a change his wife couldn't fail to notice, Giles began clearing plates.

Rachel decided not to stop him. From what she could hear of William's telephone conversation next door – and some innate suspicion meant that, unlike the rest of the table, she was listening pretty hard, going over to the sideboard when the others resumed their talk, pretending to inspect the food laid out there, to get more clarity through the wall – there was no point waiting for William to come back any time soon. The concerned 'How are you?' and the murmured 'Darlings' made it all too clear it wasn't Xandra at the other end.

Earlier that day, Rachel had found odd traces of what could only be Diana Miller dotted around the house: a pair of rimless glasses she recognised from that visit to Edinburgh; some lilac lace suspenders on the floor of the laundry room (Xandra, for sure,

157

wouldn't be seen dead these days in anything so tarty as suspenders); and finally, on the side in the kitchen, a magazine on property development that might have been William's were it not for the place it had been left, and a list of 'things to do' that fell out when Rachel picked it up. The list included a series of letters to go off to various Edinburgh-based solicitors and banks; calling some Manchester number before 'close of play' that day; and remembering to buy some special oil for gas lamps and a waterproof tarpaulin . . .

Rachel had hastily removed them all before Honor arrived – putting them into a plastic bag and leaving it in William's office – but there was no escaping the fact that William's affair was flourishing again, that there was an all-too-convincing reason for why he was spending so much time down in Suffolk these days, and Xandra was taking far greater risks than she realised – staying up in London by herself.

Matthew couldn't wait for the evening to end. For all Rachel's liberal thinking and her willingness to let Evie spend nights away from Morland Road – getting up to whatever she liked, with whomsoever she liked – out here, in Suffolk, the rules were different. So long as she, Giles and Evie – the three of them – were all under one roof there were certain standards to uphold . . . or at least give the impression of being upheld. No sex before marriage was one of them. And Matthew, that night, was more than happy to oblige.

Bidding a regretful Evie goodnight on the landing and creeping on up to his own little room, he couldn't help being glad that she was sharing with Honor – making it impossible for him to join her that night; glad that it was equally out of the question for her to join him where he had been billeted – in one of the old nursery bedrooms at the top of the house, a room with creaky floorboards directly above their host.

It wasn't that he didn't like or want her any more. On the contrary, Evie was exactly his sort of girl: urban, instinctive, rebellious. Matthew loved sleeping with her – it felt very natural to him – and the fact that he could find her company simultaneously easy and unpredictable was surely something special. So what if she wasn't academic? Nor was Matthew, not really. Everything he'd said to her – about so-called clever people simply having a trick of passing exams – he believed absolutely.

But when Honor was in the room, everything changed. Perfectly manicured Honor Montfort, who was everything he didn't like, everything that irritated . . . Why was he drawn to her? Why was he so perverse? Why was a closed door always so much more fascinating than an open one? She wasn't interested in him. His feelings would never be reciprocated. His desire was entirely hopeless . . . and perhaps that was part of its power. But that didn't mean Matthew should then take Evie up as some kind of consolation prize. It sounded corny, but he liked her too much for that. And for all her angry attitude and tough-looking exterior, Evie was still very much an innocent. She needed to be protected from herself, and the least he could do was spend the night alone.

Curling his body around Rachel's once more, holding her there in the dark, Giles vowed it would never happen again. He would never let her go. Not unless he went with her. *This is my home*, he thought, sniffing at her hair. *Not Putney, not Favenham, but you.*

159

Chapter Ten

Favenham

Overnight the wind grew stronger. Pulling back his curtains the following morning, William saw branches straining and clouds scudding – their shadows racing across the lawn. He thought of his kite: not one of the traditional diamond-shape structures with a fluttering tail in a pretty colour, but a neon-pink sleeping bag that Ben and Nina had given him for Christmas that year, that flew like a fighter plane and – in this wind – would probably take off altogether, with William attached. Particularly if they took it to the beach. He found it in the garage and, after breakfast, a group of them set off: William at the wheel, Honor in the passenger seat, Matthew and Evie in the back.

Rachel waved them off – wishing that Giles had been persuaded to go too. But kites and wild walks and blokeish tests of strength simply weren't his thing, and right now the important thing was to keep Giles in the happy frame of mind he'd been in when they'd gone to bed last night. And if that meant his morning was spent lazing in the library, drinking coffee and reading his way through Saturday's newspapers, so be it.

Rachel didn't care. All she really wanted was enough time in the kitchen, preparing lunch with Lillian so that everything would be ready for when the Beaumarises arrived.

The beach party still hadn't returned when, just before lunch, a midnight-blue Audi glided up the drive. It slowed at the divide, then forked right – round to the front of the house – and a man with a flash of white-blond hair got out. Less of it than Giles remembered, but that wasn't surprising. Sixteen years had passed since he'd last seen Edward Beaumaris. The man would have been about the age Evie and Honor were now – bright and eager, just about to leave them all for a gap year travelling round Australia.

The Beaumarises were neighbours of the Montforts. They shared a boundary at the north-east end of the Favenham estate and it was clear, just from looking at the soil, where the land changed hands. Allenham, the Beaumaris property, was sandy-yellow. And while it was a large and beautiful estate with land that stretched right out to the coast, which centuries ago had once belonged to the Montforts, William had no desire to be farming it today. It made him smile to think of the Victorian Beaumarises, with all that industrial money they'd brought with them from Manchester, trying to look grand by buying a large estate in Suffolk and not realising that most of it was worthless. William's great-grandfather had sold it to them with all the crafty charm of his forebears – and then, with the proceeds, had invested heavily in railways. With nothing to prove, socially, he could see where the true investment lay.

But the Beaumarises felt only pity for the Montforts,

believing that reduced circumstances had forced them to sell.

Poor William, they thought, *with only two thousand acres*.

Poor Robert, thought the Montforts, *with such useless land*.

And in some strange way this state of mutual pity had allowed the two families to develop a gentle friendship that manifested itself in annual shooting invitations and mutual support on agricultural committees, Christmas parties and garden openings.

And then, last month – after a long, drawn-out illness – old Robert Beaumaris had died. And while this meant that neither his wife nor his son were keen to go out much, it seemed that a quiet lunch at Favenham was ideal. They'd be delighted to come. Edward, in particular . . .

'It's been such a long time,' he'd said to Rachel on the telephone when she rang them earlier in the week. 'I can't believe it. Fifteen years, or something terrifying . . .'

'And you're really staying for good?'

'Well I can't leave my mother here all by herself. And there's no way she'd move back out to Australia. Not when she struggled so hard to get out of there in the first place! And I . . . Well, it was great while it lasted but I'm looking forward to running things over here, to be honest. There's a lot for me to do.'

And Rachel was looking forward to seeing them. She'd always had a soft spot for Edward, who'd been an immaculately behaved page at her wedding, and she ran down the steps to greet them.

'Edward . . . Lavinia . . .'

'Hello, darling,' came a familiar drawl from inside

the car – it was a deep, glamorous voice that had its roots in Australia, its finish in Europe, and a vintage patina acquired from years of smoking Turkish cigarettes. As Giles watched from his upper window, the sparkling ends of two slim walking sticks stuck out over the gravel. Then a pair of navy shoes from this season's Chanel, a pair of bird-thin ankles, and finally the rest of Lavinia Beaumaris emerged – elegant as ever in spite of her increasing frailty.

The three of them made unhurried progress into the house – with Edward and Rachel flanking Lavinia, who didn't have much strength, especially against the wind blowing in from the coast. She tried to disguise this by saying something charming about the knot in Rachel's scarf, and the white camellias she could see – still in bud – by the garden wall . . . but it was clear she was buying time. And their little party had yet to reach the top of the steps when William's car shot across the cattle grid.

The four of them got out – laughing at the force of the wind and the effect it had on the open car doors.

'Bloody hell!' William grabbed Honor's door for her as she struggled out with the rolled-up kite. 'Lucky it wasn't like this earlier,' he shouted, 'we'd all be out to sea!'

Rachel waited until everyone was inside before making introductions. Some weren't necessary: Lavinia had met Evie a number of times and knew the Montfort children quite well. But Edward was a complete stranger. They'd heard about him, of course. They knew he was the missing son, the one who had gone off to Australia and never come back again – not properly. The fleeting visits for occasional family weddings or special birthdays hardly counted when

163

Edward was back on the plane before anyone knew he'd arrived. Only his parents got to see anything of him, and even for them it was hurried. They'd tried to go out to Australia, but it had got harder as Robert had grown weaker; their visits dwindling to once every couple of years at the end. Whenever any of the Montfort children went abroad, their parents would say, laughing, 'Don't like it too much, darling. Don't do an Edward Beaumaris . . .'

And now here he was. Brushing salty hair from her face, Honor shifted the pink neon kite under her arm and shook Edward's hand. 'Hello.'

Edward smiled at her, a light smile that didn't quite engage, as if he had more important things on his mind.

'And this is Matthew Forrester,' Rachel went on round the group, 'and Evie, my daughter, and Giles, of course . . .'

While Edward shook hands with the others, Honor continued to observe him. After the manic kite-flying on the beach, the man seemed very level. She looked at Matthew, picking stones from his trainers; at Evie, chatting earnestly, with tangles in her hair; and her father, his skin burnt red by the wind. In contrast, Edward remained unruffled – with his tailored clothes and listening expression.

Leaving them in the hall, Honor went back outside again, to return the kite to the garage. He wasn't what she'd expected him to be. The way his mother sometimes spoke about him – and, more particularly, about life in Australia – she always made it sound primitive and uncultured, as if it were no match for the sophistication of Europe. Yet here was quite the reverse. Here was someone whose poise and maturity

164

made people like Abe and Matthew Forrester and the men that Honor had met at Oxford seem, to her, mere schoolboys. Standing in the dusty garage, Honor realised she'd been imagining someone weathered – someone more her father's generation – and found her interest shifting.

On her return, she passed him in the hall – still talking to her father. He did not look up. And that, it seemed, was enough. By the time they went in to lunch, Honor was wondering what she'd ever found attractive in boys her own age. She stood next to Edward at the sideboard while the others chatted behind them. They helped themselves to Rachel's lasagne, neither of them taking very much. He scooped a baked potato and offered it to her.

'You take it,' she said.

'Would you like it?'

'I – no – you go on. I'll . . .'

Smiling, Edward held the spoon above her plate. 'Yes or no?'

It would have been silly to fight him about it, silly and unnecessary. She wouldn't have minded forcing one of her brothers to go ahead of her, or even Matthew. She could have held her ground with them – ridiculed such politeness, risked a potato flying to the floor, or a smudge of lasagne on the polished wood – but Edward Beaumaris was different, and Honor held her plate forward.

'Thank you.'

They sat next to each other at lunch. Thinking about it later, she could remember nothing of what they said. Their conversation certainly wasn't noisy or clever or original. There wasn't much laughter. There was nothing outwardly impressive in the hesitations, the pauses and deflections, the polite reluctance to speak about themselves. Yet for the first time in her life Honor felt she'd found an equal – someone who played the same conventions at the same level; someone whose conversation had the unhurried beauty and ornamental complexity of a renaissance dance; someone who noticed that kind of subtlety in hers. At times it was as if a whole other conversation was taking place, in the silences, the glances, the toying with napkin rings . . . so that their movements – where he placed his glass, how she rolled her napkin, where they chose to look – were the focus. Not their words.

And suddenly it was the easiest thing in the world to do the right thing – to go back to London to be with her mother and leave the Suffolk party behind – when Edward offered her a lift to London.

'Are – are you sure?' she said. 'You know I'm really quite happy to take the train, Edward. It only takes an hour, and I—'

'Of course I'm sure.' He checked his watch. 'I'm just thinking it through. I have to be back by six to let a mate from Australia into the flat. So if we can persuade your pa to take my mother home this afternoon, we won't need to leave here until – what – three? How does that sound?'

'It sounds perfect.'

'But you'd still rather not?'

'No! No! I didn't mean that! I was just thinking that you might prefer your radio, or – or your solitude. Your space . . .'

'I get quite enough solitude and space as it is,' he said, smiling. 'I'd like you to come.'

William was more than happy to drive Lavinia Beaumaris home. 'Of course I can,' he said to Honor.

'You go with Edward. It's a much better idea than that ghastly train and we . . . No, really, darling. Go. Go quickly. Go pack. You don't want to keep the poor man waiting.'

Honor hurried off, out of the dining room, up to her bedroom. As the door closed behind her, William looked sideways at Lavinia – smoking her long cigarette.

'You don't mind, do you?'

Lavinia blew a jet of Turkish smoke into the cherry blossom that sat in the middle of the table. 'Now tell me,' she said with a lazy smile, 'what does a girl like Honor do with herself these days?'

With its hard roof and sober colour, Edward Beaumaris's car wasn't particularly glamorous. Beside the flash convertible that Abe had had in Spain last summer – complete with cooling box and matching luggage and glossy red exterior – this vehicle was barely distinguishable from a standard company car. No one would turn to look at them, and Honor liked it that way.

She liked the restraint. Here they were, travelling easily over 100mph, with barely a change in engine tone. It was only because of a lull in their conversation that she'd considered their speed at all. And now that she had, it became clear that nobody was overtaking them. Nobody could. All cars in their way were persuaded to the left, and the Audi shot clean past with Edward at the wheel. It was as efficient and superior as it was possible to be, without saying, 'Look!'. None but the most discerning would see that the engine was special – that it could, if Edward wished, take them well beyond their current speed . . . and this, to Honor,

167

was the thing. Concealed power. Quiet beauty. No need to try. It was as if the owner held something of so much worth that any need for advertisement was redundant. Nothing was for sale.

Even inside the car – where she'd have expected at least some chink or crack, some keyhole glimpse of character – everything was hidden. No chocolate wrappers, no empty cartons, no newspapers from last weekend. No empty cracked cassette cases. No scuffed and muddy road atlas, no torn-up A–Z – none visible, at least. No crumbs. No dust. No random coat. No evidence at all of the person in charge. Clean, perfect, closed. To Evie, it would have been dull. But to Honor, that very hiddenness had the sexual enigma of someone in dark glasses.

'So what made you choose this car?' she said at last.

Frowning slightly, Edward closed in on a yellow Mazda in front of them. 'You don't like it?'

'No I do . . .'

The Mazda gave way and Honor glanced across as they passed. She looked at the couple inside, at the tiny snapshot world encased in shatterproof glass. She saw the driver's chin, caught in stormy sunlight. He was talking to his passenger and laughing . . . They were close enough for Honor to see the imperfections in his teeth.

'But you'd prefer something more stylish?' Edward said.

'This is stylish.'

'It is?'

Honor smiled. 'Of course it depends what you mean,' she said. 'For me, I'd rather die than march around in orange and drive a yellow Mazda, but I've no doubt that that kind of person would find me dreary beyond belief. Evie certainly does. She's always getting at me for the boring way I dress and the way I never say what I—'

'Evie?'

'Evie – Giles and Rachel's daughter. She was there today at lunch—'

'What – the one with the dirty jumper who kept saying, "*fuck*"?'

Honor smiled again.

'You're trying to tell me she's a good judge of dress sense and behaviour?'

'She thinks I'm too restrained.' Honor's smile faded. 'And perhaps she has a point. I don't want people to think I'm cold. So if that means more opening up, then perhaps I should try a bit harder . . .'

'To be like everybody else?'

'Or maybe just—'

'Oh, Honor, the number of women I've met who'll pour out their hearts at the very first meeting, who'll tell you their deepest secrets before they even know your name . . . bore on about their current paranoia – lose any shred of mystery . . . You want to be like that?'

Honor said nothing. She didn't want to be like that at all. She wanted to be like Edward's car: discreet, perfect, understated. And she was clever enough – discreet enough, understated enough – to refrain from spelling it out. In truth, of course, she didn't need to. He wasn't expecting her to answer his question. He was simply letting her know that he liked her the way she was; that he approved. On no account should she change.

It gave her a mad rush of pleasure. Not only then and there – in that car on that afternoon – but for days afterwards. It was a rush she found she could recreate,

169

simply by shutting her eyes. Nothing could override it: not watching his car drive away, or even letting herself back into Xandra's military pre-party operation . . .

'Oh Honor, there you are. What took you so long?'

'I got a lift, Mum. It—'

'Doesn't matter. I was hoping you might have been here in time to lay the table the way I like it, but Charlotte's done it now – and it looks fine. You'd better take that suitcase upstairs, though. And don't be too long in the bathroom, will you. They're asked for eight o'clock and I'll definitely need you down by then to help with the champagne . . .'

Honor took her suitcase upstairs and was back down in good time – perfectly attired and perfectly charming – for when her mother's guests arrived. Nothing could mar the A-grade glow, the Oxbridge acceptance, the 'Yes, I passed! I did it!' effect of what Edward Beaumaris had said to her that day.

So it was just five of them for dinner that night at Favenham. And as Rachel took her place at the end of the table, she couldn't help thinking that it should have been six. For while she understood it was almost impossible these days to get all of William's family together – his youngest two were still away at school and his eldest, Charles, was working in San Francisco – in truth, it wasn't the children that Rachel was thinking about. It was Xandra. Xandra should have been here. Here, in this very chair. She might be silly and trivial, and bafflingly insensitive – there were times when they'd all wished William hadn't married her – but that didn't stop this from now being Xandra's home. Favenham was where she belonged. The place felt less, somehow, without her. And it bothered

Rachel that no one – bar Honor, with her brief reference to where she was going that night – had mentioned Xandra's name all weekend.

Yet her imprint was everywhere – in the folds of the smart new curtains; in the bright suburban plants, budding in the garden; and the pencil-thin candles, burning high down the length of the table. Perhaps William and Honor were too used to Xandra's mark, could no longer distinguish it from the house itself. And as for Evie and Giles . . . well why should they care? Favenham had never been their home. But Rachel –who'd known the house as it was before and could identify every addition Xandra had made – Rachel was finding the hole left by her sister-in-law impossible to ignore.

She watched her brother at the other end of the table, gossiping to Matthew about Edward Beaumaris.

'For *fourteen years*?' said Matthew, adding more pepper to his potatoes. 'And not once coming back to England?'

William nodded. 'Pretty much,' he replied. 'There might have been the occasional wedding anniversary or funeral he'd come back for, but never for any decent length of time. It was a nightmare for his parents. The care they took bringing the boy up, making sure he wasn't spoilt. I know Lavinia always worried that as an only child they'd indulge him, but they never did. I can't think of a single time that Edward's manners were anything less than perfect. He was always beautifully behaved, even as a teenager . . . so thoughtful. Really, the last person you'd expect to run off to the other side of the world like that, without so much as a—'

'You think so?' said Giles suddenly, from the other end of the table.

171

Surprised, William took a sip of wine. 'Well yes. I mean—'

'I'd have thought that, with nineteen years of being perfect – of never smoking or drinking or dyeing his hair some ludicrous colour guaranteed to get his mother shrieking, and generally turning into exactly what his parents wanted him to be – poor Edward was bound to flip.'

'You think his parents got it wrong, then? You think they should have encouraged him to misbehave?'

'Perhaps,' said Giles. 'Strikes me they might have squashed him slightly. I mean, if Edward hadn't holed down in Australia, it would have been something else – drugs, depression, overworking, underworking – some part of him would have cracked, don't you think?'

William absolutely didn't agree. He found that sort of view of parenting irritating and unhelpful. Not everyone had difficult children like Evie. It was perfectly possible to raise one's offspring properly. And it was typical of people like Giles – people who'd clearly failed – to assume that the raw material they were working with was flawed, instead of admitting that they themselves had got it wrong. But while he didn't agree with Giles, William didn't relish the idea of thrashing the subject out – not with Rachel and Evie listening. So instead he smiled and, turning back to Matthew, batted the ball in his direction. 'What do you think?'

Matthew smiled back – flattered by the idea that Honor's father wanted his opinion; glad that he was finally getting somewhere. With the exception of Evie – who of course was paying him too much attention – Matthew had spent the entire weekend feeling weirdly irrelevant. It wasn't that any of them had been rude, exactly. Rachel and Giles hadn't been bad, but the others

172

– the Montforts and the Beaumarises – had all displayed an unmistakeable absence of interest, a sense that he'd been judged and written off before he'd had time to prove himself. It was as if it had already been decided by some higher authority that he was simply passing through, as if he didn't warrant the attention he knew they were capable of, if only they could be bothered . . . and it annoyed him – such resolute indifference. Matthew wasn't sure why, exactly, but he wanted more than mere politeness, more than duty, more than charm. He wanted genuine interest from these people. Not because they mattered much to him, but simply because he seemed to matter even less to them.

And when Honor left that afternoon, it seemed to Matthew that the whole weekend was over. He toyed with the idea of inventing some urgent job he had to do and hopping into the car as well. But there was Evie to think of – and the whole question of what the 'urgent job' might be that didn't give away the truth of his position. So instead he'd stood on the steps with the others, watching the midnight-blue Audi disappear down the drive – and felt the sun go in.

Now, however, with a fine glass of wine in his hand, with Evie attractive again in the absence of her cousin's brighter flame, with William smiling at him – listening attentively to his views on parenting . . . Now, Matthew began to enjoy himself. With every sip of wine he grew more confident. With every glance from Evie he felt stronger. And when – later, over coffee – the others began to talk about Xandra's absence, Matthew's sense of acceptance was complete. His earlier anxieties were groundless. They had to be. Sir William could hardly be accused of treating Matthew like an outsider if he was prepared to talk

173

about his wife in front of him, in quite such disparaging terms . . .

Matthew sat quietly while the subject grew. It started with a passing remark from William as he helped Rachel carry out the pudding plates.

'Wherever did you find this china, Rachel? I don't think I've ever—'

'Xandra uses something else?'

William yawned. 'Nothing but the best,' he said, nodding in the direction of a display cabinet full of gilded tureens, elaborate serving dishes, exquisite cups and saucers – with hand-painted Chinamen and birds, caught here and there in gentle backlighting. It was the trophy end – the larger pieces – of a vast dinner service that had been given to William and Rachel's parents as a wedding present by their American cousins. It was intended only for the most formal of dinner parties, but Xandra must have had other ideas . . .

'I hope she doesn't put them in the dishwasher.'

'Lord, no,' William said, laughing. 'No, she gets some friend of Lillian's to come in and do the lot by hand.'

They both disappeared into the kitchen, out of Matthew's earshot. And by the time they returned – Rachel with a tray of cups, William with a coffee pot and a small jug of milk – the subject had developed.

'Come on, William,' Rachel was saying. 'You only have to look around you now to see how hard she's worked at – at making Favenham what it is today.'

'Oh yes?' snorted William, clearly agitated by whatever it was that had been said in the kitchen. 'And what's that?'

'Well . . .'

'It looks like a fucking hotel.'

174

Rachel looked at the tray in front of her. 'Coffee, anyone?'

Matthew was riveted. This was a woman he'd read about – on and off, for years, in magazines and gossip columns – as a paragon of social correctness. This was Lady Montfort: the woman who never made a mistake, whose parties were held up as examples of how to get it right, whose sense of design was flawless, whose fashion instincts were impeccable . . . and all along her own husband despised and ridiculed the very things those giddy girly journalists so admired.

Well, well, he thought, helping himself to spoonfuls of dark brown sugar crystals.

He sat there, warm and mellow, full of red meat and red wine, surrounded by an audience of Montfort ancestors. His eye swung back and forth – from a painted sneer above the mantelpiece to the real thing at the other end of the table; from the flirtatious glance of the 7th Lady Montfort to something very similar in the eyes of her great-granddaughter, smiling at him now across a bowl of fruit. He stirred his coffee and listened while a critique of Xandra and her deficiencies poured from William's lips.

'Perhaps, William, another time?' said Giles at last, nodding very slightly in Matthew's direction.

William helped himself to more port, passed it on to Giles, and turned to Matthew. 'You shocked?'

Matthew shook his head. 'No – no, I—'

'You're bored, then?'

'Oh, no,' insisted Matthew, keen to show he was part of it, keen to remain on the inside. 'In fact, quite the opposite.'

William's eyebrows rose.

'I mean it's just that my own parents spent a lot of time apart when I was little, so – so I . . .'

'You know what it's like?' said Rachel.

'That's right.' He looked at her, gratefully. 'That's exactly what I meant.'

'So what happened?' asked William, leaning back in his chair. 'Your mother abandon her family too?'

'In a way. She'd had enough of my father never being there – he was a hack, you see, and he was always—'

'A journalist?'

'He was a reporter,' said Matthew quickly. 'A foreign correspondent. He did a lot of travelling, and he—'

'What did you say your name was?'

'Forrester.'

William leant forward. 'What – Forrester, as in *Richard Forrester*? The chap who was killed in the Lebanon?'

Matthew nodded.

'In the seventies, wasn't it?'

'It was 1978.'

For a moment, none of them spoke. The room was silent save for the steady tick from one of William's clocks and intermittent hissing from Xandra's sinking candles. But Evie – who had known nothing of this side to Matthew's past – couldn't hold it in any longer. It was as if the whole enigma of Matthew and his unfortunate job had suddenly been explained.

'So that's why you do it,' she whispered, touching his arm. 'Now I understand . . .'

'Do what?' said Rachel, looking up.

'He's a journalist, Mum. Just like his father.'

Rachel looked rather impressed. 'You kept that very quiet!' she said. 'Here we were thinking you wrote the odd piece here and there, and all the time . . . So – so you're a foreign reporter, then?'

176

'Not quite.'

'Then . . .'

'I'm an editor.'

'An editor?' said Giles, amused. 'Christ. You don't look old enough to . . . What kind of editor? What do you edit?'

Matthew told him. Another silence followed, shorter than the first – shorter and more eloquent – followed by a snorting laugh from William, as he recalled the things he'd said about Xa.

'Well I suppose your father would be proud of you,' he said, standing up. 'Smart work, son. Great scoop! Great research—'

'You don't think I—'

'I'm sure that excellent newspaper of yours will reward such undercover efforts handsomely.'

'But that's not what I'm—'

'Not what you're doing?'

'No!'

'You're going to quit your job?'

'No. But I—'

'You can't have it both ways, Matthew. If you choose to feed from other people's lives and reputations, you can't expect them to welcome you into their homes.'

'You – you're asking me to leave?'

'Too right I am. Get out.'

Matthew left early the next morning with only Evie to see him off. It was a cool day with a restless wind that blew around the house – rattling windows, slamming doors. She stood on the steps, shivering in her cotton dressing-gown as his bags were loaded into the cab that would take him to the station.

He didn't want her to come with him. He was sorry,

but no, he had to be alone right now. He should never have come – should never have let her persuade him – only to be insulted and listen to his father being insulted . . . by a goddamn *property developer* of all things! Like that gave him the moral ground? Jesus. And okay, so Matthew hadn't realised the man had history with the *Morning Post* – some dispute a while back over an unpleasant article in the property section – but that was hardly Matthew's fault. And it can't have been that bad if he still bought the rag himself – Matthew had seen it in the library yesterday along with *The Times* and the *Telegraph* and a pile of right-wing tat. What gave Sir William fucking Montfort the right to get all puritanical and censorious about a bunch of hacks that he himself supported?

'I know,' said Evie, her grip tightening on his hand. 'I *know*, and I can't tell you how sorry I am. I'll make him apologise. I'll—'

'You think you can make that man apologise?'

'I can try, Matthew. I—'

'I'll bet he never apologised for anything in his life. You think he'll start now? With a journalist?'

'I don't know, Matthew.' She was crying now. 'I don't know. But it's not—'

'It is.' Matthew pulled free.

She couldn't follow him on to the gravel. Her feet were soft and bare.

*

Upstairs, Giles heard the taxi's engine. He looked down from his window at the scene outside – at Evie's distress and at Matthew's expression as he got into the car.

PART III

Chapter Eleven

A Different Direction

It was another late shift, another evening lost to the round of fetching and carrying with dead-eyed economy.

Ordinarily Evie wouldn't have noticed – far less cared – so long as the cash was in her pocket at the end of the week. In many ways her working life was easier than ever. After three years' experience, she no longer needed to put in a conscious effort to make every journey out between the tables work twice or three times over. These days it was automatic, and she never went to take an order empty-handed. There were always more menus to bring, or knives and forks to lay up another table, or a tray of fresh drinks waiting at the bar. And there was always something else to bring back with her: another order, a pile of dirty coffee cups, a credit card ready to be processed. She was a good, brisk waitress. Could have smiled a bit more, could have spun a little charm from time to time, but still an asset to the restaurant – whichever one it was. For there had now been quite a few, and Brasserie Beach was no more than a distant memory from another time.

But the feeling of occupational pride was entirely absent. The kind of pride that prevented Evie from accepting any offers of help from her parents or her uncle – and there had been quite a few – did not extend to the day-to-day grind. She took no pleasure in doing her job well. Instead all she had was a mild sense of time passing – each hour, another crisp note in her purse. And even though it was a different restaurant in a different part of town, even though she'd recently been promoted to deputy front-of-house – with extra duties and extra pay and a certain status in the dining room – it was still the same clattering cycle, the same neat trick of layering plates, the same numbness as another group of people got up from their table, put on their coats and trooped out into the night . . . leaving nothing behind but scribbled signatures, false gratitude and dirty napkins for her to toss into the laundry basket.

When Paul, the current manager, was away it was Evie's job to close the place up. Standing at the kitchen door, she ran an experienced eye across the room: over the mopped floor, still drying – the smell of bleach inside her head – checking, checking . . . Nothing superfluous on the surfaces, everything wiped down and shining, put away, silent . . . apart from the ticking of the fridges and the hum of an ultraviolet tube.

Switching off the overhead lights, Evie collected her bag and coat and went upstairs, inspecting the state of the floor on her way – she'd have to clean it properly before Paul got back next week. Then she checked the lavatories on the landing – good enough – and finally up into the restaurant itself where rows of empty tables stood – chairs duly upturned, legs pointing into the air with all the indignity of naked mannequins, so that the

182

floor could be thoroughly swept. There were the rows of sugar bowls, neatly lined up on the side so that they could be checked tomorrow for cigarette ends and sodden cubes and other nastinesses that invariably appeared at the bottom, night after night. There were all the vases with their sad single tulips, waiting to be redistributed once the chairs were down again. And the salt and pepper mills that would need refilling before the lunch shift tomorrow. And the knives and forks – still hot from the machines – back in their slots, ready for another day. It was all fine. And Evie stood at the exit, running her finger over the light switches so that section by section the restaurant fell dark, until the only light left was the ever-present glow from the fridges under the bar.

The outside doors of the restaurant were made of reinforced glass that had to be cleaned twice a week. Locking them carefully, Evie glanced through them one last time – past the shifting street-reflections to the motionless room inside. It was peaceful in there at this time of night. Peaceful and – to Evie, that evening – a little sad. Part of her empathised with the upturned chairs, the cooling knives and forks, the conveyor belt of sugar bowls . . .

Taking the keys from the lock, she paused briefly with them still in her hand while looking up and down the street – and then resignedly at her watch.

He'd promised he'd be there at midnight, but that was fifty minutes ago and she didn't really expect him to turn up now. Hadn't, in truth, expected it from the start. Dom was always promising things he couldn't give, or wouldn't give, or somehow forgot about. That gig he was going to in Hammersmith must have been every bit as crazy as Evie had known it would be. She shouldn't have been tempted by extravagant promises of being met at the restaurant, taken back to his flat and having him make love to her by candlelight. Not that she cared hugely about the candles. Or even, really, much tenderness. Any half-decent sex would have done. If she wasn't so desperate for a bit of physical attention, she wouldn't have made the plan in the first place. Probably wouldn't even be with Dom – who in any case would be crashed out on a mate's floor by now, or else falling senseless out of a taxi, reeking of beer and fags . . . entirely unfit for Evie's purposes. It was better all round that she go home.

In the past she might have felt hurt and rejected, or at the very least indignant. Instead there was nothing. It was the same reaction she'd have when a customer left the restaurant without smiling or saying thank you: upsetting at first, but – over time – irrelevant, and almost preferable to the kind of person who wanted to be best friends the second you gave them a menu. And now that it was late, and her feet ached and her brain seemed stuck on a repeat cycle of the day's specials, the idea of her own bed in her own room without Dom pawing at her didn't seem so bad.

Deciding to take a taxi – she was too late for the bus and the stream of orange 'FOR HIRE' lights heading out of London was simply too tempting for her tired legs – Evie gave the driver her Putney address and sat back, still wondering why – with nothing about that night so terribly bad . . . why did she feel so flat?

Okay, so her boyfriend wasn't perfect – not someone she'd be with for ever – but good enough for now. She rather liked the feeling of power and control that came with being indifferent to how Dom Franklin treated her. No stupidity, no exposure, no threat of another Matthew.

Almost two years had passed, yet Evie still winced when she remembered that time – winced not just at the cold way Matthew had abandoned her on her uncle's drive, but at the blind-bull way she'd handled it afterwards. Someone like Honor would have turned her back, nursed what sadness she had in private and busied herself with forgetting him . . . but not Evie. Oh no! Evie had to put herself through the humiliating process of calling, and calling again, and again – leaving message after message until finally, maddened by the lack of response, she'd gone round to his place in Kilburn and hammered on the door.

Matthew had opened it with a knackered expression.

'Well?' she'd demanded, eyes blazing.

Wearily he'd let her in. The room had been a mess, scattered with papers in half-formed piles and open reference books. It smelt of coffee and of Matthew at his most exhausted, and Evie – who'd been expecting to find two glasses of champagne on the table and a cheap blonde sitting on the sofa – saw instantly that this was far from the case.

And as the minutes ticked by, with Matthew explaining that there really wasn't anyone else, that he simply didn't feel comfortable going out with her any more – 'It wasn't just the things your uncle said, Evie . . .' – she wasn't sure the blonde-on-the-sofa scenario wouldn't have been preferable, and closed her eyes in pain.

'I mean, of course I loved being with you – really Evie, I mean it – we had some good times.'

She refused to look at him

'But it was never going to last, was it? Not with the kind of work I'm going to be doing soon – travelling and so on . . .'

'I wouldn't have minded that.'

Matthew put his head in his hands.

'I wouldn't!' she insisted, looking at him now with dark tears in her eyes.

And Matthew, looking warily back at her with nothing more to say, saw Evie interpreting the silence, understanding that his job had nothing to do with it, that he was trying to palm her off. He saw her expression snap suddenly back to one of anger, even disdain.

'Oh come on, Matthew. At least allow me the dignity of hearing the truth.'

So he did – or tried to. Relieved that she was able to be angry, that he was to be spared the awfulness of her crying, Matthew took a different tack – admitting that, yes, okay, while he hadn't been actively unfaithful, there was – sort of – someone else . . .

'Who?'

'You don't know her.'

'Try me.'

'Please, Evie. It's not relevant.'

'Then—'

'Especially as I've no idea if she fancies me too. Nothing will happen. It's just some mad crush and in a few months I'll probably wonder what on earth I saw in her and wish I'd never let you go.'

'Yeah, that'd be right.'

Matthew stared at his feet. 'But even if it does turn out to be a hideous mistake,' he said, in a quieter voice, 'even if nothing ever happens between me and this girl, it would hardly be fair on you to let things

186

continue – don't you think? I hope it doesn't sound too patronising, but I really was just trying to—'

'Don't you dare tell me you did it for my benefit, Matthew. I swear, I'll—'

'No of course not. I just . . . it's just, when you're with one person, and then you fall for someone else – the way I've fallen for—'

'Yes, all right.' Evie stood up. She could feel the tears building up again – weak, shameful tears – and was glad she hadn't taken her coat off, glad to be able to do this swiftly.

Matthew followed her to the door. 'I'm so sorry.'

She was struggling with the latch, finding it hard to see properly.

'You have to turn it the other way, Evie . . . you – here. Let me.' And suddenly the door was open. It was raining and the fresh wet air hit their faces. 'You will be okay, won't you?'

'Like you care,' came the muttered response as Evie opened her umbrella and strode into the night.

So, yes. All-in-all, it was much better for her to be with someone like Dom. All of the fun and none of the heartache. That side of her life was exactly as she wanted it to be. No reason for her to be feeling flat tonight on that account.

And nor did she think it was her job. Admittedly, there was a lack of status, but she was used to that now, and the pay – after tips – was pretty good. So long as she was living with her parents and needed little more than pocket money to keep her going, a waitress-wage was ample for Evie's needs. She could go to whatever films and bars and gigs she liked. She could buy whatever clothes she wanted, and take cheap holidays once or twice a year. What did Evie care for the academic rat race? She'd no desire to be like Honor who, that year, was putting herself through yet another punishing work schedule in the run-up to her finals. All for another piece of paper to put up on her wall. According to Rachel, Honor would be coming up to London next week – no doubt dressed immaculately in charcoal tweed – for a series of milk-round interviews with all the top merchant banks.

Evie opened her eyes. Regarding her own hunched reflection in the cab window, she realised that while academic Honor was something she could handle – algebra, Virgil, amino acids, past participles, Cromwell, copper sulphate, rainfall in Chile . . . none of that meant anything to Evie, Honor could have all the ticks and stars and A-grades she liked – but Honor in the boardroom? Honor in pinstripes, wielding power? That was something altogether different.

Evie had always loved the idea of the woman in the boardroom: the books of Barbara Taylor Bradford and TV soaps like *Dynasty*. She could identify far more with the kind of woman played by Joan Collins – Alexis Carrington, stalking about and standing up for herself – than the wimpy self-sacrifice of Linda Evans's Cristal, and she now felt a strange possessiveness towards the role, as if Honor were somehow stealing it from her. The thought of how they'd be in five years' time – with Evie still getting on the night bus and thinking of cabs as a treat, while Honor was whisked home in some limousine, kicking off a pair of city-slick stilettos and cracking open the champagne to celebrate the close of yet another mega-deal . . . it made Evie sick to the core.

And that was before the whole question of her parents, and the rather more practical requirement for someone in the Langton family to go out there and make a decent amount of money . . .

On an individual level, Evie's income more than covered her expenses, but the situation with Giles and Rachel was rather less comfortable. With a national recession grinding on, there was very little interest in such luxuries as hand-painted wardrobes and elaborate bathroom murals. Demand for Giles's skills had almost completely dried up – apart from occasional part-time teaching at the local adult education centre, and a standing commission to produce decorative trays for a little shop in Henley that was more of a playroom for some overprivileged friend of Rachel's than a viable business. He loathed the way she paid him – the Monopoly-board attitude she had to the money she handed over, picking each note tidily out from her old-fashioned till, her little finger pointing in the air, and laughing gaily at the noise it made when she pushed the cash drawer back in.

Rachel's income problems were, if anything, even more serious. On advice from her brother at the time of her marriage to Giles, Rachel had used her inheritance to become a Lloyd's Insurance 'name' – effectively doubling her income in exchange for becoming liable, without limit, for any insurance claim that might arise. This happy arrangement had got them safely through the seventies and eighties, but Lloyd's was now in crisis. And while it was okay for men like William Montfort – who could afford to take a few financial hits – it was a disaster for poor Rachel, who'd come to depend on every penny of extra income. For not only had that income disappeared, she was now having to pay out jaw-dropping sums as a rash of monster-claims hit her syndicate . . . with no prospect of a respite.

They tried not to involve Evie in what was happening, but it wasn't hard to see they were struggling. For a start, the house was a mess. When the tumble dryer broke last November, no attempt was made to get it mended, far less invest in a new one, and Rachel had taken to hanging up their clothes and sheets all over a kitchen that smelt increasingly of damp. The car's exhaust pipe had a disconcerting rattle. And the envelopes that fell through the door were, lately, too often branded with the familiar red ink of a FINAL DEMAND stamp.

Evie had seen all this and despaired, but until now, it hadn't occurred to her that she could do anything about the situation. It was only when faced with the idea that calm gentle Honor could go out there and actually get herself the kind of job that would one day bring in millions . . . only then did Evie feel the stirrings of ambition. And when that night she came back to find her parents still up and sitting at the kitchen table – both wearing glasses, both caught unmasked, dragged down by stress and exhaustion – Evie knew that her waitressing days were numbered.

'Evie!'

'Weren't you meant to be out tonight, sweetheart? I'm sure you said not to worry . . . that – that you were—'

'There was a change of plan,' said Evie, staring at the piles of letters and bank statements and scribbled lines of sums – white-bright in the overhead glare – slipping and toppling, wide across the table. 'What's all this?'

'Our accounts,' said Giles, hastily pulling it all together. 'We've had another Lloyd's demand, and—'

'*Selling the house*?' said Evie, picking up a piece of

190

paper from under her father's nose. It was a valuation report.

For a moment no one said anything. Giles and Rachel looked at each other while Evie continued to read the report and the clock ticked loudly on the wall.

'Hopefully not.' Rachel's voice was flat and tired.

'But—'

'But yes, you're right. We may have to move somewhere cheaper. You know the nightmare I've been having with Lloyd's.'

'I knew you had a few bills, Mum. I didn't—'

'We hoped it would pass, but now it looks as if . . . as if it won't. And that means making a few changes . . .'

Evie looked at her father, bleakly silent on the other side of the table.

'. . . but we will work it out, darling,' Rachel went on. 'Selling the house really is a final resort. There are plenty of other options.'

'Like?'

Rachel sighed. 'Well we could always take in lodgers,' she said. 'Or I could find some sort of proper job instead of wasting time on voluntary work for the Putney Project. And your father's got some great ideas about marketing his work in places like Cornwall and – and apparently Brighton's got quite a few shops that might be interested in his sort of thing. So you see there are lots of avenues for us to look at before actually selling the house. And of course there's always the chance that the Lloyd's pressure will ease . . .'

But Evie didn't like it. She didn't like her father's silence, or the cheery way her mother was talking – as if, through tone of voice alone, she could dispel the cloud of anxiety that hung over the kitchen table along with sheets that smelt of bacon. And with one parent

191

devoid of hope, and the other devoid of realism, Evie felt – for the first time in her life – an inclination towards responsibility.

If Honor could get a smart job in the City then, hell, why couldn't Evie? Sure, those graduate training schemes were out of her league. She wasn't a milk-round contender. She'd have to pass on the kinds of banks and law firms that Honor was looking at, unless it was PA work, or – God forbid – catering, but that didn't mean there weren't other jobs out there; jobs that didn't need a degree. They wouldn't pay as much or be as prestigious as the ones Honor was going for, but Evie was damned if she wasn't going to try.

The next day, she registered with three agencies. But her lack of a degree, or even basic secretarial skills, meant that the jobs they suggested to her – peeling tomatoes for a catering company in Covent Garden, packing for a removals business in Essex, delivering brochures for a travel agency – were hardly an improvement on waitressing.

So she called the banks and City institutions herself. She checked the newspapers for job vacancies, but more often than not she didn't bother – calling, instead, on spec; quickly working out how to get past the switchboard and even, on occasion, piercing the front line of secretaries and PAs; getting straight through to the heads of personnel, who would listen politely to Evie's account of herself before taking her details and saying they'd get back to her if anything turned up. But they would make it clear to her that they seriously doubted there would be any position available for a candidate with her CV. She needed to get some sort of basic qualification.

'Or at the very least, you should learn to type.'

'But couldn't you just—'

'I'm sorry. That's really all I can do for you at this stage, Miss Langton. I wish you the best of luck in your continued search, of course, but—'

'You – you couldn't just give me an interview? It really wouldn't take long. I'm sure if you *met* me, you'd—'

'I'm sorry, Miss Langton. Goodbye.'

So Evie decided to lie. Not big lies – she didn't claim to have a degree, or any previous experience in the particular jobs she was after – but it did no harm for her to say that her A-levels were rather more impressive than was strictly true, that her previous jobs had all been abroad, that typing certainly wouldn't be a problem. 'Might be a bit rusty,' she found herself saying. 'The last job was more – managerial, I suppose. They gave me a secretary of my own in Moscow, but that was only because they could tell that my typing skills don't extend to the Russian alphabet . . . Absolutely. It won't take a second for me to get back in the swing of it – and you won't be disappointed by my other office skills. I assure you. I'm extremely user-friendly . . .'

She'd buy a typewriter at the weekend and teach herself, if necessary. The important thing was to get an interview.

And it worked. By the end of the week Evie had managed to set up three interviews – all corporate, all worth over twenty grand a year. All she needed was something half decent to wear. With no spare cash, and no suitable office clothes, there was really only one person in a position to help her.

'Of course I'm sure!' said Honor, delighted. 'Just come over. Come today!'

The Montforts' house was large, early Victorian and white stuccoed. It sat in a row of similar houses in a quiet corner between Kensington High Street and Gloucester Road. Most of them were semi-detached but William Montfort had managed to buy both halves of his. With a bit of backhanding and a very sizeable donation to the Borough Gardens Trust, he had obtained permission to alter the aspect of his house so that any trace of it having once been two was now completely gone. The front door sat at the centre, up a row of shallow steps. There was even enough room for 'in' and 'out' gates. An ancient chestnut tree – that had once sat at the edge of the dividing wall – now occupied a central position. Its twigs and branches were bare of leaves and dripped with urban rain.

Evie climbed the steps and rang the bell, and was about to ring again when she heard voices inside.

'Don't mention it,' a man was saying. Evie couldn't place the voice. It wasn't Honor's brother; for sure, it wasn't Abe. 'Please,' he went on, his footsteps coming closer to the door. There was a rustling sound as he took a coat from one of the pegs on the inside. 'I was coming to London anyway, so it couldn't have been easier to drop it by.'

Evie heard Honor sigh. 'They'll be sad they missed you—'

'I'm sad to miss them! You won't forget to show Xandra that crack in the teapot, will you? I can't tell you how worried my mother was when she—'

'Of course I will. But really, Edward – it's hardly visible. And who's to say that Lavinia was to blame? She . . . here, take this one.' Handing him a black umbrella, Honor opened the door. 'It was probably

194

done by Mum herself, or Lillian, or one of the . . . Evie!'

'Hello.'

'Evie!' Honor kissed her warmly. 'God, I'm sorry. How long have you been waiting there?'

'Couple of minutes. I did ring the bell, but—'

'I must be going deaf,' said Honor, laughing and turning to Edward. 'You know my cousin Evie, don't you?'

Edward Beaumaris switched his smile to Evie. He wore a dark suit, with a perfectly knotted tie and shiny black shoes. He carried an overcoat across one arm and held a black umbrella in his other hand. He looked like an advertisement for cab accounts or dry cleaning or mobile telephones. 'Of course I do,' he said. 'How are you, Evie?'

He was trying to be friendly, even Evie could see that. But, unsettled by his polish, his confidence and his easy manner – just standing beside him made her feel inadequate – she found herself unable to respond in kind. She couldn't even meet his eye, and her gaze veered off, into the distant safety of the Montforts' hallway – as she replied, 'All right.'

Edward's smile wavered. 'Oh. Well . . .' Shrugging on his overcoat, he gave his wristwatch a half-hearted glance. 'I'd better run. Car's on a meter.' He kissed Honor on the cheek – 'Lovely to see you' – nodded at Evie, and started down the steps.

Honor watched him. 'Thank you for lunch,' she called out.

Edward did not turn back. Instead, he raised an arm in cheerful acknowledgement and – still holding the umbrella furled right up – made a dash for the car.

The second he was gone, Evie's confidence returned. Turning to her cousin with raised eyebrows and a

195

pointed grin, she waited for the door to close, and then: 'Lunch à deux?'

Honor looked back at her. A warm smell of wine and chips hung in the hall. Meeting Evie's quizzical eye, she knew at once that the true explanation of what had happened – that Edward had turned up quite unexpectedly at half past twelve to return an old tea service Xandra had loaned to Lavinia for a garden opening last summer; that Xandra had not been home to receive it but Honor had helped him with the boxes; and then, because it was lunchtime and neither of them had anything better to do, he'd taken her out to the smart little restaurant round the corner . . . she knew that it would be misinterpreted. 'Really, Evie. He was just dropping off an old tea service of Mum's.'

'And thought he'd whisk you off for lunch at the same time?'

Honor smiled, but Evie could detect some stiffness there – a trace of impatience that sharpened her curiosity. 'He had some time to spare, Evie. And so did I. It seemed like a nice idea.'

'I'm sure it did,' said Evie, amused, stepping past the boxes in the hall and following Honor up to her bedroom. 'But why couldn't he just have dropped it off at Favenham? Why heave it all up here? Wouldn't it have been simpler to keep it in Suffolk?'

'You'd have thought so.'

'I mean, who on earth gives tea parties in London?'

Honor smiled as she opened the bedroom door. 'Mum?'

Conceding that it wasn't beyond her aunt to host something as ludicrous as a tea party in London, Evie was also aware that Honor's tidy answer had, for the moment, stopped any further inquisition on the subject of Edward Beaumaris. On the surface, there was nothing suspicious about the pair of them having lunch together. And it was only Honor's reluctance to talk about it – the wariness, the blocked responses, the mild tone of defence – that alerted Evie's attention. There may well have been no agenda to Edward Beaumaris's decision to take Honor out for lunch – who knew what motivated a man like that? – but one thing was certain: it had meant something to Honor, and Evie had seen it.

Ever since the split with Abe, Honor's love life had been something of an enigma. She hadn't been short of admirers at Oxford but had somehow, over time, acquired an air of untouchability at university. She was always warm and friendly, but gave off no signals of sexual availability . . . to the extent that the students who did find her attractive would invariably decide she was too much like hard work – better to keep as a friend – and would turn instead to sexy Jessica, or any other number of female undergraduates whose bedability was simply more apparent. And Honor never seemed to mind. It was almost as if she liked being single.

Everyone assumed it was Abe. They thought that, to Honor, no other man could ever quite measure up to the glamorous actor who'd gone off to Hollywood. Even Abe himself was inclined to take this view. He knew there'd been no other men for Honor since he'd gone off to LA. And the affectionate way she stayed in touch – coming up to London in the middle of term just to have lunch with him on one of his brief trips home; remembering to send him a card on his birthday; once even collecting him from the airport – these things weren't lost on Abe. He was touched that she was holding a torch for him. And who knew, perhaps one day they would get back together. Have kids with her and settle down? It wasn't such an unappealing prospect . . . for his late thirties, maybe, when he was properly established.

Evie wasn't so sure. She knew Honor better than that – knew her cousin's acts of kindness rarely had a hidden agenda. She remembered how Honor had been really quite glad when she and Abe had split. She didn't think Abe had anything to do with it. But Edward . . . Edward Beaumaris was a different story altogether. Smiling back at her cousin, Evie followed her into the bedroom, longing to ask more. Had Edward ever tried this sort of thing before? Had he taken Honor out – at Oxford, perhaps? Or called her, even? And what was he like one-on-one? Did Honor fancy him? As much as she'd once fancied Abe?

For while Edward Beaumaris was the last sort of man that Evie would consider for herself – while he wasn't nearly as sexy as Abe or as interesting as Matthew, while he lacked the darker air, the sloppiness and irresponsibility that lured her towards men like Dom Franklin – Evie could still see that he was probably just Honor's type. He had the same blend of charm and reserve, the same social know-how, the same degree of self-control that made it hard for an outsider to know what was really going on inside his mind. He seemed to Evie, in both good ways and bad, rather perfect. She just hoped that underneath the smooth surface there was also – as there was in Honor – a streak of some-thing rather more natural and irregular.

Honor's bedroom was at the top of the house, with the corners of its already-low ceiling cut off on one side

198

to make way for the roof. Evie knew this room – with its green lattice wallpaper, its elegant basin, its lingering smell of pine from fircones in the grate – almost as well as her own. As a little girl, and even more so as a teenager in the school holidays, Evie was always spending the night with her cousin at Launceston Villas. She and Honor were forever pestering their mothers to let them stay together, and as Honor's room was larger – with space for two beds – that was where they went. Since leaving school, there had been less opportunity for that sort of thing. Evie's job and Honor's degree had taken them in different directions, and it had been a while since Evie was last up here in Honor's room.

On first sight it seemed that nothing had changed. The room still smelt the same. It had the same – now slightly dated – wallpaper; the same sage carpet; the same tricky switch on the antique bedside lamp, with its double lines of old brown flex twisting away from a hole in the base. Honor still stashed her old magazines on the shelves by the dressing table. She still had her photographs pinned to the board beyond – the same tinted ones of them as little girls shivering in swimming costumes, and those blurry ones of all their school friends in pyjamas, pulling faces. There was even a publicity shot of Abe that Honor had forgotten to take down – in black and white, with a slight waxwork quality to his skin, pinned to the bottom left-hand corner.

But as Evie looked more closely, there were other – less familiar – touches that told of another world, a new life, separate from Evie's. Different magazines sat on top of the ones Evie had known. Newer, brighter photographs of Honor's Oxford friends – a row of strangers in black tie, lined up smiling before some college ball; and hard red-haired Jessica, posing in a cowboy hat and jeans – had started to overlap the older ones.

Evie's bed was furthest from the door. Before she could even remember making the choice, Honor had taken the one closest to the light – coming at an angle from the lamp on the landing – and the other one was very much Evie's. No one else slept there. On occasion, Xandra would even tell the cleaner to leave the sheets. No point changing them when it was only Evie. Evie loved this second space. She could put her suitcase on the far side and extend her territory – her signature mess, her upturned shoes, discarded shirts and jumpers sprawling inside-out – to the wall beyond. She liked being in the corner. As with corner tables in restaurants, or corner offices, it had a kind of status that Honor – if she noticed it at all – showed no interest in wanting for herself. What Honor liked was everything in its place. She liked knowing that Evie was contained in that corner, that there would be no mixing and muddling of their things.

Today, both beds were tidily made with the covers drawn right up. The carpet had scrape-marks from being vacuumed. The windows were open, in spite of the rain, and a sweet smell of beeswax polish mingled with the undertones of Honor's scent. There was an air of order that made Honor feel calm, and Evie quite on edge. She wished she had her suitcase with her so that she had something to scatter.

'Right then.' Honor opened her cupboards and began sorting through the hangers – looking for possibles for Evie to try on. Her hands moved briskly down the rail. Her fingers battled with the hooks. Her elbows got in the way of the hangers. Her body bent this way and that, around the empty clothes, while Evie sat on the bed and waited. Every so often Honor would unhook a hanger and place it fluidly, with the clothes attached, over the other bed, talking all the while – 'You might feel awkward with the skirt – the split at the side's a bit high – but the colour's good . . . And this one's lovely, although there is a slight mark on the lapel . . . Not sure if you'll fit the trousers, but you're welcome to try them . . . Might be a bit grown-up, even for me . . . Pink might not be the message you want to give out, but' – grinning round at Evie now – 'it might work if the interviewer's a man . . .'

Evie grinned back. And as they worked through the clothes – with Evie picking out the pieces she liked, and Honor putting them firmly back – they talked briefly about Evie's interviews . . . and then about the ones Honor had had, and the series of offers she was now considering.

Evie couldn't help but be impressed. Four A-levels and two S-levels – even the predicted 2.1 degree – all of these meant nothing to Evie beside the multiple job offers from merchant banks and firms of solicitors that Honor had received in the past week.

'It's not as impressive as it sounds,' Honor added hastily, noticing Evie's expression. 'I promise you. It's just what comes from having been at Oxford. Anyone could do it. But I do have to decide pretty soon whether to go for banking or law—'

'Which pays better?'

'Banking.'

'Then there you are.'

Honor smiled. 'But Evie, a legal qualification would give me—'

'It would give you less money, and two more years at law school.'

Honor sighed. 'Dad seems to think it's important to have some other sort of training, not just a degree. He thinks—'

'Who cares what he thinks? It's your job, Honor! Your life!'

'I know. I just . . .'

'You *want* to spend more years studying and taking exams?'

Honor hesitated.

'Aren't you desperate just to get out there, roll up your sleeves and actually put the things you know into practice? Come on, Honor – if I were in your position I'd hardly be able to wait to make my first proper deal and get my hands on that first juicy pay packet!'

'And you'll probably be well on your way to that by the end of next week,' said Honor, smiling again as she changed the subject swiftly back to Evie, unwilling to confess that there was a part of her that shrank from the City-world that Evie seemed so sold on.

Yes, she'd sat through the interviews. She'd smiled and said, in her cool, calm way, exactly what they wanted to hear – that of course she was excited by the City, that she'd always been fascinated by ways of making money, that she was hungry and ambitious and clever and tough – but only because she knew it would get her the offer. It had absolutely nothing to do with what Honor was really like; or what she really wanted. And since she herself didn't even know what that was, it seemed wiser to get the job and worry about it later, rather than lose momentum on a vague soul-searching exercise that could take years.

Honor picked a favourite suit from the pile of clothes

on the bed: a sleek black jacket with well-cut trousers. 'Why don't you try this on?'

Evie took it from her – holding the hanger roughly, already scrunching the shoulder of the jacket under the dry-cleaner's cellophane. She tossed it on to her bed and began undressing.

'And what about some shoes to try on with it?' said Honor. 'They'll make a big difference. You do need a bit of a heel with those trousers – they're quite long. Even for me. And I—'

'Okay, okay.' Evie wriggled into the trousers and did up the zip. She pulled the jacket over her shoulders and, fastening the buttons, wandered to the long mirror – half tripping on the hems. The lining felt very soft against her skin. The tailored waist of the jacket felt neat and snug down the line of her back.

'You look great.'

Evie squeezed on the shoes and glanced at her reflection. 'I look like you.'

Honor smiled. 'Well, I got the Morgan Stanley offer in this one,' she said, tweaking a lapel so that it sat flat against Evie's neckline. 'Maybe it'll bring you luck . . .'

'Oh God I hope so.'

Honor hoped so too – hoped it hadn't been a mistake for Evie to lie about her skills. Evie was delighted by how clever she'd been, but Honor wasn't so sure. Those personnel people weren't fools. It was all very well for Honor to spin a line or two about her own ambitions and personality – there was no way of disproving that sort of thing. But typing abilities, and jobs in Moscow? They weren't such easy lies to sustain. Even if Evie did manage to wing her way into one of these jobs, the chances of her keeping it were – in Honor's opinion – slim to non-existent.

Waving Evie off an hour later – laden with bags of office clothes and full of gratitude – Honor couldn't help wondering if she'd actually done her cousin a disservice. Perhaps instead of gently encouraging her with offers of clothes, it would have been better to warn Evie of the risk she was taking. Perhaps she should have spoken out, and plainly, about the lengths the interviewers went to to ensure that a future employee had the right skills. But a horror of sounding patronising and a fear of alienating Evie with what, after all, were only suspicions – especially when she, Honor, had so many offers on the table – held her tongue.

Within a month, Evie started work as a personal assistant to the director of a removals company based in Croydon. Within another month she was sacked. And Honor – following her cousin's progress with a wretched heart – wished there was something she could do to help. Evie didn't seem too fussed. Her boss had been a wanker. Typing was, without a doubt, the most boring thing she'd done in years. And as for that office building, with its ugly seventies' windows and stained concrete walls . . . Christ, what a dive. What a total waste of time.

But the reality was that Evie needed work. And with waitressing no longer cutting it, and secretarial jobs out, it wasn't long before she was taking Honor's advice, swallowing her pride, and making the call to Suffolk to ask if her uncle had been serious about putting her in touch with people he knew in the property business.

Chapter Twelve

At Work

Flattered that she'd finally come round to his way of thinking, William Montfort was more than happy to help his niece find a job in property. Calls were made, relevant parties consulted, cajoled, persuaded, bribed . . . and finally – after a short, uncharacteristically honest interview – Evie had a temporary position with Marcus Graham at Chelsea Estates, a small agency in a niche market in the heart of the Royal Borough. She started the first week of October and had until Christmas to make a good impression. There was a potential permanent job going but she had to win it and, conscious that she wouldn't have many more chances to secure what her uncle referred to as a 'proper job', Evie knew that this time she had to make it work.

It didn't take her long to settle in. What she'd missed in terms of university and exam results, she'd gained from the rougher experience of having already worked for a living. Starting a new job wasn't in itself intimidating – and with the added awareness that this particular job was precious, that she'd need to make herself rather more accommodating and patient than came naturally to be certain of turning it into the substantial career she craved, Evie kept herself in check . . . and the effort soon paid off. Colleagues quickly realised she was efficient and dependable. The work they passed on to her was invariably dull and time-consuming – mainly administrative tasks like mail shots and franking, or holding the other end of the measuring tape while they prepared new sets of particulars – but it was good to know that whatever it was would be done promptly, and with enthusiasm. Evie didn't mind, not when she was learning more about the business all the time. With a team of only two partners, two 'negotiators' and one PA, Evie couldn't help but overhear how they operated. And because she was keen and interested, unafraid to show curiosity or ask questions or offer to take on a little extra respon- sibility here and there, because she always arrived first and left last and was, for once, disposed to make herself appealing, they had no problem accepting her.

All of them, that is, except Linda, the PA, who knew that Evie had been taken on as a favour for one of Marcus's more important contacts, and simply couldn't see the point of her. Before Evie's arrival, the office had been small and mostly male: just Marcus at the big desk at the back, with Nick and James at the two junior desks to his left. The only other woman was Helen, Marcus's business partner, who in Linda's eyes was simply too preoccupied, too hard-working, too middle-aged to pose any serious threat to Linda's allure when it came to daily attention from the others. When Helen was in the office at all – which was rare, as she worked so hard and was usually out somewhere chatting up future clients, or conducting viewings of the more important

206

properties, or waiting at home for the nanny to arrive – she sat way off to Marcus's right, out of sight of any random punters with passing curiosity about the properties in the windows, free of interruptions. Helen maintained her distance. And, in Linda's opinion, the office had worked perfectly well like that. It didn't need some hair-flicking ex-schoolgirl who spent far too much time outside the office, smoking.

It was Linda who'd insisted Evie take her cigarettes outside – 'It's just so selfish, Marcus. What with Helen being pregnant again.' Helen hadn't cared. She missed not being able to smoke herself, and raised her nose like a Bisto kid to Evie's trail of tobacco.

But Helen wasn't interested in office politics. These days she had more important things to worry about – like interest rates and market troughs and business drying up – than who sat where, who flirted with whom, or whether anybody smoked. That was Linda's territory. And so long as Linda made sure there was enough coffee and milk to get them through the day, so long as Linda bought Wednesday's *Evening Standard* and made sure the up-to-date property publications were set out in order and the old copies neatly filed away, Helen didn't interfere. If Linda preferred Kenco to Nescafé, that's what they'd have. And if Linda didn't like the smell of tobacco, then there would be no smoking.

But while Linda could insist on a smoke-free office, she could do nothing about what went on in the street – or, more particularly, in one of the shared company cars parked round the corner – and it infuriated her that both Nick and James had taken to joining Evie there. She tried complaining that this practice was unprofessional and meant that the office was often empty, but Helen wasn't interested – not when it was only pregnancy that was blocking her from grabbing a quick fag with the rest of them. 'It's why we employ *you*, Linda! So that you can hold the fort when everyone else is out.'

And although Marcus was a little more sympathetic, he hadn't actually done anything expressly to forbid it. So Linda sat inside and waited for the weather to get colder, for the lure of car-smoking to wane, for the others to come back in, and for Evie to find another job.

Evie, meanwhile, delighted in the hostility. She wasn't out to impress Linda – particularly now that the rest of the office had been won over – and thrived on the friction. This was mainly owing to boredom. Unlike James and Nick, Evie did not yet have any properties or applicants that she could think of as 'hers'; nothing to get her teeth into; nothing that would repay any extra diligence. So while she was keen, she still depended entirely on the others to give her tasks. Inevitably, there were lulls. And she couldn't resist toying with Linda's irritability at such times. The heavy sighing, the tale-telling, the darting eyes and self-righteous expressions Evie could elicit, simply by picking up her fags . . . it was just too tempting.

The weather was fine that Thursday afternoon, fine enough for Evie to spurn the stale car and stand outside in warm autumnal sun – dressed in a beautiful new coat she'd bought with her first pay packet, blocking the property cards in the window, smoking her cigarette . . . and it wasn't until she came back in that Linda – munching nonchalantly on an apple – bothered to tell her that Marcus had called. Half an hour ago. 'He wants you to join him at that meeting at Ovington Street.'

'He what?'

'Number thirty-four. Seems they're finally getting somewhere with those Italians. You need to pick up a spare set of keys from Winkworths on your way, he said, and bring some extra sets of particulars.'

'Christ.' Conscious that they were running out of particulars on Ovington Street – conscious that she might need to photocopy more, and that this would all take time – Evie pulled open a drawer, frantically searching . . .

'Oh, and someone called Honor rang. Something about dinner tonight?'

Honor put the telephone down and looked again at the report on her desk. It detailed the existing debt arrangements of a conglomerate that her client, MeyerBank UK, was considering backing. There were hundreds of companies in the conglomerate, all with different businesses and different financial histories and wildly complicated tax arrangements, and Honor needed to be on top of it all before a meeting with the lawyers later that afternoon.

James, her boss, was sparkly-eyed about this deal. It was the biggest he'd ever done and his decision to pick Honor over the five other newcomers in the department to help him with its day-to-day handling was a compliment of the highest order. She'd only been at Meyer's for three months and had already shown herself to be competent, hard-working, and friendly. Not to mention decorative. Exactly the sort of sidekick he'd like with him in meetings.

'Now you'll need to ask Nigel if you want any help with the tax position,' he'd said last week when informing her of his decision. 'It is elaborate, and it's

209

important we understand exactly what's going on.'

Honor nodded.

'And of course, come to me if there's anything about the proposed general structure you're not sure of. We're going to have to visit the existing plant in Poland on Monday, and then check out the sites they're looking at in Germany on Tuesday and Wednesday – that is okay with you, isn't it?'

'Yes, of course . . .'

'And David Hill – the UK finance director – will be back from Jersey on Thursday, so we'll need a meeting with him then. I don't think we want the lawyers with us at this stage, but you might want to fax Fat Parker the heads of agreement and set up a meeting for the Friday so that he can get something turned round for us over the weekend and – and hopefully, we can start negotiations the following week!'

'Great.'

James looked at her. 'You're not going to have much of a social life for the next few months, I'm afraid, Honor. Probably not until Christmas.'

'That's fine.' She smiled.

And James, smiling back, assumed that she was every bit as excited as he was – about the contacts they'd be making, the places they'd be visiting and, above all, the millions involved. She seemed oddly calm – the sums they were looking at would have made most people's eyes water – but he guessed that it was just her manner: professional, cool, serious. It was one of the reasons they'd been so interested in her interview. Not many applicants were able to convey so much enthusiasm and focus – she'd been perfectly prepared – with no hint of desperation. They'd liked her self-control.

210

But Honor – sending out the faxes and setting up the meetings he'd mentioned – felt nothing for this deal but reluctance. The money was meaningless to her. Not because she was blasé about it but because it simply didn't turn her on. The deal could have been worth a billion, or a mere thousand: her interest – or lack of it – would have been the same. And when she thought of the other graduates from her department, who would have done anything to be in her shoes that afternoon, Honor only felt guilty.

And as the week had gone by – all social commitments now cancelled so that she could read the paperwork, get to grips with the tax arrangements, then head off to Poland and Germany . . . standing around in a hard hat on building site after building site, trying to look interested while James discussed interest rates and end dates with a succession of company directors, all of whom had that sparkle . . . Honor felt like a teetotaller at a rugby dinner, and instead found herself looking with a strange sort of envy at the well-rested receptionists in the Polish corporate lobbies; or out of her cab window at a kindly faced school teacher herding a crowd of uniformed children across the road from Munich airport; or at a couple of laundry maids, laughing down the corridor in another bland hotel . . .

And now it was Thursday and she was back again in London, sitting at her desk. The trips to Eastern Europe had been a success. The deal was moving forward. In two hours' time, Honor and James would be getting into a cab and heading over to the UK headquarters of Kolzpak International to discuss final terms with the finance director . . . and still she couldn't get excited. She understood enough of the report spread open before her.

She'd spoken to Nigel in Tax. She was fully prepared. But if the deal fell through that afternoon it wouldn't have bothered her. She might even have felt relieved.

Not that it would fall through. The meeting was really just a formality, a chance for them all to get together and shake hands before more finalised terms were sent through to the lawyers and detailed negotiations got under way. It would probably be over in an hour – certainly wouldn't drag on into the night – and this sudden gap in her schedule, this last-minute prospect of a free evening (especially with the workload she'd be facing in the run-up to Christmas) was the only thing that lifted Honor's spirits.

She hoped Evie hadn't made other plans for dinner. While Honor had felt obliged to cancel her last week – she hadn't known what the Kolzpak deal would throw up, whether she and James would have to extend their trip, and it had seemed fairer to call dinner off altogether, rather than to keep Evie hanging on the off-chance – she now saw that it wasn't necessary, and waited eagerly for Evie to return her call.

But the hours passed with no response from Evie. Before leaving for her Kolzpak meeting, Honor tried again and – rather to her surprise – got through.

'Evie it's me. I—'

'Can't talk now, Honor. I'm sorry.'

'I was just—'

'I'll call you after six, okay?'

Honor looked at her watch, not sure if she'd be back from Kolzpak by then – and even if she was, she'd probably be in with James, discussing the outcome of the meeting. 'Okay,' she said. 'But—'

'Or tomorrow. Or whenever. I'm sorry Honor. I've got to go.'

The line went dead.

As predicted, the Kolzpak meeting was little more than a formality and meant that Honor and James were back at their own offices well before six.

'Won't be a moment,' said James as they passed the gents.

Honor nodded. Taking the opportunity to check her own desk for any messages and faxes that might have come in, she was about to head on when her telephone rang.

'Honor! You're there!'

'Hello Evie . . .'

'Sorry about earlier. I was up to my ears. Fucking Linda almost ruined my entire career this afternoon – not passing on my messages – and I've had Marcus on my case ever since. But he's gone home now – and so, thank God, has she. So I thought I'd get back to you before something else goes wrong!'

'That's all right.' Smiling, Honor put her briefcase on the chair – toying with its handle. She knew all about Linda Norris.

'So go on, then,' said Evie. 'What's all this about dinner? You changed your mind?'

'Only if you're free, Evie. I—'

Holding up a hand, Honor nodded at James as he passed her desk – 'Two seconds?' she mouthed – and tried, simultaneously, to concentrate on what Evie was saying.

'And I had planned to see Dom – but that's not a problem. I've got to finish some photocopying for Marcus, which might take a while – he wants it first thing tomorrow – but . . . but yes, I could easily be somewhere at eight thirty.'

'And what about Dom?'

'Sod Dom. I'll do something with him another night.'

'But—'

'He'll be fine. Really.'

'But didn't you have to cancel him the other day? I'm sure you said that he—'

'Trust me Honor, I'd much rather spend the evening with you.' Evie sighed. 'I'll tell you more about it when I see you, but basically it's not so great with Dom at the moment.'

'Oh, God. I'm so sorry . . .'

'Don't be. I'm not.'

'But—'

'I promise you, Honor. I'm fine. Just waiting for the right time to end it with him, to be honest. Although it's harder than you'd think to find a decent moment. And he's not the sort of guy to take a hint . . .'

It was at least ten minutes before Honor was at James's desk. He was already preparing for his next appointment – a business development meeting with some of the younger directors – and brushed aside her apologies as if such things were out of place in a busy modern office.

'Yes, yes. Now I've made a follow-up list of things – Sarah's just typing it up. You might want to look at it before you head off tonight, and we'll run through it all tomorrow. Okay?'

'Okay . . .' said Honor, watching him leave.

But Sarah, it seemed, had more important things to type than James's follow-up list. She never liked working for other women – particularly the ones in the graduate intake, the pretty ones that dressed well and knew nothing about banking – and found Honor's extreme politeness confusing. Sarah was used to

214

straight talking. 'I need it by seven o'clock, please' would have worked better than 'Oh – oh, Sarah? When you have a moment . . .? I'm so sorry to interrupt you, but I was just wondering . . . You couldn't possibly let me know how much longer you'll be, could you? I know you're busy, and – and of course you've got other people's work to do, but I would really appreciate it if you'd just say when you think you might have time to take a quick look at that list of James's . . .'

It didn't seem genuine. Almost as if Honor were mocking her. And the more deferential Honor became, the more irritating Sarah found her. She took Honor's courtesy for falseness. And the best part of an hour had disappeared before the list arrived in Honor's in-tray, leaving her no time to read it – far less act on it – not if she was going to be at the restaurant at eight-thirty. Instead, she slotted it into her briefcase and left the office. She'd deal with it later. Right now, the important thing was quality time with Evie.

She made it on time – just – hurrying in, out of breath, and scanning the room for a solitary Evie while the waitress checked their reservation . . . only to see that she was first. There had been no need to rush at all; she'd have had enough time not only to read James's list, but to complete half the items on it and still have been there before Evie who, in the end, didn't show up for another half-hour.

'Bloody Marcus,' Evie muttered. She took a menu from the waitress, remembering to look her in the eye but giving no margin when it came to her 'rights' as a diner and asking – slightly shamelessly, in Honor's opinion, given the style of restaurant they were in – for a jug of plain tap water.

'Called again just after we spoke, wanting me to look up some old file. Thought he could remember something about planning permission for a property that's just come on to the market again. The permission itself wasn't there, but when I read through some of the correspondence there were definite references to architect's drawings and visits from the planning authority, so I called him back to say all this and – and suddenly it was almost nine o'clock and I still hadn't done that photocopying. I'm sorry, Honor. I hope you weren't—'

'It doesn't matter.'

Evie looked up from the menu. 'You sure?'

'Of course I'm sure,' said Honor, smiling back. 'It's *you* I feel sorry for! Thought I had it bad with my boss, but it seems things are even worse your end. I'd no idea estate agents had such long hours.'

'Nor did I.' Shaking her head, Evie checked her watch. 'I mean, of course we have to work Saturdays, and people often can't view properties until they've left work so it can get pretty busy between six and eight . . . but nine o'clock? That is a bit extreme!'

Honor tilted her head sympathetically. But Evie's mind was still racing from the work she'd been doing: the perfect hot-fresh piles of photocopying sitting on her desk; the series of letters she'd been looking at so carefully, also copied out for Marcus to see, clipped briskly to the file and left on his chair. She'd managed to find the architect's number, scribbled it on to a Post-it note so she could call the guy first thing in the morning and, with any luck, chase up any further details before Marcus even arrived so that he'd have everything he'd need to ease a decent offer out of those Italians by the end of the week . . . She didn't notice her cousin's expression.

'Of course it's great about that correspondence,' she said, running her eye down the menu. 'Don't you think? Should mean that those permissions are out there somewhere – the architect is bound to have a copy – and once we've got that it'll be easy to convince the buyer he'll get the extension he keeps banging on about . . . He obviously wants the property. His wife certainly does! All they need is that top-floor mansard . . .'

And as Honor listened – as they gave their orders and waited for their wine and food to arrive – her expression changed from one of sympathy to one of confusion. For it seemed to her that Evie, far from being weary and overworked, was on a high. That old file she'd dug out – it was like she'd been on some sort of Indiana Jones mission and unearthed a priceless treasure map. And those Italian buyers she was working on – it was more as if Evie was participating in some strange seduction routine. Certainly they were more interesting to her right now than poor old Dominic Franklin – 'Oh, *please* stop worrying about him, Honor. He's fine. And,' smiling naughtily, 'and if he's not, well, that's just too bad . . .'

Honor did not smile back.

'I'd only snap at him and be a bitch. It's better for all of us that I'm here with you now.'

'But Evie, you—'

'Really. He's been a total prat these last few months, calling me at work, wanting to talk about some drummer he's found in Battersea when it's clear I've got a million things to do for Marcus, and thinking it's funny to pull me back into bed when I'm up and dressed and halfway out the door. He sits around all day in that skanky flat of his, watching daytime television and calling his mates and waiting for something to happen in the evening. Doesn't even have the get-up-and-go to organise anything himself. Just calls me – usually when Marcus is in the middle of giving me instructions – and says, "What are we doing tonight, babe?" like he's got no mind of his own. And then—'

'He sounds depressed.'

Evie rolled her eyes.

'I'm serious, Evie. He—'

'So am I.' Evie took a sip of wine. 'I'm not his fucking therapist, Honor. It's not my job to walk him through this, or find him a career, or – or provide nightly entertainment for him. It's hard enough keeping my own act together without him dragging at me, every step of the way. I'm fed up with his neediness. I don't respect his lifestyle – not any more. I've moved on. And it's about time he woke up to that and—'

'But imagine how you'd feel if he stood you up! Imagine what it must be like to have no job, and no—'

'I didn't stand him up, Honor. I left a perfectly clear message on his answer-phone. Right after we spoke.'

'And you think that's okay?'

'Yes, Honor. I do. It's how he treats me.'

'And you like it like that?'

Evie sat back, waiting for the waitress to shave parmesan over her risotto. 'A bit more there, please. Thank you. And could I have some pepper?'

'Of course.' Putting the cheese to one side, the waitress pulled a large wooden grinder out from under her arm. 'Is that enough, madam?'

Evie nodded – 'Thanks' – and, with the waitress gone, turned back to Honor. 'No of course I don't,' she said, plunging a fork into the glistening mound of rice.

'I hate it. And that's one of the reasons I'm planning to end it – this weekend, with any luck – and why I really don't care if he is a bit put-out by me not being with him tonight.'

Silently, Honor turned to her trout. Carefully lifting a segment of flesh from the fine bones of its spine, she put it into her mouth – aware, now, that Evie's mind was made up and that the subject of Dom Franklin wasn't really open for discussion any more. Everything Evie said made sense. Honor could see she was bored of him, that she'd probably never been in love with him, that it was better the whole thing came to an end. But the way Evie was talking – this new, pragmatic, each-man-for-himself approach to relationships; judging boyfriends, it seemed, more by how well they fitted around her job or how focused they were, how likely to succeed, than by anything to do with gentler ideas of love or happiness . . . it troubled her.

And Honor was still thinking about it when, an hour or so later, she paid the cab driver and let herself back into the house at Launceston Villas. It was very quiet inside. The lights that had been left on for her were mellow and familiar. The mahogany stair-rail – freshly polished that afternoon – drew a gleaming, curving, deep-brown line down the middle of the hallway. An arrangement of winter jasmine – brought up from the garden at Favenham – sat on a table to the right, dropping petals over a pile of letters that were addressed in Xandra's pale blue ink and stamped, ready to be posted.

After a day at MeyerBank, with its sleek foyer of dark-grey marble, its black leather sofas in the lobby, its exposed-steel elevators, and the sharp purity of the

219

open-plan offices upstairs with their glass partitions and pinpoint lighting, Honor found herself looking at this hallway with fresh eyes. For the first time in her life, she felt there was something special about the way it was lit, about the years of polish on that stair-rail, and flowers that hadn't arrived in cellophane. She found she could breathe again.

She realised now that there had always been an element of this gentler world in her life; in the converted stateliness of the boarding schools she'd attended, with their antique desks, their deep Victorian baths and old walled gardens – adapted, sure, to accommodate the need for swimming pools and changing rooms, but still with something of the past, some patina, in the worn bricks and dusty pathways. And it was there again in the eighteenth-century mouldings of the library ceilings, the dark dining halls and historic lecture rooms that made up the fabric of her university . . . but there was nothing of that in the City, certainly not in the parts where Honor was working. Yes, the district was steeped in history – with the Tower of London to the east, the little lanes and rickety pubs and courtyards of Inner Temple and Gray's Inn to the west, and street names everywhere that told of medieval markets and brought to mind the plagues and fires and riots of the past. But, to Honor's eye, that world was little more than a tourist attraction. It was forever being pushed aside by newer, shinier surfaces, by monochrome high-rise structures, striding over bomb sites and plague pits, lovers' lanes and sacred ground, fuelled on by a rush of eighties cash. These buildings put Honor more in mind of space stations in sci-fi movies than a living, breathing world.

Upstairs, she spotted a card she'd received from

Edward Beaumaris last week – sitting on her dressing table, waiting for a reply. It was an invitation to join a shooting party at Allenham in December, and was the first proper invitation he'd given her. For in spite of the fact that they saw each other pretty regularly in Suffolk – a wedding, a lunch, an Easter weekend, a surprise encounter in Woodbridge . . . and all of it leaving Honor very slightly breathless, with a sense that there was more to say, that she and Edward were only scratching the surface – such meetings were invariably by chance. He was always flatteringly pleased to see her, making a point of seeking her out at drinks parties, complimenting her on her dress, offering her lifts home. But he'd never taken things further . . . until now.

When the invitation first arrived, Honor had been a little disappointed. Shooting wasn't something she relished. She'd have preferred Edward to invite her to something a little less stuffy, less sexist, less stuck in the past. The sport didn't particularly interest her and the idea of spending a whole weekend with strangers older than herself, perhaps some of them with children, it had almost made Honor wonder if her attraction to Edward had been misplaced.

But now, tonight, looking at it again . . . Honor found something rather comforting about the idea of a shooting party. And instead of reaching into her briefcase for James's follow-up list, instead of turning her mind to the lawyers and tax specialists and the mountain of due diligence that would be required over the coming months, she opened a drawer on the left of the dressing table and took out one of the postcards her mother had had printed for her last year – cards with her name and address engraved along the top in black

classic lettering, with matching envelopes, tissue-lined
– and wrote out an equally formal reply to Edward
Beaumaris: in the third person, as she'd been taught at
prep school.

Chapter Thirteen

At Home

Rachel loved spending Christmas at Favenham. With Giles's parents both dead and his brother living in Canada, it had been – for a while, now – something of a ritual for the Langtons to pack up Morland Road on Christmas Eve and head out to Suffolk with a car full of presents.

This year she was looking forward to it more than ever: the prospect of a week or so away from the Slow Collapse – the peeling paint, the weakening window frames, the flow of bills through the letter box, the electrical appliances that would only work on one setting or needed a certain knack with the door, the limited hot water. She was tired of the constant economising, down to how she filled the kettle and how she worked the supermarket – going all the way to Battersea for the Asda discounts, and counting every penny, measuring and calculating so that nothing was ever wasted, but nothing was ever quite right either, and then heaving it all home, with carrier bags splitting and pinch-marks on her fingers . . .

She couldn't wait for the moment the car would be

loaded up and she'd be sitting there in the passenger seat, watching Giles double-lock the front door and come back down towards the car with that loose walk of his, that slow smile as he saw her watching him, unconsciously jangling the keys around his fingers as he'd get in beside her and slam the door.

'Where shall we go?' he'd say.

Rachel would humour him. 'Gatwick?'

'Christ, no.'

The car would pull off, down to the end of the street.

'Cornwall?'

'Too far.'

'Scotland?'

'Too wet.'

'Kent?'

'Too dull . . .'

Sitting at the junction now, with the indicator flashing.

'I know,' he'd say, with a perfectly straight face. 'What about Favenham? Haven't been there for ages!'

And Rachel would smile, tickling the back of his neck as they turned into the high street and headed out to the M25.

With the roads full of holiday traffic and queues and accidents and flashing lights, the Christmas journey was never easy. And this year it was raining, with little dribbles leaking through the gap where the passenger-seat window no longer closed properly, leaking past the masking tape Giles had put there last week and spitting on to Rachel's neck. If she shifted a little closer to the handbrake and made sure her scarf was properly arranged, it wasn't so bad. In any case, she didn't really mind. Her spirits were too high and she was too excited about where they'd be in a few hours' time to care much about the conditions of the present. She was waiting for the moment when they'd walk into the hall – the day fading outside and a fire crackling in the grate, and smelling of the apple-tree logs they'd burn at that time of year; and there, in the corner, a tree would be standing – thick with decorations – and William would be waiting for them, smiling broadly, helping them in with their bags as he filled her in on the latest local gossip and led them up to their room.

And when they arrived – an hour later than planned – that was exactly the scene that greeted her, down to the smell of the logs, the darkening sky, the sparkling tree, and William there, alone.

'I'm afraid Xa's off somewhere, wrapping presents,' he said, hurrying in out of the rain with their final bags while Giles, less troubled by the wet, took the car round to one of the garages at the back, locked it, and followed him in a few minutes later, drenched and flushed from the sudden heat of the open fire. 'Up in the nursery, I think,' William went on, 'hidden away . . . She can't have heard the car . . .'

'That's all right.' Smiling at him, Rachel unwound her scarf and inhaled the warmth of the hall.

She was high from the very predictability of it all. It wasn't just the burning logs. There were other smells – old familiar smells of home, less identifiable, caught in the fabric of the building, in the wooden panels on the walls, the dust on upper ledges that even Xandra couldn't reach to wipe, the saltiness from coastal winds, the dank leaf-strewn mud outside . . . all mingling to give Rachel a bolt-rush in her heart – a hit of security, an absolute sense of being home again, that almost made her cry.

William explained where the others had gone that

afternoon – 'Off to Woodbridge for the usual last-minute present-dash – God knows what we'll be getting from *them* tomorrow morning . . .' – and rolled his eyes with customary disdain at his wife's Christmas decorations – 'Yes, as you see, we've gone all blue and silver this year. Apparently it's the height of good taste . . .'

'It looks lovely,' Rachel said with studied loyalty as she surveyed the tree.

'You think so?'

'Beautiful. Could be in a magazine.'

'That's exactly my point. I mean—'

'I know what you mean, William.'

Her tone was reproving but her expression gave a different message, and William, noticing, pushed on mercilessly. 'Come on, Rach – don't you rather miss the stuff we used to have?' Laughing now: 'Those weird plastic toys from Norway – you remember, the polar bears? And those squashed Father Christmases that Nanny's mother knitted.'

Rachel's smile broke free.

'And tinsel . . .' William had the bereft air of a four-year-old denied his favourite pudding. 'Xa's banned tinsel, for some reason. We've got this slithery stuff instead, and *ribbons*. Bloody ribbons. Everywhere . . .'

Even this griping was part of the ritual, pulling Rachel back into the heart of the house, back to her childhood – an idealised childhood, but one that she and William clearly treasured to the exclusion of all else.

Giles watched with mixed emotions. Leaving their bags of presents by Xandra's immaculate tree – presents wrapped by Rachel in paper that had been carefully kept from past Christmases and birthdays, paper with telltale creases in the wrong places and makeshift labels from old Christmas cards, presents that would instantly spoil the glossy effect her sister-in-law was aiming for – he picked up the suitcases and took them to their room. No need to be told where they'd be sleeping, or which staircase to use.

Oh, it was easy to laugh at poor Xandra, he thought, putting their old suitcases on the smartly tasselled fold-out stands. Easy to laugh at the way she worked so hard for everything to be perfect, not realising it was possible to be too tasteful, too considered; that there was something to be said for playing it down. But in some other way, and especially in contrast to their own straightened circumstances, Giles didn't feel so inclined to laugh this year. Why shouldn't Xandra aim for perfection? What was this twisted attitude, this anti-vulgar 'less is more' approach, when he and Rachel knew only too well that less was, frankly, less? Reused wrapping paper, like torn jeans and skinny bodies, wasn't half so stylish when one didn't have the option or the money to be new or neat or fat; when there simply wasn't a choice.

Yet neither could Giles completely enjoy the luxuries on display: the professionally laundered bed linen, the towelling bathrobes hanging on the back of the door, the expensive soap in their en suite bathroom – freshly unwrapped, with the parfumier's name still perfectly carved into its surface. It pained him to think of the contrast between this life and theirs in Putney, and all the things Rachel had lost through marrying him.

Later, he watched as she put their shabby clothes on to the smart wooden hangers in the cupboard, pathetically pleased to be having, for once, the proper space for their things while laughingly observing

227

Xandra's obsessive attention to detail. The hangers were all in order, with the ones for trousers at one end of the cupboard, ones for coats at the other . . . all neatly and perfectly lined up – 'Oh *do* look, Giles! *Look* at these little lavender bags!' Giles knew that, for all her mocking, Rachel still longed for the order and control that came with having money. She wouldn't have done it the way Xandra did. She'd have toned down the details, or concentrated on subtler things – like making sure there were decent up-to-date books by the bed, instead of smothering it with artfully-arranged extra pillows – but a bit of comfort, a bit of generosity with the central heating, hot water when she needed it, and everything in its place, everything *working* . . . that was different. That did matter. Yet it was still easier for Rachel to laugh at the excesses than admit to envy, or downright need – especially in front of Giles, who could do nothing about it.

Watching her that afternoon, he realised she'd never once complained about what was happening in Putney. She didn't even tell him these days when something was broken, or needed money spent on it. She just got on with finding a way round the problem, or fixing it herself, or seeking out some friend of a friend who'd do it cheaply enough for her to pay for it out of their housekeeping account. She never troubled Giles or threw in the towel, and never, ever, spent anything on herself – no trips to the hairdresser or new clothes, and certainly nothing as extravagant as bath oil. It was only here, in the luxury of William and Xandra's spare room, that Giles saw what a sacrifice it must be for a woman like Rachel to live the way they did. And the more she laughed at Xandra's silly touches, the less convinced he was. The merriment

228

jarred. He thought of what he was giving her tomorrow – a grey hairdryer from Boots, one that she'd asked for specially because she knew it was cheap – and wished wildly that, for once, he'd ignored her and gone for something spoiling and indulgent, something from the lighter end of his palette, something that would persuade her that life with him in Putney wasn't all rotting windowsills and value-packaged bread.

Three hours later – bathed and unpacked, rested and changed – Giles and Rachel were downstairs in the library with the rest of the family, waiting for Honor to arrive so that they could go in for dinner.

Everybody else was down. There was Xandra – her present-wrapping complete, gliding around the room in a purple silk shirt and tailored black trousers, filling everyone's glasses with champagne and joining their conversations in a distracted sort of way while checking the clock above the fireplace. To the right of the fire – sat Ben and Nina, leaning over a laughing Rachel and guiding her through the complexities of an electronic game. And beyond them, Evie was chatting to Charles, Honor's older brother, who was back from San Francisco for Christmas and New Year and bored rigid by the thought of two weeks of family duty.

Looking at him – slouched on the sofa, listening to Evie with a lazy expression – it was hard to think that Charles was Honor's brother. With his sandy hair, his freckled skin and a small nose, his mother's genes had triumphed. But it wasn't just the colouring or his physiognomy that made him look so different from his sister. Charles had none of Honor's compliancy, and it showed in his lack of sheen. His hair was never

229

brushed, his clothes – in spite of armies of people to do it for him – rarely ironed. The long-haul look he'd had at Gatwick yesterday was no different from the way he'd looked when he'd boarded the plane eleven hours earlier. Such scruffiness might have been attractive in a bedroom sort of way, but Charles had taken it to a different level. There was nothing 'designer' about his stubble or the creases in his trousers.

Charles did what was necessary: ties for restaurants, white tie for balls, tweed for shooting, suits and haircuts for his job. But the underlying requirement in such dress codes – deference and respect – was invariably absent. His ties were mean and strangled-looking; the shooting breeches would be teamed with a torn AC/DC T-shirt; the threadbare tailcoat – even for those who found something to admire in the fact that it had belonged to his grandfather – was so ragged it would not have been accepted by a charity shop. And the smart chestnut cords he wore that evening – bought hurriedly by his mother last week so that Charles would have something respectable to wear over Christmas – already had what looked like toothpaste stains on the thigh.

His parents had tried. Xandra had given him an endless supply of new suits, new ties, new dinner jackets – but they always ended up at the bottom of his cupboard, as crumpled and musty as the old favourites. William had put his foot down at the vision of zigzag shreds and heavy metal helping itself to bacon and eggs while everybody else was in subtle shades of tweed . . . but the remonstrations had no lasting effect. Because although Charles would usually submit, eventually – 'Yeah, yeah . . . whatever . . .' – while he'd cut his hair, put on a tie, change his shirt,

230

there was never any corresponding change of attitude. He always needed to be told. And in the end his parents stopped trying. It was, they decided, a 'stage'. He'd grow out of it soon enough when girls appeared on the scene.

At twenty-five, however, Charles still showed no sign of doing that. His look was every bit as unkempt as it had been when he was at school and, contrary to his mother's predictions, had hardly hindered him when it came to girls. Charles still got exactly what he wanted – the pretty, sexy, feisty ones – without having to change his appearance at all. On the whole, this was down to his reluctance to date any of them for more than a couple of weeks. But for the ones that had lasted a little longer, the ones that had come down to Favenham – dressed flawlessly themselves, but still happy to giggle indulgently at the things he wore, laugh too quickly at his jokes, agree too easily with his opinions – it was clear that, for them at least, Charles's other assets outweighed his lack of grooming.

Sometimes Evie wondered if, in presenting himself the way he did, Charles was actively trying to provoke those girls he fancied. The more he fancied them, the less it seemed he trusted them – and the more extreme his untidiness became. It was as if he were testing them with some medieval system that invariably resulted in a guilty verdict. If the girl in question accepted him looking – and sometimes even smelling – so terrible, then she was clearly a gold-digger, prepared to go to any lengths. But if she rejected him – for the very same things – then she had to be superficial.

It was more likely, however, that women didn't come into the equation at all. Charles wasn't gay; he simply couldn't be bothered. He wasn't interested in taking

231

time to look nice or smell nice – for anyone. When he got what he wanted, just as he was, why should he change? It wasn't visually pleasing, but there was still something attractive, and something reminiscent of Evie, in the resistant attitude and smiling eyes. And even though Charles was a few years older than his cousin, the pair had always bonded in their mutual dislike of rules and conventions.

'And you really don't mind him telling you what to do?'

'Who – Marcus?'

Charles sat back, a chunk of ash toppling from the end of his cigarette on to the arm of a newly covered sofa. 'Yeah,' he said, oblivious. 'I didn't last three days when Dad set me up with some job like that just after I left school. All those prats in suits telling you what to do. Doesn't it drive you mad?'

'Not really.' Evie smiled. 'I quite like it.'

Charles raised an eyebrow.

'I'm serious,' She went on, 'it's the only way you get to learn anything, and right now I'm learning quite a lot.'

He looked at her with a strange expression, as if she were receding away from him, across a stretch of water.

'I don't have a choice, Charles. I've got to learn. I've got to make this job work. If I fuck up, I'm back to waitressing again . . .' she sighed, 'and I guess I've realised over the last year or so that I want to do something more with my life.'

'Like turn yourself into a yuppie?'

'If necessary.' Evie looked away. 'It's different for you, Charles. You've got—'

'I know what I've got. You don't have to remind me. But that's not the reason I'd never work for anyone

232

again. Christ, no. I'd rather go on the dole – if that's what it took – than hand my freedom over to a bunch of pinstriped wankers with closed minds and fenced-in lives.'

'You think that's what I've become?'

Charles grinned. 'Well you've certainly changed . . .'

And Evie, realising that Charles hadn't changed – that that was his problem, not hers – saw too that their days of shared rebellion were over. Charles might refuse to accept it had anything to do with his private income, but the truth was that in having to work – properly, nine-to-five, with an office and a boss – Evie was being forced to grow up. It might make her a yuppie, it might even turn her into one of Charles's 'pinstriped wankers, with closed minds and fenced-in lives'. But if it meant that she was financially independent; if it meant that she and her parents were secure – that they could keep Morland Road, that they'd never have to grovel to anyone for money, or live with the kind of anxiety that was tearing her mother apart – then for Evie, at any rate, it was a price worth paying.

And six months ago, she'd have said as much to him. She'd have fought her corner, not caring who was insulted in the process. She'd have accused her cousin of immaturity, of being protected by a trust-fund bubble he'd done nothing to deserve, on track for a wasted life. She'd have told him roundly that his own so-called job – starting up this company and that company but all of them self-funded and thin on contracts, which wasn't exactly surprising when the MD spent most of his time in bars and coffee shops, or out until four in the morning – it was hardly work. She'd have added that change was good, that it was –

233

in fact – exactly what Charles Montfort needed . . . And she'd have revelled in the fight.

Instead she let it go, merely saying she hoped she hadn't changed too much and helping herself to one of his duty-free cigarettes. It wasn't just the knowledge that Charles would never admit to being in the wrong – that rowing with him was pointless and tiring – that held her tongue. It wasn't even a reluctance to spoil the family party or make a scene. She was still quite capable of that. No, it was more down to a certain confidence Evie was discovering in her commitment to her job – commitment she didn't need to justify or defend, commitment that, in time, would speak for itself.

Charles softened. 'Aw – don't worry about it,' he said, pulling a warm box of matches from his trouser pocket and handing it to her. 'Can't see you changing deep down, you cheeky scrounger. Even if you wanted to . . .'

Evie, taking the matches, grinned back at him. She put the cigarette in her mouth, opened the matchbox, and was about to strike one when they heard the car on the drive.

'They're here!' cried Xandra, putting down the champagne bottle and turning to her husband. 'Darling . . .'

William went to open the door. And a minute later, Honor was there in the room with them all – smiling and glowing, unwinding a wonderful Scandinavian-style scarf, undoing the buttons on a dark-green velvet coat with fresh cool air flowing in behind her – followed by Edward Beaumaris, carrying her suitcase and a large bag of Christmas presents.

And as Honor greeted everyone it became apparent

that Edward had driven her down from London, that he'd gone out of his way – waiting until she was able to leave work, happy to go back with her to Launceston Villas so that she could change and pick up her things, happy to save her making the tiring journey all by herself.

'Poor thing,' he said, glancing over Evie's shoulder for a moment to look at her again. 'She's had a long day . . .'

Evie lit her cigarette. 'It's not that *same* nightmare deal, is it? The German one that wiped out November and meant she couldn't go to Nina's play?'

Edward hesitated.

'I thought that was over,' Evie went on. 'I thought '

'It is over.'

'Then—'

Edward smiled knowingly. 'I'm sure she'll tell you all about it herself when she's got a moment. It's quite exciting, really. But' – he glanced at his watch – 'I really should get going. My mother's all by herself and I promised I'd be there for supper. We're seeing you tomorrow, though – aren't we?'

'Are we?'

'Aren't you coming for lunch?'

'I've no idea . . .' Evie looked round at Charles for confirmation. He was still slouched on the sofa. 'Is that—'

'Yeah that's right,' said Charles, stifling a yawn. 'We'll see you tomorrow, Edward – and maybe in church as well. Not sure I'll be up for it, but there's been talk of going to the Allenham service this year. I think our vicar's ill or something, and Mum can't bear the stand-in.'

Edward smiled. 'Great. Well . . . bye, then . . .'

235

'Bye,' said Evie and Charles in unison. They watched his smooth departure: a light kiss on Xandra's cheek, a courteous shaking of William's hand, the brief nods at Giles and Rachel . . . and Honor – still glowing, still wearing her unbuttoned velvet coat, followed him back out into the hall, their voices and footsteps fading.

'So kind of you, Edward. Really. I—'

'Not at all.'

Evie sat back down next to Charles. 'I wonder what her news can be.'

Charles parted the curtains with his forefinger and looked out – at the car on the drive, its dark metal shining in the rain; at the diagonal dashes, caught in the headlights; and at his sister, alone under a black umbrella, waving Edward off into the night.

'Hmm.'

'You think it's to do with work?'

'God knows.'

'She – she seems pretty happy, though. Don't you think?'

Charles grinned. 'Then she must have seen sense and handed in her notice,' he said, letting the curtains fall back into place and reaching for his glass of champagne.

And he was absolutely right: Honor had resigned. Announcing it joyfully to everyone as she went in to dinner, she seemed to carry them all with her so that nobody – nobody but Evie – questioned the wisdom of what she'd done.

'Hooray!' Charles cried, grabbing her and kissing her. 'Well done!'

'Thank God for that,' Xandra murmured to Rachel as she led her to the sideboard, put serving spoons into the vegetable dishes, and told her to help herself. 'You should have seen the mess Honor's hair was in last month, and the state of her skin . . . Poor darling. I made her go to Franco last week, made her take the whole afternoon off so that they could give her a decent facial as well – get some moisture back, at least . . . And thank God I did. But that air conditioning or central heating, or whatever it is they have in those offices at this time of year, honestly, Rachel, it's *lethal* . . .'

'So what'll you do now?' said Ben.

Honor smiled. 'I've absolutely no idea,' she replied happily. 'Might go travelling, I suppose. Might even drop in on Charles . . .'

'Oh God . . .'

'And my friend Jessica from Oxford – you remember her don't you, Ben? Came to stay last summer? Well, she's off to San Francisco, in the new year – just been offered some amazing job out there – so there's really no excuse for me not to go out and see them both. And then . . . oh, I don't know . . . New York? Moscow? Anything! *Anywhere*, but building sites in Poland and Marriott hotels . . .'

'What's a Marriott hotel?' said Ben.

Honor looked at him affectionately. 'Ben-boy,' she said, 'I hope you'll never know.'

Even William seemed happy for his daughter. 'Well of course, ideally, I'd like her to have stuck at it for a year,' he told Giles, as they opened the wine. 'But she wasn't enjoying it. And the hours they were making her work . . . I mean, it's all right for a man. But how's a girl ever going to find a husband – a decent husband – when she's stuck behind a desk at ten o'clock every night?'

Evie watched them all congratulating Honor. She looked at her cousin – at the broad smile and gleaming

237

skin and the light in her eyes as she talked about all the things she might do with her life, now that she was 'free'. And the more Honor spoke of the things she'd hated at the bank – focussing her criticism on the tough modern attitudes of her colleagues; the absence of gentleness; the importance of always having to appear to know more than one did; the hard women-directors who'd come back to work a week after giving birth; the ugly ambitions and values that were openly on display, openly encouraged, openly rewarded – the more distant Evie felt from her. For these were things that Evie rather admired. She looked up to women like Helen – Marcus's partner – with her high-achieving mentality, her determination to keep her career *and* her family, her professionalism, her confidence, her smart ability to work the system . . . Since arriving at Chelsea Estates, Helen had become something of a role model for Evie. Yet the sight of Honor's happiness and relief at being spared a similar life, and the approval of everyone around her – even Giles and Rachel seemed in favour of a 'gentler' path – filled Evie with dismay.

And when, a few hours later – as they were getting ready for bed – Honor told Evie a little more about the day she'd had: the anxiety of handing in her notice, the rushing back and forth across London, and kind Edward, insisting she shouldn't drive in such conditions and taking her down himself . . . It struck Evie that her cousin's high spirits weren't solely to do with her resignation.

'He really didn't need to do it. I think his original plan was to leave London at midday – it certainly would have taken him half the time – but when I called to find out which route he was taking—'

'You called him about that?'

'Absolutely.' Honor rinsed her mouth and put her toothbrush back in the holder. 'He's brilliant about anything logistical. So organised. So calm. Whenever we go anywhere in London he always knows exactly how to get there – whether to take a cab or drive, and how much time to allow . . . Never arrives late. Which makes it all the kinder – don't you think? – when he knew it would mean hitting the roads at the worst possible time. And yet he still went out of his way to wait for me. Insisted on it. Just so I'd have a calm journey and wouldn't have to struggle with the rain and all that traffic . . .'

Evie got into her bed. It was warm and fresh – someone had been in and turned on her electric blanket – and she lay in perfect comfort, watching Honor pad around the room, unpacking her suitcase, putting skirts on hangers and perfectly folded jumpers into drawers.

'Do you fancy him?' she said suddenly.

Honor turned to face her.

Evie smiled from the pillows. 'Well he clearly fancies you. And I was just wondering if—'

'Oh Evie! Do you think so?'

Jesus. Evie rolled her eyes. 'Why else would he have waited for you today? You dumb nut! Of course he bloody does! He's not going to waste his time hanging about on Christmas Eve for someone he only quite likes.'

Honor closed the drawer. 'He does have incredibly good manners, Evie. Perhaps he was just . . .'

'Just what?'

'I don't know. Just being nice?'

Evie snorted.

239

'I – I'm only saying it's not certain,' Honor went on, frowning now, as she snapped her empty suitcase shut and lifted it into one of the top cupboards. 'Not to me, anyway – that he feels anything. I know he takes me out to dinner—'

'Dinner?' This was news to Evie.

'Sometimes. Once or twice. And he took me to an auction last week, which was wonderful, but he never makes a move, Evie. He – sure – he must enjoy my company but don't you think that, if he fancied me, he'd—'

'Perhaps he's worried you don't fancy him.'

Honor was silent.

'Which brings me back to my original question,' said Evie, amused. 'And I have to say, I think you probably do.'

Honor opened the window, turned off her electric blanket, and got into the other twin bed. An old wooden table sat between them, with a lamp on it, and an alarm clock, and a couple of magazines. It was impossible now to see her face.

'So you think I should say something to him, then?'

'If you fancy him you should.'

'But what if he doesn't—'

'He does, Honor! He does!'

Unable to resist it, Evie pushed back the covers and sat forward – peering round the side of the table so that she could see her cousin's reaction. Honor wasn't smiling. She lay flat on her back, her newly-cut hair dark and sharp across the pillow, staring at the ceiling, or perhaps somewhere far beyond, and radiating a certain wild serenity that said something far more serious about her happiness and excitement than an ordinary smile could have done.

Evie lay back down, rather wishing she hadn't looked at Honor just now and that she hadn't told her cousin so plainly and robustly what she'd noticed in Edward Beaumaris's behaviour that evening. For she could see now that this wasn't really about 'fancying' at all. There was nothing light or frothy – no passing distraction – in the way Honor felt about him. She was serious. And to encourage her onwards was no longer amusing – not unless Evie believed it was right.

It was hot and stuffy in Allenham Church that Christmas. Not only had the heating been fired up to a full seasonal blast, but the congregation had swollen to almost twice its usual size – on account of the unfortunate Favenham stand-in vicar – and had to squash into the pews. Dried out by the sudden change in temperature, the holly berries in the flower arrangements had shrivelled hard and dark and were dropping from their twigs.

Edward and Lavinia Beaumaris had been there for almost twenty minutes when the Montfort party hurried in with only seconds to spare. There was no room left in the nave, but the warden, recognising Sir William and feeling that a man in his position – with his family name in brass all over the walls and engraved into the floor of the church – should not be made to stand at the back, led the entire party up to the spare choir stalls by the altar. They processed up the central aisle as if they were special guests of honour and the rest of the congregation had been waiting solely for their appearance.

Neither William nor Xandra noticed this special treatment. They sat on their carved thrones, flicking

241

idly through their hymn books, and muttering to one another.

'Heavens, it's hot . . .'

'It's these bloody pipes' said William, stretching down to feel them. 'They're right under our seats.'

Taking off her gloves, Xandra undid the fastenings of her fur coat and fanned her face with the carol sheet. 'They never get it right, do they? One's either shivering with a ghastly red-raw nose, or one's sweating away in an ugly flush. It's an impossible thing to dress for . . .'

Honor got up from her knees – catching Evie's eye as she settled back into her stall. Evie grinned back. 'Thank God I didn't bring my fur,' she murmured. 'What a piece of luck . . .'

But Honor barely heard her. For with the organ shifting into a triumphant introduction of the first hymn, the rest of the congregation now standing, and the vicar and the choir coming towards them up the central aisle with their white flowing robes and a great brass cross raised high – carried slightly at an angle – Honor turned to look at the procession, and at the mass of flushed Christmas faces of Allenham and Favenham . . . and saw, amongst them, Edward – looking back at her.

Honor smiled – bright, straightforward, welcoming. And Edward returned her smile with one that was more complicated, as if he were thinking about something – something to do with Honor. She'd no idea what it was. But in that moment, with the organ blasting at her ears, some distilled essence of Edward's thoughts seemed to pass directly into her – across the shimmering heated air and the worn stone floor of the church.

242

'O come, all ye faithful!'

Remembering the things that Evie had said to her last night, Honor turned to the carol sheet. It wasn't the words she needed. It was the safe solidity of the print before her eyes, and the paper – tangible – in her hands.

Allenham House was easy walking distance from the church, but the combination of a drizzly day and Xandra's fur coat, and the fact that the Montfort party had already driven to the church from Favenham, meant they arrived by car.

Evie had been there several times before, mostly for drinks parties, when it had been dark, but she still knew what it looked like from the outside: the old brick walls, the five Dutch gables along the front, the mass of Jacobean-style chimneys and the steps leading up to the door. She'd often heard her uncle being rude about its Victorian origins – the false air of history it exhaled, the boarding-school gloom that hung about its windows – and, driving up that Christmas morning, catching a distant glimpse of it through the heavy mist of the park, she had to agree with him. There was something bulbous about it, something a little top-heavy. It stood square on the flat landscape: grey and grand and veiled in rain.

And the interior was no different. Lavinia had clearly tried with holly over the portraits, a large fire blazing, and a tall if somewhat sparse Christmas tree. But the faded velvet curtains, the musty antlers on the walls and a brownish light emanating from the chandeliers . . . it was all a little murky. The hall – with its double height and exposed floorboards – resonated with their voices. And looking up at a ceiling of black

243

beams and pale arches, caught in its draughty solemnity, Evie had the shrinking sensation of being back in church.

She looked at Edward – pouring Xandra a glass of champagne; chatting easily as he guided her between the sofas, towards the fire where his mother stood talking to William – and saw at once why, at nineteen, he'd shot off to Australia, and why he now spent so much time in London. Perhaps it was in contrast to the oppressive gloom of the house, perhaps it was because he was more relaxed on his own ground, perhaps he was just a born host . . . Whatever the reason, he certainly seemed more natural today, more talkative, more willing to laugh and engage.

'You got a drink, Evie?'

'No. But—'

'Have this.' Smiling, he passed her the glass of champagne he was carrying. 'Or would you prefer something else? I'm sure we could find you some gin, or vodka, perhaps?'

'No this is great, Edward. Just what I need . . .' Evie took a large gulp.

And Edward, amused, stood ready with the bottle – refilling her glass just as soon as it was down. 'Sermon too long?'

Evie grinned in answer, not trusting herself to talk with bubbles still tickling at her throat.

'He can go on a bit,' Edward agreed. 'With so many people in from Favenham, I suppose the old boy couldn't believe his luck! Never had so many punters captured there in front of him, all at one time.'

'Must have thought it was Christmas,' said Evie, taking another sip.

Edward's lips twitched. And even though he had no

smart reply, Evie was pleased by his reaction. It was a relief for her to see that he wasn't quite so smooth and grown-up and humourless as he appeared. Perhaps there was hope after all.

And as they all went in to lunch, she resolved to be better disposed towards him. Honor clearly thought the man was wonderful. So, Evie knew, did Giles – fully admiring the way Edward had come out of the strict repressive childhood inflicted by his parents, yet still able to have a civilised relationship with them; still willing to come home, take up the reins and play the dutiful son. Giles was genuinely amazed that Edward hadn't gone off the rails. He thought Lavinia and Robert had been staggeringly lucky that their son's only rebellion had been a few years in Australia.

Even Rachel seemed fond of him. She told them again what a sweet page Edward had been at their wedding, laughingly reminding him of the grey silk breeches and lacy shirt he'd been made to wear.

'Oh, God, Rachel. Did you leave me no dignity?'

'But you looked lovely! Didn't he, Giles?'

Giles rolled his eyes.

And Rachel, turning back to Edward, went on, 'I promise you, you did. Your hair was still quite long back then, and *curly* . . .'

'I was eight,' said Edward, glancing at Honor with a helpless expression. 'Can you imagine anything more excruciating?'

'But Edward you were beautiful! Next time you're at Favenham, I'll get William to dig out the photograph album.'

'Oh do,' said Honor naughtily, still looking at Edward as she sat down at the table. She was enjoying every second of his embarrassment. 'Oh please. I'd love to see it . . .'

And as Edward's look of helplessness switched to one of reprimand, she enjoyed it all the more. With every passing minute, she was growing more certain of his feelings towards her. Unlike before, when she'd been tight with anxiety – not knowing how he felt about her, not wanting to get it wrong – Honor was suddenly able to enjoy what was happening between them, loosen up and ride the wave as the things Evie had said last night were, bit by bit, confirmed.

'Well I'll certainly be taking some time off,' she said, smiling, when Edward asked what she was planning to do once she'd worked out her month's notice.

'Very sensible.'

'I'll need a bit of space to think through exactly what I do want to do with my life.'

'Of course you will.'

'And I'm quite keen to do a bit of travelling.'

Edward looked up from his mince pie. 'Travelling?'

Honor nodded. 'Still haven't been to see poor Charles in San Francisco, which is terrible when you think he's been out there nearly three years. And my friend Jessica from Oxford's just landed herself some high-powered job out there as well, so I've really got no excuse. I was thinking I might get one of those round-the-world tickets and – I don't know – just see where I end up . . .'

She looked at Edward, at his bending head, and the particular way he was concentrating on his food.

'Not that I deserve another gap year . . .'

Still, he said nothing.

'But – but if I'm going to do a trip like this at all, it

does seem quite a good time to go . . . don't you think? When I'm young and free and—'

'Sure.'

Honor leant forward, trying to see his face. 'Is everything all right?' she said.

Putting down his spoon, Edward glanced across the table and saw that everyone else had finished. They were waiting for cheese and biscuits, and toying with the crackers. Then – looking back at Honor – he said quietly, 'I'll tell you later.' And Honor, with that extraordinary overriding tact he so admired in her, simply smiled at him and let the subject go.

But it wasn't until four o'clock – with darker shades of charcoal and slate creeping into the washed-out grey sky of earlier – that Edward had an opportunity to explain himself.

In the meantime, there was lunch to finish and crackers to pull, presents to open and the Queen's Speech to listen to . . . all in a wider family context. It felt slightly awkward now for Honor to continue sitting beside Edward at the table – knowing that he had things to say to her; knowing that she simply had to wait. They both tried to start up new conversations on different subjects, but invariably the flow ran dry and it wasn't long before other conversations began drifting into earshot.

'It just seems like quite a smart thing to do, with prices so low at the moment.'

'And as a first-time buyer, you'd get a pretty competitive interest rate.'

'Exactly!' Evie beamed at her uncle.

'You'll want to watch *where* you buy, though, Evie. It may be worth looking at places north of Notting Hill, or perhaps up by the City – Hoxton, even, or

247

Clerkenwell? My guess is that you'd want to avoid places like Chelsea and Kensington until—'

'I don't think she'll have much of a choice William,' said Rachel, amused that her brother thought Evie could begin to afford a flat of her own in Kensington. She and Giles were rather amazed to hear that she was thinking of getting one at all. It seemed a little advanced. But while they didn't want to push her out of Morland Road, the idea of her bedroom being free for lodgers . . . it was certainly tempting from a financial perspective.

'. . . I mean, ordinarily I'd say go for the safe areas,' William went on – still looking at Evie. 'Especially if it's about making a financial investment. With places like Knightsbridge and Belgravia, you never lose out—'

'You never make much either.'

William shrugged. 'Depends on the market. We haven't done badly with Launceston Villas.'

'But you bought that in the seventies, Uncle William! It's hardly—'

'Still did bloody well.'

Evie smiled. 'So, you think Hoxton, then?'

'It's all right up there, Evie. Some pretty little streets, lots of galleries and restaurants – and right next to the City. We've got a huge apartment block development this end of Old Street, and sure, it's not the best time to be developing anywhere, but that's probably the one place on our books right now that'll be certain of showing a profit . . .'

Evie took a sip of wine. 'What kind of profit?'

'Oh – twenty or thirty? Something along those lines.'

'Gross?'

'Net. And that's if we sold it off tomorrow. With any luck the market will have picked up by the time it's complete and we'll get an even better margin. Forty, if we're lucky.'

Uneasily, Honor looked round at Edward. She'd always felt uncomfortable with people talking about money and guessed – correctly – that Edward would feel the same way. Interest rates and profit margins . . . at Christmas lunch?

Edward looked back, catching her eye and the two of them smiled. 'Sorry about this,' she murmured.

'That's all right.'

Honor shook her head. 'Honestly. You'd have thought they might have been able to give it a rest – today of all days.'

'I suppose it's hard when you love that sort of thing the way they do, when it's an obsession . . .'

Honor cracked open a walnut. 'It's exactly what I hated about MeyerBank. It's what I hate about yuppies.'

'And it's exactly why you did the right thing yesterday, handing in your notice.'

Again, the pair of them smiled.

'You were never cut out for the City, Honor.'

'Thank you.'

And Evie – aware that they'd been glancing at her, aware of the smiling and the murmuring, and all with a slight quality of hiddenness that instantly alerted her to something not being right . . . Evie tuned in to the tail-end of their exchange and felt a physical heaviness about her heart. It was the same heaviness she sometimes had in the bath – when the plug had been pulled but she still went on sitting there, with the line of buoyant bathwater falling and falling, and her body getting colder and heavier against the white enamel.

Like Charles, they thought she was a yuppie. They

were probably right. But the shared disdain – and the way they were bonding through it – was unmistakeable. Suspecting that it was Edward who'd talked Honor into handing in her notice; Edward, who'd lured her into a distaste for a way of life that was, in Evie's eyes, simply hard-working, straightforward, meritocratic – Evie felt a surge of renewed antipathy towards him. Sure, her career was all about money – sure, she was interested in market patterns and interest rates – but was that really so bad? And how would Edward Beaumaris's oh-so-fine principles change if he found himself cleaned out? Hmm? Would he be so rude about people wanting to better themselves if there'd never been a wad of cash around to prop him up? Cash that, no doubt, only existed because of the hard graft of some despicable 'yuppie' Beaumaris ancestor . . .

She watched silently from the car window as, after lunch, Honor elected not to come back to Favenham with the rest of them. She wouldn't be long – just wanted to see the stables conversion that Edward had been telling her about . . . he'd give her a lift back later.

'You're converting the stables?' said William, interested.

'Oh we're still at very much the planning stage,' Edward explained rather quickly. 'I just thought Honor might like to take a quick look at the old layout before—'

'Well! I think that's an excellent idea! Half wondering whether to do something similar myself. Although I suppose your buildings would stretch to at least three flats, wouldn't they? Whereas ours are only—'

'Four, actually – if you count the existing groom's

cottage, although we may still decide to keep it as one house. It all rather depends what my mother wants to do.'

'Of course. Of course. But a groom's cottage? How fascinating! You know, I'd love to have a look myself sometime if—'

'Darling,' said Xandra's voice from inside the car. 'Just quickly.'

'Absolutely not. We're all waiting for you. I've got a hundred and one things that need doing at home before it gets dark . . . and . . .' Xandra leant forward, reached right over the driving seat, pulled at her husband's trouser-leg and hissed something inaudible.

Hurriedly, William got into the car. Glancing out at his daughter – standing happily next to Edward on the drive, dressed in a waterproof coat of Lavinia's and a pair of borrowed gum boots – he fumbled for a moment with the ignition. 'Of course . . . Well, bye then, you two. Take your time.'

Smiling gently as the car moved off, Honor waved for a moment. Then she dropped her hand, turned her back on the departing vehicle and accompanied Edward in the opposite direction, back, around the side of the house, suddenly out of view. She was looking at him as they turned the corner, looking and smiling in a way that made Evie rather wonder if they were going to see the stables at all.

Honor never went to San Francisco that year, or New York or Moscow or any other long haul destination. By New Year, she was going out with Edward Beaumaris. And when in March they announced their engagement, nobody was remotely surprised.

Chapter Fourteen

Honor's Wedding

Neither William nor Lavinia approved of long engagements. And while Xandra would have liked a few more months to get everything absolutely perfect, she could see the advantages of a September wedding. People would be back from holiday, but not yet into the shooting season – not properly. It would, with any luck, be warm enough. And while the garden was never at its best at that time of year – just dahlias and daisies and a few straggling roses – she was confident that, with the right sort of advice it wouldn't matter. The fruit trees would be wonderful, and easy to cheat if they weren't. Fake apples and plums could be bunched on to branches and no one would know they weren't real. The whole place would radiate fertility. They could even work towards a harvest festival theme – particularly in the church – with sheaves of corn, and—

'I just want something simple, Mum.'

'Of course, darling. But corn would be beautiful, don't you think? We could wind it up the pillars. And have baskets of fruit overflowing—'

'And vegetables,' said Charles from behind a dodgy-looking tabloid.

He was back from San Francisco for good now. His apartment out there had been packed up and the furnishings were being shipped home. His three self-funding companies had been dissolved and he was living once more in London, waiting for the next academic year to start, when he'd be attending business school.

And there were no prizes for guessing what – or rather, who – was behind this sudden decision. For Jessica, Honor's flame-haired friend from Oxford who'd just been offered a job out there, had known better than to wait for Honor to come out in person to make the introductions. Instead, she'd simply asked for Charles's number and called him the night she'd arrived. And – being such a very high achiever – it was really only natural that Jessica would then waste no time finding her way into Charles's bed, his mind, his wallet . . . only to realise something had to be done if this man was going to be her husband. All that money and property . . . it had to be managed properly.

Charles was lazy and self-indulgent, but he wasn't stupid. He'd met girls like Jessica before. He knew she wanted him to propose to her and had no intention of obliging. But that didn't mean he had to forgo the distinctively masochistic pleasures that came with being pursued and bossed around by a decisive, leggy redhead. And when Jessica said she thought business school was essential – and was happy to do all the legwork for him, make the necessary applications – Charles dutifully went along with it. When she made it clear she rather despised people who dossed about in cafés all day, rarely shaved and never got up before

253

twelve . . . Charles obediently took to getting up when she did, using the new razor and gel for sensitive skin that she'd gone to the trouble of finding in some specialist drugstore on the other side of town. Whatever it took to keep her in his bed, really – bar, of course, the one thing she really wanted.

And when Jessica landed herself a better job that would take her back to London later in the year, Charles decided to come home too. San Francisco without her seemed somehow rather dull. And although Jessica was the one driving the move back to England it was Charles, in the end, who'd arrived home first. Jessica (who was being made to work out her three months' notice period) thought it best that he get moving. He could use his parents' place as a base for househunting, find them a nice place in Chelsea or Notting Hill or somewhere like that, so that everything would be perfect for when she came back in June.

Charles just loved the audacity of it. With Evie's help he'd already found a couple of possible apartments – though of course nothing would be finalised without Jessica's say-so. And in the meantime, the preparations for Honor's wedding were providing him with more than enough entertainment.

Unsure of his tone – but thinking that marrows and aubergines might look rather wonderful in a garland at the altar – Xandra turned to her son. 'Perhaps,' she said. 'So long as they—'

'Oh, go on.' He put down the paper and grinned at her. 'Why waste money on orchids and lilies when a few sacks of potatoes from Tesco would do just as well? I'm sure Edward would be thrilled . . .'

Xandra decided to ignore him. Men never understood this sort of thing – the importance of how a wedding looked, the need to come up with something memorable, beautiful and unique – something people would talk about for months afterwards. Her reputation as a hostess was riding on this wedding, and Xandra was determined that people should gasp as they entered the marquee.

And gasp they did.

Deciding it was easier to leave it all to Xandra – so clearly in her element – Honor and Edward took a back seat in the preparations for their wedding. It was, after all, being held at her parents' house. It was Montfort names at the top of the invitation. All done at Montfort expense. Why shouldn't it fall to Xandra and William to decide what wine to serve at dinner, and how many dahlias to plant along the borders?

So with carte blanche from her daughter on the decorations, and carte blanche from her husband on the expense (for William had learnt early on in their marriage that it was invariably easier to give his wife enough money to find something that would make everyone happy than embark on some pointless discussion about apples versus plums, or whether to have white or cream tablecloths) Xandra went to town.

And Abe – sitting over the remains of the wedding dinner and staring at the splendour of it all – found it hard not to think of how things might have been if it was he, not Edward, taking Honor to the dance floor now, whirling her into married life. It was hard for him not to feel as if Honor was 'his' – even now, four years after they'd split up; hard, to accept that in his absence life in England had moved on – and that Honor, in spite of all that warmth and friendliness towards him in the intervening years, had fallen in love with someone else. For there was no doubting she loved this husband of hers . . . Abe found he couldn't look at the dance floor.

'You okay?' said Evie, taking the seat next to him and offering out her cigarettes.

Abe took one. 'Yeah,' he said. 'Yeah, I'm all right – I guess.'

His voice had become slightly American and Evie – thinking of the effort he must have gone to, to be here today – hoped he wasn't regretting it. 'Must be quite a hike from LA.'

Abe shrugged.

'Fifteen, sixteen hours?'

'Something like that.'

'What time did your flight get in?'

Abe lit his cigarette from a candle. 'About midnight.'

'Oh God.'

'Three weeks ago.'

'Oh God!' Evie laughed. 'So it's not just Honor's wedding you're back for, then?'

Abe hesitated. 'No. No, I . . .' He seemed to be struggling with something. 'No,' he said again, shifting in his chair. 'The thing is, Evie, I'm kind of back for good.'

She looked at him.

'It wasn't so great in LA, to be honest. It wasn't bad – don't get me wrong. I could get work, but it was never . . . up to much. I was made a lot of promises that never came good, and I . . .' he smiled again – a front-smile, the kind of smile that said more about the way he wanted to be seen than what he really felt. 'Sounds strange maybe, but I missed it here in England. Missed living in London. Missed my friends—'

'Well we certainly missed you,' said Evie, picking off

256

some ears of corn that were dangling from Xandra's table arrangement.

Abe swallowed. He looked out at the dance floor – knee jiggling wildly, giving Evie the impression that it had cost him a lot just now: to say what he'd said to her; to admit it hadn't worked out. Especially here, at Honor's wedding.

'Abe . . .'

'Hmm?'

'You don't have to stay, you know, if it's all too much.'

'I'm fine, Evie.'

'Yes I'm sure you are. But even so . . .' She placed a hand on his shoulder. 'It can't be easy for you here, can it? I mean, what with—'

Turning his back to the dance floor, Abe shrugged Evie's hand from his shoulders. 'I'm fine,' he said again – struggling, now, to mask the strain with the same front-smile from before. 'I think it's great that your cousin's getting married. Great to see her happy. It's not as if she and I were ever *that*—' But the effort must have been too much for him. Unbuttoning his morning coat, Abe felt in his inner pocket. Then, seemingly satisfied, he removed his hand – empty – and looked at Evie with clearer eyes. 'You wouldn't mind if I left for a moment, would you?'

'Not at all. I was only—'

'Won't be long.' He stood up, smiling. 'Don't go anywhere now . . .'

Unable to smile back at him, Evie nodded – but didn't bother to hang about. She knew Abe would be longer than five minutes. Even if he did remember to return to her, the whitened one-way chatter would hardly be worth the wait. She saw him later, dancing oddly with some friend of Nina's. And then by the bar, gabbling to Charles – mumbling, chuckling, exclaiming, whispering, with eyes as bright as the moon.

And he was nowhere to be seen when – at one o'clock – the car came for Honor and Edward and sped them away beneath a sky cracking with fireworks.

From a distance, Evie watched them go, watched their coupled hands as they said their goodbyes and got into the car. And as it moved off, she walked out across the lawn to stand by an orange flare that marked a turn in the drive, glimpsing – through a slanting rectangle of moonlit glass – the briefest passing detail of Honor's tailored shoulder, a sketched neckline turning in to her husband, and a pale dash of cuff and wrist as Edward reached forward to say something to the driver.

So it was done. And when Evie thought of the alternatives: of Abe, feverishly tapping out another line of cocaine; or of MeyerBank – that thrilling mesh of steel and glass, that sharp modern world where someone of Honor's nature was as wasted and misplaced as a handwritten letter, or a smile on the Underground . . . when she thought of those things, it seemed to Evie that Honor had made the right decision after all.

Sure, it was a retreat. For in spite of today being about the future – the children that Honor and Edward would have, the places they'd live in over the years, the highs and lows of married life, for richer, for poorer; in sickness and in health; the awesome weight of a promise – Honor was still moving, really quite decidedly, into the past. She hadn't included 'obey' in her vows – but in every other way it seemed that that was what she was choosing. She'd let her father give her away. She'd stood – silent, young and beautiful –

258

while the men closest to her made short, elegant speeches about the bride's intelligence and achievements, qualities that suddenly seemed more like charming accomplishments than anything vital or useful, or relevant to life as the wife of Edward Beaumaris – except, perhaps, the raw genetic potential she'd contribute to their children. And while Evie knew that it was all in the spirit of pretty tradition, that nothing sinister was intended, that this was in many ways what every wedding was about . . . part of her could not discard the initial sense she'd had, back at Christmas – when Honor had joyfully announced her resignation and gently fallen in with Edward – that this was some kind of delicious surrender; that one day Honor might wake up and wish she'd fought a little harder.

But why should Honor fight? And what, exactly, would she be fighting for? The privilege of working in a world that trampled on her good manners and asked her to throw aside the gentle principles of her nature . . . all for a certain sort of pay packet and status she simply didn't care for? Why struggle with difficult men like Abe Wyatt when safe, organised, attentive Edward was there – to collect her, and care for her, and support her, and understand her . . . never embarrass her, never forget about her . . . laying down a cloak of old-fashioned courtesies so that she'd never again have to step into a puddle? Why should Honor choose the hard way, merely to satisfy the standards of a modern world? Why not just surrender, and be happy?

Without a doubt it had been a success. And Xandra glided through the guests who'd returned for lunch the following day – encouraging them to help themselves from the selection of pasta salads and strange-looking bread displayed at the buffet table along with carefully-sourced pâté of foie gras and game and every conceivable variety of ham . . . pointing out the freshly barbecued tiger prawns and marinated chicken legs further down the line, and the serious-looking chef at the far end whose sole purpose was to make individual omelettes and scrambled eggs for anyone still in breakfast mode . . .

'Oh do go and ask him for something, Rachel. He can't stand there redundant with his puffy white hat and pristine frying pan all afternoon . . .'

Xandra could not resist a moment of pure self-congratulation.

Even the sight of that awful red-haired leech Charles had picked up in San Francisco – that friend of Honor's so plainly on the make it made Xandra want to throttle her – talking now to the farm manager's wife with all the condescension of a chatelaine-in-waiting, could not spoil the moment.

All around, she could hear greedy exclamations and see plates piled high. She could catch snippets of conversation as she passed . . .

'Just adored that veil. So *intricate* . . .'

'And the cake? Oh my God! I must have had at least three slices, and I know for a fact that Tim Elliot had six. He was carrying them about – all six of them – like a dog with a . . .'

'Can't think how they managed to persuade some-one like Marianne Helzinger to come all the way over from the States, just to sing for—'

'Perhaps she was here for the Edinburgh Festival.'

'Perhaps. Although I wouldn't put it past Xa-Xa to . . . oh, hello darling! We were just talking about you!

Amazing day, yesterday . . . absolutely amazing . . .'

Xandra smiled graciously. 'I don't know . . . But do go and grab some lunch,' she said, waving a hand in the direction of the chef. 'And sit anywhere. There's no plan . . .'

Rachel watched from the end of the buffet queue – balancing out the horror she felt at what the whole thing must have cost, with genuine happiness for William and Xandra. For all his show of indifference, William was clearly proud of how yesterday had gone. The way his house had looked, his garden, his daughter – even the sight of his wife was a source of pleasure to him these days. Okay, she'd spent a fortune on her wedding clothes, but it had absolutely paid off. She'd looked fabulous – at least ten years younger, slim without being scrawny, brown without being leathery. Her hair was glossier than most of Nina's friends'. Whatever they did in beauty salons these days, it certainly worked. For along with the figure of someone half her age, Xandra also seemed somehow to have held on to her vibrancy and sex appeal. And today, in some ways, she looked even more attractive – glowing in the yellow tented light. Less formal, in her linen dress. More relaxed, now she knew how well yesterday had gone – laughing with one of his shooting cronies, who seemed to be standing rather too close to her for William's liking.

Picking up a bottle of white wine, he approached the little group and put an arm around his wife's shoulders, making some remark to the others that Rachel couldn't hear – but the gesture was unmistake-able. And seeing Xandra looking back at him with much the same expression as Honor had had yesterday when looking at Edward, Rachel couldn't help but be

261

pleased for them . . . until she remembered Diana Miller, and the promise she'd made last week to drop in on their way back to London.

Ever since Diana had agreed not to go public about William after all; ever since he'd decided to play to her tune – giving her the houseboat in Woodbridge, letting her more comprehensively into his life, even allowing her on occasion to play at being mistress of Favenham when Xandra stayed in London – the affair had rambled on. Diana still lived and worked in Edinburgh but had, increasingly, found reasons to stay in Suffolk. To begin with, she had only been there at weekends. But when she saw how William tended to stay down for the weeks as well, when she realised that Xandra – on the rare times she came – would also be there at weekends, Diana made little adjustments to her working life so that she was able to stay on until Mondays, or even Tuesdays . . . Then last year, at great expense, she'd bought a laptop computer and had the boat wired up so that she could work directly from Suffolk all week – needing only to go to Edinburgh for meetings and site visits.

But for all the adjustments Diana had made, William – it seemed – carried on just the same as ever. And when Xandra or the children did come down – which in the run-up to the wedding had been frustratingly often – the rules were rigid: there would be no visits, no calls, no contact whatsoever. And Diana was starting to mind. Of course she understood the arrangement. She could see that, temporarily, it was necessary for her to lie low. But it was still hard – when the whole county was talking about Honor's wedding, when everybody else would be going to it, and all Diana could do was sit on her houseboat with her computer and wait for William to call. And there was really only one person she could talk to about all this. Only one person would understand how painful it was for her to be kept, once more, on the outside.

'It won't be for ever,' Rachel had told her on the telephone, while pressing at the kitchen wall and seeing yet more flakes of paint coming off on her fingers. 'In two weeks' time the whole thing will be finished. Honor will be off on honeymoon. The marquee will have been taken down. Xandra will have hurried off to some health spa or other to recover . . . and everything will be back to normal again. You just have to be patient.'

'Patient? I've been *patient* for six – seven – years . . .'

Rachel frowned. 'This is the life you've chosen, Diana. You can't—'

'Except I haven't! I haven't *chosen* this life! I – Christ, Rachel. You think I *want* to be a mistress?'

Rachel was silent.

'You – what? – you think I *like* skulking around and telling lies and never having him with me for Christmas or to go on holiday with in the summer? You think I'm *happy* with this set-up?'

Feeling slightly alarmed, Rachel tried pressing the paint-flakes back on to the wall. 'I'm sorry. I – I thought this was what you wanted,' she said, trying to stay calm. Why did Diana always make her feel so unpleasant and insensitive? 'I thought this was what the whole . . . . upset – back when you were so hurt because William wouldn't let you buy that houseboat . . . I thought that this was what you wanted from him.'

'It was. It is.' Diana swallowed. Rachel could hear how close she was to tears. 'In a way. But it's hardly . . .'

'No of course not. I do see—'

263

'I just want to be like everyone else, Rachel! I – I just want to be a wife. A mother . . . I just want a normal life! Is it so much to ask, to be like you, or Lucy Harper, or Clare Armstrong, or – or anyone else?'

'You sure you want that?' Hating herself – but at a loss for anything else to say that would make Diana feel better – Rachel grabbed hold of an argument she didn't entirely believe. 'I mean, you might think you want a life like mine, Diana, but I'm sure there'd be things about it you'd hate. You – you wouldn't have been able to keep your wonderful job, for a start—'

'Oh poor me.'

'And how would you feel if you suddenly found out that – that this husband you think you want so much was having an affair with someone else?'

Diana was silent as the point sank in, and then said – roundly – 'A fuck of a lot better than I'm feeling now, Rachel. Believe me. You've no idea what it's like to be treated like this – like some sort of pariah . . . uninvited . . . like a bad witch in a fairy story . . .'

'No. Sure. But—'

'At least women like you – *proper, respectable, married* women – can talk about your problems. But me . . .? I can't speak to anyone! Don't you see? And I – I'm just so lonely, Rachel . . . so terribly, terribly . . .' She was sobbing now.

'You can talk to me.'

'I know . . . I know . . .'

Rachel sighed. 'Of course I can't understand exactly what it's like, but I do sympathise. Really I do.'

'I know. And I'm grateful, Rachel. I'm sorry to . . . burden you with this . . . your brother, and every-thing . . .'

'That's all right.' Rachel softened, her face full of

human concern as if it were Diana there in front of her instead of an expanding hole in the plaster. 'But listen, Di. Would it make any difference to how you feel about any of this if . . . I don't know . . . if I came to see you when we're down? I know it's not the same as you coming to the wedding, but it would be no problem for us to drop in on our way back to London and – and make sure you're okay. I'd love to see your little boat, and I'm sure Giles would be thrilled for an excuse to get away early. We could come for tea maybe, and fill you in on the gossip . . .'

Which was how, that Sunday, Rachel and Giles found themselves leaving Favenham promptly at four o'clock – opening their car windows for the air was still quite hot, blinking in the afternoon sunlight, pulling down their sun visors – and turning left at the end of the drive, taking the little road with the dry grass verge that led towards the coast.

Giles said he'd take a walk along the bank. And Rachel, only too aware of his feelings on the subject of Diana Miller, was happy to let him. He'd only have sat there in a cloud of disapproving silence – or, worse, chattered on about how lovely the wedding had been with a perky air of 'serves-you-right'. Whichever it was, his presence would have put a block on any real conversation. No. It was much better for everyone involved that he stroll off in the direction of ice-cream vans and newsagents and let the two women get on with it.

Diana was waiting for her, sitting out on the deck of her houseboat, soaking up the last of the sun. From a distance, it all looked rather idyllic. The boat was really more like a barge, with a broad, black hull and pots of geraniums along the sides and a charming gypsy air. But as Rachel approached, the charm began to disappear. It wasn't so much the smell of mud, or the muddle of green-tinged rope, or the garish jazz blaring from a tape recorder on a neighbouring vessel, as the oppressive stagnancy in the air, a stagnancy that hung about anything designed for movement – caravans, boats, water, limbs – and left to stand too long.

And as soon as Diana got up from her deckchair – dressed in a pair of jeans that showed every ready-meal she must have eaten in the last year, a tide-mark of dye halfway down her once-perfect hair, and something . . . *reduced*, was the way Rachel put it to Giles later . . . about the way she was standing – it was clear that Diana too had caught the malaise.

Because of the jazz, they went down inside to talk – and that was even worse. Rachel had thought that the damp at Morland Road was bad, but this was another league. The whole interior was filled with the smell of rot – a smell so strong that it was hard to breathe properly. Mould had already crept into the smart Jane Churchill curtains that had accompanied Diana when she'd moved in. Indeed there was something clammy about every surface Rachel touched – teacups, plates, worktops, books . . . all left a film of moisture on her hands. And when she thought of how hot and dry it had been at the weekend – all through the summer, in fact – it seemed to Rachel that something must be terribly wrong for Diana's boat to feel so saturated and run-down, and for Diana – apparently – not to have noticed.

'Giles not with you?' Diana said, managing to light her fourth match; touching it to the gas on the stove and putting a kettle over it.

'No. No, I . . .' Rachel smiled. 'To be honest, I thought we'd have a better time by ourselves. Thought we'd be able to talk more freely . . .'

Diana nodded.

'But he does send his love.'

Again, Diana nodded. Joining Rachel at the table, she helped herself to a biscuit from the half-eaten packet she'd put out – and then, remembering her manners, offered the packet to Rachel. 'So go on then,' she said, munching cheerfully. 'How was it?'

Rachel didn't trust the biscuits to be dry. She could feel something cool creeping from the cushion she was sitting on, up into the material of her skirt, and wondered how Diana could stand it. 'Lovely, really. Honor looked beautiful—'

'Of course.'

'And they were very lucky with the weather.'

Diana took another biscuit. 'And William?'

'Oh – oh, he seemed fine.' Rachel kept her tone very even. 'To be honest, we didn't speak much, what with all the other guests . . .'

'And Xandra getting him to do things, no doubt.'

Rachel hesitated.

'Poor darling.' Diana got up again as the kettle began to whistle, and began making their cups of tea. 'She's been really terrible recently. Even worse than usual. He had to write out all the table places – can you believe it? Four hundred people, or something . . . Meant he couldn't even do our usual Friday lunch. And then she made him go all the way up to London – did you hear about this? – to collect service sheets that she'd insisted, apparently, on getting revised because they'd spelt the organist's name wrong. And she had him spending most of last week tying apples into hedges, and sorting out the car park, and the seating in the church, and then struggling with his speech, and – and God knows what else, while she just waltzed off to the manicurist . . .'

Smiling hard – but unable to look Diana quite in the eye – Rachel took her cup of tea.

William loathed speeches at weddings, and months ago had delegated his responsibilities in that area to Charles. As for the rest, it was equally implausible. So far as Rachel knew, her brother had spent the last two weeks standing idly by, watching the tent go up, and the florists at work, and the band rehearsing; marvelling at the bizarre sight of perfectly ripe fruit being tied back on to the trees . . . and generally getting in everybody's way. Xandra had been desperate to get rid of him. In the end, she'd had to ban him from the house, suggesting with some sarcasm that he go out and follow the progress of his wretched harvest, and, particularly, to admire the beauty and efficiency of a giant combine harvester the farm had bought at great expense that year, a machine that Xandra had come to resent ever since she'd discovered it cost almost as much as one of those delicious luxury yachts she'd seen in Italy last summer.

Laughingly, William had done as she'd told him – telling her, almost as an afterthought, that it was only because of the harvester that he'd now be able to afford the yacht. But of course, if she really didn't like it then—

'What?'

Turning, he'd grinned at her from the open doorway – up to where she was standing, at the top of a ladder, creating an elaborate 'harvest garland' above the fireplace in the hall. 'Well, I had thought to wait until

268

the wedding was over before telling you about it, my little cornflower. But since you brought it up, I suppose I—'

'You're buying that yacht?'

'Well not that *exact* one, but—'

'With the dark blue bottom—'

'Hull, darling. Hull.'

'And the double decks? And that quiet engine? And – and the five bedrooms? Just like the Fieldens' . . .'

'Seven actually, if you count the crew—'

'Oh my God!' Xandra nearly fell in her attempt to descend the ladder. 'Oh my *God* . . .'

Rachel had heard all about it from Nina, who'd been called in to finish Xandra's harvest garland while her parents disappeared upstairs . . . ostensibly to look at brochures. But even Nina – wrinkling her nose as she gave her account – could tell that brochures were hardly the first thing on her father's mind.

And when Rachel thought of how beautiful Xandra was looking at the moment, of how happy and focused she'd been in the run-up to the wedding, clearly doing what she did best . . . it was suddenly all too clear why William wasn't so keen to drive out to Woodbridge and lie in clammy guilt with his run-down mistress on her run-down barge.

'But of course you were absolutely right,' Diana was saying as she reached for the last dank biscuit and put it in her mouth, 'about this state of affairs not lasting for ever. And in way it's rather wonderful – don't you think? – to be in a place where you love someone enough to put up with the difficult times because . . . because of the way you'll feel when everything's right again . . . Sometimes I think it's only when you make the sacrifices that you know how much you love them.'

269

'I – I suppose so. I hadn't—'

'And one day, when the children are all grown up and married, and there's no need for him to keep the whole façade in place . . . And it won't be so very long! Really. I was thinking – Ben's nearly seventeen, isn't he? Exactly. I'd say in five years – ten, tops – and it'll pass terribly quickly . . . And then we won't have to skulk around any more! We . . . we'll really be together – properly, openly – and all this waiting will only make it more wonderful, more precious, when *finally*, we can come out about it and – and tell everyone the truth.'

Chapter Fifteen

Shelley's Present

The earth was pale and the air warm at Allenham the day Honor and Edward returned from honeymoon. With nearly a month of no rain, it felt more like August than late September, with the green lawns faded to sepia and the borders tinder-dry.

But Lavinia was still glad there was sunlight for Edward and Honor, here, today, at the start of their married life. She was on the steps to greet them, both sticks in one hand – leaning lightly at a slant – while she shaded her eyes with the other and watched their car pull up.

'Oh God,' said Edward, turning off the engine. 'Sorry about this.'

Honor smiled – a tanned African smile. Then she wound her hair back freshly into its tortoiseshell comb and got out of the car. 'Lavinia!'

Edward followed her up the steps, still wearing his sunglasses, a suitcase in each hand. The three of them stood at the top of the steps, laughing and kissing and asking questions. How was Kenya? How were the tents? What animals had they seen? And what about

Lavinia? What had she been up to? Any news on the home front?

And it soon became clear that while Honor and Edward had spent the past fortnight looking for big game and lazing about in the sun, recovering from the excitement of their wedding, Lavinia had spent most of that time preparing for their return.

'I won't stay,' she said, switching her sticks to both hands as she turned to go back into the house. 'Just making sure it was all in order for you both. I'm afraid there are an awful lot of presents in the billiard room.' Gesturing to the left: 'It seemed as good a place as any . . .'

'Absolutely,' said Edward.

'And I wasn't sure what you'd have in mind for dinner tonight, darling. I asked Mrs Wilkins to put a few things in the fridge, and there's bread and coffee and so on, but if you'd like to come over for dinner with me . . .?'

'I think that'd be great.'

Putting down the suitcases, Edward took off his sunglasses in the cool of the old hall and looked at his wife. And Honor – keen to co-operate – smiled quickly at Lavinia and said she'd love to come to dinner. How kind of her to think of them.

'Not at all.'

When they'd told her they were getting married, Lavinia had been adamant about moving out of Allenham. Not only did the house officially belong to Edward, it was much too big for her to occupy alone. She didn't even *want* to live there any more. No. She honestly preferred the idea of Glebe Farm, with its low ceilings and charming garden. It was just the right sort of place for a woman of her age.

'But you're only—'

'Seventy-three is old, my darling,' Lavinia had replied, stubbing out her cigarette and searching for another. 'Whichever way you look at it. And I'm not even a fit seventy-three . . .'

This was true. With her fragile bones and smoky voice, Lavinia Beaumaris – for all her glamorous clothes – seemed, if anything, older than her years. Add to that a whippet-thin physique, a bird-like diet and a lifelong loathing of exercise, and it was clear she had no interest in regaining her physical strength. She was happy to be a little frail, a little dependent. It made her into someone people naturally wanted to assist. Porters, Mrs Wilkins, strangers in the street . . . nobody could bear to see delicate Lavinia do so much as carry her handbag.

But what Lavinia lacked in bodily strength was more than compensated for by the force of her personality. And when she announced that she was moving out of the big house, declaring that it was now Edward and Honor's time, that she'd thought it all through and knew exactly where she was going and how it was all going to happen . . . it was quite impossible to refuse. Especially when Edward seemed so excited by the idea, presenting it to Honor as the most wonderful sacrifice his mother was making, not clinging on into her dotage. They should be eternally grateful.

So Honor kept quiet. Silly of her to be wishing that they might have had a few irresponsible years in London, just the two of them, before taking on a project like Allenham. Silly and ungrateful. It wasn't as if she didn't know Allenham was the ultimate destination. So it was a few years earlier than expected. So she wasn't going to get *exactly* what she wanted. But with

273

a husband she adored, a gentle domestic sort of life, a beautiful house to renovate . . . ? Good God. She could hardly complain.

Her first task was the wedding presents – hundreds of them, packed away in the billiard room – all of which needed to be unwrapped, catalogued and their givers thanked.

They started the following day, with Edward busily unwrapping while Honor wrote the details of who had given them what into a special present book from Xandra.

'This,' she'd declared, handing over a smart beribboned package emblazoned with royal warrants and a Bond Street address, 'is essential.'

Honor had smiled inwardly at the idea of anything from Bond Street being 'essential' and undid the ribbons.

'It's the only way you'll keep track of all those wretched presents,' Xandra went on. 'I should know. I've still got the one your father and I had. Certainly comes in handy when you . . . Well anyway, darling, it's nice to have a record.'

Remembering her mother's words, Honor sat yawning on the billiard room window seat with the leather-bound book in her hands, while Edward proceeded methodically, opening the cards first, reading out the names and addresses for her to inscribe in their Bond Street book before taking off the wrappings. And as more glass jugs appeared, more salad bowls, candlesticks, crystal bowls, paperweights . . . the harder it became to feel grateful.

Wearily the paper was torn away. Wearily the name was written in. There was no need even to make a pretence of pleasure – not when it was just the two of them, sitting alone in the billiard room. They could be as indifferent as they liked. The thank-you letters would tell a different story, of course – but for now, nobody would know. And by the end of the first day, Honor was exhausted with the strain of it all – of receiving so much, yet remaining so completely devoid of anything near the kind of gratitude she knew she should be feeling.

'Charles and Maeve?' said Edward – another silvery box on his knees, reading out the names on the little matching card.

'Penscombe-Jones. Friends of Mum's.' Honor wrote them into the present book. 'Is there an address?'

Edward opened the card again. 'The Old Rectory, Chelford . . .' he read out. And as Honor wrote it down, he tore off the paper and opened the box. 'Another vase,' he said, not bothering even to take it out. 'Blue and white china, flower pattern.' Putting it on the billiard table, he turned to the next package.

Honor automatically filled in the details. 'China vase,' she wrote. 'Blue and white, flower pattern.' Then she brought her pen down to the next line and waited for Edward to open the next card and read out the name.

But Edward remained silent. Looking up, Honor saw that he'd opened the card of the next present and was reading it with a strange expression.

'Well who's it from then?'

He looked up suddenly – as if her question had woken him.

'Who's it from?'

'Shelley Maclean.' He spelt it for her. '489 Pilkington Drive, Sydney, Aust—'

275

'Who's Shelley Maclean?'

'She's a friend from Australia.'

'A *special* friend?'

Edward hesitated, then got to his feet, came over to the window seat and sat beside Honor, passing her the card. 'In a way,' he said awkwardly.

Honor read the card. 'Hope you'll be happy,' it said, in looping ink 'lots of love, Shelley.'

She looked round at Edward with an amused expression. 'Well, my darling, I think *you'll* be writing the letter for this one, if you don't mind. Much as I love to do these little things for you, I'm afraid I draw the line at—'

Edward smiled, taking the card from her. 'You got the address down?'

Honor read it out from her book as he checked it against the card. And then, tearing the thing in two, Edward tossed it into the pile of rubbish and picked up Shelley's present. Inside was a small stuffed koala bear, the sort of koala bear that would have sat on the shelf of some airport souvenir shop along with hundreds of identical bears in identical gift boxes with multicoloured artwork scribbled round the sides.

'Oh God.' Honor giggled. 'Another one for the charity pile?' Until she realised Edward wasn't laughing too. He was looking at the bear with that same strange expression – and clearly hadn't heard a word.

She picked up the next present, quickly passing it to him as she tore open the card. 'Oh look – it's from Gina and Mark. Okay Edward? You ready?'

'Yes. Yes.' He put the koala to one side. 'Gina and Mark . . .'

Head bent forward, Honor scribbled '*Gina and Mark Fleetwood*' in the next entry and tried not to think about the koala bear lying carelessly beside him – or what he planned to do with it.

'. . . PN14 5DL,' said Edward's inscrutable voice. 'That's P for Penny, N for Nigel . . .'

PART IV

Chapter Sixteen

Putney Rot

The front door to Evie's new flat needed fixing. She was still in Hoxton, but after two years of living in a classic first-time buyer's basement box – a box that, nonetheless, with a bit of paint and attention and a favourable surge in the market, had almost doubled in value – Evie had, earlier that year, upgraded to an apartment in a new development off Pitfield Street. This time everything was brand new and perfect. All she'd had to do was move in . . . except that, now she was there, it was clear the smart front door wasn't quite as perfect as it seemed.

It looked all right from the outside. White and smooth and clinically precise against the acid greens of the common parts of the building, with the same porthole of frosted glass and the same width-long metal door handle that all the apartments had been given. All part of the hospital-chic look everyone knew was about to take off . . . But the inner fire-door structure, the way it took ages to close and then – at the very last minute – noisily and suddenly crashed shut: that particular hospital feature really had to go.

It was fine when she was alone. But now that Ian was in her life . . . Of course, he preferred it when they went back to his place, but it wasn't always convenient to get out to St Albans, especially when they had evening commitments in London. And anyway, Evie liked her own territory. When he did come back to Pitfield Court with her, and then got up at seven o'clock on a Sunday morning to go jogging, that front door drove her mad.

She could doze quite happily while he opened the gym bag he always carried – always equipped with spare clean kit and towel, always ready in the back of his car no matter where he'd spent the night. She could stir sleepily while he sat on the side of the bed and pulled on his trainers – listening to the soft flick-flick of the laces as he tied them, and the muted clicks of plastic as he pulled out his Walkman and headphones and checked the cassette. And then the noises would grow more distant. The perky squeaks of his trainers on the rubber stair-covering, the metallic click-click as he opened the front door, a long deep silence, and then . . .

Damn door. Evie opened her eyes – fully awake now, from a combination of irritation and habit. As she and Ian invariably got up at six on weekdays, hopes of a Sunday lie-in were perhaps a little optimistic – even when he wasn't off jogging. But as silence returned and she lay in amongst the pillows, looking at the minimalist features of her bedroom – the sleek teak edges of her dressing table; the smooth brilliant-white walls curving seamlessly up into an arc over her head so that it was impossible to tell where wall ended and ceiling began; the wafer-thin slats of the window blinds; the soft mushroom suede of her bedside lampshades; the discreet row of knobs and buttons by

282

the bed that operated the blinds, the radio, the alarm clock, the lights . . . all she had to do was reach out from the duvet – it was hard to stay irritable for long. Hard to believe sometimes that this state-of-the-art apartment really belonged to her at all. If it hadn't been for that call from Ian – who, when he found out that the developer was desperate to be shot of this last apartment, had dialled Evie's number there and then, insisting Linda extract her from a client so that she could give him permission to put in an offer immediately on her behalf . . .

'Oh God, Ian. I don't know . . .'

'Okay.' His voice was slightly echoey. 'I'm standing here in the kitchen . . . There's lots of light. Lots of space. Two bedrooms – both upstairs. Two bathrooms. All immaculate. And a huge sitting room with a balcony . . . It's a proper, decent flat—'

'Square meterage?'

'Well over a hundred,' said Ian. 'Maybe even one-ten . . .'

Evie's eyes grew wider, her cheeks pinker. 'Go on.'

'They were asking a hundred and eighty grand, but he says he'd be happy with one-fifty – which makes me think you'll probably get it for one-two-five if we put an offer in right now.'

Evie bit her lip. 'Sounds great. Of course I will need to—'

'There's no time for that,' he said, reading her mind. 'By the time you get over here, the moment'll be lost.'

'But—'

Ian sighed. 'There are no obvious structural problems – not at first glance. It's a great location: just round the corner from where you are at the moment. And it really does look top notch, Evie. Decent wooden

283

floors throughout, and some excellent fittings. Granite worktops, two fan ovens, huge American-style fridge, excellent sound system, stone gas fire in the sitting room . . . all there. And fully furnished, with lots of teak and suede and glass and chrome. I have to say, for one-two-five, you'd be mad to turn it down.'

Evie glanced for a moment around her office: at Linda, sticking stamps onto envelopes; at James, wasting time on some private call; at her clients, browsing lazily down the rows of overpriced properties in the window.

'Okay,' she said, face now completely pink. 'Get it.'

'You sure?'

'I'm sure.'

Ian smiled. 'Good girl. I'll call you back when it's done.'

And now she was there – properly there. In truth it wasn't quite her style. Minimalist decor needed a tidy approach and Evie's clutter was always spoiling the look of the place. Ian had insisted she get a cleaner, so there were moments in the week when everything was perfect – but it was hard to keep it that way. There were times when she rather suspected that Ian himself did the odd bit here and there when she wasn't looking. She'd discover her towel neatly folded, flat on the heated rail, on a Sunday night. Or yesterday's knickers – mysteriously in the laundry basket, when she'd no recollection of being so organised as to have put them there herself. The magazines in the bathroom would always be stacked properly after he'd come over, with the outdated ones thrown out. He hadn't yet made little V-folds in the loo paper, but it was only a matter of time.

And, much to her surprise, Evie loved it. Instead of

being irritated by such fastidiousness, she was oddly reassured that he liked to do that sort of thing for her. It was nice that he liked to take care of her, and that his care could extend to something as tiny as sorting through her bathroom magazines. There were times when it reminded her of Honor. And if Honor, her greatest friend, was similarly tidy, similarly focused, perhaps it wasn't so surprising that her lover should be of a similar disposition.

In any case, he wasn't the sort of person who expressed his emotions very well. He was serious and driven and extremely successful – which was what had attracted Evie so strongly in the first place. A man like Ian Davis was never going to write her poetry, or buy her something silky, or waste three hours at the office dreaming about her breasts or planning a trip to Paris. He was going to tidy her bathroom and negotiate a great deal on her flat. He was going to speak to someone about getting her pension sorted out, and check the details of her health insurance. And Evie understood that, for such a man, those were the signs of love. More importantly, she wasn't so sure that silky frippery and flowers and clichéd trips to Paris really cut it with her. They seemed slightly useless and unnecessary, not to mention old-fashioned. And the longer she spent with Ian, the more certain she was that his style of loving – practical, supportive, ordered – was the style that worked for her.

They'd been together now for almost three months, and last night Evie had finally got around to introducing Ian to her parents. She was certain they'd love him. After the likes of Dom Franklin, Harry the drummer, poor, hopeless Billy, and – God, she couldn't even remember his name – that Irish barman from way back . . . Even Matthew Forrester had had certain drawbacks, with that awkward career and that rather fundamental lack of interest in Evie. After so many losers, Giles and Rachel would surely be delighted that she'd finally found someone with focus and direction and a good stable job. Someone with a bit of maturity; someone capable of commitment.

Lying amongst the pillows that morning, Evie thought back over how the evening had gone. How respectful Ian had looked in his suit as they'd stood on the steps of Morland Road and waited for her father to open the door; of how hard her parents had tried – with a delicious leg of lamb, a decent bottle of wine, and the kitchen tidier than she'd seen it in months. The candlelight had certainly helped, and the roasting lamb and garlic had almost obliterated any smell of damp.

Evie hoped the evening hadn't cost her poor parents too much. For while Uncle William's decision to hire a team of top lawyers to represent the Lloyd's syndicate that both he and his sister had signed up to had effectively eased concerns on that front – while bankruptcy was no longer an immediate concern for Rachel and there was no pressing need for Evie to chip in – it was still a daily struggle to make ends meet. Letting Evie's room certainly helped, but even though Rachel had taken a job at the local library and Giles had found weekend employment at a friend's gallery in Kew, it still only kept their heads just above water, and wasn't nearly enough for the repairs and improvements that now seemed vital if the house in Morland Road was to retain its value.

And Ian couldn't help but notice the neglect. Evie saw his gaze flicker over the kitchen ceiling as they made their way in to supper. She saw him hesitate at the wobbly step on the stairs. And even though his conversation was perfectly polite, complimenting Rachel on her cooking and asking Giles about his work, about the sort of people who commissioned murals and the kind of money that could be made from the Arab market, it wasn't until they were having coffee in the sitting room that he seemed able, finally, to relax. For once Rachel had been able to shift their talk away from Giles's Arabs and on to the subject of Evie's new flat and Ian's involvement, it seemed there was no stopping him. There he sat in Giles's armchair, offering his views on everything from the rise in the property market – and his own plans to open offices in Manchester and Liverpool – to the government's approach to interest rates and the pros and cons of taking on the Euro.

Amused – proud, even – Evie listened as Ian explained to her father why it was so important that control of interest rates be given to the Bank of England.

'If only that ghastly man would see the advantages of letting it go, instead of thinking he knows best all the time. It could all be so much simpler. But instead we get flung here and there by a government desperate for short-term approval, and no thought given to the long-term fiscal damage of playing interest rates that way.'

'Ian's even written to *The Times* about it,' Evie added, just in case Giles – who seemed a little dozy that evening – failed to grasp the importance of Ian's point.

'Oh has he?' said Rachel quickly. 'How fascinating! Was it printed?'

Still frowning at the thought of the mess the Chancellor was making of the economy, Ian finished his whisky and, catching Evie's eye, stood up. 'I'm afraid I don't know,' he said, doing up the button on his jacket. 'I only sent it on Thursday. But I am optimistic that they'll print it. I managed to get five or six signatures from some of the other agencies, so I'm hoping they'll pay it more attention than the last letter I wrote. But of course one can never be certain. I'm writing an article on the same thing for *London Property* magazine – which'll be out in October – but who knows what damage the Chancellor will have done by then . . .'

Giles and Rachel saw them out, both standing at the door and waving as Evie and Ian drove off down Morland Road. It was only when they got back to Pitfield Court that Evie realised it was only ten thirty.

Still, it had meant an early night, and Ian had been delighted. Talking about his plans for the next day – being in bed before eleven meant he could go for that early jog after all, and then they could have their café breakfast and time to read the newspapers properly, and he'd still have four or five hours to get ready for his trip to Manchester on Monday – he'd undressed and got ready for bed. And Evie – aware that this was the attitude that brought about success, aware that early nights and taking time to prepare were what made the difference between men like Ian and men like Dom – Evie was full of admiration for his discipline and focus, his resistance to distraction. Sex could wait. And while she might draw the line at an early-morning jog, there was nothing stopping her from following Ian's example when it came to the other things. With any luck, she too would have her own property business by the age of thirty.

And with that in mind, she pushed back the sheets – determined to be showered and dressed by the time

Ian returned. Knocking herself against the hard wooden edge of her new bed – the sleek Japanese design meant she was always doing that, and had blue bruises all round her shins – Evie stumbled into her en suite 'wet room' and stood under a power-jet of water, her back tingling from the pressure.

'Well, if you're going to retain any value then absolutely you must. Sooner the better. Morris can be round first thing Monday if that works for you, or . . . no I've just spoken to him about it, and . . . no, no – that's fine. Really. He often works weekends. I had to call him about another job anyway, so it really wasn't a problem . . .'

Evie stood in the doorway, wrapped in a towel, watching Ian at her desk – glued to the telephone. He was still in his trainers, still sweating from his jog, and already it was business. Business, at eight o'clock on a Sunday morning. She hoped for his sake that whoever he was speaking to was okay with that, or else lived somewhere like Hong Kong.

'Ten? Twelve? Something like that . . . which might sound quite a lot, but— Sure. And you do need someone decent for this sort of thing. It's certainly not something you should scrimp on, and— What's that? Oh – oh – well he reckons he'd have a report for you by Wednesday, so— I know. You should be able to get contractors sorted by the end of the week. And if you'd like any help with that side of things, then— sure, Giles. I understand. But why don't I give you a couple of numbers anyway? Just in case . . .'

Giles? Hoping wildly that there was another Giles in Ian's address book, Evie lingered at the door. A client, perhaps? A commercial contact, with some sort of private concern? Or—

289

'And thanks again for last night. It really was wonderful to meet you both, and do please thank Rachel for that delicious supper . . .'

Oh God.

Realising it was much too late to do anything about it now, Evie turned back into the bedroom, rubbing her hair with the towel and rolling her eyes with an air of hopeless amusement. God, poor Dad. Poor Ian . . . only doing his best. He must have seen the state of the kitchen and smelt the damp and been worrying about it all night. She hoped Giles hadn't bitten his head off.

But Giles, it seemed, had been a model of restraint. It was about time, he said in a slightly flat tone when they spoke about it the following week. About time that something was done about the damp. Ian had been absolutely right. And his instincts had just been confirmed by that man Morris's report. Work did need to be done that year. It was very much a case of acting swiftly before the trouble cost ten times more to rectify.

Of course it was unfortunate that Morris had been quite so expensive, but Ian wasn't to know how desperate the situation was. And, needless to say, it was awkward that they were going to have to delay getting started on the work – again, for financial reasons – but there simply wasn't a way round it.

'And – and that's really why I'm calling, sweetheart. I mean, we don't want to offend Ian. In fact, we're really touched that he's gone to so much trouble. But—'

'How much is it going to cost?'

Giles sighed.

'Come on, Dad. You can tell me.'

'Well it probably doesn't sound a great deal to you, Evie . . .'

'Just spit it out.'

'Ten grand.'

Evie was silent.

'It was over five hundred simply for the report.'

'Oh God.'

'Which we can just about manage, if we wait until the end of the month before paying him. You think that'll be okay?'

'Of course it will, Dad! It's common practice.'

'But we really don't want to embarrass you with any of this. So if you think we should pay instantly, then . . .'

'Absolutely not.'

'Great.' Giles sighed again. 'And – and then there's the whole question of how to handle the delay. I mean, if the report is telling us to get started "yesterday", what's Ian going to think when we just seem to be ignoring it, and everything he's done for us, and—'

'Ten grand, you say?'

'Well I expect we could find someone to do it a little more cheaply, but basically yes. It's a big job, sweetheart . . .'

'Sure.' Evie scribbled something at the bottom of her task list. 'Sure. Okay. You leave it with me, Dad – I'll call you back in a couple of hours. But please don't worry about Ian, or coming up with ten grand out of the blue. I – I'll work something out. Okay?'

And Giles, with an odd sense that he really could leave it with his twenty-five-year-old daughter, put down the telephone with a strange combination of shame and pride running through his veins.

By lunchtime, Evie had called Morris to double-check the findings of his report and whether the work really was essential. She'd then called Ian to be certain that Morris really was up to scratch and that there was no need for a second opinion. And finally, having spoken to her bank to check the status of her savings account, she called her father back and told him exactly what was going to happen.

'Right, Dad. Now the first thing to say is that if you want to do nothing – if you want to hang on until you feel comfortable – then absolutely, you do it. There's no pressure, you understand?'

Giles smiled. 'It's not that I *want* to hang on, sweetheart. I simply don't have the—'

'Fine. Great. Well then, if it's still okay with you, I thought maybe I could help out a bit with the money side of things.'

'Darling, you—'

'I'm serious. From a purely materialistic point of view – and I hope you don't think I'm presuming too much here – I am rather expecting one day that I'll be inheriting the place . . .'

Giles chuckled. 'What about the poor cats' home?'

'You've always loathed cats.'

'But your mother—'

Evie grinned. 'I'm sure that when you point out to her that I might be rather more effective than a couple of stray cats when it comes to fixing this current problem, she won't feel quite so inclined to—'

'True. True . . .'

'So assuming she's persuadable . . .'

'I think she might be.'

'You could say it was in my interest,' Evie went on, 'to be certain of the place still standing when the pair of you finally pop your clogs.'

'Fair enough,' said Giles, suddenly serious. 'But darling—'

'And as I happen to have that sort of cash in my bank account – or will do, by the time I get my bonus – I'd like to invest it in getting the work done. I— no, Dad. I'm absolutely sure about this. It makes sense from whichever way you look at it. And I— no. No, I'm— Okay then. You speak to Mum about it and let me know. You find the contractors, if that makes you feel any better. Just make sure they're properly registered and certified and— okay! Okay! Just let me know.'

Work started in November. After discussions with a number of possible contractors, Rachel and Giles decided to hire Mike, an old friend of Giles's who'd never made it as an artist and had taken on building jobs to bring in extra cash. Not only was his quote a fraction of the others, there was something reassuring about his honesty. Mike had made it very clear that, while he knew exactly what needed to be done, damp-proofing wasn't strictly his expertise. He'd have to involve qualified specialists to ensure Giles and Rachel had the right certification – but as this qualified as 'training', he certainly wouldn't be charging for that side of things. As a result, he'd probably take a little longer than the others to get the work done properly. Together with what they knew of his standards – Mike could never do anything half-heartedly; his obsession with perfection was one of the reasons he was so much better suited to joinery and plasterwork than anything more randomly creative – not to mention their desire to give him the contract, and help him out financially . . . all these things made Mike the obvious choice.

It seemed highly dodgy to Ian. He made a point of finding out exactly which qualified specialists Mike intended to consult, and whether they'd really be able

293

to certify his work, and what the insurance position would be once the project was complete. And although it seemed the proposals were viable, he still didn't like the sound of it. Didn't like it at all.

'It is their house, Ian. There's a limit to what we can—'

'Fine. But don't say I didn't warn you.'

And while the work started on time, while Mike was always there in the morning on the dot of eight and made sure he left the place each night as clean as was humanly possible – painstaking in his efforts to do a perfect job – Rachel sometimes felt he tried too hard. He spent ages clearing out the kitchen, taking the cupboards off the walls and wrapping them in protective covers; packing up all their cheap plates and glasses with the care of a Sotheby's expert; and chipping away at the plaster as if he were creating, not destroying. He'd start clearing up at least an hour before he was due to leave, an hour that could have been spent getting on with the next task. He'd insist on getting the damp specialists to view each step of the work – which meant waiting days, sometimes even weeks, for the right person to be available just to give the nod on something as basic as the level to which the tanking should reach . . . a level that, even Rachel could see, was clearly no higher than ground.

The other problem with Mike was that he kept noticing extra things that needed doing. So while they waited for each stage of the damp work to be completed, he would occupy himself by sorting out the wiring in Giles's studio, or the dripping taps in the top bathroom . . . only to uncover other horrors that Rachel would have been quite happy to leave.

'I'll have it done in no time.'

'But—'

'Please, Rachel. I insist. You'll only be paying for the materials, and it'll be so much nicer to have the place right-and-tight when I'm gone. I promise you, you'll thank me for it later . . .'

But November moved into December with no sign of any replastering. Even the new rendering looked unlikely for some time, and the chances of getting any expert out to look at it in the run-up to Christmas were slim to non-existent. The house remained a building site. An immaculate building site, but that was hardly the point, and gratitude wasn't the first response Rachel had in mind whenever she came back in from some errand or other and opened her front door.

With every week that went by they were losing money. Not only because, while the work was being carried out, there was no chance of getting lodgers into Evie's room. There were also the inevitable disruptions to Giles's projects. He could hardly use his studio while it was being rewired by Mike and then repainted. And when Rachel caught Mike in there at seven o'clock one Friday evening, polishing floor-boards, she flipped.

'For God's sake, Mike. It's not a ballroom.'

Mike got up from his knees. 'I'm sorry. I only wanted it to—'

'I know you want it to look perfect for Giles, but honestly, you know as well as any of us that it'll get dusty and paint-spattered within seconds of him getting back in, with his mucky oils and his tools and – and all the rest of his rubbish. That's the whole point of him having a studio in the first place!'

'Just let me finish this corner here and I'll—'

'No!' she cried, grabbing the rag and polish from

Mike's hands, putting them firmly into his bag and shoving it back into his arms. 'No, Mike. You're done in here. You've made it look great. Really, you have. We both love the colour, and the lighting you've installed is fantastic. But – *enough*. You understand?'

Mike looked at her, stunned. And then – to both their relief – the doorbell rang.

'Christ,' Rachel muttered, heading down the stairs assuming it was Giles at the door, back from another humiliating trip to Martha's shop in Henley. 'He can't have forgotten his keys *again* . . .'

But it wasn't Giles. It was William, standing on the doorstep in the darkness, looking back at her with an expression not dissimilar from Mike's. 'Can I come in?'

'Of – of course . . .' Rachel stood aside, her mind spinning. 'Is everything all right?'

William did not reply, but the very fact of his arrival – unannounced, at eight o'clock on a Friday night – together with the look on his face . . . it was enough for Rachel to know what the answer would be. He stood staring at the hallway, stripped of furniture with the carpets up – now propped in tidy rolls against the wall, along with the rest of Mike's tool boxes and materials. Everything had been carefully stacked and piled – it looked more like an ironmonger's store than a building site – but it was hardly the hall that William remembered. He took it in with a dazed expression. 'Good God.'

'I'll be off then, shall I?' said Mike on the staircase.

Hurriedly Rachel nodded up at him while ushering her brother into the sitting room. It was the only room which had at least a semblance of normality. 'I . . . yes, Mike. I think . . . thanks for . . .'

She stood in the doorway as her brother went

through, trying to think of a quick, decent way of closing things off with Mike. She didn't feel she should apologise – someone needed to point out how ludicrous it was getting, how maddening it was to wait so long for something that should have been fixed weeks ago – but neither did she want to offend him. She just—

'It's all right.' Mike smiled at her forgivingly. 'It's been a long day. But you have a nice restful weekend, you hear? Get Giles to take you somewhere nice, or – or give you a good long massage . . . and' – still smiling – 'and I'll see you bright and breezy on Monday!'

Exasperated, Rachel saw him out and came back in to her brother. 'Wretched man.' She shut the door. 'The *audacity* of it – acting as if I'm the one that needs—'

And then, stopping short, she noticed that William was sunk on the sofa, leaning forward with his head in his hands. It was a disturbing sight: her brother – always so confident, so physically upright, so easy with his bearing . . . crushed and broken double. Forgetting all about Mike and the half-polished floor upstairs, Rachel sat close to William and quietly put an arm around his shoulders. For a while they sat in silence. Then William sighed and sat back – so that Rachel had to remove her arm – and looked at her dully. 'Xa's left.'

Rachel went pale. 'She found out?'

'Well actually, in the end Diana had to tell her, but—'

'*What*?'

'But that's neither here nor there, to be honest. Not now. The point is, Xa knows. Knows everything. And I . . .' Clenching his right hand into his left, William found he couldn't speak.

'And now you want her back,' said Rachel for him. There was no question in her tone.

William nodded.

'You love her.'

He nodded again. 'And it's because I bloody love her, Rach – it's because I realised I could never leave her, not in a million years, that we're now in this . . .' He shook his head. 'I just wanted to do the right thing. But as Diana's been so low, what with her job and her father being ill and . . . this and that. Things haven't been so great. And I never wanted to hurt her, not after everything we've—'

'Sure. I understand.'

'So I just didn't see so much of her.'

Rachel looked at him.

'I – I was so certain it would be best – best for Diana, quite apart from anyone else – if I waited until she got back on her feet again before saying anything that might have pushed her over the edge. You know how shaky she can be.'

'Sure.'

William sighed. 'Except, of course, things didn't get better. She lost three contracts last year, and then her father died in April, and then she really started to lose it. Wanted to know my every movement. *Why* had it taken a whole extra hour for me to get down from London? *Why* couldn't I drop everything and come over to see her in the middle of Sunday lunch? *Why* hadn't I called her from Italy? When it would have been quite impossible, Rach. When she knew – when I'd told her specifically – that I wouldn't be able to get much privacy on a yacht . . . stupid, tiny things . . . And last week it just . . . all . . . came to a head. And she said – insisted – I had to make a choice. There and then. I had to decide: it was her or Xandra . . .'

'And you chose Xa.'

William swallowed. 'The weird thing is, she seemed

to take it pretty well at the time. Said she always knew I'd never leave. Said she was glad to get it sorted out now, while she still has the flat in Edinburgh and – and there's work she needs to do, work that's better done on-site . . . she really needs to get back there. So we parted on quite good terms, all things considered. I took her to the station the next day, offered to get the boat packed up for her and oversee the sale . . . And it was fine, Rach. Really quite civilised. But then something must have happened, because the next thing I know I'm getting a call from my lawyer saying I need to instruct some other firm because my wife has already hired them to – to initiate fucking divorce proceedings!'

Rachel closed her eyes.

'She won't speak to me – hasn't taken a single call. I had to find it all out from Honor – all about how some woman had rung Xandra, and told her to go out to Woodbridge and look at the barge . . . which of course was full of incriminating junk . . .'

'Oh God.'

'And I just . . .' William looked at his sister, eyes swimming with tears. 'I can't bear it at Favenham at the moment. With all the children away, and – and everywhere I look, it's—'

'Oh William . . .'

'We've got at least three shooting parties between now and Christmas – not to mention Christmas itself. And then . . . God only knows what else. And I just can't cope any more. I—'

'Of course you can't. No one's expecting you to. You – you leave it all with me, William. We'll get a room fixed for you here upstairs, no problem. We'll cancel your shooting and—'

'Cancel the shooting?'

299

'Or – or handle it, anyway. One way or another. And you certainly mustn't worry about Christmas. The important thing is for you to get some space and time to think what to do about Xandra, and how you're going to win her back . . .'

By the time Giles returned from Henley, it was all fixed.

What with all the building work going on at Morland Road, it had not taken much for William to persuade his sister that it was really best all round if she go back with him to Suffolk. For a start, there'd be a decent amount of space at Favenham. No interruptions, no sudden power cuts, no irregularities in the water supply. It was, William confessed, something of a shock for him to discover that his sister had been living for so long in what he considered to be completely uninhabitable conditions. Surely it suited her to be away from Putney while the work was completed. Surely it suited Rachel and Giles to be away from Putney while the work was completed. It wasn't just the inconvenience of living on a building-site. It was the whole financial muddle they'd got themselves into that really baffled William. Couldn't Rachel see that the pathetic part-time jobs they'd taken on recently hardly justified the expense of remaining in London? And as for any useful income they might receive from letting the spare room . . . they may as well forget it, with the house in such a state. No. It was enough. Rachel and Giles needed to wake up and see sense – quit their pocket-money jobs and take advantage of the free bed and board that William was offering. They simply couldn't afford not to. And in any case, wasn't it preferable to take refuge in the comforts and luxuries of Suffolk instead of battling with all this mess and dust and unnecessary bills falling through the letterbox? Certainly, it wouldn't be a problem for him to have her there. She shouldn't hesitate on *his* account. Why, he'd love having her there! And if Rachel could help out with the shooting parties . . .

'Of course I can.'

And – and Christmas, if it . . .

'Absolutely.'

Then it really did seem the perfect answer. With his sister there to support and advise him, perhaps even to act as a go-between with Xandra – William was starting to wonder if there was a chance of reconciliation after all . . .

'Although I certainly wouldn't want to drag you away from poor old Giles, if—'

'Oh, Giles won't mind!'

Giles looked back at them both, seeing, all too clearly, the joy his wife was feeling at the prospect of time away from Putney.

'He could even come too, if he likes! We could give the dreaded Mike the run of the place. He could work as late and as diligently as he pleases . . . and' – turning at last to Giles – 'and you could get some proper peace and quiet, darling. Actually finish some of those trays you promised Martha she could have in time for the Christmas rush. You'd make much more money from sticking to your proper work, instead of wasting time at Harold's Gallery. And – and who knows? Perhaps Xandra will be home by Christmas, and we'll be coming back to a perfectly finished, damp-free house!'

It all made a depressing sort of sense. Standing there with Martha Orme's latest order tucked away in his inside pocket and three sample trays in his hands, Giles simply didn't have the heart to refuse.

301

Chapter Seventeen

Abe's Play

Davis–Jones Developments occupied the top two floors of a discreet modern office building in Mayfair, and Evie – who, after five months of being with Ian, should really have grown more used to this side of his life – still got a thrill from walking into the lobby and asking for the boss.

'Ian Davis,' she'd say, idly pulling at one of the glossy Davis–Jones brochures that had been piled to one side for prospective clients with time to spare. 'He is expecting me.'

'And who shall I say . . .?'

'Evelyn Langton.'

Tonight was no different. The tree outside the building had been covered in tiny white Christmas lights, and there was a Xandra-like effect in the lobby. Approaching from the street, Evie could admire the stage-like scene through a sheet of reinforced tinted glass – all that space and warmth, with those rich-red damask walls, those wide empty sofas, that mellow lighting, and that wonderful bushy fir tree with its sparkly-perfect balls. It all sat in painful contrast to the

302

chilly subways of Marble Arch, not two hundred yards away, and the pale, cold faces of the people going down into them. As someone who could never quite escape the idea that she herself might end up in such a subway on such a night, Evie hurried inside – just grateful to be one of the lucky ones. The odd slip here or there – a foolish investment, an inattentive eye, too many drinks on too many weeknights, or the wrong person with the wrong influence – it was all too easy, she felt, for a girl like her to end up on the dark side of the glass.

'Do take a seat,' said the receptionist, looking up from her telephone. 'He'll be down in just a moment.'

Evie looked at the clock above the girl's head and hoped Ian wasn't going to be difficult. It was already past six thirty. He'd promised he'd be waiting for her down here in the lobby, that they'd be ready to go straight away. He knew they couldn't be late and – usually with Ian – that was more than enough to ensure a prompt response. But the lack of interest he'd shown in coming along tonight had made her slightly uneasy.

'Okay. Fine,' he'd said when she first raised it. 'I understand that *you* have to be there, Evie. But why do I—'

'You don't.' Evie sighed. 'I just thought—'

'It's not as if I know the man.'

'Yes, Ian. And I know it's not your scene, but poor Abe really does need all the support he can get right now. And – and if Honor and Edward are prepared to come all the way up from Suffolk—'

'Honor – your cousin?' Ian had yet to meet her.

'That's right. *And* she used to go out with him. She – trust me – she's got no reason to schlep up to London for some dodgy play of his, except to be kind. Her husband even less . . .'

'And they're both going to be there?'

'That's right. And her mother. *And* Charles, her brother, who might even be bringing his girlfriend . . .' She looked at him. 'I know it's a lot of boring members of my family, Ian. But it really would mean a lot to me if you—'

'Okay, okay . . .'

'You'll come?'

Smiling, Ian had opened his diary. 'Friday the fourteenth, you say?'

In the two years that had passed since Honor's wedding, Abe and Evie had become good friends. Better, in many ways, than before. From Abe's point of view – back in London and looking for work – Evie was one of the few remaining links to his old life. The combination of a flagging career and his having been away in LA for so long had meant that Abe's former circle of friends was almost non-existent and with so much time on his hands these days, he often sought out Evie's company. As for Evie . . . the very reduction in Abe's circumstances, if anything, made her fonder of him. Abe wasn't so dissimilar now from the offbeat men Evie had once dated – the Doms and Harrys and Billys who'd so attracted her before Ian had come along. And while she was very happy with Ian, while she had no desire for anything more than friendship from Abe, she still did rather like having him around – liked the irregularity of his world and the flavour of naughtiness he brought into hers.

So when, back in October, Abe told Evie that he'd been offered a role in some low-key fringe production, Evie had been determined to support it. She knew such work would hardly have thrilled him in the past, but a lot had happened in the intervening years – or, perhaps more accurately, not enough – and Abe was no longer in a position to pick and choose.

After two years of being back in London and telling everyone he was simply waiting for the right part to come his way – that he could easily take a role in *Casualty* or *The Bill* but that it was important for him not to degrade his image at this stage in his career, important not to 'slip' – Abe had found it a hard attitude to drop. With major parts in both *Cavaliers and Roundheads* and *Spanish Boots* to his credit, it seemed mad to step back into soapsville. Okay, so LA had been a stretch too far, but that didn't mean he was auto-matically destined for the other end of the spectrum. Surely something would turn up. And while *Florida Beach* had been a mistake – thankfully, one that would never reach the UK – he was all the more determined to hold out for something equal to his standing. It was for that very reason he'd ditched Karen Rossetti.

'Honestly Evie, the kind of stuff she was pushing my way. It was dire. Truly dreadful.'

'And this Nigel person? He's good, then?'

'Nigel Fournier. He's brilliant. Not as well known as Karen, but that's only because he's just started work as an agent – and in a way that suits me . . . not nearly so many other clients to distract him. And it's not as if he's inexperienced. He used to be a casting director, so he's got loads of contacts. But – but most importantly, Evie, he's on my wavelength. He understands what I want from this profession. He believes in me . . .'

Evie wasn't so sure that Nigel Fournier sounded as good as Abe was making out. Certainly he seemed a step down from Karen, and Evie's suspicions merely hardened when she discovered the man was gay and in his sixties. And as the months went by, with Abe attending various BAFTA previews with Nigel, having endless 'business lunches' with Nigel, going to Cannes with Nigel, and book launches with Nigel . . . even having his hair cut with Nigel, and still no sign of a job, or even a decent audition, Evie rather gave up asking. She wasn't sure she could face another of Abe's elaborate displays of success, another fine-tuned performance of a man on the brink of greatness . . . Not with the subtext of failure now so heavy and so loud. Didn't trust herself to play along. So when, over lunch one afternoon in late October, he told her casually that he'd decided to take on a part in some little play in a small theatre just off the Bayswater Road, she hardly dared believe him.

'But Abe, that's wonderful!'

'You think so?'

'Of course I do! Why, you must be thrilled!'

'You don't think it's degrading, then?'

'Degrading?'

'Fringe, darling. *Fringe*. And not being paid. Especially after—'

'Don't be silly,' said Evie, who hadn't got a clue about such things. 'It's not like you're stripping, or doing a tampon ad.'

'Mm,' said Abe, wishing the script was better. But it was certainly good to be working again. A director of Miles Keith's experience could hardly harm Abe's precious CV. According to Nigel, the man had done some great art house movies in the seventies. And that was before they got on to all the other – rather less obvious – advantages to this project that Abe was still hoping to milk.

306

'And you should see the babe they've lined up as my love interest,' he said, grinning now at Evie. 'She— Here.' Leaning forward, he pulled the latest issue of *The Stage* from a plastic bag at his feet, and turned to a marked page where the grainy mugshot of an ordinary-looking blonde gazed out seductively, just above his thumb. The whole magazine was shaking. 'Not bad, eh?'

Evie tried not to notice the shaking. 'She's gorgeous.'

'Well . . .' Pleased, Abe put the magazine back into his plastic bag. 'She'll make Honor jealous, if nothing else.'

And with that – with the mention of Honor's name – a cloud crossed over their lunch. It had become something of a habit, recently, for Abe to bring Honor up in conversation. He'd barely seen her since coming back to England – not now that she was married and living in Suffolk – but it still hadn't stopped him from thinking about her. And the more he talked about her, the more it seemed to Evie that her cousin had become, for Abe, something of a yardstick in terms of his own life. She couldn't help thinking that the intimacy they'd once shared was, like *Cavaliers* and *Spanish Boots*, representative of a happier time, a time he'd lost, a time he'd casually thrown away in search of something better.

But, unlike his former acting projects, Honor wasn't a mere memory. She wasn't stuck in celluloid. She was alive, in the present – admittedly married, admittedly in Suffolk, but still not entirely out of reach. Something could yet happen. Things could change. And Evie, suspecting that some dogged part of Abe saw some kind of opportunity in that fact – some scope for still coming out on top, some sense that their story was far

307

from complete – saw now that all hopes of this new play diverting his attention into something fresh and positive were futile. Honor was still very much at the forefront of his mind.

'You – you will at least try and get her to come, won't you?' he said, a little later, as he walked her back to the office.

'Sure, Abe. But you do know she—'

'Of course.' He laughed. 'It doesn't matter. I was only thinking she might enjoy it. Poor girl, stuck out in some dreary ploughed field – I'd have thought she'd love an excuse to come up to London . . .'

Evie need not have worried about Ian making them late. On the contrary, she'd barely had time to get comfortable on one of the smart lobby sofas when he was down and ready – doing up his overcoat, ushering her out through the sliding tinted doors and saying goodnight to the receptionist. Perhaps a little mechanical, a little tired. But then he could often seem that way when he got back in from work – his mind still clearly at his desk, still lost in the finer complexities of some building contract or half-formed business plan.

'So when does it start?'

'Seven thirty.'

Ian looked at his watch.

'We should have plenty of time,' Evie went on. 'It's only down the road. And they're serving free drinks to the Angels before the curtain goes up, so we might—'

'Angels?'

Evie smiled. 'It's what they're calling anyone who's given money towards the production. I – I just thought it would be nice to show—'

Ian stopped short on the pavement, looking at her.

'It was only fifty quid, Ian. I wasn't—'

'Fifty pounds? For a glass of warm white wine?'

Evie turned away, fiddling with her car keys. With Ian so down on Abe, and down on fringe theatre – indeed all theatre, so far as she could make out . . . he was never going to accept the idea of supporting a friend in this way. Particularly a 'friend' like Abe – a fantasist, a loser with a dodgy lifestyle and a depressing drug habit; a man who, to Ian, was quite clearly using Evie to get his three pathetic seconds in the spotlight.

Wishing she hadn't told Ian quite so much about Abe's background – understanding that his indignation was purely on her behalf – Evie was only too aware that she could hardly be cross with him now for wanting to look out for her. Why should Ian understand her reasons for bothering with Abe – for going to so much trouble to persuade half her family to be there for him that night – when sometimes she herself wondered why she did it? What actual difference was there, after all, between someone like Abe and all those hopeless boyfriends she'd so gladly discarded, and so frequently criticised?

But somehow a friendship was different. There was less – less of *herself*, at any rate – at stake. No skin off Evie's nose if Abe went on a bender, or failed to call her back, or eyed up some passing waitress. And then there was the – perhaps overdeveloped – sense of loyalty Evie carried for the few friends she had; a sense of herself as a protector, in some way – particularly towards those friends of hers who were too vulnerable or naïve or gentle for the real world. With people like Phil and Nigel in his life, there was no doubt in Evie's mind that Abe needed someone close by with nothing to gain from being with him.

309

But how to explain all that to rational, sensible Ian, whose idea of friendship was so much more balanced, and who felt that there were certain rules, certain standards to maintain . . . on *both* sides? For him to learn now that she'd actually thrown good money at Abe's theatre project – with absolutely no hope of a tangible return beyond that glass of warm white wine – it would, Evie knew, be incomprehensible.

'Well anyway,' she said, unlocking the car doors by remote control and watching the headlights flash. 'I don't expect it matters much if we miss out on the drinks, so long as we're there for the play itself.'

Saying nothing, Ian got into the passenger seat.

'It won't be long, Ian. I promise you . . .'

Ian did up his seatbelt. 'Well let's get on with it then,' he said, tapping his knee as she indicated left and pulled out into the traffic.

The Leinster Pit was a dingy fifty-seater in the basement of a pub in Paddington. On ordinary nights it was a venue for what the pub advertised outside as 'Live Jazz!' – attracting the same small group of grizzly punters, interspersed with occasional tourists who'd invariably leave after five minutes when it became clear that the set was little more than a jamming session with overamplified drums and ear-splitting trumpets.

But tonight was something different. Tonight, there was a certain sort of buzz. Flyers had been scattered over the tables, and all along the bar. A board had been erected at the top of the staircase, with black-and-white photographs of the cast in rehearsal together with publicity mugshots of each actor, and a short bit of background blurb. Everywhere there were posters:

310

'*Brainpower!* The new Miles Keith sensation! Starring Abe Wyatt as Tony, and introducing Rhianna Francis as Grace . . . "Outstanding!" "Sexy!" "Original!" "Terrific!" '

And instead of its grizzly regulars, the place was full of fresh-faced smiley – disconcertingly smiley – drama students. They were pacing busily and handing out yet more flyers to an odd selection of punters that ranged from predictable bohemian hangers-on, with dyed-orange hair and flowing clothes, and talking in very deep voices . . . to cast-members' parents – meek-looking, middle-aged, thanking them profusely . . . to a rather impressive turnout of pinstriped estate agents – checking their watches and wondering if this really was the place Evie meant . . . to, finally, a group of rare-looking creatures who were clearly more suited to royal enclosures than pubs and jazz and experimental theatre, creatures on the verge of extinction – with a collective demeanour that drew an invisible cordon around whatever place they occupied, a cordon which even the happy drama students knew better than to penetrate.

But no critics, Abe noticed – from a gap in the screen behind the ticket desk. No casting directors. Not even any agents. Nigel Fournier had said he'd come, but in the end he couldn't make it either. He was ill, he'd said, 'And the last thing I'd want to do would be to give it to *you*, my angel. Not on your big night. I'll come along at the end of the week, when you're properly into your stride . . .'

And now, with less than ten minutes to go until the curtain went up, Abe realised he was glad that Nigel wasn't there to see him in such a reduced context. Glad of the low profile. He chose to ignore the other

311

implications of the message: that Nigel wasn't paying proper attention, that he wasn't prepared to support Abe, or bring any casting director to see him. It was easier to look on the bright side. And anyway – much more importantly – where the fuck was Phil?

Abe looked out again, sneaking a quick look at the groups congregating by the bar. Some of them he recognised. There was Honor's brother with a red-headed girl he didn't know. There was Evie . . . and presumably that was Ian, still in his overcoat, inspecting the cast photographs with a gloomy expression. And there – good God – was Xandra, fully made-up and straight from the hairdresser, with something furry round her neck and ludicrous high heels. Abe could catch her heavy floral scent from halfway across the room.

Having expected to see William there that evening – perhaps even Rachel and Giles – Xandra was feeling simultaneously relieved and deflated to learn that none of them was coming. She hadn't seen William for months – not since waving him off to Suffolk that fateful August morning, kissing him hurriedly through the open window of his car with the telephone insistent in the background, and then running in to answer it as William drove off . . .

'Oh – oh hello,' a woman's voice had said. Xandra couldn't place it. 'Is that Xandra Montfort?'

'Who is this?'

'I'm so sorry to bother you, Xandra. I hope it's not an inconvenient time. But . . . well . . . my name's Diana Miller. I'm a friend of your sister-in-law – Rachel Langton?'

'Oh yes?'

'And also of your husband . . .'

Xandra had been planning Abe's opening night for weeks. She'd gone to great lengths to find something to wear that would make William sweat. Fur, high heels . . . Not really her taste, but he loved that sort of thing. And she knew exactly what she was going to say to that sister of his – the oh-so-perfect Rachel towards whom Xandra had always felt so affectionate but who, by all accounts, was now taking over at Favenham. Oh, Xandra had a few choice phrases up her sleeve for Rachel.

Only they weren't there. And then Xandra wondered if tonight might be when the Favenham carol service took place. If so, William would probably be doing his duty with the opening lesson before hosting the mince-pie affair that happened afterwards . . . Which, of course, he never did anything about – always leaving it to Xandra, thinking what could be easier than rustling up a few mince pies and laying on some booze? – completely unaware of all the cooking involved (for it never was just mince pies) and having to get all the decorations ready in time and arrange a place for people to leave their coats, and then all the clearing-up afterwards . . . just when she'd most like to be in London, doing her Christmas shopping before the streets got too crowded. This year, however, it would be Rachel at the helm – and Xandra allowed herself a smirk as she thought of her sister-in-law handing mince pies around a room that would be getting far too hot, and fretting at the sight of eight or nine children racing past the pair of Quing Dynasty pots that stood either side of the fireplace . . . while old Tom Driver and Jimmy Newton tucked into William's gin.

Briefly Xandra wondered how Giles would be coping: probably told to guard the bar, or – more likely

313

– to keep an eye on where everyone would be parking. William had always fussed about parking. He'd tried to send Charles out to oversee matters a couple of years ago – and been given very short shrift. Ben had been no better. But Giles – mild, kind Giles – was probably out there right now, wrapped up in that dreadful old duffle coat, his breath visible in the chilly torchlit air as he directed all the visiting cars into a nearby field . . . struggling to explain to sour Mr Graham why he couldn't drive his eighty-year-old mother right up to the house.

Xandra loosened her furry scarf and smiled at her daughter, ordering drinks.

'In fact, why don't we get a bottle?' she said. 'Honor darling?'

'Yes, yes . . . you got that, Edward? A bottle of Chablis for Mum. And I'll have a glass of water.'

Abe's heart began to pound. Turning to look out of the window again, at the street and the dark and the Bayswater traffic, he saw nothing but vacant parking spaces. There was no sleek Merc. No restless silhouette. No Phil. Sweating, he glanced at his watch – five minutes to go – and suddenly the idea of getting up in front of all those people terrified him. The play was dismal. The costumes made him look fat. And that first scene, where he was to come on stage wearing nothing but a towel . . .

Where are you, Phil? Where are you?

At least it was short, thought Evie – exactly an hour later – as she squeezed past a group of people at the ticket desk muttering about a wasted evening, and made her way over to the bar . . . followed by a silent Ian.

Evie reached for his hand. 'Just a quick drink,' she murmured in his ear, 'and then we'll be off, okay?'

Ian gave her a penetrating stare, like a dog wanting to be let out.

'We can't just leave, Ian. At least not without seeing him. Not when it—'

'I could wait for you in the car.'

'You could.'

Both were silent. And Evie, suspecting that this was a stand-off she was likely to lose, was glad – for once – of an interruption. Having made a great show of resisting, Nick and James from the office had decided to come after all . . . and were now descending upon her with expressions of humorous accusation.

'I know! I'm sorry, guys. I'd no idea—'

'It wasn't so bad,' said Nick, laughing. 'Poor man. He seemed ill. There was one point when I thought he might actually collapse – that bedroom scene . . .'

'Wasn't he supposed to be that way?' said James, scratching his head as he reread the synopsis in his programme. 'I mean, the story's pretty bizarre. You'd never have a brain surgeon that jittery – he could hardly hold that wine glass, far less a scalpel – but . . .' Looking up from the programme: 'What? You think it was *him*, do you? You think—'

'He was certainly sweating. And what about all those silences?'

Both looked at Evie, who smiled – hopelessly. 'God knows. You want something to drink?'

As there were no proper dressing rooms, Abe had arranged to meet Evie – and anyone else who was up for it – back in the main bar of the pub. He'd befriended the barman, who'd agreed to reserve a corner table for Abe's party after the play . . . and it wasn't hard to tell

315

which table it was: open bottles in ice buckets and a mass of expectant wine glasses suggested quite a party. Giving up on Ian – leaving him to make up his own mind about what he wanted to do – Evie led the others over to the table and hoped it wouldn't take Abe too long to appear from whatever it was actors did backstage at this point in the evening.

Realising she was probably expecting too much from Ian – why shouldn't he wait for her in the car, if that was what he wanted? . . . it wasn't as if Abe knew him: probably wouldn't even notice if he was there or not – Evie found her indignation swerving towards Honor, standing alone beside the flashing fruit machines, dressed immaculately in a pair of charcoal-coloured woollen trousers and a spotless dove-grey chiffon shirt, with all the air of someone on the verge of leaving.

'I can't stay, Evie. I'm sorry.'

Evie frowned at her.

'I – I'll call you tomorrow,' Honor went on. 'Maybe fix something up for the weekend? Edward's going back to Allenham but I'm around until Wednesday, staying with Mum and doing Christmas shopping – that sort of thing. Would love to see you properly. And – and of course I'll call Abe. I promise I will, Evie – when I have a moment, and when I can actually speak to him. But it's a madhouse in here! And we really must get moving. Edward's fetching our coats and then—' Looking back at her cousin's unsmiling expression, she said again, 'I'm sorry, Evie. Really I am. It's just been rather a long day . . .'

'What, shopping for Christmas presents and having your nails done?'

Honor bit her lip. 'And there's Mum. I know you can't tell from looking at her but – honestly Evie –

316

things haven't been easy since . . . well . . . you know how it is. It took a lot of courage for her to come out with us tonight.'

'Sure. Whatever.'

'I don't expect Abe'll even notice we've gone.'

And Evie, looking at her, wanted to shout, 'Of course he'll bloody notice! Come on, Honor. One lousy drink won't hurt.' It wasn't as if Abe were some lost bit of Honor's past. He was still her friend. They'd been close all through her time at Oxford. He'd been at her wedding. And while Honor's married state had meant that the little lunches and laughing telephone calls had rather dwindled in the past two years, the friendship was still very much alive. He deserved better than this.

But life was too easy for Honor at the moment – suspended above the daily grind by a combination of inherited money and a happy marriage. The horticultural course she was taking kept her nicely busy, but not manic; and the gradual changes that she and Edward were making to Allenham now that Lavinia had moved out – coming to London to look at new collections of curtain material or the latest style of refrigerator; or to drop in on the opening of some contemporary art exhibition in Cork Street in case they saw something perfect to go above the mantelpiece in Edward's newly decorated study – although the Victorian landscape that was hanging there at the moment was perfectly good for now . . . It just seemed the height of luxury to Evie, simply to have the time to consider such things at length.

Honor didn't even have children to worry about. Not that Evie disapproved of this. Far from it. In her view, twenty-five was still far too young for nappies and pushchairs . . . and Evie was relieved – relieved

317

and pleasantly surprised – to see that Edward hadn't forced it after all; that, contrary to her expectations when the pair of them had married, he was letting Honor enjoy being young and free from that sort of responsibility; that he understood there was no hurry. From time to time there'd been muttering from Honor's parents, but – thank God – the muttering had been ignored. Honor was living a lovely, carefree life. And while Evie was glad of it she felt, tonight, a rare flash of criticism towards her cousin.

With everything so rosy and perfect for Honor at the moment – why, even William and Xandra's sudden separation wasn't the blow to her stability that it would have been at the time of her eighteenth-birthday party, not now she had Edward – was Honor really unable to spare a few minutes for one small drink with poor crushed Abe? Or didn't she have time for her old friends any more?

'I – I only mean he must have hundreds of important people to see right now,' said Honor, noticing Evie's expression. 'Don't you think? This being his first play, and – and . . . everything. I thought if we just slipped away, he wouldn't even—'

'He was looking forward to seeing you, Honor.'

'He was?'

Evie frowned. 'And with the play being so . . . with it having so many . . . It just wasn't very good, Honor. Surely you—'

'Wasn't it?' Honor sighed. 'Oh dear. Poor Abe. I have to say, Edward would agree with you – he was being very rude about it just now – but I didn't think it was so bad! I mean, it can't be easy for Abe if he's never done theatre before. And I didn't think much of the actress who played Grace – she had a slightly annoying

318

voice. But some of those silences . . . and all that repressed aggression . . . It reminded me a bit of Pinter.'

And Evie, conceding that this was genuine – that it simply hadn't occurred to Honor that Abe might need support, Evie was about to back down when she spotted Abe suddenly through the crowd – rubbing at his nose and blinking. He seemed perky, jovial – greeting people and smiling – nothing like the man he'd been on stage. It didn't take a genius to work out what had been holding him up just now.

'Xandra!' he called out – the whole bar could hear him. 'How good of you to come! You want a drink? You . . . great! Well, there's a whole table over there – see? And if none of that's any good just tell me and I'll get Hal here to fix you up with something special . . . You've met Hal? Hal, this is Xandra – you don't mind me calling you Xandra, do you . . .? Oh, thank God for that. You know, I never *dared* while I was going out with Honor, but now we're friends – right? I do love those trousers you're wearing, by the way. Most women your age can't get away with suede, but I think they look fabulous . . .' He gabbled on, peppering his talk with manic laughter, while wriggling his nose and mouth for a sneeze that never came. 'You know, Xandra, I really appreciate it, you coming out to see me when – ahhh . . .' He hugged her suddenly.

'It's nothing, Abe. Really.'

Abe held on, his sweaty arms round Xandra's little shoulders. 'Well it's a damn sight better than my parents. Jesus. Did you ever meet them? No . . . no, I – well my mother's all right I suppose – in a wet sort of way – but my father . . . What is it with fucking barristers? Why do they always think they know everything?'

319

'I'd better rescue her,' Honor murmured, kissing Evie goodbye.

Evie watched them leave. She watched Xandra and Edward lie to Abe about how much they'd enjoyed the play. She watched Honor lie about hoping to see him soon. And then she watched, with growing horror, as they greeted another punter, emerging from the theatre door . . .

'Matthew!'

'Honor. How are you?'

'I'm fine! Really well. Just leaving, sadly, but—'

'Won't you stay for one more drink?'

Honor seemed genuinely regretful. 'I'm so sorry,' she said. 'It's hopeless. I—'

'Honor . . .'

'Oh Mum, this is Matthew Forrester. Matthew – my mother.' She was going to make a connection and explain to her mother how Matthew had covered their party at the Wellesley Hotel, but Xandra wasn't interested.

'It's a pleasure to meet you, Matthew,' she said briskly. 'But we do have to run. Come on, darling. Edward's waiting.'

Giving Matthew an apologetic smile, Honor followed her mother and husband out into the street.

Matthew stood in the centre of the room, looking round for faces he recognised – and Evie watched him. He seemed different, she thought. Bigger, somehow, without being fatter. And perhaps that wasn't so surprising. Evie might have moved on from those early days, but for some reason she still knew exactly what was happening in Matthew Forrester's life – and, more particularly, his career. She knew about some scoop he'd pulled off at the Tory Party conference a year or so

320

ago. She knew he'd left the diary section and was now contributing regularly to his paper's political analysis. She'd followed his progress with grudging admiration.

'Hello Evie.'

'Hello.'

Matthew met her eye and smiled. 'Enjoy the play?'

And Evie, looking back at him – looking back, and instantly regretting it – she barely heard the question. With Matthew now so close and smiling gently, eye-to-eye, the moment of calm observation she'd had a moment ago, the easy way she'd been able to watch him with Honor and Xandra and think, quite detachedly, about the developments in his career . . . it vanished. And suddenly it was as if the intervening years hadn't happened at all; it was as if she'd scurried away from his flat in Kilburn – angry and miserable, out into the downpour – just last week, and the idea of having a civilised discussion with him about the strengths and weaknesses of Abe's new show was absolutely beyond her. She didn't even try to play along.

'I'm sorry, Matthew. I . . .'

Again he smiled. 'Just wondering what you thought about the play. It seems to have had something of a mixed response.'

'Oh I see! I'm sorry. I – I just wasn't expecting—'

'Abe invited me.'

'*Abe*?'

His smile seemed to twist a little. 'I imagine he hoped I might be able to find him some sort of publicity. It's not really my area any more of course, but I thought I might be able to help out. My successor at the diary's pretty malleable and there's always a chance they'd find a slot for someone like Abe . . .'

Evie couldn't hide her astonishment. Thinking back to Honor's party at the Wellesley Hotel; back to Abe's dismissive remarks in the cab home, when he'd looked at the business card Matthew had given Evie and discovered what he did for a living . . . back to Abe's view of journalists – all journalists – as irritating flies, and the disparaging way he and Honor would talk about such people . . .

'You're surprised?'

'I just didn't think that he . . .'

Matthew helped himself to a glass of Abe's fine wine. 'It's amazing what people will do when they're desperate, Evie – particularly when they're desperate for publicity. Usually I refuse. But something about this little show sort of . . . grabbed . . . me . . .'

Wondering why it was he'd stopped talking, why he was suddenly looking over her left shoulder, Evie turned around – and saw that it was Ian, in his overcoat.

'Oh Ian! Oh God—'

'It's okay.' The tone of Ian's voice and the smile he gave her . . . it was oddly mild, until Evie remembered his refusal to present himself as anything other than balanced and controlled when there were strangers about, and his utter distaste for open disagreements. And even though the smile was clearly more for Matthew's benefit than Evie's, even though – in another context – its falseness would have irritated her, she was somehow glad of it tonight. Glad that she and Ian would not appear at odds.

'Just thought I might go and check on the car, darling. Make sure it's still there . . .'

Evie smiled back. 'Then I'll come with you.'

The decision was instant. Easily made. No matter

322

that she'd just accused Honor of letting Abe down by not staying on to the bitter end . . . All Evie could think about was getting away from Matthew. Putting a hand on Ian's arm, she felt the comforting gaberdine of his trenchcoat. The very neutrality of its colour and cut seemed to offer an escape from the way Matthew was making her feel – the sweaty fever down her back, the heady weakness she might get from looking over a steep, sharp drop, half-wanting to throw herself over, half horrified at the impulse.

'Well goodbye then,' said Matthew, bending to kiss her cheek.

Safe now, with Ian's sleeve clenched tight in the palm of her hand, Evie looked back at Matthew. Looked straight and smiled properly. 'Goodbye,' she replied. 'It was good to see you.'

'You too.'

They moved away. And as they did, she saw Abe hurrying purposefully towards them.

'Hang on a second,' she said to Ian. 'I'd better just—'

But it wasn't Evie that Abe wanted. 'Matthew!' he cried, brushing past them. 'Oh – wonderful! You're here!' He was sniffing heavily. Evie saw the shine on his skin; his eyes shrunk to pinpricks. A sharp black fringe flopped over his forehead. He smelt of sweat and cigarettes. It was really quite astonishing that he could remain attractive, even in that state.

'Bye Abe,' she said.

The pinpricks swung towards her for a moment. 'Oh – oh Evie . . . oh, bye . . .'

But his mind was just too jumpy, too airy – fizzing and crackling and darting around the surface of the party like some unstable compound on a pool of water. Already, he was turning back to Matthew – burning off

323

a white light of charm as he put a hand on Matthew's shoulder and guided him off in the other direction.

'You're not going anywhere, are you mate? I know Rhianna would love to meet you – and Miles. They're by the ticket desk, if you . . . Sure – just let me know.' Another sniff. 'I really appreciate this. I – you think you have a story? We can always dig around for one if that's any help . . .'

Evie and Ian left the pub in silence and made their way round the corner – into the mews where her car was parked. Just ahead of them, striding out across the cobbles, was the hard silhouette of a man wearing a knee-length coat and narrow trousers. He, too, seemed headed for the mews. The pale grey oval of his close-cut head was bent in concentration – listening to some message on a mobile telephone as, with his free hand, he opened the door of a silver Mercedes and quietly slid inside.

Two days later Matthew's review was out. Evie read it on the Tube, squashed amongst rain-spattered commuters.

Despite having a company car, she did not always drive to and from work. Often it was quicker and easier to leave her car at the office and go by Underground, especially when she'd been drinking with colleagues or when the traffic was dismal and she needed to get home early . . . as was the case that day. Ian had some papers he wanted to show her: some particulars and photographs of a three-bedroom family house in Chelsea.

'Sounds great,' she'd said when he called her at the office earlier that afternoon. 'You think the vendor might be interested in instructing us?'

324

'Not exactly.'

Evie frowned. 'Then . . .'

'I was thinking you might want it.'

'What – me, personally?'

'Why not?'

Evie laughed. 'But Ian—'

'Just hear me out, will you? And then make up your mind.'

Explaining that the vendors were desperate to sell – that some sudden personal crisis he'd happened to discover about the couple that morning now led him to believe that the place could go for as little as 60 per cent of its proper price – Ian couldn't bear to let it slip away. Not, at least, without offering it to Evie. For himself, he'd no desire to move back into the heart of London – he liked living in St Albans, liked the larger houses and the sense that he was surrounded by responsible, like-minded people – but Evie's situation was rather different and her Hoxton flat (which they both knew was worth a good fifty grand more than the price she paid for it) was a real possibility when it came to finding the cash. Certainly, she'd have no trouble selling it. With all the fashionable publicity the area had received recently – together with the modern layout of Evie's flat, and the fittings still so new . . . Ian already knew of five or six people looking for something that fitted its exact description. Handled correctly, the place could go for as much as £200,000. It was, in short, the perfect time for Evie to realise the investment she'd made back in the summer. Moving twice in one year wasn't ideal – he realised that – but surely the prospect of making three or four hundred grand in the process would more than compensate her for any temporary inconvenience . . .

325

So Evie was hurrying home – high, from the idea of making quite so much money in quite such a short space of time. She'd heard about estate agents pulling off this sort of thing in the eighties, but had never thought it could happen to her. Not so soon, at any rate. Not in the current climate. Telling herself it was probably nothing, that the vendors had probably found another buyer by now, or maybe their crisis wasn't as serious as Ian had thought, maybe they'd hold out for a decent price after all . . . Evie turned her attention to the newspaper in her hands, and her thoughts to Abe's play and what – if anything – Matthew might have written.

It was tight and steamy in the Underground carriage – too cramped for newspapers – and there were frowns and winces as Evie opened her copy. She rustled it quickly into position, arranging the pages, folding them back and back again, until the entire paper was reduced to a block the size of a novel with only Matthew's article in view. And as the train lurched on, as doors opened and closed, as tourists and shop assistants joined bankers and lawyers and the whole incongruous lot rolled north to Old Street, Evie blinkered her attention to the print before her eyes.

Her first reaction was one of relief. The article might not have had Matthew's name attached, but he was clearly behind it. Clearly responsible. And in spite of the way he'd held off over Diana Miller, Evie still didn't think it beyond a man of Matthew's mindset – she'd read his political articles; she knew how acidic he could be – to prefer a nasty juicy story over one that gave bland blanket support. And she was glad for Abe that her fears had been unfounded. There was no mention of forgotten lines; no reference, even oblique, of drugs abused or the dismal state of Abe's health. But there was also something about it that made her uncomfortable without quite knowing why. Only when she got back home and was showing the piece to Ian did she realise what it was.

'"... the talented Abram Wyatt"?' he read out loud, adding the question mark himself, '"shines in this subtle play about one man's obsession with precision"?'

Evie looked at Ian, sitting on the sofa, reading the article out to the end.

'And – and this is by that friend of yours?' he said, looking up. 'The one you were talking to when we left?'

Evie nodded.

'So he's a theatre critic . . .'

'Not really.' Evie smiled. 'Strictly, he's on the political desk. But I suppose he must have thought he could help Abe out a bit and, judging from the article, I'd say he's more than—'

'The political desk?' said Ian, sitting forward – the paper still in his hands. He read the *Morning Post* from time to time. 'What did you say his name was?'

'Matthew Forrester. He—'

'What, that *boy*?'

Evie frowned.

'That – that lad, with the jeans and the baseball shoes and the studenty hair?' Ian went on, astonished. '*That's* Matthew Forrester?'

'Yes . . .' said Evie slowly. 'But he's not a boy, Ian. He's over thirty.'

Ian smiled.

'And he has had a fair bit of experience. Not in politics, maybe. But they made him editor of the gossip section a few years back, which – poor thing – he hated, but it doesn't seem to have done his career much harm. And now he—'

'But he looks almost my age in his picture!'

Evie smiled. 'I guess that's the intention.'

'And his writing, Evie – it . . . Jesus.' Ian examined the article again, shaking his head in disbelief. 'I've quoted this boy in client reports! I . . . If he's the man I'm thinking of, Evie, then he's seriously good—'

'You sound surprised,' said Evie, amused.

But Ian wasn't listening. 'Won some prestigious award last year – I'm certain of it. Yet – yet the man still finds time to make it down to the Leinster Pit . . .' he murmured, staring at the article and the picture of Abe – standing in front of his co-star with hands outstretched, a scalpel in one of them. 'He sits through a dismal performance, turns up at the party afterwards to find the star attraction trashed, and then – then he goes away and comes up with something like this?'

'I think he just wanted to do Abe a favour.'

Ian shook his head. 'Well whatever Abe did for him in the past, it must have been pretty special.' Throwing the newspaper to one side, he felt in his briefcase for the file on the Chelsea property. 'Now. I've got some of the details with me here – and we're getting some more tomorrow – but really, the sooner you can make a decision, darling, the lower the price will be . . .'

And Evie, in spite of herself – and in spite of all the bitterness and anger she'd nurtured towards Matthew over the years – was filled instead with warmth. Remembering all the unpleasant things Abe had said about Matthew in the past – knowing he owed Abe nothing – Evie could not help but be stirred by Ian's reaction.

This gesture of Matthew's – this generosity towards

Abe – it robbed her of reasons to stay hostile. How could she keep her fists clenched tight in the face of something like this article? Even the memory of what had happened back at Favenham that spring – the way he'd ended it with her, so brusque, so cold . . . even that seemed somehow acceptable. When she remembered the way her uncle had spoken to him, and – yes, she could face it now – the sad fact that Matthew simply couldn't have been *that* interested . . . and, frankly, why should he have been? What on earth did a girl like Evie have to offer a man of Matthew Forrester's calibre? . . . in the light of all this, what else could he have done? With hindsight, a clean break probably was best. Kindest, even.

Taking the Chelsea papers from Ian, she tried to concentrate as he outlined very carefully, step-by-step, the risks and rewards involved in bidding for a property in rushed and vulnerable circumstances. Bit by bit she began to feel that familiar coolness seeping back into her brain. Yes, there were problems for her to address with this new property, but these were the sort of problems she knew she could handle. Facing them gave her that same sense of restored control she'd had the other night – mixed, perhaps, with something very slightly closed; something a little sanitised . . . rather like some hot August afternoon when she'd have to get into her car to go for a viewing and – after five minutes of baking hell – feel a sudden gust of airconditioning sweep across the sweaty surface of her skin.

Chapter Eighteen

Pipe Dreams

'It'll only be a couple of hours, Ian. He— sure, I know. But he seemed so keen to have us there – have us *both*. And it's a great-sounding place . . .'

Evie sat at her desk – head cricked round, the telephone wedged between her jaw and her collarbone – listening to Ian's objections while simultaneously correcting a draft set of particulars that Linda had just typed out for her.

'His club, apparently. It— no . . .' She chuckled. 'No, it's a thespy-arty sort of place. The kind they write up in magazines because – because Yasmin le Bon goes there, or whoever . . . in Soho, that's right – which isn't so far from your offices, and no doubt costs Abe a fortune in membership subscription, but— no, *he's* paying! For everyone. He—' Evie sighed. 'Of course I believe him, Ian. Come on. He's not that bad. Might drink a bit. Might take a few drugs . . .'

Linda looked up.

'. . . Might take a few drugs,' Evie repeated in a lower voice, swivelling her chair so that she no longer faced into the office. 'Might be a bit flaky – I don't know – but he's never once, in all the time I've known him, scrounged off anyone or *left his wallet behind*. He— no, Ian. You can't say that sort of thing without—'

Hearing the agency's shop-bell ring, she glanced up to see a harassed-looking middle-aged woman come in with a dog on a lead. The woman had been out in the street for some time, inspecting the properties in the window and making notes. She was scruffy and inelegant but there was something about her expression, her lack of glamour, added to the fact that she'd been making notes, that caught Evie's attention.

'Well do what you like,' she said suddenly. 'I thought you might be interested to meet Matthew properly, and if Abe's offered to pay for us all I'm surprised you're not jumping at the chance. But if you— fine. Okay. I've no idea what's in the fridge, but— sure. Whatever. Bye.'

Getting up from her desk, Evie hurried forward into the office – hoping to catch the woman and her dog before Linda passed them on to Nick or James. She still had to watch for these moments. Couldn't rely on Linda to spread the applicants fairly between them, and this was definitely an applicant with potential. 'Can I help at all?'

Within five minutes, she'd found six properties that matched the woman's criteria and was picking out the right sets of keys from the cupboard and pulling her coat from its hanger. The woman was delighted to get started. She didn't seem bothered by the fact that Christmas was just round the corner. The sooner she found somewhere the better.

'How wonderful,' she said, happily flicking through the particulars Evie had given her. 'My husband will be thrilled. Are you sure you don't mind Henry coming with us in the car?'

Evie looked down at Henry – a fat yellow Labrador with very muddy feet – and decided that a dirty car was, in this case, worth the effort. 'Not at all.'

Two hours later, she was back in the office, with three second viewings already booked for Saturday morning when the woman's husband would be free. From the way the woman was talking, it seemed as if it was simply a matter of which of those three properties he would prefer. Evie sensed the quickest, easiest deal of the year – the woman was just so friendly and polite, so easily pleased, so keen to make a decision . . . the perfect applicant. Evie was determined to hold on. She'd hoped to get away early for Christmas, but the idea of squeezing in one final deal beforehand was too tempting.

'Right,' she said, smiling at the dog – and then at the woman – as she handed over her business card and opened the door to the street. It was dark and clear and cold outside. 'I'll see you Saturday morning, then. Ten o'clock. Redcliffe Gardens . . .'

It was only when she sat back down at her desk and checked twice through the pile of telephone messages that had accrued in her absence . . . only then did Evie notice what wasn't there and realise that she'd been rather hoping that Ian would change his mind, that he'd have left some backtracking sort of message to say he'd be coming after all. But it wasn't going to happen. Ian wasn't coming. And, biting her lower lip, Evie turned her thoughts to the evening ahead and the prospect of having to go alone, without him by her side.

*

When Abe discovered Honor was planning to be in London for a few nights without Edward, he'd been determined to take advantage of it. Having already invited Matthew out to dinner to thank him for that career-enhancing review, the idea of getting her to join them seemed really rather clever. She'd never accept dinner with him *à deux* – Abe knew that – but with Matthew there as well she might just be persuaded.

'And – and Evie?' Honor had said.

Abe hesitated. Having Evie meant having Ian, and he really didn't think . . .

'Oh come on, Abe. You can't *not*—'

'I know. I know . . .'

It seemed almost too good to be true to then hear that Ian wouldn't be coming. And Abe – with a sense that the wind was behind him, that his run of bad luck was finally at an end – got out of the cab that evening with a spring in his step and hurried into his Soho club. He was early, but that was no bad thing if he was going to get the corner table he wanted.

Half an hour later, her palms sweating, Evie stood with Honor at the entrance to the club.

Not wanting to face Ian that night, she'd decided to accept Honor's invitation to shower and get ready at Launceston Villas – which was, in any case, no distance at all from the office. Feeling like a teenager, she'd stood on the fluffier, newer-looking bit of carpet where her bed used to be – the twin beds were now firmly clamped together in recognition of Honor's married state. She'd looked at the photographs on the clipboard by Honor's dressing table and wondered what those two giggling girls would have made of the women they'd become.

'I've booked a cab for eight,' said Honor, poking her head around the door. 'Okay?'

She was, as usual, perfectly dressed. Her hair gleamed. It seemed as if the pair of rings on her wedding finger – sparkling and twinkling as she caught back the edge of the door to stop it from banging open – seemed as if they'd always been there. And Evie, smiling her assent, realised that the younger Honor would have known exactly what the older Honor would become. There'd never been any doubt.

Waiting now to be let into Abe's club – while, behind them, the street hummed with watchful tourists, unlicensed cabs and damaged-looking teenage boys – Evie was glad that Honor was wearing gloves; that those sparkly rings of privilege weren't quite so beckoningly evident. Smashed glass glittered in the gutter. In front of them, there was a reinforced door with a small black camera in the top right-hand corner.

'Evie Langton and Honor Beaumaris,' she said for a second time. 'Guests of Abram Wyatt?'

'Hang on.'

The bright light of the video intercom shone over them both. There was then a short pause before the door buzzed open.

Upstairs on the first floor, they handed over their coats and signed their names in a large black book before being ushered further up, past bars and sitting rooms and private dining rooms, and on to a perversely unfinished-looking restaurant at the very top – with plain floorboards, chunky wooden tables, coarse curtains and weathered chairs. Xandra would have found it most confusing. Abe and Matthew were both there, sitting drinking.

It was easy to spot Abe. He'd taken a seat facing out

334

into the room and, as they entered, was leaning forward to say something to Matthew. He wasn't dressed flamboyantly, or talking particularly loudly – but still, without even looking up, he radiated that peculiar energy that involved an entire room, not simply the person he was talking to. It was the same energy that had once caught the eye of Karen Rossetti, an energy that made people look at him before they even knew quite why.

Matthew sat at a right angle to Abe, in profile to the door. He was leaning back against the wall, smoking – his face well outside the hemisphere of candlelight that rose from the middle of the table; deliberately obscure. And it was Matthew, not Abe, who saw them at the door.

'Ah . . .'

Abe followed his cue: looking out, jumping up. 'Oh, excellent! Excellent!' With Matthew still stubbing his cigarette out, Abe was on his feet and coming forward – 'Thanks, Naomi' – kissing them both and leading them back to the table. 'You found us! Wonderful! Now come and sit down . . . Honor, you go in – that's right – next to me. And Evie . . . you okay there? You sure? You . . . Great. Now' – to all three of them, almost as if he were making an announcement – 'how about some champagne?'

Taking a wine list from the waitress, he ordered two bottles of vintage Krug and two further bottles of disconcertingly superior-sounding claret. 'I hope that's all right,' he said, smiling as he sat down. 'If anyone wants fish, we can always order white as well, but—'

'Abe . . .'

'What?'

Evie looked at him, straight. 'It's too generous,' she

335

said. 'It's enough that you're taking us all out. It's more than enough. You mustn't feel you have to . . . I mean, we'd all be quite happy – more than happy – with house wine. You know that.'

But Abe merely laughed. 'Oh, *Evie* . . .' he said, leaning forward and kissing her cheek. 'Evie sweetheart, just indulge me – can't you? It's not often I have something to celebrate.'

Evie hesitated – looking to the others for support. Abe needed to change this absurd order. He simply couldn't afford Krug and Haut-Brion. He could hardly afford his heating bills, for God's sake. They shouldn't be letting him do this.

But something in the way Honor and Matthew were both looking back at her – their wariness; a patent unwillingness to side with her – made Evie hold fire. She knew them both too well to think it was greed, or a sense that Abe owed them something, that prompted this reluctance. They . . . no . . . Evie's brain searched feverishly . . . no, it had to be something better, something higher, something to do with the importance of not denting Abe's pride. If it had been just one of them holding back, she might have ploughed on. But with both staying quiet, it put Evie in the rare position of wondering if she was wrong. Perhaps, tonight, Abe's pride was more important than his bank balance. Perhaps it was better to take a more deferential line – let Abe spend his money as he wished and handle the consequences. Clearly neither Honor nor Matthew felt it was their place to question his generosity. And their combined approach had a decided influence on Evie's.

'Oh well,' she grinned at Abe. 'If you're sure . . .'

'Of course I'm sure!'

So she drank her Krug with gusto. And although she

couldn't help but be indignant when, a little later, Abe tasted the wine and seemed slightly disappointed . . . Adamant he should return it, adamant that at least Abe should get some value for all this money he was spending – 'Don't you dare let them fob you off with a dodgy bottle! You – here. Give it to me' – Evie took the glass from Abe's hand, found the wine waiter, made him taste it, and bring another bottle . . . but aside from that, she made no further attempt to dissuade Abe from his course. She said nothing when the menus arrived – strictly à la carte and no prices – choosing lamb rather than lobster, but avoiding any obvious efforts to save him money by going for soup and fish-cakes. And instead, she joined the others in keeping the conversation in the happier – if somewhat optimistic – realms of Abe's future career.

'So it's really been a sell-out?' Honor was saying.

Abe smiled. 'Only thanks to Matthew's review,' he dutifully replied – raising his glass in Matthew's direction. 'Without that, I'm not sure it would even have lasted the week. Far less the—'

'Rubbish.'

'It's true, Matthew. Really. I can't tell you the difference it's made. There's even talk of it going to the West End.'

'But that's wonderful!' said Matthew warmly. 'And I have to say, it only backs up my point. It – come on Abe,' he urged. 'There has to be something inherently good at the heart of your play to get that sort of result. I'm no proper critic – and I've no idea how these things work – but I'm pretty certain no one gets air-lifted into the West End on the back of some half-baked review in the *Morning Post*!'

Abe hesitated. 'It – it is only talk,' he said. 'There's

nothing certain . . .' But with all that lovely Krug inside him, and all that lovely food to come, and all the pretty people flowing into the club . . . the other actors, and writers, and models, and producers . . . they all noticed Abe, all happened to meet his eye because that's just what people did, no matter how important they were, because that was Abe's particular talent . . . and all of it happening on the right side of the club's reinforced front door, all passing inspection; all ushered through and up . . . away from the smashed glass and the vomit and all the ugly noises of the gutter . . . Abe couldn't help but feel blessed. His luck was turning; his time had come. He was still, in spite of everything, a member of the club. And now, with Honor beside him, so admiring, so pleased for him, so seemingly impressed . . . he barely needed the artificial stimulants in his pocket.

'Came last night,' he said, in answer to her question about his agent. 'Seemed pretty happy with the way things are going. It's not the same one as before.'

'Oh?'

'But that's good!'

'Oh!' Honor smiled.

'See, the problem with Karen is that she never really got me,' Abe went on, filling her glass. 'I mean, obviously she's good at what she does – and she represents some big names – but . . . but some of the decisions she made for me, the projects she pushed me into . . .'

'Like Spain?'

'In a way. And America was a disaster. Way too early for me to make that sort of transition . . .'

Honor nodded.

'Especially when she wasn't prepared even to come

338

over and represent me in person. You need a certain level of support in this business. It simply isn't possible on your own. And there's nothing like having someone totally devoted to *your* interests.'

Honor smiled.

'And Karen just had too many other people to think about. She never had time for me. She'd never have come to see something like *Brainpower*. She wouldn't have thought it important. Whereas Nigel . . .'

Honor listened as he babbled. Perhaps it was all true – why shouldn't it be? But the longer he talked, the more obvious it became to her which way the wind was blowing. It wasn't that any of it was lying, exactly. It was the way he felt he had to highlight the things that were good; and that particular sort of vagueness with the things that weren't. West End opportunities that might present themselves; casting directors that might want to see him; film parts he might be up for – all possible, but none of it certain. None of it, that is, except for Matthew's kind review.

She glanced across at Matthew – playing with his cigarette packet while discussing the London property market with Evie – and thought back to that early Oxford weekend when Evie had come up and brought him with her. She remembered the horror she'd felt when she realised it was her – Honor – he'd fancied . . .

'But that's amazing,' he was saying. He seemed genuinely taken aback. 'I'm clearly in the wrong job! You – Christ, Evie – that's brilliant. You must have made a fortune.'

Evie shook her head. 'Much as I'd love to take the credit . . .' she said, smiling, 'I have to say it was completely down to Ian.'

Matthew didn't look convinced.

'It's true, sadly. My only skill was in deciding to take his advice – which I suppose in itself was pretty smart of me. But Ian was the one who found this extraordinary house in Chelsea . . . and the flat in Hoxton, too, come to think of it . . . and steered me through the negotiations. He's a complete genius, especially when it comes to sniffing out the right investments.'

Matthew bent his head a fraction more, intent on pressing out the crumples in his cigarette packet. 'And other things as well, no doubt,' he said with a casual laugh.

Looking back at him for a moment, Evie decided to say nothing – choosing simply to radiate contentment instead. Fuck it. All she had to do was make Matthew believe she no longer cared for him. After all, it was no more than the truth: Matthew had been out of her life for years and she was doing perfectly well without him. What better way to achieve this air of indifference than give the impression that Ian was something of a god?

Matthew clocked the beatific smile. Sighing, he put his cigarettes to one side. 'So things are pretty good for you right now, aren't they?'

Holding her smile, Evie nodded.

'Great job, great house, great boyfriend . . .'

'Ah well.' She shrugged. 'It wasn't so sunny a few years ago, I can tell you. I've really had to work to get where I am. It hasn't been easy . . .'

Matthew bit his lip.

'And when I think of all the shit I've had to deal with, and all that failing, and all those put-downs, I have to say I rather think I deserve a bit of a break,' she went on, helping herself to more wine. 'Having been so

340

useless at school, and useless with money, and useless with jobs, and useless wi—'

'With choosing men,' he finished for her. 'Good God, you've had some shockers there!'

Amused, Evie met his eye. 'Well maybe *some* . . .'

Fascinated, Honor looked at them: at Matthew – so intent on what Evie was saying, so deeply focused it was as if there was no one else in the room . . . not even Honor. And then at Evie – who, for some mysterious reason, seemed particularly beautiful that night. Certainly she'd made no obvious efforts with her appearance. Her hair fell in exactly the same way – a little more curve, perhaps, a little more shine, but nothing that could explain the distinctly seductive quality it seemed to have acquired in the last half-hour. Then there was the line of the top she'd been wearing all day at the office: scooped and fitted, clean against her skin, with a brush-gleam of silver at her neck. No special effort, nothing expensive, but again unmistakeably transformed. Perhaps it was simply the way she was sitting: more upright, more balanced . . . heightened, in some way. Or perhaps it was just the lighting in the room. For all its superficial attempts to appear plain and unconsidered, it was clear to Honor the longer she sat there that someone had thought a great deal about the design of the restaurant, generating an impression of simplicity while giving its clientele maximum comfort and flattery. Everyone looked great. But still . . . there was something special about Evie right now, and it was hard not to conclude that Matthew was the reason.

'Oh God. Please.' Evie was laughing. 'Please, Matthew – it really couldn't matter less. Not now!'

341

'I still think I could have behaved better. Treated you better. It—'

'Listen to me, will you? It was years ago. Years. And I was hopeless back then – so stupid and chippy, so caught up in that mad crush I had on you . . . God knows what possessed me. I'm surprised you didn't lose patience weeks earlier. I must have been a nightmare!'

'No you weren't, Evie. You—'

'Oh, but I was! Believe me, you did exactly the right thing – for both of us, as it's turned out – don't you agree? I mean,' she was laughing again, 'can you imagine if we were still together now? How unsuited we'd be, how—'

'More champagne?' said Abe, suddenly.

Honor turned. 'Oh – oh, I'm sorry Abe.'

'Come on.' Smiling, he tipped the bottle over her glass. 'You've hardly had a drop! And we've a whole other bottle to get through, so you're really going to have to start making an impression on your evening's quota because I'm certainly not having any of it wasted! It's—'

'Really, Abe. I . . . Thank you, but I won't.'

Abe stared at her. 'But you love champagne! I know you do! You—'

'I'd just rather not tonight. I'm sorry, Abe. I know it's wonderful – and I do love champagne . . . you're absolutely right. But . . .'

Abe put the bottle down. 'You're not pregnant, are you?'

Evie and Matthew turned.

'Oh no!' said Honor, laughing. 'I – no! God, no! I . . .'

'Then why won't you drink with us?' Abe demanded. 'What is it? Krug not good enough for you

342

any more? Is it Cristal, these days? Or Dom Perignon? Or—'

'Abe, man.' Matthew put the bottle back into its ice bucket. 'She doesn't have to drink.'

'But—'

'Don't bully her.'

Confused – bullying was the last thing he wanted to do to Honor – Abe looked anxiously at Honor. 'I'm sorry,' he said quickly. 'I didn't mean—'

'It's all right.' She smiled back at him. 'But please, Abe – please put any ideas of me being pregnant out of your mind, will you? I'm nowhere near ready for anything like that.'

'You are *married* . . .' said Evie suddenly, giving her cousin a crafty look.

'Sure, Evie. But I'm also only twenty-five.'

Evie raised an eyebrow. 'Some people would say twenty-five's an ideal age to have kids.'

'Well I'm not one of them,' said Honor, rather too quickly. Then, trying to keep the tone light, 'Of course Edward and I will want children at some point but, right now, we have other things to do with our lives . . .'

What, like gardening courses and interior decorating? thought Evie, to herself.

'There's absolutely no hurry.'

'So you're not pregnant, then?'

'No!' cried Honor. 'And, for the record, I'm not planning to be pregnant for some time yet!'

Evie gave her an affectionate smile. 'Well in that case, Honor, there's absolutely no excuse for you and Edward to go on hiding away in Suffolk like a couple of old hermits . . .'

Cajoling Honor and Edward into moving back to London had become something of a project for Evie in the past year or so. While it seemed they'd opted to postpone the baby stage – and while, of course, that decision had Evie's wholehearted approval – she still couldn't understand why they persisted in living out in the middle of nowhere. There'd be all the time in the world, once children arrived, for open fields and ponies and good fresh air. Now, surely – as a young married couple with lots of money and no responsibilities – now was the time for Honor and Edward to be living it up in London. They needed diversions and excitements, and – for sure – a more varied social life than their current diet of shooting parties and garden openings that country living had to offer.

Evie also suspected that, with the right kind of prodding, Honor might even agree with some of this. She knew how much her cousin enjoyed coming to London. She could tell Honor was tempted by the idea. And now . . . aware that, in Abe and Matthew, she might have found some useful allies – aware, too, that with Edward absent, she might have rather more influence than usual – Evie was delighted at this sudden opportunity to address the subject again. Certainly, Honor didn't seem averse to it – smiling and rolling her eyes as Evie went on.

'It's a great time to buy, you know,' she said, looking mischievously at the others. 'Only yesterday I was measuring up the most beautiful house in Notting Hill – in Stanley Place? You know – just off Ladbroke Grove . . .'

'Please, Evie. Don't tempt me. I—'

'*Stanley Place*?' said Abe, twinkling. 'That must be just around the corner from Stanley's restaurant.'

'That's right.' Evie twinkled back.

'God, how delicious . . .' Abe rolled his eyes. 'Nigel

took me there last month and – *oh* – the truffle ravioli . . .'

'Only this particular house is at the quieter end.'

'Even better.'

'I know. There's the most beautiful cluster of cherry trees or apple trees somewhere up that end – the blossom's just magical in the spring – yet it's still close enough to Notting Hill and Portobello and all those pretty shops you love so much, Honor. And honestly, the house itself is something else . . .'

'My aunt used to live in Stanley Place,' said Matthew, turning to Honor with a more serious expression. 'When the whole area was a bit more bohemian . . . and she loved it. I remember it had the most beautiful garden – really exceptional – and so much space . . . I promise you, it was almost like living in the country.'

Smiling, Honor bit her lip. 'It does sound dreamy . . .'

'Well you have to see this one then,' said Evie as if the matter were already settled. 'At least *view* it, Honor. I could take you there tomorrow. It's got the most stunning French windows in the drawing room, leading out on to a balcony, and steps down to . . .' looking at Matthew, 'to, as you say, the most exceptional garden. And it's got six bedrooms, and the most perfect little study for – for Edward, I suppose it would be – and a laundry room, and even a self-contained flat in the basement if you—'

'Stop it! Stop!'

But the more Honor objected, the clearer it was to all of them that the idea of moving back to London really grabbed her. And the more they probed, the more it seemed that the reasons she and Edward had for staying out in Suffolk were hardly conclusive. It wasn't even as if Edward had so much work to do down at Allenham these days. In the two years since their wedding, he'd managed to establish himself as his father's successor – and with a new farm-manager he liked and trusted, and a young bright agent to consult on the more strategic elements of how to make the best of his property, the place could almost run itself. Certainly there was no pressing need for them to stay there permanently. And, as Evie so rightly said, the country was for children. Right now, Honor and Edward should be in London. It was a great time to invest.

Honor needed no more convincing. She'd be on to Edward tomorrow about it, just as soon as she got home . . .

It was after midnight by the time they'd finished dinner and were down again at the reception desk – collecting their coats, thanking Abe and kissing each other goodbye.

'Thanks Abe. Completely unnecessary, but still wonderful' – Matthew grinned at him – 'and deeply unethical. I won't hesitate to give you any number of glowing reviews now – no matter what kind of rubbish it is!'

Laughing, Abe shook the hand he was offering. 'But – but you'll come with me to Max's, won't you? It's only round the corner. Just a quick snifter, before . . .'

Taking his coat from the girl at the desk, Matthew put it on. 'Sorry mate. I'm in trouble enough as it is, without—'

'Trouble?'

Matthew smiled. 'It was bad enough leaving poor

346

Sally in the lurch on my last night in London. If she knew that – well, that we weren't exactly alone . . .'

Abe opened his eyes very wide. 'You mean you didn't tell her?'

'I—'

'*Matthew*!'

'Well . . . well as you only told me yourself this afternoon, I could hardly—'

'No reason not to tell her too.'

'Absolutely,' said Matthew, regaining his composure as they followed Evie and Honor down the stairs and out into the street. 'And no doubt I will when I get a moment. But my position won't exactly be improved if she discovers we went on to Max's bar . . .'

Sally. Standing apart from the others on the cold Soho pavement, Evie's bravado vanished. Who the fuck was Sally?

'And I've got to be up at six to catch a flight to Washington.'

'Washington?' said Honor, interested.

Matthew smiled at her expression. 'Oh – nothing very distinguished, I'm afraid. The usual guy's just had to go suddenly into hospital and apparently we have to have *someone* out there over Christmas in case the world blows up, or Hillary does a runner or – or God knows what . . . And for some reason the editor picked me. It's only until they know how serious it is and can find a proper replacement. And,' sighing now, 'I'm just the poor sod they happened to pick on. Much to poor Sal's fury . . .'

'And – and Sally's your girlfriend?' said Honor, very carefully – casting a quick glance at Evie to be certain she was listening.

Matthew nodded. 'Although she of all people

347

should understand – being in the same line of work.'

Girlfriend. Journalist. So, no doubt clever and tough and . . . God, how depressing.

'But that's great!' said Honor, pressing on. 'And – and does she write the sort of things that we might have come across?'

Matthew smiled again. 'Well, Honor, that depends if you like long speculative articles with headlines like "My Bigamy Hell" or "How I Got My Perfect Breasts".' And then, suddenly spotting a passing cab, he hailed it. There was a shriek of brakes as the cab pulled in. 'You want this one?'

Honor hesitated. 'What about Evie,' she said, raising her voice a little. 'Evie?'

'Hm?'

'Would you like this cab?'

Evie took it. Bidding the others a brisk farewell, she got in and slammed the door.

Abe didn't mind going to bars alone – particularly not a bar like Max's, where most of the staff were now mates. He only wanted one shot of whisky. Or brandy . . . he still wasn't quite sure which, but it wasn't going to be a long one. He just wanted the comforting sensation of amber liquid trickling down his throat, and the warm feeling in his stomach. He could sit on one of the leather stools and ask Cindy, the barmaid, about that casting she'd had last week in Bristol . . .

Matthew let himself into the rented basement flat he was living in – to the sight of his life packed up into a couple of suitcases, bound and labelled for Washington. He'd said goodbye to Sally earlier that day and was glad to see she hadn't come back. The place was perfectly silent. Without bothering to switch on the lights, Matthew sat in the neutral armchair provided by his landlord, overlooked by a cheaply framed poster of Van Gogh irises, and put his head in his hands. Outside, someone passed along the pavement – a pair of stepping shadows crossing the room, neutral and anonymous against the dirty orange air of the night-time street. A sharp gust rattled the windows, stirring the slatted blinds. Something dry – a withered leaf, an old receipt – fluttered briefly at the glass before dropping down to the basement concrete. For a moment there was silence. And then, a little further off, a bin lorry beeped as it reversed.

'Darling?'
  'Mm.'
  'Darling . . .'
  'What is it, Ian?'
  'Are you sleepy?'
Evie lay completely still, her mind full of Matthew and Sally.

'I just thought . . .' Ian wriggled closer, putting a hand on her shoulder and reaching round to kiss her mouth. His breath was in her airspace. Still, Evie didn't move. It was all she could do not to push him from her.

But the idea of a conversation was infinitely worse. Evie was nowhere near ready for anything so final, wasn't even certain it was really what she wanted. Matthew's proximity was wrecking her sense of direction. There had been times tonight when he'd seemed . . . almost . . . regretful. But she now realised that must simply have been charm on Matthew's part – a charming display of regret because he knew he was safe, what with God-like Ian and everything. She had

349

Ian. He had Sally, and Washington, and God only knew what else. They'd – both of them – moved on. So what was the point in Evie ruining her own life, just because of some old crush she hadn't quite resolved?

And so, deciding that it was quicker and simpler to go along with Ian's desires than to turn on the light and try to explain herself, Evie rolled over and – splitting her mind from her body in a way that, a few years back, she'd have found quite impossible, immoral even – quietly let it happen.

It was still and bright at Allenham the following morning when, just before lunch, Honor's glossy new four-wheel drive crunched across the gravel and came to an abrupt halt. She couldn't wait to get home. All down the motorway she'd been thinking of last night and what the others had said about moving back to London. The more she thought of it, the more certain she became that, for now at least, it was the right thing for her and Edward to do.

It wasn't that she was unhappy at Allenham. Lord, no. She loved Suffolk. Loved the landscape. Was even growing to love the bulbous architecture of their house. She knew that it would always be her home, and that – one day – she'd have no desire to be anywhere else. But without children, wasn't it a little . . . premature? – to be living so far from her friends? With just the two of them in that great building, and Lavinia down the road, there were times when Honor felt that she and Edward were more like a retired couple than newlyweds. And now that Edward had the farm running so smoothly – now that he'd sorted out the agent and put in a new manager – was there really any need for them to stay out there

350

permanently? It wasn't as if they couldn't afford a second house in London.

Leaping lightly from the car, Honor left her suitcase and shopping sprawled along the back seat – she could deal with all that later – and made straight for the dry stone steps, eager to find Edward and talk to him about this new idea. She'd already worked out when they'd be able to get back to London together and view that house in Stanley Place. And if Edward agreed – at least to the viewing – then she'd have a couple of days to arrange for a few more properties for them to inspect at the same time . . . She couldn't wait to get started.

'Darling!' she called out, tossing her handbag on to one of the chairs in the hall.

The place was silent. 'Edward?'

She opened the door of his study, to find an empty desk with, surprisingly for Edward, his papers in disarray. A window had been left open and a few of his letters had slipped to the floor.

Frowning, Honor came back into the hall and then – noticing it was nearly lunchtime – made straight for the kitchen. It was quite a walk: through a small side door by the staircase in the hall and down a long stone passage. Honor hurried through. She could smell something cooking – something like fish pie. She could hear the one o'clock jingle of the local radio station Mrs Wilkins listened to, and a low professional voice reading the news headlines.

'Hello!' she said, coming in.

Mrs Wilkins stood up from one of the lower doors of the Aga with the fish pie in her hands.

'God, how delicious . . .' Honor sniffed at the pie. 'Sorry I'm late,' she went on. 'Traffic was terrible coming out of London – and I've no idea where

351

Edward's disappeared to, I'm afraid. You haven't seen him, have you? Had a quick look in his study just now, but . . .'

Mrs Wilkins put the pie down on the table and Honor could tell, simply by the sound of the pie dish landing – a little too suddenly – and the way Mrs Wilkins let it drop and skid – the lack of interest she showed in it – that something wasn't right. Looking round, Honor saw that the table was laid only for one. 'What's happened?'

'He's gone to the hospital,' said Mrs Wilkins, turning off the radio and finally meeting Honor's eye. 'He – he had to take Mrs Beaumaris. She . . .' Mrs Wilkins sighed and frowned.

'She what, Mrs Wilkins? What's happened to her?'

'She's not well.' Mrs Wilkins leant heavily on the Aga-rail. 'Not well at all. Terrible stomach pains, apparently, and she could hardly get up this morning, poor soul. Looked like death when I saw her in the car earlier, and that was . . . oh' – looking, now at the kitchen clock – 'two, three hours ago.'

Honor sat at the table. 'Any idea when they're coming back?'

Mrs Wilkins shook her head. 'I expect he'll call when they know,' she said.

It didn't take long for Lavinia's test results to arrive – not that they were really needed. Yes, she'd been discharged from hospital and – yes – she'd come home with a serious quantity and variety of painkillers. But it was clear, just from looking at her, that something was badly wrong.

For while she'd never shown much interest in appearing healthy, Lavinia's sense of glamour had always had a glorious energy all of its own. The sharp way she dressed, and an awareness of modern trends in the detail of her shoes, or a slight flash of lace at the hem of her skirt . . . such touches had always conveyed the impression of a woman who cared, who hadn't given up – not by so much as a millimetre. It was an approach to dressing that more than made up for any bodily weakness, and that was how Lavinia liked it. She'd always considered physical robustness in a woman to be slightly vulgar – certainly clumsy – and did what she could to avoid it. And because she'd seemed fragile for most of her adult life, nobody had noticed in the last few months as Lavinia had become genuinely sick. Intermittent stomach pains and occasional sleepless nights had been brushed aside with an extra coat of lipstick and a smart new pair of gloves.

But now, with this sudden turn for the worse – with pains she could no longer ignore, in spite of all those pills, and a total loss of appetite, and then all the humiliations of the hospital tests – Lavinia had stopped trying. She lay in bed with her hair askew, her eyes dull and her skin devoid of make-up – and it was more this change of attitude, this sudden absence of style, that made her condition seem particularly bleak. The classy impression of frailty that Lavinia had cultivated for decades was now, for the first time in her life, horribly, mockingly real.

Learning some days later that Lavinia definitely had cancer, and that there was a strong possibility it had advanced into her vital organs . . . it was, to Honor, mere confirmation of a fact so evident it barely needed saying. And Edward, it seemed, preferred to take that line. Certainly he showed no desire to talk about it directly. And Honor – knowing that her husband was hardly the sort of man to parade his darkest fears, knowing that there was much to admire in his fuss-free attitude – was almost relieved to see him handle himself in this way. It was an approach she understood. Taking her cues from him, she knew instinctively, without ever having to mention it, that any idea of them moving back to London was now quite out of the question.

Chapter Nineteen

Playing Doubles

In the end it was sympathy for Honor, rather than any real desire to spend a weekend at Allenham, that prompted Evie to accept the invitation. She'd been working harder than ever that spring and needed her weekends to relax, not drive three hours in heavy traffic to a place that was bound to put her on edge. No matter how much she loved being with Honor, the prospect of a whole weekend with Edward Beaumaris still filled Evie with dread. And the fact that Ian would be coming too did nothing to alleviate her reluctance.

She'd done her best to forget that strange evening at Abe's club – with Matthew being so interested and attentive, so flattering, so *possible* . . . and then, moments later, so clearly and obviously *not* possible. It hadn't taken long to find out about Sally Jarvis. By Christmas, Evie knew exactly which newspapers and magazines the woman wrote for, just how good she looked – with a byline photograph that made her appear more attractive than any of the people she interviewed – and how phenomenally tough and successful she was. And then, of course, there was that job he'd taken in Washington, which really put the nail in the coffin. So Evie – desperate not to sink back to the person she'd been when Matthew had last walked out, desperate to stop him from ruining her life a second time – Evie had pulled herself together in the past few months, clinging to Ian, determined to make it work.

Not that Ian was making it easy for her. She looked at him now – standing there on the other side of the four-poster bed they'd slept in, pulling on a pair of pristine tennis shorts.

'I thought you said you didn't play.'

Ian fastened the zip. 'I said I haven't *for a while*. And anyway, it doesn't mean I can't wear the appropriate clothes.'

'Sure Ian. But—'

'I might not be born to this kind of life,' he went on, as he wriggled into an equally pristine T-shirt and glanced at himself in the mirror. 'I might not have your aristocratic pedigree' – Evie winced.

– 'or a posh family home, but I do at least know what to wear.'

An hour later, after breakfast with the others – both dressed in jeans – Evie wondered if Ian was now regretting his whites. Wondered if he even knew he'd got it wrong. For Edward, with classic politeness that was hard not to admire, had immediately gone up to change after breakfast. His shorts weren't white but at least he'd tried, and Ian's legs didn't look quite so naked as the four of them made their way to the court.

It was some distance from the house. And as Edward led them out across the drive, past the mellow brick of a formal walled garden and then down into an orchard that Evie had never known existed – their passage narrowing to single-file along a path of sparkling grass; bending to avoid the sweep of a branch weighed low with blossom while, all around, birds were singing and soaring in the bright blue air . . . she inhaled the growing summer and couldn't help wondering if her sympathy for Honor had been misplaced. Certainly, it was hard to conceive of Honor being 'stuck' out here in Suffolk. After a week of angry London traffic and the choking fumes of tarmac being laid in the street outside her office, ducking to avoid the gang of battered-looking pigeons that gathered every afternoon around the half-eaten sandwiches that the workmen left behind, Evie's brain swelled like a sponge at the dazzling green of Edward's orchard. She struggled to remember exactly what it was that she loved about the hard grey scenery of her London life.

'Rough or smooth?' said Edward, spinning his racquet on the palm of his hand.

'Rough.'

He caught it and looked. 'Rough it is. You'll serve?'

Evie glanced at Ian – who was inexpertly tipping tennis balls out of their tins and watching them bounce into the net. She elected to receive.

In fact Edward wasn't as good as she'd expected. He had a swift serve that no one could return, and he had a certain style as he walked about the court. But Honor was really the best of the four, and certainly the most steady – able to knock gentle balls in Ian's direction; balls that he stood a chance of returning.

Evie wished that Ian would lighten up. Every time he served a double fault, he'd sigh and fret and roll his eyes, wailing 'What am I doing *wrong*?' It was like looking after a child.

'You need to toss the ball higher,' she instructed him. 'That's right. That's great. Well done. And again . . .?'

But Ian couldn't do backhands. The ball hit the side of his racquet and flew out, high over the surrounding mesh, landing in the long, wet grass of the orchard.

'Bugger.'

'Just leave it, Ian. We—'

'Ian?' yelled Edward, from across the net. 'Ian – leave it! We've got hundreds. It'll be soaking wet, and . . . Evie, can you tell him?'

But Ian was deaf to their wishes. 'I've marked it,' he muttered, heading out. 'If I don't get it now, we'll lose it altogether . . .'

It wasn't that he couldn't play. It was that he minded so terribly, and couldn't see it was just a game, approaching each shot with the same deadly intensity of purpose and absence of humour as one of his property transactions. And Evie was so caught up with observing this unattractive side of her boyfriend, she barely noticed what was happening – or rather, what wasn't happening – on the other side of the net.

It was only when Ian finally worked out how to volley and sent a ball so perfectly down the middle of the court that neither Honor nor Edward took it – nor, more significantly, even bothered to call it – that Evie began to wonder if everything was all right. She realised that while they both seemed happy enough to banter over the net, Honor and Edward said almost nothing to each other. When Honor served her third ace in a row, Edward didn't even bother to turn round, far less congratulate her or look pleased. And when Evie tried to copy Ian by sending another ball directly between them, the opposite happened: both went for it with vigour and collided. Honor's racquet slammed so hard on to Edward's exposed shin that it drew blood and caused him to crash to the ground.

358

'Oh *hooray*!' cried Ian, into the void. 'Well done, *darling*!'

There was silence as Edward got to his feet.

Honor reached for the fallen racquet. 'Are you all right?'

'I'm fine.'

They both looked at the damage – at the trickle of blood, drawing a slim red line from knee to sock.

She handed him the racquet and tried to put a hand on his arm – but it didn't seem comfortable there. 'I'm so sorry. I didn't mean—'

'Really, Honor. I'm fine.' He wasn't looking at her. 'Just get me a plaster or something, will you? And – and maybe some Pimm's while you're at it?'

'Sure.'

With Honor gone, Edward and Ian played singles. Evie was happy to sit out and watched, fascinated, as Edward set about teaching Ian how to improve his backhand. Not caring about his bloody shin, he sent ball after ball over the net for Ian to hit back. This was accompanied by a stream of patient running guidance, interspersed with attempts to make Ian laugh and relax so that soon the balls were gliding back effortlessly over the net, plum to the heart of Edward's racquet.

'What a great guy,' said Ian afterwards, undoing his shorts and wandering happily into their en suite bathroom. He wanted to be clean and fresh for Edward's mother, who was going to be joining them for lunch. 'What a really *great* guy – to take so much trouble . . .'

There was a thundering rush of water as he turned on the taps – a thundering rush that faded as he shut the bathroom door.

*

359

But Evie didn't like it, and there was little to alter her opinion when, at seven o'clock that evening, she and Ian were back once more in their bedroom – this time getting ready for a dinner party William was holding at Favenham. There'd been no major upset. Just small things, like the way Edward omitted to offer his wife any wine at lunch, so Honor had to get up and pour herself a glass. Or the way he praised the flower arrangement his mother had done for the table centre-piece, drawing everyone's attention to it, but failing to comment on the haddock soufflé that – in Mrs Wilkins's absence – Honor had gone to great lengths to prepare.

And it wasn't just Edward. For, rather to Evie's surprise, Honor was little better – 'not hearing' his request for ice cream to go with their apple crumble; and then later, suddenly disappearing in the middle of the afternoon so that Edward was forced to leave off showing Ian his father's old telescope and take Lavinia into Ipswich to have her hair done.

'You think she did it deliberately?' said Ian. He was standing at the long mirror with his chin in the air and his eyes squinting forward – trying to find the catch on his bow tie – while Evie sat at the dressing table, scrunching gel into her hair and observing his reflection in the mirror.

'Did what?'

'Ruining Edward's afternoon with that stunt she pulled.'

Evie didn't reply. Ian clipped his bow-tie in place, and then, turning for his dinner jacket, continued, 'Oh come on. Surely you noticed her disappearing just when his mother was expecting to leave. It—'

'What are you saying, Ian?'

'I'm just—'

'Because—'

'I'm not saying it was only Honor,' he pushed forward – double-interrupting. 'Don't misunderstand me, Evie. I'm sure he's every bit as bad. I just couldn't help wondering . . .'

Evie stopped scrunching and turned to look at him.

'Just wondered if everything was all right,' he stumbled on, surprised by her lack of awareness. Had she really not noticed anything strange? Was offhand behaviour between married couples normal in circles like this? 'I mean – obviously . . . on the surface, everything's great . . .'

'But what?'

'Oh I don't know.' Absent-mindedly he picked her jeans up from the floor and stood folding them. 'So you think they're happy, then?'

Evie shrugged. 'They seem all right,' she replied, turning on the hairdryer.

She simply didn't feel like gossiping about her friend. Of course Ian was right. Of course she'd seen the awkwardness. But the last thing Evie felt like doing was chatting it over with someone who barely knew them, even if that someone was Ian.

She was, however, looking forward to dinner at Favenham – in particular, to seeing her parents again. The decision that Giles and Rachel had made at the end of last year – to come down to Suffolk for a few months while repairs on Morland Road were completed – had crept on into May, with no plans to return anytime soon. On the contrary, they'd gone ahead and let the place. But although Evie was glad to think of the rental income this would provide for her parents, she missed not having them in London. She hadn't seen Giles or

Rachel for months – or Charles for that matter – and with the atmosphere at Allenham being what it was, a few hours of something more comfortable and familiar was certainly appealing.

But it was clear to them all, within seconds of arriving, that things at Favenham were far from comfortable.

'But – but that's as good as calling her a . . .'

Someone was shouting from somewhere down by William's office. They could hear it as they got out of the cars.

'You bastard! You complete and utter—'

'Just come in here, Charles. You too, Jessica. I'm not prepared to have a shouting match with either of you now. I just—'

'Why not now? It's as good a time as any. We already know what you—'

'In here.'

A door closed. But while the precision of the words was lost – while it was impossible to work out now what was being said – the tonal ups and downs of the continuing row were still fully audible to the rest of the house.

The Allenham party stood in an empty hall, taking off their coats and looking at each other.

'Oh dear,' murmured Lavinia as, very gently, Edward helped her off with her coat and handed her back her sparkly evening bag. She was still far from well, but over the last few months her health – or at least her state of mind – had made a marked improvement. These days, from time to time, she did accept invitations, even if only to show off her new shoes or some piece of jewellery from her late husband. She found conversation tiring and would invariably leave directly

362

after pudding, feeling terrible for two or three days afterwards and needing every moment of care that Honor was prepared to offer. But it was encouraging that Lavinia wanted to go out at all, that she hadn't given up. '. . . what do you think can have happened?'

Nobody knew. For a moment, Honor hesitated – unsure whether to join the others heading down to the library or seek out the row in her father's office.

'Leave them, darling,' said Lavinia, reading her mind. 'Really Honor, you'll only make it worse.'

'I know. I just—'

'You come along with us, you come and have a drink. Come on . . . let them sort it out by themselves.'

'But Jessica—'

'Jessica will be fine. Girls like that always are.'

So Honor followed them into the library, which was full of people trying to pretend they couldn't hear the rumpus going on at the other end of the house . . . that it was the most natural thing in the world to be greeted by their host's brother-in-law.

'Wonderful! Wonderful!' said Giles, his face projecting the opposite message as he offered them champagne. 'The others should be down any minute – I think there's some sort of problem in the kitchen . . .'

But Evie was having none of it. As soon as was possible, she pulled her father to one side and hissed, 'What's going on?'

Giles looked at her.

'Come on, Dad. I've never heard Charles shouting like that in my life. And what the fuck's *Mum* doing in there? She—'

'Jessica's pregnant.'

'What?'

Giles put down the champagne bottle. 'She's nearly

four months pregnant – presumably with Charles's baby. And your uncle, as you heard just now, isn't exactly overjoyed.'

'Jesus.'

'They told us about an hour ago. She's still thin as a rail – I'd never have guessed – but apparently, according to your mother, some women are like that, especially if they're as fitness-obsessed as Jessica . . .'

Evie looked at the Montfort coat of arms above the fireplace. 'I wonder if it's a boy,' she said.

Giles sighed. 'I think that's William's main concern. Because of course, if Charles and Jessica do have a son without being married, then there's the whole issue of the title, which won't pass down – not unless they hurry up the aisle before he's born . . . It's all completely ridiculous of course. I mean, who's going to care about some tinpot baronetcy?'

'The son would.'

Giles looked at his daughter, surprised.

'When he grows up and some younger brother or cousin gets all the goodies?' said Evie. 'Talk about having your nose rubbed in it.'

'Maybe . . . but – but anyway, Jessica doesn't want to know the sex – she wants it to be a surprise.'

'I bet she does.'

Giles frowned.

'Well, it's her best hope of getting Charles up the aisle, isn't it?'

Giles looked shocked.

'I'm serious. No one'll bother if it's a girl. But if it's a boy – or *might* be a boy – Charles would have to be quite a bastard, so to speak, not to marry the mother just in case . . .'

Giles wanted to say that titles didn't matter – or

364

shouldn't matter – and that if the child was brought up with the right values then that would be enough. He wanted to make Evie see that the real question was whether Charles and Jessica loved each other; that what they'd be needing right now from their parents was love and support – maybe even delight at the prospect of a grandchild. Not wild accusations. But before he could respond, they heard a loud crash as a door flew open, and more shouting voices, this time closer, in the hall.

'Don't just walk out when I'm talking to you! You – damn it, Charles – you—'

'Fuck off.'

'Charles . . .' said Rachel's gentler voice. It sounded out of place. 'Charles, please. We only want what's best for the baby. For everyone. And—'

'You walk out now, young man, and you're never setting foot back in – you hear me?'

'William, don't. Please. He'll only—'

'Come on, Jessica.'

'*You hear me?*' William bellowed.

But Charles – out on the steps now, with Jessica's hand in his – merely laughed at his father and said that, seeing as the house technically belonged to him, William was hardly in a position to make statements about whether or not he was permitted to set foot in it. Then the pair of them got into his car and, with eight or nine faces staring at them through the library windows, drove off into the night.

'Olivia!' said Rachel, entering the library moments later and greeting the woman closest to the door, before turning quickly to the next. 'Janey . . . Lavinia – how lovely to see you!'

*

365

It was only when the last of his guests had departed – with just the Allenham party remaining – that William felt able to let his own mask slip. He came back in from waving off Olivia and Jeremy Henderson and slumped on the sofa with a shattered expression. All round the library, squashed here and there on the little sofa-tables, the mantelpiece, the piano, wherever there was space, were abandoned coffee cups and half-finished glasses of champagne. Not knowing which glass was his – not caring – William grabbed the nearest and knocked back its contents as if taking some unpalatable medicine.

'You did brilliantly,' said Rachel, coming to sit beside him. She refilled his glass with some cooler champagne from an ice-bucket by the door.

William shook his head.

'You did.'

At the far end of the room, Honor was playing the piano. It was a Schubert sonata, one she'd learnt at a sufficiently young age for her fingers now – over a decade later – to fall automatically into position with very little mental effort. Ideally, she'd have liked to be leaving as well. After Charles's bombshell, she was hardly in the mood for family chit-chat. But with Edward already gone – he'd taken Lavinia home directly after supper – she was now depending on the others for a lift, and since Evie saw so little of her parents these days, Honor was reluctant to interrupt the affectionate father–daughter conversation taking place on the sofa. Ian's scrutiny of her fingers was perhaps a little disconcerting, but a small price to pay for not feeling obliged to talk to him instead. And so she played on, slightly mechanically, with her left foot down on the mute-pedal so as not to intrude too

366

heavily on the rest of the party.

William observed his daughter fondly for a moment – and then the fondness flickered out.

'Wretched children,' he muttered. 'Wretched, useless . . .'

Rachel frowned.

'Well what's a father supposed to do?' His voice was getting louder. 'Tell me Rachel, what's the answer? When the ones that get married refuse point-blank to breed, and – and the ones that are at it like rabbits won't go near a church . . .'

The piano-playing stopped.

'It's almost as if—'

Honor stood up. 'I'm sorry, Evie,' she said, coming over to the sofa and looking at her watch. 'You don't mind if we make tracks, do you? I—'

'Of course not.' Evie was on her feet. 'Come on, Ian. We're going back.'

'It's almost as if they were doing it deliberately,' William went on, eyeballing Ian – who didn't know better than to look at him just then. 'Deliberately – to annoy me.'

Ian was silent.

'Don't you think?'

Ian swallowed. 'I – I'm sorry, Sir William. I'm not really in a position—'

'Bloody children. Should have disinherited the lot.'

And so it fell to Giles to act as host once more and see the others out. With William muttering on the sofa and Rachel realising she'd have to stay there too – simply to keep the man from saying anything else he'd be sure to regret – Giles stood alone on the Favenham steps, waving for as long as he imagined Evie might see him.

Coming back in, he poked his head around the

library door. William was still on the sofa but was now bending forward, his head clasped in his hands. His failure to react to the opening door was not, Giles knew, down to deafness. William would for sure have heard that old door open. He just no longer cared to be polite. And Rachel, sitting there, stroking his back, seemed more than happy to indulge him.

'I'm heading up,' said Giles.

Rachel gave a business-like nod. 'They're just young, William,' he heard her saying as he closed the door. 'And – who knows? – it might even work out better for Charles in the long run, if they don't get married. Especially if Jessica's the arch gold-digger you take her for . . .'

Giles waited for Rachel in the bedroom, propped up against the pillows, reading an old Agatha Christie. He'd almost reached the end when Rachel crept in at dawn with an oddly maternal expression on her face – one of fulfilment and exhaustion – that he hadn't seen since Evie had been a baby.

'Everything all right?'

Rachel sighed. 'Oh I don't know . . .'

Giles almost expected to hear that William had taken five ounces and had been winded, but simply refused to settle.

'It wasn't helped by all that alcohol, I suppose,' she said, clambering on to the bed and lying against him – fully dressed, too tired even to think about taking off her clothes or going into the bathroom. 'Of course, some of those things he said to Charles were unforgiveable. He brings it on himself – I know he does – but it's hard not to feel sorry for the poor old bear. He's just not used to things going badly . . .'

Giles said nothing.

'And of course there's only so much that I can do to help him.'

Giles closed his eyes. 'Then why,' he said, unable to stop a tone of raw impatience creeping into his words, '*why* go on trying?'

Rachel stiffened. 'I go on trying, Giles—'

'And don't say it's because he needs you, or because there's no one else, or any of that rubbish.'

'But darling, that's exactly why! He—'

'Can you honestly say you helped your brother tonight?'

Rachel was silent.

'Don't you think that sometimes your "help" might have the opposite effect?'

Still Rachel said nothing. Filled with a sense of her own high motives, a sense that she'd been good and kind to William throughout this mess and – if anything – deserved praise and support from her husband, she was dismayed to find Giles taking this line with her. She knew what he was referring to. It wasn't the fact of them continuing to live at Favenham. For Giles, while disliking it, had nevertheless accepted the necessity of that decision, of grabbing the opportunity it gave them to make money from the project. (Indeed he was pleased to think that this new rental income would mean they'd have no need to rely on Evie's original offer to fund the repairs.) No, it was the way she'd failed to condemn Diana, back when they'd first discovered what was happening – making it so easy for that side of William's life to continue.

'I suppose that means that you do,' she said sadly, heaving herself from the bed. 'But I can't abandon him when he's struggling, Giles. I just can't.'

Giles's failure to reply was enough for her to know

what he thought. But Rachel – overcome by another wave of exhaustion from all the effort she'd expended on her brother that evening – simply didn't have the energy to deal with her husband's disapproval now. She felt sick enough as it was about Diana. Wretched Diana who, according to gossip from friends in Edinburgh, had already moved on to someone else's husband and by all accounts was having some success this time around. Certainly, everybody knew about it – including the devastated wife.

But it was easy to judge with hindsight. It hadn't been a straightforward decision at the time – Giles knew that. Couldn't he credit Rachel with trying to do the right thing? Couldn't he find it in himself to support – or at least accept – this attempt she was making to help poor William, instead of seeing it as some sort of weakness?

By the time she came back from the bathroom, Rachel felt calmer – more willing to talk. But Giles's bedside light was off and he'd turned his face to the wall.

Evie and Ian left for London after breakfast the following day. With Monday meetings to prepare for and the weekend property reports to read, they were both keen to get on and left with brisk energy – Evie's little car sweeping a wide arc in front of the house and accelerating up the drive.

Honor came back into a house that was heavily silent. She'd been expecting them to stay for lunch and stood in the hall for a moment, looking at the two names scrawled in the visitors' book – the ink on Ian's was barely dry – and wondered what to do with her morning. Edward would no doubt find some reason to

370

get out of the house, or else hole up in his study, reading the papers and watching television. He never joined her in the sitting room these days. Lavinia wouldn't be getting up at all – not after last night's exertions. And Honor . . . all Honor had in front of her that day was a bit of clearing up to do and a frail mother-in-law to tend.

But while having Evie to stay had made Honor realise how much she missed her friend – the laughter, the energy, the wonderful transparency . . . Evie hadn't needed to say a word about Ian's whites at breakfast yesterday for Honor to know exactly what she was thinking and, these days, that level of connectedness to another person was increasingly special to her. But there was still something about them leaving early that made Honor heave a sigh of relief. That same level of connectedness she so valued had also brought complications – the transparency was two-way – and Evie had obviously been concerned about the glimpses she'd had into Honor's married life. Her worried expression on the tennis court yesterday morning when Edward had hurt his leg; and again at lunch, with those mix-ups over the wine and the ice cream . . . none of it had been lost on Evie. And then that whole humiliating scene with Honor's father the night before, and the squeeze from Evie's hand on the landing as they'd gone to their separate bedrooms,

'You sure you're okay?'

'I'm fine, Evie,' she'd said, squeezing back and releasing. 'You sleep well.'

Honor was the sort of person who'd rather be miserable alone. She didn't like an audience – particularly not an affectionate one – and as she pulled Evie and Ian's sheets off the bed and shook the pillows out of their cases, she was glad not to have to be putting on a show any more – letting the tears fall freely without worrying who might see.

She didn't cry for long – putting things in order always helped her feel calm – and with the dining room swiftly cleared of breakfast things, and all the sheets and towels churning in the washing machine, Honor was just warming some soup to take upstairs on a tray when Lavinia appeared, tired and frail in her dressing gown.

'Lavinia?'

'Hello darling.' Lavinia leant against the kitchen table. 'That smells good . . .'

Honor gave the soup a stir. 'Shouldn't you be in bed?' she said.

'Shouldn't you be entertaining your friends?'

Smiling, Honor tried to explain why Evie and Ian had left early – work, business, things to do . . . not that she expected her mother-in-law to sympathise. To Lavinia it was the height of rudeness for a weekend guest to leave before lunch on Sunday, especially with no prior warning, but she'd yet to find the words to express the extent of her disapproval when Edward strode into the kitchen.

Like Honor, he wasn't expecting his mother to leave her bed that day, and – heading straight for the fridge – failed to see her at the table. Opening the fridge door, he took out a plate of cold roast beef left over from Friday's dinner and a couple of tomatoes and asked his wife if the newspapers had arrived.

'Aren't they in the sitting-room?' said Honor. She was concentrating hard on pouring Lavinia's soup into a bowl without spilling any, and made no effort to look at him as she spoke.

Shrugging, Edward took a plate and a tall glass from the cupboard. He carved off some beef – just enough for himself – sliced the tomatoes and, grabbing a can of Coke from the fridge, poured its contents into the glass and left.

Lavinia watched him go. She looked at Honor's back – bending to take a couple of bread rolls out of the Aga – and opened her mouth to say something. But then her courage must have left her, or maybe she just thought better of it, because her mouth simply closed again and it wasn't until Honor asked if Lavinia wanted butter or margarine on her toast that the tension in the air dispersed.

PART V

Chapter Twenty

Being There

'I'm leaving now, Linda. I   fifteen minutes. But if you really can't stall her then I'll just have to deal with it when— Yes, I *know* that, but—'

With a mobile telephone clamped to her ear, Evie slammed the front door behind her and – not bothering to double-lock – strode down the steps and out into the otherwise-peaceful Chelsea street she now thought of as home.

'Well the longer we stand around talking, the longer it'll take. Just tell her I'll call back when I've had a chance to look at the terms. They only arrived today, for God's sake. She's not my only client. Not even a particularly important client, if we're talking about— fine. Thanks.'

Evie snapped the mobile shut and walked briskly over the Kings Road in the direction of her office. It was wonderful not having to drive to work any more or battle with the vagaries of London Transport; wonderful to know that it would only ever take fifteen minutes door-to-door. And she was just starting to calm down and catch her breath when she realised that, if Ian got his way, the chances of her being able to do this for much longer were slim to non-existent. It made her want to stop there in the busy traffic and weep.

Of course she was grateful to him for finding the little house in Chelsea – for getting such a very good price for it back in January, for encouraging her to give the place the overhaul it needed to realise its true investment potential, for taking so much trouble on her account. But Evie couldn't help but resent the way that, already – barely nine months in – Ian was thinking about selling.

It wasn't just his manner – the way it was always 'we' these days, not 'you'; 'our house', 'our options', 'our investment'. Or the way he'd arranged for some Swiss contacts of his – rich and charming as they were – to view the property at ten o'clock that Friday morning, blithely assuming that Evie would be able to rearrange her working schedule at absolutely no notice, and at no point offering to show them round himself. Oh no . . . *his* meetings were far too important to reschedule.

No, it was really more Ian's attitude to houses that bothered Evie so much – his inability to see a property as anything other than an investment, as opposed to a living home. She hadn't cared about the basement box in Hoxton; even less, the hospital-chic apartment in Pitfield Court. But this dear house that she'd spent the best part of a year healing and decorating, with its pretty front and its mellow sitting room, the huge fireplace she'd specially installed with a carved mantelpiece that her father had found in some junk shop at the back end of Woodbridge and had painstakingly restored himself . . . It just wasn't something she was ready to give up.

378

She knew why Ian was doing it. With an autumn market on the up, a freshly painted house in Bramerton Street with a brand new kitchen, charming 'features', and new carpets throughout . . . it still had that magic gloss that could seduce the kind of crazy offer every estate agent dreamed about. Ian knew what Evie's living standards were like. Within six months, the place would have acquired a worn-in air that invariably reminded buyers they were getting something second-hand. He couldn't bear to let this precious time of newness slip by without at least a crack at selling high.

And as the professional side of Evie could hardly disagree with that standpoint, she found it hard to justify the more personal – and frankly sentimental – part of her that longed to stay put for a while, to have a proper home, and opt out of whatever financial advantage there was to be had from moving on. She was ashamed of feeling this way, of being such an amateur and breaking the very rules she strove so hard to uphold. Rules she'd even, on occasion, attempted to instil in some of her more susceptible clients. So she'd agreed to play host to Ian's Swiss friends' viewing. She'd called the office to reschedule – grimly withstanding the disdain of Linda's response to the sheer unprofessionalism of a woman in Evie's position turning up at the office at midday when she had a morning of appointments in her diary – and told herself, quite firmly, that Ian was right.

'Okay, Linda. Hand it to me then –'

Linda nodded at the pile of papers in Evie's in-tray. 'It's all there. She has put a call through to Marcus, I'm afraid—'

'Oh for God's *sake*.'

'But as he's not in today, I guess you've still got time

to butter her up and get her to retract the complaint before—'

'*Complaint*?' Evie spluttered. 'Jesus . . .'

Linda shrugged. 'She just wants to get the thing signed off before the weekend, Evie. And after all the trouble she's had selling the place . . .'

'Self-inflicted trouble, wouldn't you say?'

'. . . it's hardly surprising she's a bit jumpy.'

Taking off her coat – throwing it crossly over the back of her chair – Evie stood at her desk and picked the latest offer on Mrs Brook's flat out of her in-tray, together with three angry messages. The offer was still well under the asking price. The purchaser had no interest in Mrs Brook's carpets and curtains, or the specially designed sofa, or the potted plants on the pathetic patch of paving that she persisted in calling her 'garden'. He wanted the dishwasher and fridge – but only as part of the purchase price he was offering. And he was insisting on an exclusivity period of fourteen working days. It was an offer that, a year ago, Mrs Brook would laughingly have rejected. But now she was desperate. And Evie, torn between a desire just to have the thing off her desk – how easy it would be to tell Mrs Brook what she wanted to hear: that it was a decent offer, that she should get on with passing it into the hands of her solicitors and have the thing sewn up by Christmas – and a knowledge that, with the market rising again, Mrs Brook would do well to hang on for a few more months . . . Evie was still deliberating when the telephone rang.

'Hello darling,' said a treacly voice.

'Abe.'

'I've just got – oh . . .' – giggling – 'oh God, I've dropped it now! Bloody thing . . . it . . .'

Sighing, Evie sat down in her chair. 'Abe, listen. Call me back when – when at least you've had a cup of coffee. You're not making much sense at the moment, and I'm sorry but I don't have time right now to—'

'No! No! . . . No, I . . . Damn. I just . . . Here it is! Just wanted to say I think it looks great! I – I've just opened it thish minute, Evie, and I . . . It looks great, darling. Just great. You've made . . . made it look like a fucking palace! Honestly, it . . . seems a bit of a bargain now, for only two hundred and ninety!'

Evie reached for the pile of new particulars on the other side of her desk and, pulling the top three towards her, selected the one that featured Abe's flat in Hollywood Road. It had been sent out to him last week. 'You only opened it this morning?'

'Yes! At – at least I think so. I've been away . . .'

'But you like it?'

'Love it, darling. Fucking love it.'

'That's great, Abe. Well, the second we have any interest, I promise you I'll be round there. So you must remember to—'

'Yes, yes . . . I know. Got to keep it smart, right? Got to make my bed! Got to wash my dishes! Got to—'

'That's right. Now Abe, I can't talk on I'm afraid. It's a bit busy here at the moment, but—'

'Shure – sure, sweetheart. Just wanted to say—'

'I know, Abe. And thank you.'

'You're a shtar, Evie ... . an angel . . .'

Evie smiled, in spite of herself. 'I'll call you at the weekend,' she said. 'You get some rest now – you hear me?'

Ending the call, Evie turned to the fading file on Mrs Brook's flat and dialled the Earls Court number. And as the seconds passed and the telephone continued to ring, she glanced again at Abe's Hollywood Road particulars, sitting open to her left.

Abe was right to be grateful. They didn't usually go to so much trouble for properties under five hundred grand – particularly a two-bedroom flat like this. But she knew how important it was for him to sell the place and sell quickly. Take advantage of the autumn surge – with people back from holiday and wanting to complete their moves before Christmas was upon them. With the rise in the market, she wished that Abe had the means to hold on to his flat. It would be worth double – maybe more – in a couple of years, and there was a strong risk that, in selling now, it would take years for him to get back on to the London property ladder. But Evie still knew it was the right decision to sell. In truth, what else could Abe do? He had no money. The place was heavily mortgaged. And with his current lifestyle – where nights and days blurred into one; where the bars grew cheaper and the people seedier; and even Nigel Fournier had stopped calling – Abe simply didn't have the clarity of mind or purpose to let a flat successfully. He could barely handle the responsibility of owning a property at all, far less find some sort of alternative job to raise the income necessary to pay his mortgage and fund his excessive tastes. He'd just have to sell the place, pay off his debts and rent a room that matched his circumstances. It wouldn't be much fun for him but it was, Evie felt, the only way Abe would wake up to what he was doing to himself . . .

'Hello?'

'Oh – oh, Mrs Brook? It's Evie Langton here, from Chelsea Estates. I'm sorry I couldn't call earlier – my meeting went on a bit, I'm afraid – but—'

382

'Well have you seen the offer, then?' snapped Mrs Brook.

'Yes, Mrs Brook. I have.'

'And?'

'Well of course it's wonderful to have an offer. I – I have to say, I wish it were slightly higher –'

'So you could get more commission, no doubt.'

'And with the market being what it is,' Evie went on – she was really quite good at ignoring barbs these days, 'with the market being what it is, Mrs Brook, it would be quite understandable if you wanted to hold out for a better offer, or even—'

'Hold out?' shrieked Mrs Brook. 'Have you forgotten how long this flat's been on the market, Ms Langton? I realise girls like you aren't exactly the brightest lights on the Christmas tree, but—'

'So you'd like us to accept Mr Patel's offer, then?'

'I most certainly would.'

'And agree to his conditions about exclusivity?'

Mrs Brook's silence made Evie wonder if she'd understood that part of the purchaser's terms.

'In other words,' she went on, 'he wants a lock-out period of two weeks when you won't be able to show it to any other potential buyers, while he completes his searches and his survey and so on. Of course, it's not binding – not legally – but—'

'I think I know what "exclusivity" means, Ms Langton.'

'Great. And you're happy to go along with that?'

'If you say so.'

'I really need *your* decision on this, Mrs Brook.'

'Well do you advise me to accept it or not?'

Again, Evie had to bite her tongue.

'For crying out loud, girl – it's what I'm paying you

for, isn't it? To give me a bit of advice now and then? To be around when I call during office hours? Is that really so much to ask?'

Evie took a long, deep breath. 'If you're serious about accepting Mr Patel's offer,' she said very slowly, and in her most professional voice, 'if you don't want to take advantage of what's happening in the market – and I quite understand that, after two years of trying to sell your flat, you might want to take an offer that's actually on the table – then yes. I think you should agree to his terms. And while I feel it my duty to point out to you that exclusivity arrangements aren't legally enforceable – that you're only honour-bound, and if you decide you want us to continue showing then we can certainly do that – but I do need clear instructions from you on this point.'

'Fine.'

'So – so we accept?'

'Yes, Ms Langton. We do. I'd like written confirmation sent to me directly, and of course to my solicitor.'

'Absolutely.'

'And I'm expecting that, in the weeks to come, I'll be getting a somewhat more professional service from Chelsea Estates than the standard I've had to deal with this morning.'

Evie hesitated.

'Do I make myself clear?'

'Yes, Mrs Brook. Yes you do.'

Evie replaced the telephone with a shaking hand. Aware that both Linda and Nick had been listening, aware that, for all her attempts at remaining professional, the essence of the call would not have been lost on either of them, Evie was in no mood to explain herself to anyone . . . particularly not to Linda and Nick, who both had reason to relish any potential setback to her career. She grabbed her coat again and made for the office door.

'Just getting some lunch,' she muttered. 'You want anything?'

'No, no . . .'

She knew they'd be smiling at each other behind her back – and was glad to see, on her return, that Linda had at least been forced to take a couple more calls for her. Two message slips were waiting on Evie's chair, filled out in Linda's boxy handwriting. The first was from a different client, agreeing to reduce the asking price of his house in Paultons Square by twenty per cent. Sitting in her chair, Evie leant across the desk, found the relevant file and clipped in the note with a satisfied expression. That house would go now. If she got on with it, calling every single interested applicant she'd remembered to note down on the inside of the file – starting with that promising-looking couple from America – she might even get an offer by the end of the day.

Putting the file to one side, Evie then turned casually to the second message: 'Matthew Forrester. Appointment booked – 4 p.m.'

Still wearing her coat, still holding the message slip, Evie glanced across the office. 'Four p.m. . . . today?' she said.

'Hm?'

'This message, Linda – this appointment you've booked for me . . .'

'I'm sorry. Your afternoon looked free. I assumed you—'

'No that's fine. I am free. So . . . so he's coming in today, then? At four?'

385

'That's right.' Catching Nick's eye, Linda went on – speaking very slowly as if Evie were stupid. 'He's coming. Today. At four. Exactly as I've written down . . .'

'Sure. I see that. I just – did he say what he was coming for?'

'Well, I imagine he wants to buy a flat, Evie. Or sell one . . . but you could always call him if you're not finding any of this clear enough. The number's there – see? Where it says, "Number" . . .'

'Yes, yes, all right.'

Evie had heard nothing from Matthew since that evening at the end of last year when Abe had taken them all out to dinner – and Matthew had then hurried off to Washington the following morning and, once again, out of their lives.

She knew he was back in London. He'd been back for a while. The Washington job, as he'd said at the time, was only temporary. Political analysis – not foreign reporting – was his area, and over the summer Matthew had been promoted to official parliamentary sketch writer for the paper. He was making quite a name for himself. Sometimes, she'd hear him on the radio – even, once, saw him on television. But he'd made no attempt to contact her. And why on earth should he? More importantly, why should she care? As far as Evie was concerned, Matthew Forrester was nothing more than an ex whom she felt a certain sort of nostalgic affection for – in much the same way as she'd glance fondly at an old dolls' house that had once occupied her for hours, but would still have no desire to pull open the front and play with all the little things inside.

386

He arrived early, just as she was finishing her call to the States. '. . . no . . . absolutely. I quite understand. I just thought you'd like me to let you know. As I say, the seller only came down a couple of hours ago and – and we do have quite a few clients interested now, so . . . well, I'll let you speak to your husband, shall I?'

Frowning, Evie bent over her desk so that her face was hidden from the front of the office.

'. . . no, it's *Paultons* Square, Mrs Goldmann. The one with the roof terrace, remember? And the shower room you liked? . . . exactly. The asking price was a million, but he's come right down to nine-thirty. That's right: nine hundred and thirty thousand. Pounds sterling . . . yes, I know. But he has come down quite a bit, Mrs Goldmann. It's a sensible price. And you really don't want to alienate him at this stage if you're at all serious about— sure. Great. You have the number . . . ? Okay then, Mrs Goldmann. I'll speak to you tomorrow.'

Matthew was standing at Linda's desk, his weight resting on one leg while he looked at the various papers Linda was handing him. It was all so casual, so incidental. Just another man in off the street, talking to Linda, standing against the sales display, looking at particulars . . . Except, of course, to Evie – struggling to deal with the sight of that person she still loved and dreamed about, physically there, in the functional scenery of her daily life – to Evie, it was startling. She'd known he was coming in, she was prepared, yet the impact of his presence now was far greater than that surprise encounter at Abe's play. She hadn't known the Leinster Pit. It was as unfamiliar to her, as rare, as Matthew himself now was. Nothing had been normal that night. In many ways it had been rather appro-

387

priate for her to find him in such a place. But here, now, in her ordinary little office? The sound of his voice was almost more than she could bear. His voice. Linda's voice. One so special, the other so mundane . . .

Putting the telephone down, she walked over to them. 'Sorry about that.'

'Don't worry.' Matthew smiled and kissed her on the cheek. 'It sounded pretty important, and I'm being beautifully looked after here by . . .'

'It's Linda. Now, I've given him the August sales lists, Evie – and the details for Callow Street and Hollywood Road. He wants two bedrooms, some-where not too noisy, and—'

'Thanks, Linda.'

'I'd say Redcliffe Gardens wasn't right, but he might like to see it just in case he—'

'Thank you, Linda.' Evie repeated, with a little more force. 'I'll take it on from here, shall I?'

She took Matthew back to her desk – pulling up a chair for him and sitting opposite at her own, with all the paraphernalia of her working life between them: the piles of particulars ready to mail out, the office diary, telephone, Post-it notes, property magazines . . . and a dog-eared pad of A4, scrawled all over, with telephone numbers at erratic angles, and no respect to margins or lines. She wasn't a tidy worker, but there was something more impressive than tidiness – something energetic – there instead.

'So how've you been?' she said, busily clearing some space. 'How's work?'

'It's fine.'

'And Washington?'

For a moment Matthew looked confused and then, smiling suddenly, 'Oh, no! No, I was never going to

388

stay in Washington,' he explained. 'I've been back since February. It was just a temporary placement, just until they found someone more – more suitable, I suppose.'

'So you're in London, then?' She said, hoping it was convincing – this show of ignorance about Matthew's working life.

He nodded. 'Yup. I'm in London . . . Same job – pretty much. Same life, same grotty rented flat . . .' he continued to smile at her.

'*Same girlfriend?*' she longed to ask.

For a moment neither of them spoke.

'So tell me what you're looking for,' said Evie, only aware of the double entendre after the words were out. Because from the expression in Matthew's eyes just then, it seemed to Evie – however far fetched – that there was really only one answer. Embarrassed, she went on, 'A – a flat, right? And are you set on two bedrooms, or would one be enough? We – see here? – we've got masses of studios and one-bedroom flats but if you— Right. Okay. And how do you feel about basements? They . . . sure. I understand. Well there's this one here on Elystan Street – great location, second floor, a bit on the small side maybe . . .'

It wasn't fair. If he'd moved on and up, why not say so? Why come in here and tease poor Evie with penetrating smiles and holding her gaze too long and all that rubbish, when he now had Sally Jarvis for a girlfriend? It annoyed Evie how much she came across Sally Jarvis these days. Invariably it happened at times when she was hoping to switch off, and she'd pick up an old magazine or tabloid newspaper and find herself face to face with yet another piece by Sally sodding Jarvis on how mothers in their forties might carry off

389

the combat look, or the true story behind Michael Barrymore's marriage or, on one occasion, Sally's picture in some social column, carrying off the sexy-librarian look to perfection.

As for Matthew . . . there were hundreds of other estate agencies he could have gone to. It wasn't as if Evie worked at Foxtons, or Faron Sutaria, or one of the usual places that a man like Matthew might first try. And while he'd explained that the only reason he was in a position to buy a place like this at all was because of money inherited from his father, money he should have invested in property long ago . . . that hacks at the *Post* were paid a pittance – Might have been different if he'd taken that job at the *Sun*, but that wasn't why he'd gone into journalism . . . For all that, there was a distinct air of prosperity about him now. She wondered if he was getting some sort of kick out of seeing her like this – gloating, perhaps? Showing her that he had money to invest, even if it was from his dead father? Maybe it amused him to put her in the awkward position of serving him. Who knew? Presumably he thought that Evie didn't care for him any more, that she only had eyes for Ian – and like the idiot she was she'd done nothing to disabuse him of that impression, but – but still . . .

What *was* he looking for?

'Or there's that place in Hollywood Road that Linda was telling you about, although it's a bit over budget, and . . .' she hesitated, 'and you might have a problem with taking on a flat that belongs to someone you already know.'

'Someone I know?'

Evie looked up. 'It's Abe's,' she said.

Taking the sets of particulars out of Matthew's

hands, she handed back the sheet for Hollywood Road. 'He's selling. I – I know, Matthew. It's a crazy time. Anyone with any sense is doing what you're doing and looking to buy—'

'But he needs the money.'

Evie nodded. 'We've suggested two-ninety – which is actually pretty competitive – so that he can sell quickly and get on with sorting himself out. Just look at this other place. It . . . oh, where is it?' Glad of the sincerity of the distraction, glad to have something else to worry about other than what Matthew was up to, Evie scanned the sales lists. 'See here? Fawcett Street? Just round the corner. Exactly the same deal, only it's second floor, not first, and it hasn't got a second bathroom. And they're asking ten grand more . . .'

Matthew looked at the photograph of Abe's apartment. He took in the boyish techno-decor, the large windows and contemporary fireplace.

'Two-ninety, you say?'

Evie nodded. 'Should really be asking three-ten, according to my boss. I don't know how much further the market's going to rise but, put it this way, Matthew, if I had the money, I'd be in there like a shot.'

Matthew looked at the floor plan.

'But it might be a little weird,' she conceded. 'I guess it's a personal thing. You could change the look of it a bit . . . that might help. It is absolutely what you say you're looking for . . . but . . .' Quickly pulling other sets of particulars from her pile – none of them as glossy as Abe's and all of them more expensive – Evie continued, 'Why don't you look through this lot and tell me a bit more about what you're looking for . . . You say you want two bedrooms – is that two proper bedrooms or would a galleried study-cum-bedroom space be as good? And what about bathrooms . . . ?'

Now that she had a specific job to do, it was fine. In a way she rather liked having Matthew here on her territory. Liked knowing she was good at what she did – liked seeing him seeing it. So long as she didn't meet his eye too readily, and so long as there was some random prop for her to play with – pens, papers, car keys, particulars, anything to hide behind, and something else to talk about – chattery words to cover what was really underneath, cover it with a blank two-dimensional quality, like music in a lift . . . then everything would be all right. There was nothing to worry about.

Listening attentively to Matthew's replies, Evie sifted through the other properties on offer – only selecting ones that met his criteria – and within ten minutes it was clear there were quite a few he liked, including Abe's. Glancing at the clock on the wall behind her desk, Evie calculated she could take him to two of the properties – maybe even three – that very afternoon. She only had to send out that confirmation of agreed terms to Mrs Brook and her solicitor, which was something she could easily ask Linda to do. In fact, given the circumstances, it was entirely appropriate that Linda should be doing it. Her only concern was whether Abe would be at Hollywood Road while they were there and what sort of state the place would be in.

Leaving Matthew to browse through the particulars, she dialled Abe's number . . . but there was no response. He was either out or fast asleep. Either way, she decided it would do no harm to turn up – not when Matthew was a friend. And so, leaving an upbeat message saying that she'd got him his first viewing, that it was Matthew – really! Matthew! – and that they'd be there by six, Evie pulled on her coat, grabbed her bag and, collecting the keys from the cupboard behind Linda's desk, followed Matthew out into the street.

The lights were off in Abe's flat as Evie and Matthew approached. The windows were dark, and there was no reply when she rang the bell. Mildly relieved by this – for in spite of all the possible benefits of buying from a friend, there were just as many pitfalls, and it was certainly easier to view the place without Abe there – Evie took out the set of keys. 'Must be out,' she said, opening the street door, switching on the staircase lights and standing back for Matthew to go in first. 'Goodness, it looks better in here,' she went on, following him up the stairs towards Abe's door. 'I have to say, when we came to do the valuation it was awful. Full of unopened mail and,' she chuckled, 'and God knows what. We did get the cleaners in for the brochure photographs but I wouldn't have been surprised if he—'

She tried to unlock the flat and found that, far from opening the door, she must have turned the key in the wrong direction and double-locked it instead – and had to go through the whole process again.

'Sorry about this, Matthew. Never know if people lock their doors properly or . . . ah! Here we are.'

The door opened. 'Now there's a little hallway here if I can just find the lights . . .' Again, she stood back for Matthew to go first. 'You've got a sort of cloakroom to your left, and . . . no, that's just a cupboard. The main reception's straight in front of you . . .'

Matthew opened the door. But even before he opened it, Evie sensed that something wasn't right. While cheerfully directing him through, she'd already half-detected what then hit them both with the force of something that had been trapped for some time: the stagnant smell of vomit, mixed with something else, warm and sour and unidentifiable.

Her first thought was: thank God it's only Matthew. And it wasn't until she was in the room with him – peering round his shoulder – that she realised the extent of the problem. For there on the beechwood floor, in amongst the sheepskin rugs, the ashtrays and the glass, was not only Abe's vomit, Abe's blood, Abe's urine . . . but Abe himself, unconscious.

Matthew took off his coat. 'Abe?' he said, swiftly kneeling at Abe's body and feeling for a pulse. 'Abe!' he said again, this time a little louder, inspecting the ashen face. 'Abe mate, can you hear me?' But Abe did not respond. Rolling him over into the recovery position and clearing his mouth, Matthew turned to Evie – standing, frozen, behind him. 'Call an ambulance, will you?'

'Of course.' She looked around for a telephone, in amongst the chaos.

'Just get on the phone, Evie. Use your mobile. Or . . . fuck it. Here. Use mine.'

Ashamed, Evie took the mobile, bent her head and dialled 999 while Matthew – with that same disarming presence of mind, that rare streak of the practical that made him stand out from the ranks of equally bright, but infinitely less effective, rivals at the paper, Matthew began putting into practice the basic artificial respiration techniques he'd been taught at school and hadn't forgotten.

The ambulance was there in minutes but it felt infinitely longer as Evie sat with Matthew and Abe on the beechwood floor. The Hollywood Road sales particulars rang around her head. '. . . and plenty of entertainment space . . .' they said.

Plenty indeed, thought Evie, catching sight of a cigarette butt floating in a glass of red wine. Beside her, Matthew was still crouching by Abe – still pumping away at him, immersed in stench – and as Abe began to cough and splutter, a curling blue light flashed over their heads. It touched the ceiling, skimmed the curtain and pulsed on round.

'Let them in, would you?' said Matthew, supporting Abe's head as he turned to the floor, stroking his back as he gagged.

It was nearly midnight by the time Evie left the hospital. Abe was going to be fine. They'd pumped his stomach and restored him to consciousness and dealt with the gash round his head. He was being kept in for observation – would probably be there for a couple of days – but there was nothing more that Evie and Matthew could do that evening. It was better that they go home.

'You'll be okay?' said Matthew, seeing her to her car.

'Yes fine. Thanks, Matthew. I—'

'We can see the rest of those flats some other time.'

'Absolutely.' She smiled. 'Of course. I'll call you on Monday, shall I?'

Without thinking, Matthew opened his wallet to take out a business card. And it was only when he handed it over that they felt an echo of before . . . back in the foyer of that smart Park Lane hotel. Evie – prickly Evie – young and glowing in her black Spanish dress, and Matthew – preppy Matthew – with his combed hair, his neutral dinner jacket and thoughtful expression.

They both caught it. And as the card passed between them, their eyes were up and down the road; anywhere but each other. It was hardly surprising their fingers collided.

'Oh – oh, thanks!' she said, laughing cheerfully as she slammed the car door, tossed the card on to the dashboard and felt for her seat belt. 'You have a good weekend, yeah?'

Matthew smiled back. 'Yes,' he said. 'And you.'

Ian wouldn't hear of it. Absolutely not. No way. *Niente*. Sure, he could see that it wasn't a good idea for Abe to be on his own at the moment, and – yes, okay – he understood it wouldn't exactly be a good selling point for that flat in Hollywood Road if it contained a recovering drug addict. But if Evie really thought for one moment that Abram Wyatt was moving in with them – right here in Bramerton Street; sleeping – or whatever else he did during the night – in the very next room; filling their bathroom with his pills, their kitchen with his liquor, and their evenings with that endless egocentric chatter about whatever overblown project he thought he'd be up for next – which they all knew was about as likely as him going to the moon – then Ian was moving out.

Evie looked at him – twitching the edge of their bright-white duvet so that it lay perfectly over the bed. Twitching it sharply. She felt a sudden urge to jump all over that clean flat surface. 'You mean that?'

'I certainly do.'

'Even though he's desperate, Ian? With nowhere to go right now, and no one to look after him, and – and his whole world crashing in . . .'

'He's brought it on himself, Evie.'

396

'But—'

'No.'

A spark of morning sunlight flashed in Evie's eye. 'No?'

Ian sighed. 'I'm sorry sweetheart,' he said, picking up his briefcase and heading out of the bedroom – his voice fading as he passed through the doorway. 'Really I am. But it's Abe or me, I'm afraid. And that's my final word.'

Evie followed him down the stairs, a loose dressing-gown belt trailing behind her, step by step. Her heart was beating so wildly, she felt she might explode.

'Then it's him,' she said. It was almost a whisper.

Ian looked up in disbelief – at Evie: leaning over the banister with unbrushed hair flopping about her face, and wearing that childish expression of defiance. He hated it when she was like this. 'I'm serious, Evie.'

'So am I.'

Shaking his head, Ian left the little house. He didn't slam the front door. Didn't make any sort of fuss. Didn't even call – and went home that night to St Albans. He wasn't going to confront her or let himself be dragged into some sort of undignified scrap. Better to wait for her to come round – which, of course, she would. Eventually. She wasn't completely irrational. Just needed a bit of firm handling now and then; needed to be shown there were limits . . .

And it was only after a week had gone by that he began to think something might be wrong. Calling the Bramerton Street number, he was greeted by Abe's smoothest acting voice on the answer phone.

Ian's blood ran cold. 'Okay,' he said, into the machine. 'It's Ian. It's Friday. I'll be collecting my

397

things tomorrow morning – sometime between eleven and one – and I'll leave my keys when I go.'

Evie wiped it from the tape. Upstairs, she could hear Abe coughing in the shower. It should have sounded terrible. But to Evie, just then – after three whole years of pristine sheets and perfectly wiped surfaces – to her, it was a wonderful noise.

Chapter Twenty-One

Honor and Evie

It had just stopped raining and the streets were full of water. With every slight movement in the air, small pockets of it would drip from the upper branches of the trees, or trickle noisily from faulty drainpipes – or whatever Evie happened to be walking beneath on her way back to the office. She still had her umbrella up. And even though it afforded her no protection from the spray that flew up every time a car sped past, even though her coat was covered in mud-wet splashes and her black suede shoes were ruined, she seemed immune to the onslaught. Almost seemed to relish the cool damp London air against her face, and paraded her splash-marks with a swing of careless pride.

Over a month had passed since Ian had collected his things and she hadn't missed him once. On the contrary, she was actively enjoying her freedom, and the opportunity it gave her to look after Abe. She loved seeing him grow steadily better; loved knowing that, for the first time in her life, she had the ability to be genuinely helpful to somebody else – particularly somebody like Abe, towards whom she felt such affection. For when Abe wasn't shivering and craving, when he wasn't waking her up in the middle of the night or hurrying off to a sudden AA meeting, or regurgitating some of the more evangelical aspects of the therapy he was taking . . . she enjoyed having him there with her. Evie didn't care if the bins weren't emptied, or the bathroom was left untidy, or there was suddenly no milk in the fridge. After three years of rigid order, there was something decidedly reassuring about a bit of mess and irregularity – certainly to Evie. And then there was all the laughter. In spite of everything that had happened to Abe – in spite of his lost career, his shaky health, his puffy face, his shrinking finances – he could still make Evie laugh more than Ian ever had.

And while Matthew hadn't wanted to buy Abe's flat, there had still been plenty of interest from other applicants – one of whom, much to Evie's delight, had put in an offer over the asking price and was now pushing for early completion. She was glad that at least that side of things had been easy for Abe, glad that he'd felt able to trust her to get the best deal for his flat. An extra five grand would make a real difference to him now.

Things were going well at work. For with Helen's recent announcement that she was pregnant again and, as of January, had no intention of working from the office any more – sure, she'd still have a stake in the company; still bring in what business she could; still act as a consultant and even – if it suited her – take on the occasional prestigious property, the balance of power at Chelsea Estates was shifting. To help him with strategic decisions and overall responsibility for the business, Marcus was going to need a replacement partner. He didn't want the anxieties that went with being solely in charge. He liked sharing the load, liked being able to go away on holiday without worrying that the whole operation would collapse – and there was only so much that Helen could do from her sitting room in Clapham, even with all the marvels of computers. So last week he and a heavily pregnant Helen had taken Evie out to lunch to discuss the situation with her.

Yes, Evie was young. And yes, she still had a lot to learn. But she now had the grounding and the discipline – had, in the past three years, proved more than competent at coping with the more complicated aspects of selling residential property, and there was something about her instincts that both Marcus and Helen liked, something that couldn't be taught. In principle, she was just the sort of person they could imagine in Helen's place. They still had terms to discuss. Nothing would be made public for at least a couple of weeks while they thrashed out an appropriate contract. Evie would certainly need separate legal representation and, for now, it was vital that she say nothing about their offer until the whole thing was done and dusted, vital to keep it secret. But in principle, what did Evie think?

Evie couldn't believe what they were saying. At only twenty-seven, with no degree, no special qualification – beyond the various token modules she'd taken with the National Association of Estate Agents – and only the most limited experience, was she really going to be Marcus Graham's new partner, and sit at Helen's desk?

Marcus smiled at her expression. 'Well only if you like the idea, Evie. It's not compulsory.'

'No of course I do! I love it! I just—'

'You won't be getting the same pay as Helen I'm afraid. Not yet . . .'

'That doesn't matter.'

'Although we would, of course, be offering you some sort of nominal stake in the business.' Evie's eyes widened. 'Mainly to ensure your continued commitment, and – and give you the right sort of incentive to make the business flourish.'

'It's in our interests every bit as much as yours,' Helen added, emptying the rest of the champagne bottle into Evie's glass and smiling too.

Evie had smiled back as she'd picked up the glass, and had barely stopped smiling since. Now, walking back along the quiet Chelsea streets, in amongst the November drips and splashes, with a warm, dry scarf around her neck, Evie wasn't sure she'd ever been this happy, or could ever be quite so happy again. With Ian gone, and Abe getting better, and her career rocketing . . . and now, to top it all, Matthew had invited her to dinner.

It had been the end of another morning of viewings, and they'd been heading towards the last property – an overpriced one in Lennox Gardens – when Evie, flicking idly through her papers for the right set of particulars, had made a passing reference to Ian moving his things out of her house.

'What?' said Matthew, braking sharply.

Evie looked at him, surprised. 'We split up,' she said. 'But surely you . . . Didn't Abe tell you?'

'No!' cried Matthew, indignant. 'No, he bloody well didn't! He – Christ, Evie –'

'It's fine,' she said, amused. 'Really, Matthew. It wasn't working. And when Ian had the gall to start saying poor Abe couldn't move in with us – in with *me*, if we're being pedantic here – even temporarily . . .'

'You ended it.'

She nodded.

'And – and you're really okay, are you?' he said, pulling in at the first opportunity and stopping the car so that he could look at her properly.

Laughing, Evie told him she was more than okay. Should have done it months ago – years, even . . . and Matthew, laughing with her now, said that he was glad. He'd never warmed to Ian.

'Nobody did,' she muttered. 'As I'm only finding out now . . .'

Matthew smiled. 'So how about dinner to celebrate?' he said casually. 'You free tomorrow night?'

It was almost more than she could bear. Sure, she'd seen a fair bit of Matthew in the past few weeks – but it had only been for professional reasons or strictly to do with Abe, whom he visited from time to time. She'd had no reason to think that anything had changed. That odd moment when he'd passed her his business card outside the hospital – it never occurred to her that the tension was anything other than one-sided.

Evie couldn't wait to run the whole thing past Honor, whom she'd planned to see the following day for lunch and perhaps a spot of early Christmas shopping. She was desperate to ask what Honor thought of it all. Did it really mean he fancied her, or was it just as friends? And what about Sally Jarvis? Did this mean she was out of the picture? And – and – and what, oh what, should she *wear*?

The office was full when she got in. Everyone was there, everyone except Linda, who – in line with everything else that was, just now, so perfect in Evie's

403

life – had taken a holiday that week. Smiling, glowing, striding in, Evie greeted the others, shook off her coat, and sat happily at her desk.

Not caring that the call was personal – it wasn't as if she had anything to prove on that front any more – Evie picked up the telephone and dialled Honor's Suffolk number.

'Hi there!' she said cheerfully. 'It's me. Just calling about tomorrow . . .'

There was a long silence.

And then, '. . . oh my God! A girl, you say? . . . Oh that's wonderful, Honor! What – actually *at* Favenham? Jesus . . . poor Jessica! No, of course I understand. How exciting! Of course you must stay up there with them! We can have lunch any time. I've got masses of days off in December – haven't nearly used up my holiday entitlement . . . and – and everything was okay, was it? Really? She didn't . . . Oh, good. Oh, Honor! Charles must be over the moon . . .'

Evie decided she'd still take the day off. Perhaps it was even a blessing that Honor had cancelled. Without the distraction of Honor's company, Evie could probably get her entire Christmas list sorted that day. And, in truth, there wasn't much Honor could add to the whole question of Matthew and what – if anything – was behind his invitation to dinner that night. She just needed to keep herself occupied. And so, with an appointment at the beautician for midday and a blow-dry scheduled for four, Evie resolved to devote the rest of her day to early Christmas shopping. The prospect of getting through her entire list of family presents before December had even arrived was really quite appealing. She couldn't wait to get started.

'Hey – hey!' Abe put out a hand to stop her. 'Nowhere will be open yet – not unless you're thinking of doing the whole lot at Boots . . .'

Evie looked down at him, sitting snugly in one of the sofas in their local café – and wondered how much time he spent drinking coffee on his own in here these days.

'Boots!' she said. 'Of course. What a brilliant idea! I'm sure Xandra would be thrilled by some own-brand shampoo, or—'

'Not if you're still hoping for a purple alligator-skin handbag to match that purse she gave you last year,' said Abe, getting to his feet.

Evie chuckled. 'Well maybe not Xandra, then . . . dear, generous Xa-Xa . . . but I'm sure some of them wouldn't mind. Charles, for instance. He never—'

'While you're thinking about it . . .' Abe reached for her empty mug. 'Just one more little cappuccino, hmm? Oh, go on, Eves . . . just one. Or some orange juice? They squeeze it freshly here, you know. And the croissants—'

Breaking off, Abe looked at Evie – who'd stopped pulling on her coat and was standing, half-frozen, transfixed by something that was happening beyond the café window. 'Evie?'

'Hang on a second.'

Hanging on, Abe followed the direction of her gaze and saw – in flashing glimpses, through the busy Kings Road traffic – Honor getting out of a large four-wheel drive. He saw her lean in for a moment to kiss Edward at the wheel and then stand back, slamming the door shut and waving him off into the traffic. She seemed pale, he thought. Slightly sad, even, standing alone with shoppers bustling around her, although that closed, blank look was, he knew, her default expression.

405

She only came alive when there was someone else to consider.

'Bloody hell,' breathed Evie.

Abe turned, surprised.

'She – damn it, Abe – she's supposed to be in Suffolk! Helping Charles's girlfriend recover from giving birth . . .'

Still Abe looked confused.

'She cancelled lunch! We spoke only yesterday! And – and here she is, bold as brass . . .' Evie pulled her coat back on and grabbed her shoulder-bag from the empty chair. 'I'm sorry, Abe. I'm not letting her get away with this . . .'

And she was gone, hurrying out of the café and dashing across the road, leaving screeching brakes and blaring horns in her wake as she gained on Honor's neat solitary figure – walking, slow and oblivious, in the direction of Sloane Square, stopping every now and then to look at the Christmas displays in the shop windows as she passed . . . lost in a world of her own.

'Honor?' Breathlessly, Evie grabbed at the navy wool shoulder – dragging it round, forcing her cousin to face her.

Startled, Honor turned.

'You . . .' Evie caught her breath. 'What the *fuck* are you doing?'

Honor's face had been pale already, but now she was almost white. 'Oh God,' she said, closing her eyes.

'Oh God indeed. You said you were in Suffolk, Honor! You said—'

'I know what I said.'

'Then . . .'

'I'm sorry, Evie.'

'Sorry?' Evie stared at her. 'Is that all you can come

406

up with?' And then, to Evie's fury, Honor glanced at her watch.

'Jesus, Honor. What is this? You arrange to spend today with me – *weeks* ago. You don't bother to tell me it's off until – until very late yesterday, when *I'm* calling *you* to confirm. And when I tell you I really need to see you . . . when I explain that it's about Matthew, and his invitation, and – and just how important it all is—'

'I know, Evie. I'm sorry. I –'

'You – you come up with some story about your brother's baby daughter being born, which I hope isn't entirely fabricated . . .'

'No, of course it's not,' said Honor, looking again at her watch.

Evie grabbed her wrist. 'Stop *doing* that!' she cried. 'You . . . you of all people! Can't you at least show me the courtesy of listening properly . . . and explain why you feel you have to lie to me these days?'

'Okay,' said Honor quietly. 'I will, if you give me a chance.'

So Evie let go and waited, with shoppers pressing all around them, the stream splitting and rejoining, chattering through them, bags brushing past them, gathering at the traffic lights, waiting for the signal. And as Honor began to explain herself, Evie realised, to her horror, that Honor had every reason to be secretive; that, once again, it was she – Evie – in the wrong . . . and the bustling street seemed simply to fade away. For it was all she could do to absorb the news that Honor's only reason for being in London that day was medical – and that Honor would, in all probability, be childless for the rest of her life.

'It's not definite,' Honor added. 'I mean, there's still

a lot that can be done for us. It – it may still all be fine. That's why we're having all this treatment. It's why we're here in London today . . . and why we couldn't stay in Suffolk. But it's never certain when they can see us, Evie. For reasons I won't go into now, they do everything very last-minute at the hospital. When they say come, we come . . . which – which is why I suddenly had to cancel you. I had no choice. But I'm so sorry, Evie. I—'

Raising a hand to stop any more apologies, Evie silently shook her head. It wasn't just the threat of childlessness facing her cousin that stopped her in her tracks. It was the discovery that Honor had lived with this for almost three years – and had said nothing to anyone, anyone at all; that those past three years had been filled with trips to infertility specialists, not only in London but all over the world; that Honor had already been through five cycles of fertility treatment, and was now in the middle of her sixth . . . it was this sense of her own ignorance and prejudice that filled Evie with shame.

And when she thought of all those comments she'd made about how wise Honor and Edward were to wait a few years . . . and Honor herself, lying so beautifully that evening at Abe's club about wanting to wait as well . . . and then all the times Evie had assumed her cousin was in London merely to have her hair done, or her nails, or something equally spoiled and trivial, when in fact Honor was flat on her back in some cold surgery; or receiving the news that – yet again – the treatment had failed; or injecting herself with all manner of terrifying drugs. All the times she'd thought that Honor and Edward were off on another self-indulgent holiday, another trip to New York, or San

Francisco, or Paris, or Switzerland, when they were really stuck in the system of another grey-walled clinic in another grim attempt at the loveless mechanics of artificial conception . . . It rendered Evie speechless. 'Sorry' simply wasn't a big enough word.

And then there were all those – presumably far worse – comments from William and Xandra and God only knew who else, asking what was stopping them from—

'bloody getting on with it? Twenty-six isn't so young, Honor. Believe me. And by the time you hit thirty . . .

I was only reading last week, in *Tatler*, about some poor woman who left it too late . . .

If only you knew what a joy it is to have children! Then you might show a little more interest . . .

And what about poor Edward? He is almost forty, darling. He might not want to pressure you, but I'm sure he must be hoping . . .'

And finally, to top it all: Jessica's effortless whoops-how-did-that-happen? pregnancy.

By the time Honor was finished, Evie felt actively sick. 'Oh God, Honor.'

'It's not so bad.' Smiling, Honor kissed her cousin. Evie could see that there were tears in her eyes. 'Really, it isn't. We've still got a chance. It's not all over – not by any means! We're both so determined and, thank God, the money's not a problem. Compared to hundreds – thousands – of couples, we're just so lucky. I'm sure it'll work out eventually. But I do have to get to the hospital by ten, Evie. According to the nurse, the timing's pretty vital.' She glanced down the road for an empty taxi. 'But I will call you when it's over if you like, and maybe we—'

409

'I'll come with you.' Honor shook her head. 'You don't want me there?'

Honor hesitated. 'Not really, Evie. I'm sorry. It'll take for ever, and I . . .'

'You're worried Edward would mind?'

Honor smiled – a different, wintry smile. 'Certainly he'd mind,' she said, spotting an orange taxi light and sticking out her arm. 'He won't be there himself, of course. Once he's done his bit, he can scoot off to his meeting – poor thing. He's got a nightmare day today. But – but he would mind. You're right.'

'He doesn't want anyone to know?'

'Neither of us do.' Honor got into the cab. 'So you won't – you wouldn't . . .'

'Of course not.' Evie could feel herself about to cry too – and was suddenly glad that Honor was leaving and wouldn't see how upsetting she found it. 'I promise you I won't. Not anyone.'

Honor's hospital appointment was set to take some time. It was the day they'd be taking her eggs out – what eggs there were – to be injected with Edward's sperm. All Edward had to do was turn up that morning and 'produce'. Evie imagined him there now: sitting back in some badly-lit room, perusing well-thumbed porn mags while filling his plastic pot.

Honor, on the other hand, would need a full anaesthetic. She'd be there the whole morning, and would take a few hours to come round. She'd be dozy and weak when she left the hospital.

'Perhaps not in the best condition to see you,' she said half an hour later, telephoning Evie from the hospital bed as she waited for the anaesthetist to arrive. 'But as Edward won't be ready to leave for

410

Suffolk until five, I'll have an hour or so to kill if you still want to meet up.'

'He's not collecting you himself?'

'Sometimes he does,' said Honor quickly, 'but today's not great from his point of view. He—'

'Honor . . .'

'It's not a problem. Really, it isn't. Not when you've done it four or five times already. Trust me – I'll be absolutely fine! Just need to go easy. Of course they *say* you have to have someone there to meet you, but that's only to cover themselves. It's no worse than being a bit drunk. I promise you . . .'

'Well, I'll certainly be there.'

'Evie, really I—'

'What time will you be out?'

'Two, three o'clock? But it depends how long they take – how many eggs there are, and so on. And then how quickly I come round. It's really boring. And I—'

'But when's the earliest?'

Honor sighed. 'One o'clock, maybe. I don't know. It—'

'Right,' said Evie, mentally scrapping her beauty appointments. 'I'll be there for you in the main lobby at one. And if you're not ready until three, or even four, then that's absolutely fine with me. Okay?' In the background Evie could hear sounds of opening doors, of voices and rustling and general busying.

'Okay . . . okay, I – I have to go Evie. I'm sorry. I—'

'Good luck, darling,' said Evie, thinking of poor, pale Honor – all alone in a smart private hospital, dressed in a vile impersonal green gown, holding her arm out to the anaesthetist. 'See you later . . .'

It was almost three when Honor finally emerged. And

411

while Evie wasn't sure whether the extra two hours were good or bad – whether it meant that there were masses of eggs for the doctors to retrieve, or whether Honor had simply been struggling to come round from the anaesthetic – it didn't take long for her to find out.

'Not great, to be honest,' said Honor as they waited outside the hospital for a taxi to take them back to Bramerton Street.

Evie took her arm. 'We'll get you home just as soon as we can. I'll get you comfy on the sofa, and make you another cup of tea, and—'

'No – no, I'm all right!' Honor laughed. 'Took a while to come round but otherwise, they think I'll be fine . . . No damage there, apparently. No sign of anything wrong . . . except . . .' She swallowed, 'except that there were no eggs again. No useable eggs, at any rate . . .'

Forgetting about the taxi for a moment, Evie turned to Honor. 'What – nothing?'

Honor bit her lip.

'But I thought . . . I thought they'd called you in specially because—'

'Oh, I had the follicles, which is all they can see on the scan. I had masses – some of them quite big – which I suppose is why they were keen to get moving . . . but nothing inside. Nothing viable, anyway. So,' she sighed, 'so I guess it's back to the drawing board . . .'

To Evie's relief, there was no sign of Abe at the house – but, taking no chances, she decided to get Honor up into her bedroom where the two of them could talk freely.

Her mind was buzzing with questions. The more she thought about the back-to-back cycles of fertility

412

treatment Honor had endured, the more she worried for Honor's health. Not that she knew much about the subject – only what she'd gathered from skimming the occasional magazine article, or picked up on the news. But she couldn't help wondering if Honor and Edward had the right approach. Shouldn't they take a bit more time between each attempt? Go on holiday, relax, get healthy, eat the right kind of food and have a lot of sex . . . For all she knew they might, with a little less force, even be able to conceive naturally.

'No, Evie. Believe me. It's long past that sort of solution.'

Okay. Well even if it was fine, physically, for Honor – every six months – to go through what she'd been through today, not to mention the sudden hormone surges and energy fluctuations that went with each course of injections . . . surely there was an emotional side to consider. Honor wasn't a machine. And Evie couldn't help thinking that she needed a break – a good long break – from the pressure to conceive.

'You're only twenty-six!' she said, giving Honor a cup of tea and sitting beside her on the bed. 'You've got ages to get this right, Honor. It—'

'I've got four years.'

Evie frowned.

'After thirty, every woman's fertility starts to lessen—'

'But some have children in their fifties, Honor! And I'm sure I read somewhere that thirty-seven's the critical age—'

'Not for me, I'm afraid,' Honor said, sipping her tea.

'And that's the doctors' view? They told you that?'

'Some of them have. The ones in New York certainly did. And Paris . . .' She smiled. 'They're a bit gentler

413

over here, which is nice for me – but it drives poor Edward mad.'

'He doesn't believe them?'

Honor sighed. 'It's hard, I think – when you've been longing for kids as long as he's been. All his friends have got families now . . .'

'His *friends*?' spluttered Evie.

'It is different for him, Evie. He's pushing forty.'

'And?'

'And – and he's scared, I suppose.'

'Scared?' cried Evie. '*Scared?* What's Edward got to be scared about? It – Jesus!' She was laughing – horrified disbelieving laughter. 'It's not like *his* fertility falls away at any point! It's not like *he's* got to have all those injections and lie on a slab every six months while some strange doctor prods and pokes about inside him! How *dare* he?' And then mid-rant she noticed Honor's expression. She saw Honor look away, saw her put the cup of tea to one side and shift round against the pillows into a sitting position. It felt as if she'd already left the room. 'I'm sorry,' Evie said, more quietly.

Honor nodded, feeling for her shoes. 'You're just looking out for my interests,' she said. 'I know that. But the thing is, Evie – the thing you're forgetting – is the degree of sacrifice Edward is making, staying married to me. It's not his fault we're in this position—'

'Not your fault either.'

'Except it is,' said Honor gently. 'It's my body we're talking about. My eggs – or lack of them. My deficiency.'

'That's only—'

'I don't think you realise how many men leave their wives when they find they can't have children, Evie.

414

It's a big deal – and even more so for a man. They just aren't interested in adopting. They want their *own* offspring. It – it *really* matters . . .' Her eyes filled with tears. 'And yet, in spite of all this, Edward's sticking with me. He's prepared to fork out thousands – maybe hundreds of thousands – to have a child *with me*. He's prepared to go through endless undignified interviews with doctors all over the world. He's willing to put up with all the questions and all the intrusions and – and the whole hell of infertility . . . for me. That's how much he loves me.'

Evie's expression did not alter.

'And while I'm happy to talk to you about all this, Evie, while I trust you to say nothing to anyone, and – and am sure you'll be full of great ideas for us, I just won't listen to you rubbishing Edward. You hear me? I'm lucky he's with me. I'm lucky he's doing this. I'm lucky! I'm lucky! And if it means we do things his way – if it means I take on a few extra cycles than perhaps is normal – then that's something I'm glad – more than glad – to do for him.'

Evie was too stunned to reply. The firmness in Honor's voice, the barely contained indignation on behalf of her husband . . . it wasn't something she cared to provoke further. Honor might believe all this stuff about men leaving their infertile wives, and not wanting to adopt, and – and all the rest of it. But Evie wasn't convinced. Not for one moment. There were plenty of men, she was sure of it, who loved their wives enough to consider a childless marriage. Plenty more who'd be happy to adopt. And anyway – while it might be Honor's body letting them down – it was wicked, she felt, positively wicked, for Edward just to let her take the blame for this. To take advantage of her wretchedness – sending her down into some grim hospital-dominated underworld while forcing her to dance to happy, carefree music on the surface.

She looked at Honor, miserably. And Honor – catching something of Evie's thoughts in the expression on her face – sighed as she picked up her coat and bag.

'You don't understand it, do you?' she said.

'No – no, Honor. I just—'

'You still think he's a monster.'

Evie swallowed. 'No,' she said again. 'But nor do I think that he's doing you a favour by staying with you. I – I think that when men stay with their wives, no matter what, it's usually because they love them.'

Honor smiled. 'But of course he loves me! That's exactly what I'm trying to say to you! That's exactly my—'

'If Edward really loved you, Honor, he wouldn't be letting you think that your inability to give him a child makes you . . . somehow . . . useless. He should be showing you that it doesn't matter . . .'

'Except it does matter. It matters a great deal. And I—'

'Okay – okay, it matters.' Evie waved a hand impatiently. 'I'm not saying it's irrelevant . . . but – but nor is it everything, Honor. There are lots of things that a woman can do with her life, a lot of ways of – of being special to her husband, besides giving him a baby. Your – your lovability, for want of a better word, isn't dependent on whether you can have children! It's to do with you – *you*, as a person.'

'You think we could be happy without children?'

'Why not?'

Honor was silent.

'Why not?' said Evie again, warming to her

416

argument. 'You've got a beautiful life, Honor. Both of you do. You're married to someone you love, you live in a beautiful home, with lots of money and friends and – and people who love you. Edward's got all his farming and his shooting and his business projects. And you – you could do something really incredible with your time, if you put your mind to it. Just think of how you were at school, Honor. You could easily start up your own business, if you wanted, or go travelling, or write a book, or go back to Oxford and do a PhD, or . . . or anything! Without children, you could have the sort of career most women can only dream about. In fact,' Evie's eyes brightened, 'in fact, when you think about the world's most successful women – women like . . . I don't know . . . like Elizabeth I, or Marilyn Monroe, or – or Jane Austen! Or Mother Theresa.' Evie put a hand on Honor's arm. 'What I'm trying to say, Honor, is that it is perfectly possible to live a completely fulfilled life without children. That – that sometimes it's even an advantage, especially when it comes to one's career . . .'

Honor looked at her stiffly.

'. . . wouldn't you say?'

'I'm sorry, Evie. I see your point. But – but, truly, you don't know what it's like. You don't understand. You can't. You'd never say such things if you did.'

'I'm only—'

'Infertility is a nightmare. Believe me: a total nightmare. And for you to suggest to me, now, that a career might be some sort of *substitute* . . .' Honor gave an awful empty laugh. 'It's – if I didn't know you better, Evie, I'd find it almost offensive.'

Evie looked back, shocked. With the word 'offensive', it was as if Honor had slapped her.

417

'Maybe you can't see it yet,' Honor went on, 'because you're not married. Or because you're so ambitious, or so obsessed with your own precious career that it does seem all-important . . . And who knows? Maybe it is. Maybe for women like you childlessness isn't such a problem. Maybe when the time comes, you really won't care. But for me? I do. I care desperately. My life – the life I've chosen, the life I want – it's meaningless without . . .' She was crying now. 'And for as long as Edward is willing to stick with me so that we can have a baby, then – then I'm sorry, but I'll think myself the luckiest woman alive. I'll go through whatever medical treatment is necessary. And I'll fight anyone – including you, Evie – who dares question that decision.'

Chapter Twenty-Two

Second Thoughts

Trembling, Honor left the little house. Evie did not try to stop her. Instead she stood in the middle of her kitchen – face flushed, smarting from the sting of Honor's parting words – and frantically tried to made sense of what had just happened. Having always had the utmost respect for Honor's judgement – her balance, her row-free existence – it was hard for Evie not to wonder if she herself had perhaps overstepped the mark. On the other hand, she – Jesus. What did Honor want? Would she really prefer to be told by her friend that – yes, it *was* a dismal state of affairs, and – yes – her life *was* all but over unless she could have a child? Did she want Evie to say, yeah, fine . . . your husband's doing a great job letting you stew away thinking you're somehow at fault here? And of course you don't need anyone else to look out for you or pick you up from hospital or – or start talking about other constructive ways to live a life without children? She – damn it – was it really so wrong of Evie to offer support and concern and ways of looking at the situation that were perhaps more positive? Surely that was what being a good friend meant!

In any case, there was nothing Evie could say that wouldn't smack of insincerity, and she was done with falseness. For Honor had been completely right in her assessment of Evie's attitude to children and careers. Evie truly didn't think – had never thought – that being someone's wife, and someone else's mother, was the be all and end all of a woman's life. To her, Honor's aspirations were dated. Ridiculously, hopelessly, *depressingly* dated. It had, perhaps, been tactless of Evie to start talking about alternatives when poor Honor was still recovering from the news about her empty follicles but Evie still believed – at heart – that she was the one who saw it clearly.

The best thing to do was to leave it for a while. Let Honor calm down a bit – go back to her husband and her safe old-fashioned life, get over what had happened that day at the hospital. In time, no doubt, they'd try again. And perhaps next time they'd be lucky – and then there would be no need for Honor to think about alternatives. She could retreat, with every excuse, into the maternal role she'd always been expected to play; never have to face the modern world again . . . and Evie would be happy for her.

But it would still involve a loss. The loss of that other Honor she might have been, unfettered by children, forced on to a different path. It wouldn't be an easy life, but the person coming through at the end of it – a person who'd been stretched by the challenge of a sudden swerve away from the conventional pattern, a person forced to seek fulfilment in other spheres – would surely be more interesting than . . .

Well, whatever. Honor didn't want that sort of life

and, frankly, who could blame her when the old-fashioned model was just so much more suited to her nature and her tastes? Evie had to back off. Honor had made her decision when she'd agreed to marry Edward. Perhaps even before then. Perhaps when she'd quit her job, or even as early as the time when she and Abe had gone their separate ways.

Honor, it seemed, didn't 'do' struggle. She simply turned away. And nothing short of enforced childlessness would get her to change direction now. Even then, Evie felt she'd probably still prefer a fruitless marriage to Edward – shrinking away from the rocky search for other sources of fulfilment in favour of her ivory tower, putting up with a vague sense of purposelessness in her life over the rough rude dirt of the unfamiliar street.

But for all her attempts at self-justification – firmly resolving that, yes, of course she was in the right, Honor was just a bit wobbly after her operation, wasn't thinking straight – Evie still rather wished that she wasn't sworn to secrecy. She longed to run the episode past Matthew, sitting in front of her now, refilling her glass with wine and explaining why he too was single again.

'It just wasn't right,' he was saying. 'Worked fine when I was out in Washington and Sally was here in London . . . but I guess that rather sums it up. When I got back home, it was obvious. Not completely sure she's accepted it yet.'

Their eyes met.

'I – I mean, she definitely knows it's over,' he said quickly. 'I made it very clear. But Sally does tend to see what she wants to see. And as she's off now to spend

Christmas and New Year in Aspen, it was all "Yes, yes, Matthew, we'll talk about it when I get back..." which, now I'm thinking about it, is yet another reason why it was never going to work. It's weird. For someone whose career's supposed to be all about listening, and understanding, it turns out she's hopeless. Hopeless. Except when it comes to fashion and gossip.'

For a moment neither of them spoke. And then Matthew went on, in a more contemplative voice, 'The strange thing is, on paper, Sally should have been rather good for me. Too good, even. I mean, she's pretty. She's clever, well travelled. And there's no doubt she's making a success of her career. We've got masses of people and interests in common – a bit like you and Ian, maybe – but . . .' he frowned, 'but there was always something missing.'

'Like something was missing between you and me?' said Evie, naughtily. She was fishing now. She knew there'd never been anything wrong between them on that front. Matthew might have had a crush on someone else back then – almost certainly he would have found Evie wanting 'on paper' – but she'd never been in any doubt of the—

'Christ, no!' Matthew looked suitably appalled. 'Christ, Evie. Certainly not from my point of view. And . . .' pausing for a moment, he looked down, gathering his words with great care. 'And the more I go through life, Evie, the more women I date, the more I see of the—'

And then, quite suddenly, he stopped.

'Is that yours?'

'Is what—'

'There's a mobile ringing.' He leant to look under the table. 'I think it's coming from your bag.'

422

Evie could hear it now – getting louder and louder. People were turning to look. 'Okay, okay . . .'

Hauling the bag on to her lap, she rifled though it, grabbed the telephone, and was about to switch it off when she saw the number on the display. She glanced at Matthew.

'You need to take it?'

Evie nodded. 'I'm so sorry. I . . . Honor?' Putting a hand across her free ear to block out the worst of the restaurant noise, she huddled against the wall behind her chair, speaking in as low a voice as possible.

'No, it's fine. I'm just here with Matthew.' Smiling slightly: 'No, really. It's okay. You go ahead.'

There was a long silence.

'No, of course I don't. I'm sorry too . . . no, I am, Honor. Truly, I am. I should never have said those things, especially the— sure. I suppose I was still in shock for you – desperate to find something positive to say . . . but it's not the first thing you want to hear when you're just out of hospital – I do see that . . .'

Matthew picked up the pudding menu, but it was impossible not to listen.

'Well, it's typical of you to put it that way, Honor, but I think we both know I was . . . okay. Okay, let's drop it. And – and you got back all right? . . . And Edward? Was he . . .? Oh that's good. I'm glad . . . And you're really feeling okay, are you? You promise? . . . fine. Sure . . . Of course I will. Speak tomorrow, then – all right, Honor. Lots of love, yeah? . . . Okay, bye.'

Honor put the telephone down. She was standing alone – back now in her bedroom at Allenham, with the curtains still open – and saw her world reflected in the evening glass of the windowpanes: the solitary woman in her elegant bedroom, dark against the glow of an antique lampshade . . . all criss-crossed with rigid Georgian bands of whitewashed wood.

Somewhere beyond the glass – outside, in the darkness – Edward had yet to come back in from whatever it was he'd rushed off to do on their arrival. He hadn't said what it was. Most likely some minor irregularity to do with the farm: a barn door open when it should have been closed – they'd both seen it from the road – and an unfamiliar vehicle in the yard. It was right that he should go. But the timing and manner of his going – not telling her, not bothering to carry her things inside, as if today were just like any other day – Honor tried not to mind. Indeed, she told herself, there was more than a little truth in Edward's unspoken assessment of what had happened that day. For them, there was nothing unusual in not being pregnant. Nothing to say – nothing that hadn't already been said a thousand times before . . . why should he make a fuss of her? *If Edward really loved you*, Evie had said that afternoon, *he wouldn't be letting you think that your inability to give him a child makes you . . . somehow. . . useless. He should be showing you that it doesn't matter* . . . Well, he was. That was exactly what he was doing. It didn't matter – apparently. Life went on. Barn doors needed to be closed.

Honor sat on the edge of the bed. She thought again of Evie in the restaurant with Matthew. She replayed their conversation in her mind – the happy warmth in Evie's voice, even when she was sounding concerned; the babble of voices in the restaurant beyond. Honor had never liked dating. Private dinner parties and peaceful nights in had always been her preference. But tonight was different. Right then, Honor would have given a great deal to have been able to exchange the cool, tasteful silence of her bedroom for the chatter and laughter of a London restaurant.

Evie put the telephone back into her bag, and exchanged it for a packet of cigarettes. 'Sorry about that. We had a bit of a row earlier, I couldn't leave it. Not when she was the one to call first. It would have been—'

'I understand,' said Matthew. And then, unable to resist the instinct to probe before the subject grew cool, 'So, Honor's been in hospital, has she?'

Evie was silent. She took a cigarette from the packet and put it to her mouth.

'I'm sorry. I couldn't help overhearing.'

Evie lit her cigarette. She'd promised Honor she wouldn't say anything, and in any other circumstances she would have kept her word. She'd have told him quite plainly that she couldn't talk about it and then quickly change the subject. But the fact that Honor had rung while Matthew was right there in front of her, the fact that it was Matthew – Matthew who minded so much about trust, and who so deserved to be trusted; Matthew, who was looking at her now with so much concern, Matthew, whose opinion of the subject she so longed to hear . . .

'I'm sorry,' he said again.

'It's okay, Matthew. It's my fault. I should have taken the call outside. I just . . .'

'You'd rather not tell me?'

Evie shook her head. 'It's not that,' she said. 'In fact, I'd love to tell you – I'd love to know what you think – but . . . Oh, sod it.'

It was too much. Explaining to him that she was hesitating only because Honor had asked her,

425

specifically, to say nothing about it to anyone; explaining that she was only breaking her word because she felt Matthew might be of some use in all this, that he might have some idea of how she could help her friend . . . she told him what had happened. Hurrying through the bare facts of Honor's infertility and the back-to-back rounds of IVF treatment that she and Edward had endured through most of their married life, Evie arrived at the source of her own particular concern: Honor's refusal to see that there was more to life than children.

Matthew frowned. 'Like . . .?'

'Like having a career! A woman doesn't have to be defined by whether she's married or has children . . . not any more. We . . . surely *you* can understand this, Matthew! You're not stuck in some sort of Victorian time warp. You can see we've moved on from that sort of mentality . . . from – from thinking that if a woman has no husband or children then her life is pretty much over . . . that she's worthless, that she has no purpose. If – if anything, it's the opposite.'

'The opposite?' he said.

'In a way. I mean, you only have to look at the kind of women who really make something of their lives, who go on to write masterpieces, or win Nobel Prizes, or run countries . . . I – I know there are exceptions, of course there are, but you see what I'm saying, don't you?'

Matthew didn't smile back. 'You're saying that a woman can't be successful and at the same time get married and have children.'

'I suppose I am.'

He paused for a moment. 'And – and if I'm reading you correctly, Evie, you're saying it's "old-fashioned" to want those things.'

'Certainly, to want them at – at the expense of . . .'

'A career?'

'A life, Matthew. A *life*. How's a woman going to do anything significant with her life if she spends all her days ironing some man's shirts and wiping sick off the carpet? Or feeling guilty because she's hired someone to do it for her. It's not what we're about any more! Not modern women, at any rate . . .'

While Evie had been talking, their bill had arrived. Matthew pulled it towards him and reached to the back pocket of his trousers for his wallet. 'So what's the answer then?' he said, with studied lightness. 'No marriage and children?'

'Not if you want to be successful!'

He glanced through his wallet, seemingly casual. 'You really believe this?'

'You're saying you don't?'

For a moment, Matthew said nothing. And then, taking out a credit card, he passed it to the waiter, turned to her and said, almost angrily, 'No, Evie. I don't. I – I know I used to be down on marriage. I know I used to think they were shams and so on . . . but I've changed my mind. And in spite of everything I saw with my parents, and everything I said before, I have to say that I now think promising to spend the rest of your life with someone you love is – absolutely – the most romantic thing you can do. I think having a child with them would put every other achievement in the shade. And I'm afraid I think that calling it old-fashioned is like saying that kissing is old-fashioned. Or dancing. Or smiling. Or making love. So I'm sorry, Evie, but in this case I have to say that I'm with Honor. And I don't think a career is, even remotely, a substitute for having a child with the person you love.

427

You only have to look at someone like that poor girlfriend of your uncle's . . . What was her name? The one we all got in such a flap about – with her high-flying career, and all that money she'd made, and all those awards she'd won – Diana someone . . .'

'Diana Miller.'

'That's right. She had a great career, didn't she?'

'Still does. But Matthew, she's—'

'Hardly fulfilled. Hardly happy . . .'

'She—'

'. . . hardly a role model for the next generation.'

Evie couldn't believe what she was hearing. It was all right coming from Honor, in a way. Honor, after all, had never lived in the real world. With her money and her background and – most significantly – her disposition, it was hardly surprising she had felt no need for change. She was perfectly content with the old ways. They suited her. Or had, at least, until this dreadful news about her infertility. But *Matthew*? Matthew had no excuse. Entirely modern in his outlook – with a job that necessitated an awareness of contemporary standards, contemporary attitudes, contemporary aspirations . . . surely Matthew could see that – no matter what had happened with mad Diana Miller; her case was hardly comparable – that there was something desperately wrong with Honor's situation?

'Desperately sad, maybe. But hardly—'

'So you think Honor's doing the right thing, then?' Evie was speaking quite loudly now. 'You can honestly say, with your hand on your heart, that you think it's fine for me, as her friend, to let her cling on to these crazy dated notions of marriage and motherhood – notions that are certain to make her miserable – instead

428

of encouraging her to look to other ways of finding fulfilment?'

Matthew sighed. 'I suppose I just think it may not be so easy for Honor to let go,' he said, taking back his credit card. He sounded tired. 'I think that if you ever get to experience the kind of love that makes you want to marry someone and have children with them, Evie, then those things won't seem so "crazy" to you any more. Or even remotely dated.'

They left the restaurant in a sober mood. Evie sat quietly in Matthew's car – he still had that old sky-blue Renault from all those years ago – while he drove her back to Bramerton Street. Once more she found herself wishing she'd kept her mouth shut. More particularly, she wished she hadn't taken Honor's call. He'd been about to say something important to her – she was sure of it. But then the call had come, the subject had changed, and Evie had rushed on in with everything she felt about Honor – pouring out the internal anxiety of her day, determined to make Matthew see it from her point of view . . . and the moment had been lost. Whatever Matthew had been about to say to her, he certainly wasn't going to say it now.

But Matthew, it seemed, had other ideas. Parking briskly in a space outside Evie's house, he switched off the car engine and said, quite suddenly, into the silence, 'I'm sorry about that.'

Evie turned.

'Really I am,' he added. 'Of course I agree with what you were saying, about Honor needing to find some other focus in her life if she can't have kids. It might not have been the most tactful thing to have suggested so soon . . .'

He smiled at her. Without thinking, he reached across the gearstick and put a hand on Evie's. It was supposed to reassure her. In the context of what he'd said about Evie being tactless, it was his way of telling her that the error was hardly grave. But the sensation of his hand over hers had an effect far beyond the one he'd intended, and an old surging reflex – one that Evie had never felt with Ian, one she'd almost forgotten about . . . as if some internal valve had finally opened and blood was rushing into a part of her heart that had fallen dormant – rendered her speechless for a moment.

'Now listen,' he went on. 'It's late – I can see you're tired. But – but I don't suppose you'd like to do this again sometime, would you? I swear I won't get so hot and bothered, and I absolutely promise to keep what-ever boring, old-fashioned opinions I might have to myself . . .'

Evie felt the cue. But before she could pull herself together and tell Matthew he wasn't old-fashioned or remotely boring, there were three sharp raps at his window and Abe's face appeared in the rectangle of glass. He was smiling at them, a strange low-watt smile that Evie now recognised as one of the results of the meetings he now attended. It was almost someone else's smile, as if Abe were merely acting happy; as if to be truly happy would kick-start a lethal cycle of ups and downs that simply wasn't worth the downs . . . and the terrible needs that such downs might drive him to satisfy. And while Evie knew that Abe's meetings were his lifeline, while it was these meetings – more than anything else – that kept him on the straight and narrow, she still missed the natural brilliance of his former smile.

'Abe!' Matthew opened the car door and got out, shaking his old friend's hand. 'Abe man, how are you?'

Evie opened her own door and stepped into the empty street. With Abe and Matthew on the other side of the car – Abe answering Matthew's question in rather too much detail – she reached in for her handbag and, throwing the car door shut again, closing that sky-blue shell, came slowly round to join them on the pavement.

'Oh that's good,' said Matthew, toying with his car keys as Abe chattered on about his health. 'I'm glad. Really glad. And of course you can't hurry these things, but I . . . absolutely. One step at a time.' He glanced at Evie. 'Don't you think?'

Evie smiled.

And Matthew, taking advantage of the lull in their chatter, stepped forward to kiss her cheek. 'I'll call you tomorrow,' he murmured.

Evie nodded. 'Better call my mobile. I've got a few viewings. Nothing important, but—'

'Great.' He was in the car. 'Bye then! Bye Abe . . .'

Abe watched him go. He saw the jangling car keys. He noticed the speedy exit, the casual 'I'll call you tomorrow', and Evie's trusting reply . . . and followed her back inside, his face dark as he turned to bolt the door.

Later – lying in bed and listening to Evie pottering about in the bathroom, humming to herself – Abe turned the question over in his mind. He didn't have a problem with Matthew. He liked Matthew. Matthew had been a good friend to him in the past year or so. Getting to know Matthew had made Abe realise that the man's qualities far outweighed his deficiencies . . . but that didn't mean that the deficiencies had vanished altogether, particularly where women – and one woman in particular – were concerned.

For while Abe didn't doubt Matthew was fond of Evie, while he could see that something more than friendship had prompted him to ask her out, Abe still couldn't get it out of his head that Matthew wasn't truly in love. Ever since the evening they'd first met – way back, at that party Honor had given in her rooms at Oxford before he'd even gone to LA – even then Abe had understood, deeply and completely, that Matthew could never be in love with Evie. Not when he was so chronically in love with her cousin.

He knew it because he, Abe, was similarly afflicted. He couldn't help himself. God knew it, he'd tried. It was just the sort of girl Honor was. And while it had taken Abe the six intervening years to realise this quality in her (at twenty-one, he'd assumed that falling in love would be something that happened frequently and easily; that girls like Honor, girls who made him feel that way, would flit in and out of his life indefinitely . . . that he'd be able to take his pick) he'd never been in any doubt of his original feelings.

And neither had he been in much doubt of Matthew's. No matter that he'd been out of it that first evening at Oxford, Abe still *knew* – knew like you know when someone else is thinking what you're thinking; when they've sensed the same shift in the breeze, or felt the first drop of rain. He didn't need to be sober to figure out such things. And when Honor subsequently told him the news that Matthew and Evie were over, that Matthew had ended it – that he'd done it at Favenham, of all places, and that, according to Evie, it was down to a crush Matthew had on some 'mystery woman', it was mere confirmation of a truth

432

Abe already knew. He was glad to hear that Matthew had found the decency to back out. Better late than never, he'd thought quietly to himself.

Now, however – six years later – Matthew was back where he started. True, Evie had changed since then, and considerably for the better. It was understandable that Matthew should feel attracted to her. Indeed, there had even been moments in the past few weeks when Abe himself had wondered . . . Although of course he couldn't inflict himself in that way on anyone right now, not at his current stage of recovery. And even if he could, he knew it wasn't fair to Evie. It was, Abe felt, a sign of his love for Evie – a different love, the love of a friend – that he held back. Evie deserved better than to be someone's second prize.

But perhaps Matthew felt safe this time around, with Honor married off and unobtainable. Perhaps – in Matthew's eyes – the mere fact of that marriage was enough to bump Evie into being first prize. But Abe still didn't like it. He didn't like the fact that Matthew was succumbing to a temptation that he himself had resisted. Didn't like it that his dear good friend was walking blind into a deception – admittedly a benign deception, although in Abe's book, such things didn't really exist – and he felt it his duty now to warn her. It wouldn't be easy. But after everything Evie had done for him in the past few months, it was absolutely the least he could do.

And so, catching her early next morning before she'd left for work, Abe asked if Evie could spare half an hour. 'No more than that, I promise. I know you like to get in early. But I do need to talk to you about something. Something important –'

He knew of a café in Chelsea Harbour. It didn't have

chairs, or anywhere to sit and was a fair distance from Bramerton Street, but the coffee was good. They could take it and drink it, perched on bollards overlooking the gin palaces and speedboats in the marina, while he told her what was on his mind.

Whether it was embarrassment or natural honesty – with perhaps a sense that Evie was pretty robust and didn't need to be handled with kid gloves – or whether it was simply the therapy he'd been having, with its emphasis on saying things as they were, not cushioning blows, of plain-speaking from the cruel-to-be-kind school of thought . . . whatever it was, Abe made no attempt to sugar his words that morning. It didn't occur to him to phrase his concerns in a way that would protect Evie from the truth. He didn't see the truth as anything other than good.

'So go on then,' said Evie, taking the plastic lid off her polystyrene cup and tipping in some sugar. 'What is it?'

Abe gathered his resolve. 'It's Matthew.' He looked at her. But Evie seemed more interested in closing the plastic lid without spilling any coffee. 'Sweetheart, have you any idea what was really going on when – when he left you last time?'

Now she frowned. 'There was another woman,' came the considered response. 'Some crush he had. But that was years ago. He—'

'And do you know who that woman was?'

'No,' said Evie, getting annoyed. 'And to be honest with you, I'm not sure I want to know. It's all so much water under the bridge. I'm hardly—'

'It was Honor.'

Abe looked at the mute profile.

'Matthew was desperately in love with Honor,' he

434

went on. You wouldn't have seen it, Evie, because you weren't thinking that way then. You were just mad for him, and happy to take it all at face value. But I could see the way he looked at her . . .'

'What, at Oxford?' said Evie, with a hard, short laugh. 'When you were oh-so-sober and reliable?'

'Not just Oxford. It was the same the night of my play last year. And, sure, you'll say I was in no fit state to figure out what was happening then either, or – or at that dinner we had at my club . . . but why else do you think he wrote such fabulous things about me in his review, other than to make Honor think better of him? It certainly wasn't me he was out to impress! And why else would he go to such lengths to be with the four of us on his last night in London before heading out to Washington, instead of with his girlfriend?'

Evie struggled with the implication. Was it really so impossible to think that she, not Honor, had been the one to lure Matthew away from Sally Jarvis that night? Was she really so very second-rate? Holding her cup of coffee close under her chin, she looked out towards the boats in the marina.

'More importantly,' Abe rammed on, 'why do you think – if there was nothing to hide – why was he so very secretive about whoever it was he had a crush on, back when he dumped you?'

Evie didn't know.

'Believe me, Evie – it's very hard not to fall in love with your cousin. She's in a whole other league – I don't know a single woman like her . . .'

'Sure. Fine. We all know she's wonderful. But she's married, Abe – in case you hadn't noticed.'

'You think it makes a difference?'

'Well,' Evie spluttered, 'well, you'd hope it would!'

435

Abe was silent.

'And – and anyway, why exactly do you think I'd mind about all this?'

Still, Abe said nothing.

'I'm just helping him find a flat to buy.'

'That's really all?'

'Of course it is. He . . . sure, he's become a sort of friend again, and yes – I still enjoy his company. Who wouldn't?'

Abe looked at her and sighed. 'I just wanted to look out for you, Evie. Just didn't want you to get hurt.'

'Me? Hurt?' Shoving her polystyrene cup into the mouth of a smart black Royal Borough bin, Evie gave him an easy smile. 'Jesus . . . you don't need to worry about that!'

It wasn't until she was in the taxi – out of view, and earshot – that Evie's smile disappeared. She thought of all those other moments that Abe had never even witnessed: Matthew's dogged resistance to all those attempts she'd made to get them to meet again after that first time at Oxford; Honor's own subtle doubts about Matthew – veiled concern that Evie had taken for snobbishness. Then there'd been Matthew's suddenly understandable lack of physical interest in Evie that weekend at Favenham. And, finally, that muttered explanation that there was – sort of – someone else –

Who?

You don't know her.

Try me.

Please, Evie. It's not relevant.

Like hell it wasn't. Abe was right. For even if Matthew had done the sensible thing and abandoned his crush once Honor had married Edward Beaumaris

– even if his current pursuit of Evie was sincere – there would always be the knowledge that Honor was the one he really wanted, the plain hard truth that Evie would always be second best in the heart of the man she loved. Thinking of the wistful speech that Matthew had made to her last night about love and marriage and having children, Evie realised it must have all been spoken with Honor in mind, and her cheeks burned bright with shame.

When Matthew rang her mobile, she didn't pick it up. When Linda finally took his call on the office line, Evie was hurrying out for lunch. Choosing a time the following day when she knew he couldn't answer his own telephone – a time he'd scheduled an important interview with an ex-athlete who'd recently decided to go into politics, an interview he'd been pressing for for ages – she rang to say she'd got his message but dinner that week, or even the week after, was really out of the question. She was sorry, but life was getting on top of her. She really needed to write a few letters, do some ironing, catch up on her expenses.

By the end of the week she'd passed his file over to Nick. She didn't really deal with the lower-bracket properties these days – wasn't the best person to help Matthew any more, especially as she'd so patently failed to find him anywhere suitable and it was now almost December. No, Nick was the man for the job. Much better that Nick take over.

Chapter Twenty-Three

Lavinia

'Okay.' Honor had the telephone clasped to her ear and was looking through next year's diary. 'So that takes us to the eighteenth of February. Will Mr Hassan be back from his skiing holiday by then, do you think?'

It was mid-December, under four weeks since the last IVF result, and already Honor was calling to arrange the next cycle of suppressants and stimulants. She could tell that the nurse didn't like it. Wanted Honor to wait – 'Give yourself a chance to recover, dear' – but Honor was filled with urgency. This wasn't about her age or how many more good fertile years were left to her. Those things, as the nurse well knew, were fine and healthy. But the nurse was rather less informed about the state of her patient's marriage.

Ever since their return from the last treatment in London, Honor had been unsettled. Although in many ways, things were smoother between them again – certainly less confrontational than when Evie and Ian had visited in the spring – there were other things that worried her more. It wasn't that Edward had been unpleasant to her, or rude, or lazy over his share of caring for Lavinia. True, he wasn't as habitually affectionate towards Honor as he'd once used to be . . . but that, in isolation, didn't bother her so much. No more erosion than was natural, she felt, after three or four years together. In comparison to the careless way her father had treated her mother over the years, it was an infinitely more civilised marriage. In essence, Edward was exactly the same as he'd always been: a little formal, a little distant, and not so long ago she'd found that style of love refreshing. She'd liked the space, liked having the freedom to breathe, instead of gasping for air in the face of Abe's desire.

But as failure layered on failure with every empty cycle, Honor was starting to realise that she wanted – needed – more. Faced with the nightmare of a perpetually silent nursery, she wasn't sure she could withstand so much silence from her husband as well. Often he was out of the house or shut away in his study, reading. Even when they were in the same room he seemed absent – cordoned off – but how could she complain when he'd always been that way? How could she begin to tell him that his elegant air of indifference didn't work – wasn't right – in times of trouble?

Honor struggled constantly with this thought. There were moments of defeat when she felt it was a simple case of blood and stones – no point chipping away if the blood wasn't there to start with – and times when she was certain there was something she could do. He wasn't a bad man, he had a heart, if only she knew where to look.

The blood didn't need to be red hot. If Edward couldn't be her lover – and, absolutely, she understood that years of clinical demands on when and how they should make love had rather flattened that side of things – then couldn't he at least be her friend? Someone who might sit with her and hold her while she cried, someone who wouldn't leave her do it on her own; someone who'd make it his business to see that she was truly okay instead of taking her at face value? She needed someone prepared to confront, with her, some of the sadnesses and frustrations thrown up by the prospect of such emptiness – even as Evie herself had done the other week. Honor might once have been the sort of person who preferred to cry in private but not any more, not where her husband was concerned.

She longed for evidence of life in him – ups, downs, tears, laughter; even rows and shouting would have been preferable, she felt, to the well-mannered surface he always presented no matter what was thrown at him. His brand of distant courtesy no longer made her feel safe. Indeed, it had the opposite effect. And Honor, like some poor mistaken perfectly camouflaged creature – tricked by its own trickery – was getting the oddest sensations from her choice of mate. The very politeness she'd so valued, so missed, when working in the City – that politeness she'd taken as a sign that someone cared – was now being thrown back at her as precisely the opposite. All Edward could give, it seemed, were the *signs* of caring, of love. Not love itself. And Honor was no different from a large grey beetle, expending all its energy on a pebble.

'Darling?' she said, coming into his study with the diary in her hand.

For a moment, it seemed he wasn't there – and then she realised he was simply leaning down to the bottom drawer of his desk, putting some papers away. He sat up, red in the face from bending.

440

'I'm sorry to interrupt you . . .'

'That's okay.' He smiled.

'Just wanted to let you know I've been speaking to Alison at St George's, and it seems that Rami Hassan can see us again in February – which is great, don't you think?'

He continued to smile.

'So I've made an appointment for the eighteenth. You are free then, aren't you?'

Edward reached for his desk diary.

'It's a Friday.'

'Sure.' He scribbled something in. 'Thanks, Honor.'

Leaving him there, Honor felt more like a secretary than a wife: booking in another appointment for them to find themselves a baby, as if it were some two-dimensional suited client they'd scheduled in, not a primal blood-drenched naked little life . . . and something of her despair must have shown on her face at that moment because Lavinia, making her way through the hall to the sitting room just as Honor emerged from the study, was asking her – out of nowhere – if she was feeling all right.

'Me?' The denial was total reflex. 'Why, I'm fine, Lavinia! It's you we should be thinking about!' Honor put her diary and papers on a chair. 'You want a hand with that tapestry bag? Here – let me take it . . .'

The next day was a Saturday and, as was now customary on the last weekend before Christmas, both Edward and Honor had been invited to spend the day shooting with her father at Favenham.

With Lavinia's health so poor, however, weekends were increasingly difficult for Honor and Edward to accept invitations together. Mrs Wilkins was happy to

441

tend Edward's mother during the week, but she had her own family to consider at the weekend – which meant that, unless they employed someone else to come in on Saturdays and Sundays, it was up to Honor and Edward to share the job of caring for Lavinia. And as, with shooting invitations – even ones from Honor's father – it was invariably Edward's presence that was required, Edward who'd actually be shooting, Edward whose absence from the line of guns would throw the whole day awry, Honor had agreed once again to be the one to stay behind.

He was outside on the gravel, putting his gun case and a fresh box of cartridges into the back of his car. 'It's a nine thirty start, isn't it?'

Honor nodded. 'Not that there'll be much action until at least ten, knowing Dad. You remember last year . . .' Edward slammed the car boot shut. 'You've got masses of time. Send them my love, won't you?'

'Of course.' Edward walked round to the front of his car and opened the door to the driving seat. Getting in behind the steering wheel, he pulled the door between them, put the keys in the ignition and, turning to her, mouthed, 'Bye,' through the shatterproof glass.

'Bye,' she echoed, standing back for the car to swing out and away from her down a wet December drive.

Back inside, Honor went straight upstairs and helped Lavinia out of her bath – steadying the bird-like feet on an unforgiving floor and finding a fresh towel – before starting work on the house. It didn't need cleaning or even much tidying, but she'd found in recent months that she rather liked doing housework. When the tasks weren't obligatory, there was something rather pleasing about the process of putting things in order; a

442

certain relief in knowing that she still had control, however petty, over some areas of her life. Certainly it helped to fill the silence, and Honor would always feel much better after an hour or so of ironing, or wiping last night's tumblers dry until they gleamed, or sorting through a jumble of receipts and papers, down to a flat, clean desk.

Today, with Christmas decorations to put up, there was an added incentive to her industry. Honor worked solidly until lunchtime: clearing breakfast, sweeping fireplaces, tidying papers, before turning to the piles of holly that had been cut down and left in an old garage in readiness for her return from London. The only room she left untouched was Edward's study. He'd never complained when, in the past, she'd gone in. But from the tired way he'd ask where she'd put his stapler, or what had happened to that package addressed to his lawyer, she could tell he'd rather she didn't go in there. Even though she'd refilled the stapler and put it neatly back into the drawer, even though the lawyer's package had been stamped and taken to the post office, Edward had always seemed more forgiving than grateful to find these things done for him.

By one o'clock the entire ground floor was finished – all that remained was the tree, which Honor couldn't do until someone bigger and stronger than her was able to drag it into the hall. And so it was, with some sense of satisfaction, she prepared a light lunch for her mother-in-law and took it up on a tray. 'It's just soup I'm afraid, Lavinia – Mrs Wilkins's pea and mint.'

'That sounds lovely.' Taking off her glasses, Lavinia put her book to one side and leant back against the pillows, observing Honor. 'Thank you, darling.'

There was a moment of silence as Honor dealt with

443

the tray, feeling for the catch that released its little legs, and then easing the whole thing over her recumbent mother-in-law.

'Another pillow? I can easily get one from the cupboard if you'd like. Or—'

'No I'm fine, darling. Thank you.'

'And you're sure you're okay with the light?'

'Absolutely.'

Honor smiled. 'Then I'll leave you to it,' she said, and was on the verge of turning when Lavinia raised a hand.

'Actually, Honor. There is one thing . . .'

Honor stopped. For a brief second, no more than a breath's worth, neither woman spoke. They merely looked at one another through the musty air of Lavinia's room, their eyes meeting with such a very particular seriousness that, by the time Lavinia opened her mouth, Honor could predict exactly what was coming.

'I know,' said Lavinia.

Honor nodded and lowered her gaze. She didn't trust herself to speak.

'I'm so sorry, darling,' Lavinia went on sadly. 'I suppose I could have turned a blind eye to some of those envelopes you've been getting. Although I have to say the ones last year from New York were so blatant I wanted to sue them myself for breaching your confidentiality. How *could* they?'

Still, Honor couldn't answer.

'But we're living too close these days for that sort of privacy, sweetheart. All those letters and faxes, those indistinct telephone messages from strange-sounding clinics. And then your sudden trips to London and God only knows where else . . . I was bound to notice something eventually.' Lavinia gave a self-deprecating smile. 'And when you remember you're saddled with a dreadful grandmother-in-waiting, just longing to see you refusing shellfish, or whatever it is pregnant women can't eat these days . . .' But Honor didn't return her smile, and Lavinia quickly dropped the levity. 'I'm sorry, darling – I'm sure you'd prefer me to stay quiet about it all, just as Edward would . . .' She reached for Honor's shaking hand. 'So alike, you two,' she murmured. And then, looking straight and clear into Honor's eyes: 'But I'm afraid I just can't do it any more. I can't bear seeing you both so miserable. Can't bear having to pretend with you that everything's fine, when it's just so clearly not.'

Swallowing hard, Honor looked up with tears in her eyes at a blurred Lavinia, sitting against the pillows.

'Of course I can't really imagine what it must have been like . . .'

'It's been fine.' Honor gave her a determined smile. 'Really. Not half as bad as some of the dreadful things you've had to deal with recently, Lavinia. And—'

'Except that I'm old.'

Honor's smile softened. 'That's hardly relevant!'

'No . . .' Lavinia shook her head. 'No, darling. It is. What's happening to me – however grim it is, however depressing – it's natural. It's life. People die. But you – you and Edward . . .'

'We might be struggling a little. It doesn't mean—'

'You've been struggling for years, Honor. And yes, I know your parents have had their own troubles, so it's only understandable they might not have noticed what's been going on . . .' Her smile this time was odd, almost as if she were apologising for something. 'And dear Edward . . . he can't be the easiest person at times like this. In fact I'm sure he's not. He's like his father – never say what they're thinking, especially when it's serious . . . and – and I suppose I just don't want you to feel that you're alone in all of this. You – you understand?'

Honor was crying now.

Reaching forward, Lavinia pressed her arm again. 'But you mustn't feel he's given up,' she went on, her voice filled with fire. 'You hear me? Don't think about the past. Don't go there. He's with *you* now. It's *you* he loves, it's *you* he married. That girl . . .'

Honor looked up, surprised.

'. . . she was just—' Lavinia stopped short, realising too late her mistake.

'What girl?'

'Exactly,' came the swift response. 'What girl, indeed! And the important thing now is for you and Edward to—'

'What girl, Lavinia?' Honor looked stricken. 'What are you saying?'

Lavinia closed her eyes. How could he not have told her? It wasn't a particularly terrible secret, and so much better to get such things sorted out at the start of a marriage rather than wait for his poor wife to discover like this. It only made the whole episode seem so much more significant than the banal situation it really was. Some random woman, hopelessly unsuitable, and a young man not ready to settle down. Oh sure, he'd *thought* he was in love with her, but honestly he wasn't. Just a few sharp words from Robert . . . that was all it had taken. A few mild threats about inheritance and so on. Edward had soon seen sense. She hadn't been heavily pregnant – only a couple of months gone – and, thankfully, had really been rather decent about it all. Surprisingly co-operative . . .

446

Honor remembered the tacky koala bear that had been waiting for them on their return from their honeymoon, and the looping writing of that card from Australia.

Hope you'll be happy. Lots of love, Shelley.

She thought of Edward as he'd been this morning – the blood in his cheeks as he rose from that bottom drawer of his desk to answer Honor's question about the hospital appointment . . .

'I'm sorry, Lavinia . . .'

'Honor?'

Honor didn't turn back. She was already halfway down the passage, heading for the stairs.

It was all there. The drawer was crammed full – with notebooks, and photographs, and a grey koala bear still in its airport packaging. Honor pulled it right out. She sat on the floor with the drawer beside her and – hating herself – opened the first of the notebooks.

It wasn't so much the diaries in the end. Or even the stupid koala bear. The fact that he hadn't bothered to take it out of its packaging suggested to Honor that, whatever Edward might once have felt for Shelley Maclean, he'd certainly moved on. But the photographs were a different matter. One here of her husband, tanned and laughing, his hair a mess, with sea and sand all around; his eyes meeting the click of the camera – or, more particularly, the person behind the camera – with a depth of happiness and affection that to Honor was completely unfamiliar. And again, this time in a suit with the shirt collar undone and his arm round the shoulders of a beautiful girl . . . And the more Honor looked at them, the more apparent it was to her that, even if Edward was no longer in love with Shelley, there'd certainly been a time when he was . . .

and that whatever it was he and Shelley had shared, it far surpassed his relationship with Honor. He wasn't a stone. There was blood enough pulsing through him – just not for his English wife.

The two-dimensional man in the photographs was a man in love. Fully alive. But the flesh-and-blood man in the sensible car who had driven off that morning for a day's shooting . . . ? That was a man who'd settled for second best – something right enough, but only on the surface. A man reduced to something far flatter than any of the photographs in his bottom left-hand drawer, a man who'd made a terrible mistake when he'd asked nice sweet Honor to be his wife.

And Honor, to her horror, realised that the very things that had attracted her to Edward Beaumaris in the first place – the slight distance about his person, the dark glass inscrutability, the controlled way he conducted himself – were the things that should have warned her he had something to hide. He was the actor, not Abe. There was something dishonest at the heart of it all . . . Yet Honor had liked it, had found it more interesting – and less demanding – than anything direct, upfront, and undiluted. It was almost as if she needed the shadiness, as if standing naked in full bright sunlight was simply too much for her.

She wasn't surprised when he denied it.

Shelley Maclean? Good God! He was barely mature when he'd met the woman! And even at the time it had only been a crush. It was never going to last. That old drawer in his desk? Why, it was just a bit of nostalgia! He should have cleared it out years ago. It was only because he'd forgotten about it . . .

'And the baby?'

Edward began dismantling his gun, laying out all the parts in preparation for cleaning, and shaking out the oily rag he kept in the pocket of his gun case. 'Well, of course that was unfortunate . . .'

'*Unfortunate?*'

'Come on, Honor. It wasn't as if we'd planned to have a baby. Neither of us was ready for anything like that. It would have been madness.'

'And you still think that?'

Edward peered down the length of his barrels, looking at where the pellets from the day's cartridges had roughened and blackened the sides.

'You really think it was the right decision?' she went on. 'Even now? After everything we've been through and – and the possibility that you'll never have a child of your own?'

Pricked by her sharper tone, Edward put the barrels down and looked round at his wife, standing anxiously by the back-room door – arms clasped, hands over elbows in front of her slim frame – waiting for his reply.

'Of course I do,' he said, in a tired flat voice. 'It's you I love, Honor. It's you I married. It's you I want to have children with, no matter how they're conceived . . . and we will have them, darling. I promise you we will.'

But his smile was shallow and his bottom fixed to the wooden chair. He made no attempt to touch her. Just picked up another section of his shotgun and reached for the oily rag.

Turning, Honor walked out. She went back into the kitchen, filled the kettle and took two cups and a teapot from the cupboard. Listening to the rumbling of water coming to the boil, she sat expressionless at the kitchen table, looking ahead – in her mind's eye – down the flat desert road of their marriage.

Chapter Twenty-Four

Rachel's Christmas

Giles stood at the checkout with two full supermarket trolleys under his command and ran his eye for a final time down Rachel's list.

Strictly it was Lillian's job to do the weekly food shopping. But Lillian had injured her leg and for months now had needed someone to give her a lift. William was never going to do it – his air of superiority was such that nobody even thought to suggest he act as Lillian's driver. And while Rachel had seemed quite happy to step in, Giles was having none of it. Why should Rachel go? With all Xandra's duties to contend with – sometime cook, gardener, housekeeper, social secretary, hostess – she was already run off her feet. Giles was damned if she was going to drive anybody anywhere for the sake of an already-spoilt brother. So it was Giles who went; Giles who took Lillian to the local supermarket every Thursday; Giles who – unable to bring himself just to sit in the car and wait while the poor woman limped up and down the aisles – came in to help; and Giles who, after a couple of weeks, saw that it was really rather silly for both of them to be there

450

when he could do it all just as well on his own . . .

Ever since that awkward weekend when Charles and Jessica had announced her pregnancy, and Rachel had come down so heavily on her brother's side, Giles had decided to keep a low profile. In the back of his mind there was always the fear that, given the choice between him and William, Rachel might go the other way . . . and Giles had no wish to put that to the test. Better for her to come naturally to him. Better, in short, not to fight. It was only a matter of time before they returned to Putney.

But the intervening months had not been easy. The longer they stayed, the more – as Giles had known he would – William took advantage. It never seemed to occur to the man that Giles and Rachel were there because he needed them; because he couldn't survive on his own. On the contrary, William had the air of someone doing them the most enormous favour. Blithely assuming that Rachel would run the place as Xandra had, with everything perfect and rigidly structured – his wardrobe, his fridge, his larder . . . all fully stocked and not a thing out of place – William was oddly frustrated by a perceived lack of order in his house. He loved being rude about Xandra's 'hotel style', but it was increasingly clear to everyone that he'd started to miss it. And while Rachel did her best, William never seemed to appreciate her efforts, never praised her, never noticed when she went out of her way. It made Giles want to shake him.

On the other hand, at least such indignities were self-inflicted. Rachel had no one but herself to blame when she was still up at eleven o'clock at night, cooking something special for his next weekend party. But Giles's chores were a different matter. Poor Giles, roped into doing his brother-in-law's weekly food shopping, or taking on car-park duties after the village carol service. If it wasn't for the thought that it was merely temporary, that he'd be going home in January with a healthy bank balance and a happy wife, Giles wasn't sure he'd have borne it.

In any other circumstances, he'd have loathed spending that morning in a Christmas-crazy supermarket. The tinny jingles from a mass of overhead speakers, the dismal reindeer horns that the staff had been forced to wear, the perpetual screeching from over-excited children . . . Instead, he was smiling at the checkout girl and making room for a hassled-looking mother to get past. He was putting everything on to the conveyor belt – briskly, lightly, intelligently – with the air of a man enjoying himself. No clotted cream? So what? Double would be fine. The wrong sort of smoked salmon? Who cared? Nothing could dampen his mood. For in under a month, they'd be going home. By mid-January he and Rachel would have packed up the Volvo and be on their way back to Putney, with a beautiful new house waiting for them, no overdraft, and a couple of thousand to play with from the balance of the rent that had been coming in since April.

Letting the place had been William's idea. Giles's heart had sunk at the prospect of another eight or nine months in Suffolk, but the idea of ten grand landing in his bank account was simply too hard to resist – especially when he now had all those extra expenses to consider. It wasn't just a desire to pay Evie back in full that had prompted the need for more money. With Giles and Rachel out of the house entirely, the builder had had free rein with the place – and Rachel, no longer maddened by the absence of a kitchen, or day

452

after day of banging and scraping and the sense that she was living in a hardware store, Rachel had been rather more willing than before to indulge Mike's inclination to get things perfect and take advantage of how little money he was prepared to do it for. Of course they should redo the lighting in the bathroom – how silly of her not to have thought of it earlier. Yes, the hallway really did need a new lick of paint – dear Giles's *trompe l'œils* were looking terribly out of date. And once the idea of tenants had been raised, there was yet more money to spend on getting the place up to standard for that. A shower was essential. And a gas fire in the sitting room, not smoke-free logs. And new carpets throughout . . . although *not* in the bathroom.

'*What?*' Giles had said – appalled at the idea of bed-warm toes on chilly tiles.

'It's what people prefer these days. More hygienic, apparently . . .'

Giles grunted.

'. . . Well it's up to you, darling.' Rachel poured him another cup of coffee. 'But Evie's friend did say it was worth at least another hundred a month – maybe more – and I just thought—'

'Oh well then!' Giles grinned suddenly at his wife. 'Decision made.'

By April, the tenants were in. By November the Langtons' joint account was – for the first time in ten years – finally in the black. The last instalment of rent had arrived that morning and on 4 January the place would be empty again. All Giles and Rachel had to do was wait for the rest of the month to pass and Morland Road was theirs once more. Giles was counting the days and hours like a schoolboy looking to the end of term.

He quite enjoyed helping Rachel drape lights over the Christmas tree and poking holly behind the antique picture frames, helping her towards a rather less showy kind of Christmas than Favenham had seen in recent years – and not just because Rachel preferred it that way. Doing a Xa-style Christmas was, she now realised, back-breaking. Rachel was grateful for any help that came her way, and Giles was more than happy to oblige. Certainly he didn't mind the shopping, and had merely chuckled to himself when, over lunch, William informed him that a couple of his men would be needing the disused garage that had become Giles's studio – just for the afternoon, to spray-paint a new gate they'd made to replace the one at the bottom of the park.

'I mean, it's not as if you'll need that space today, is it? Not if you're off to Tesco, or wherever it is you go these days.'

Pricked by her brother's thoughtlessness, Rachel had looked up sharply from the shopping list she was compiling. 'Can't you find another place for them to do it, William?'

William frowned.

'Just because he's helping with the shopping, it doesn't give you the right to march into Giles's studio and—'

'*Giles's studio?*' said William, amazed at this reference to his garage.

'How would you like your study reeking of spray paint?'

'But—'

'It's okay,' Giles cut in. 'Really it is. I'm not planning to do much work now in any case – not when the others get here – and I'm sure that by the time they

454

leave it'll be fine. Really, William. You go right ahead with your spraying.'

William rolled his napkin away and got up from his chair. 'Thank you, Giles,' he said with exaggerated gratitude.

Giles didn't care. Before going to the supermarket, he showed Rachel the bank statement that had arrived in the mail that morning. He knew it wouldn't be news to her. It was all part of the plan. But there was still something thrilling about seeing it there in print, and Rachel – equally thrilled – had not been able to stop herself from sharing the moment with her brother after Giles had gone. She thought William would be glad of it. Xandra might not be coming back, but life at Favenham was settled now. It was time for everyone to move on, and scenes like the one in the dining room just now only emphasised the point. She hadn't meant to snap at him. She was tired. And this positive news, backed up by a tangible statement that she could actually show him, it seemed a good pretext for seeking William out in his office and clearing the air.

William was barely conscious of any air to clear. Amused, he took the statement and looked at it while his sister chattered on.

Oh, there was nothing surprising about it, she knew that. They'd always planned to be back on their feet by Christmas, but it was still reassuring – didn't he think? – to see it there in black and white. At last they were independent again. At last they could afford to go back to Putney and with any luck pick up from where they'd left off. Get back to—

'What's that?' Putting the statement down, William swivelled in his office chair and looked up at his sister. 'I'm sorry, Rachel. I didn't quite . . .'

'Pick up from where we left off,' she repeated, with a sudden sense of what was to come. 'You know – go home again. Get out of your hair. God knows you must be desperate for us to leave. You've been so amazing, so patient . . . and now it's actually happening! We're finally leaving. And you'll have your precious garage back, and that extra spare room for your parties, and no one doing the crossword before you get to it.'

'And you really think you can go back to Putney? On' – coughing, he gestured to the statement on the desk – 'on that?'

'We're in the black, William. And right now that's all we need.'

'To pay off your creditors, sure. But what makes you think that's going to be enough long term?'

Rachel smiled. 'Well it's enough for us,' she said affectionately. 'I realise you might have higher standards, William, but it's different for Giles and me. We haven't been this strong in years. It's wonderful. And it's all thanks to you,' she placed a sentimental hand on his shoulder, 'for letting us stay with you here and – and being so kind and generous. Truly, I can't tell you how much we owe you – or what it's meant to me to be here again.'

'And now you want to leave.'

Her smile faltered. 'It's not that we *want* to leave, William. We just—'

'I can see why old Giles might want to go back to Putney,' William went on. 'Risk falling into debt again, and bury his head in the sand about what kind of old age the pair of you are facing . . . That kind of attitude is clearly in his blood. But you, Rachel? Don't you think it might be sensible to stay at Favenham a little longer? Build up a bit more capital? Imagine how great it would be if you stayed here for, what, another year, perhaps? You'd come away with another twelve thousand. Maybe more. When one looks at what's been happening recently in the property market, I wouldn't be surprised if rental values soared this year. Ask Evie if you don't believe me.'

Rachel was silent.

'Now I know it's not what you want to hear,' he continued, folding up the statement and handing it back. 'And I know it'll be a difficult strategy for you to persuade Giles to accept. But I'd never forgive myself if I didn't make you see that at your age and with your resources . . . you're vulnerable, Rachel. And you might want to think twice about whether you can afford to pass up on that kind of money.'

By the time Giles returned, the damage was done. Rachel came out from the kitchen into chilly early-evening darkness and helped bring in the shopping. William had advised her to talk to him soon, before the poor man got carried away. And with everybody arriving that night, there wasn't much time. Rachel steeled herself. She'd wait only until the car was empty and the final bags had been brought in. Then she'd shut the door and grab the moment, before weakness got the better of her.

'Well, that's it!' she said with brisk cheer, heaving the last load in. The door was shut. The moment had arrived.

Kissing her, Giles looked at the pile of supermarket bags they'd amassed on the kitchen table. 'Hope it's all there,' he said. 'I did check and double-check.'

'I'm sure it's fine.'

'And the girl said they'd be open the day after Boxing Day from twelve until four so if I've been a

457

plonker and missed anything crucial then at least you'll know we're not entirely stranded.'

'Great.'

'Not that I am a plonker, of course.' Grinning, he nudged at her. 'You're supposed to disagree with me when I say things like that, Rach!'

'I'm sorry.'

Rachel closed her eyes. She could feel him looking at her, but didn't need to look back to know that his smile would be fading. Now, she told herself. Now. Now. Opening her eyes, but still unable to meet his – looking instead at the white mass of bags – Rachel took a deep breath. She wanted to discuss their plans for January, she said. And what to do about the house in Morland Road . . .

Giles sat at the kitchen table. He couldn't go on standing while she spoke. Every word sapped his strength: the way she said 'the house in Morland Road', as if it were some sort of impersonal asset, instead of simply 'home'. Then there were words like 'pension' and 'responsible' and 'market value' . . . which made him feel so useless, so hopeless as a husband, so lacking in the business acumen that kept men like William Montfort happily rolling in money. And when it transpired that Rachel had already rung the letting agent to check what the position was vis-à-vis the current tenants – would they be interested in taking the place for another year? – it seemed to Giles that she had already made up her mind. They needed this extra money, she said. How else could they feel properly secure?

Her certainty threw him. Forgetting that he had, in fact, considered all these things at length before they'd even come to Favenham, forgetting that provision had been made for their old age, that all the sensible insurance policies were in place, that their cash flow would be fine now that Lloyd's was under control . . . Giles put his head in his hands.

'Darling . . .'

He looked at her.

'Darling.' She sat beside him at the table. 'Please. All I'm saying is that it would be jolly nice to have a few more thousand put away somewhere. We do have to think about what's going to happen as we get older, and – and what if, God forbid, we have to go into a home. You see what I'm saying, don't you? Even if all we do is sit on it, and ultimately leave it to Evie? Or . . .' tentatively, she smiled, 'or maybe we could go on holiday? Haven't had a proper holiday in *years*!'

Giles nodded, staring at the patterns in the waxed tablecloth.

'I'm just asking you to think about it. There's nothing we can do now, in any case, until the twenty-eighth. The agency's shut until then. But I didn't want you to get all excited about going back to London when – when it may be more sensible to stay on here for a bit.'

Again Giles nodded. He even said he would think about it. Of course the extra money would be nice. He didn't think they needed it – at least, not in the way she thought they did – but he could understand her fears, and her longing for a holiday. Getting to his feet again, he kissed her on the cheek. 'Won't be long,' he said, feeling for the car keys in his pocket. 'I found Lillian that cut-price wrapping paper she wanted. Should really take it over before I forget.'

Rachel heard his footsteps fading down the passageway. Then a door opening, then closing. And

459

then nothing. Slowly she began emptying the bags, and in one of them she found the shopping list she'd written out for him with everything dutifully crossed-off.

Charles and Jessica were the first to arrive – on Christmas Eve, in time for tea – in a car jam-packed with presents and baby paraphernalia. They'd come straight from Launceston Villas, from a sad and lonely Xandra with only Julia Reed for company over Christmas. Julia Reed was Xandra's great friend. After years of squabbling with her own husband, Julia's divorce had finally come through – and she'd been instrumental in encouraging Xandra down the same path. But in spite of her friend's gossipy presence, Xandra was acutely aware that it wasn't the same as being with her family, and her darling baby grand-daughter.

Once, all she'd thought about was the effort of 'doing Christmas': about how wonderful it would be to be shot of all that catering and hosting and present supervision and making sure the spare bedrooms were just right for the Langtons when they arrived. What a bloody nightmare, she'd thought. Back then. And even last year, with the shock of their separation still so raw – with Diana Miller's words still ringing in her ears – there had been a certain novelty about spending Christmas away from Favenham. Xandra and Julia had gone to the Caribbean. It had barely felt like Christmas at all. But this year, waving Charles and his new family off to Suffolk, and then Ben and Nina not far behind – the former laughingly removing a parking ticket from the new car she'd just given him for his eighteenth birthday – it was hard for Xandra not to torture herself with memories of the wintry beauty of Favenham. The smell of pine needles, the warm feelings of belonging, of sitting in the library after lunch on Christmas Day, surrounded by her children, William teasing Ben about his haircut . . .

Instead all she had was Julia banging on about golfing holidays for middle-aged singles in the Algarve and some dreary-sounding man they both knew wasn't a patch on Julia's charming, if slightly unreliable, former husband.

William was infinitely less bothered. His sister might not be able to get his socks quite as perfectly folded as he liked, but there were definite advantages to having her around instead of Xandra at this time of year. No nagging at him to light the fire in the library, or lay the table, or check there was enough drink in the cupboard. Rachel did all that now. No sulky face when he came back late from shooting with the Ovendens. No irritable comments on his choice of tie. No questioning his judgement when it came to making decisions about whether, and where, to go for a walk; whether to accept the Gilchrists' invitation to drinks; or which church service to attend. For Rachel, unlike Xandra, invariably deferred. Welcoming his four children home that evening – sitting with them in the library, drinking tea that his sister had just made and eating his third slice of chocolate cake – William was happy just to have them with him again for Christmas; happy to see that, with minor exceptions, life really did go on. Even the presence of Jessica and that baby seemed somehow less offensive than he'd imagined they might be.

His only concern was for Honor, who'd arrived shortly after the others, unaccompanied by her husband.

With Lavinia virtually bedridden, Honor and

461

Edward had not felt able to bring her with them that evening. They were hoping she'd be strong enough to come for Christmas lunch tomorrow – it was something they'd have to play by ear – but for now it was simply the pair of them expected for dinner. Kissing her father's cheek, Honor unbuttoned her velvet coat and failed to meet his eye.

'Edward's coming later,' she explained. 'Had a couple of things to sort out at home. Nothing vital, just getting Lavinia settled . . . He'll definitely be here in time for supper.'

William took her coat and hung it wearily in the cupboard. He knew what had happened. A few days earlier, he'd gone over to see them and had found Honor alone in the kitchen, in tears. William wasn't used to people crying on him. With supreme effort, he'd hid his distaste, put an arm around his daughter's shoulders and, assuming this was simply to do with Lavinia's cancer, asked her what was wrong.

He certainly hadn't been prepared for Honor's reply, and the sudden flood of information about the poor girl's sex life and reproductive system – her ovaries, her follicles, her eggs, her periods . . . and all kinds of complicated-sounding tests on her fallopian tubes, her hormone levels, the fluctuations in her body temperature, and then all the daily injections she had to take, self-administered, as the IVF programmes began . . . and, worse, the occasional image of the virtually non-existent sex life that his daughter and her husband had been forced to endure before they were allowed to move on to IVF: dismally clinical, rigidly timed . . . was it really necessary, William wondered, for her to go into quite so much detail?

But Honor had lost all sense of proportion. She had

462

been unable to respond to Lavinia's concern – however kind the old lady's intentions had been towards Honor that afternoon, Edward was still her son. And the sense of relief as, finally, she felt able to unburden herself when her father had asked what was wrong . . . it was overpowering. She'd barely registered William's embarrassment.

And as she'd moved on from the subject of her own infertility to the whole issue of Edward's ex-girlfriend . . . and then Edward's adamant response, his refusal to admit that anything was wrong, his hard determination to stay married to her at any cost . . . all William had been able to think was that his daughter was being unbelievably silly.

It wasn't as if they couldn't have children, not for sure. Edward was right to be encouraging Honor to keep trying. They'd get there eventually. And if, God forbid, they couldn't . . . then . . . then shouldn't she be glad that he still wanted her?

Honor was silent.

'I mean, I can see why you're unhappy, darling. I can see that you're longing for a baby. Of course you are. What woman wouldn't? But why complain about Edward? Seems to me that so far his reaction has been faultless! And as for that girl in Australia . . . why, everyone has a past these days! You yourself—'

'I was never in love with Abe, Daddy.'

'Yes, but—'

'Not in the way that Edward was with Shelley.'

William had sighed. 'And I'm sure Edward loves you too, Honor. Differently perhaps, but that's no bad thing. The kind of woman one marries often bears no resemblance at all to the kind of woman one . . .' William had trailed off. 'Even if he doesn't love you in

463

quite the way you'd like, he clearly wants to stay married.'

'But that's—'

'And frankly, I'd be grateful if I were you. Edward Beaumaris is a decent man. He looks after you extremely well. He doesn't seem to mind about your dodgy fertility, and clearly doesn't want to have anything more to do with this other woman. I . . .' William had frowned. 'I'm sorry, Honor. I know it's been upsetting. I can see you're in shock, and this is probably the last thing you want to hear at the moment, but I'm afraid I'm going to say it anyway. I think you're jolly lucky. No, I do! To have a husband as principled and as loyal and – and, frankly, as committed . . .'

He didn't actually tell her to pull herself together, but the implication was clear, and it seemed that Honor was doing her best to take his advice. With her eyes dry and her head calm, she'd waved her father off and gone back in – determined to make the best of it, which included sticking to their plan to be at Favenham for Christmas. All she needed was time, William decided. Time to appreciate what she had with Beaumaris: that he made her a good husband; that they were clearly suited; that – in short – she was incredibly lucky he hadn't dropped her the second it was clear she'd need help conceiving a child. Honor had made her bed – an extremely satisfactory bed it was too – and the last thing anybody wanted, least of all William, was another divorce in the family.

But seeing her today – with Edward coming separately, with her eyes unsettled and something garish about her tone – William could see the strain that she was under. Probably thinking about it too

464

much, he said to himself. Women these days . . . encouraged to spend far too much time *thinking* about their lives, as opposed to *living* them. All Honor had to do was pull herself together and be grateful she had such a splendid husband. Not fret about his past.

He tried to brush it from his mind. But as the evening progressed – with Honor growing ever quieter and stiffer as Beaumaris arrived, and then Evie; and then they all went in to dinner – William rather wished that Xandra was there. Xa would have known how to deal with this sort of thing. Willingly, she'd have sat up for hours with Honor, explaining – no doubt rather more convincingly than William had been able to do – why it was that she should stay married to Edward.

'So in the end she got her way. Again. She just pulled on her coat, picked up her bag, and left, with the mailshot still to be finished, and a whole pile of letters – *my* letters – still to be franked, and—'

'You've got to be tougher, Evie.'

'I'm trying!' Laughing, Evie put down her wine glass. 'Believe me, Uncle William, I've never grovelled to her, or let her get away with anything obvious. But it's the little things, the way she always leaves at four thirty, instead of five like everybody else. And—'

'Is that what her contract says?'

Evie looked at him. 'I've no idea.'

'Well, find out. No point getting upset with her for leaving early if she's contractually entitled to do that. But my guess would be that she isn't, and then you've got some leverage. Just quote the relevant clauses and watch her squirm. Trust me, she'll find it pretty unsettling.'

Filling her glass with more wine, William grinned at Evie.

Evie grinned back.

'And it's the same with the filing and the telephone,' he went on, putting down the bottle. 'Find out from that boss of yours what falls within her job description—'

'Oh, I know what falls within her job description. But it's one thing to know what she should be doing, and quite another to enforce it. Short of physically barring the door, I don't see how I can make her stay the extra half-hour . . .'

Chattering on, Evie was glad she was sitting next to her uncle; glad of the distraction, of the way she could bluster on about Linda Norris and turn from the rest of the table. From Honor, sitting opposite, sleek and perfect, smiling at the people she loved best with all the empty professionalism of a Ritz-Carlton concierge.

They'd barely spoken since that day in London when Honor had walked out, preferring the anonymous stream of shoppers on the Kings Road to any more conversation with Evie about the rights and wrongs of holding out for a baby and spurning a career. There had just been that single call Honor had made to Evie's mobile in the restaurant, with Matthew listening in while she apologised for walking out, apologised for snapping . . . and of course Evie had forgiven her. But that was before Abe had spoken, and Evie's sudden pain as she understood why it was that Matthew's love was lost to her – together with all those feelings of envy and resentment towards the beautiful cousin who'd unwittingly lured him away . . . such things, however unintentional, were infinitely harder to forgive. And although Honor had tried to reach her

466

a number of times since then, and had even left messages – on one occasion, sounding really quite low – Evie simply hadn't been able to return them. Yes, Honor was childless. Yes, she was going through a difficult time. But – fuck it – at least the girl had married the man she loved.

Looking at Honor now, however – at the brilliant teetering smile of a woman devastated from yet another failed attempt for a baby – Evie found it hard to sustain the feelings of resentment. It wasn't Honor's fault Matthew had fallen in love with her instead of with Evie. It wasn't her fault she was beautiful. She'd done nothing to encourage Matthew's interest. It was hardly fair to punish the poor girl for something she could clearly have done nothing about. Full of sudden remorse for not returning her friend's calls, Evie found herself wishing she'd been more sensitive that afternoon in November; wishing she hadn't been so critical about Honor's marriage to Edward, which was probably the one thing in her life right now that still made Honor happy. She longed, in short, to be a proper friend to Honor, instead of someone on the outside of her smile.

'And on no account must you do it yourself, Evie. There comes a point in life when one should simply refuse to take on menial jobs. Because if you go down the other route – trying to be unselfish – that sort of thing . . . And God knows the number of women who make this mistake . . . Before you know it you'll be tidying *her* desk, answering *her* telephone, watering *her* plants. And that's no good. She'll just think you're a doormat.'

Nodding, Evie took another sip of wine.

'I bet no one else in your office types their own letters,' William went on, warming to his theme. 'I bet she's up to date with everybody else's paperwork.'

467

'But what do you think I should *do*, Uncle William? How do I turn it round?'

William smiled. 'Well,' he said, taking a sip of wine, 'I suppose it depends how scrupulous you are, Evie. Whether you're prepared to play a little dirty now and then . . .'

And as he began suggesting all kinds of interesting methods from the school of grey morals, Giles – at the other end of the table – struggled to hold his tongue. What was wrong with the man? Wasn't it bad enough that he was failing his own daughter? Giles had caught him earlier, chattering away to Rachel about poor Honor's fertility troubles with all the discretion of a loudhailer. Sure, most of the others had been upstairs unpacking and having baths and generally getting ready for dinner at the time, but Giles – coming into the library – had been amazed to find his brother-in-law mid-rant.

'Ridiculous girl,' William had muttered, handing Rachel a glass of champagne and returning to the drinks cupboard. 'You'd have thought she'd be *grateful* to Edward for wanting to stay married in spite of her rotten ovaries. But instead she ties herself in knots about this absurd relationship he had in Australia – years ago – quite unable to see that the kind of woman one falls head over heels for in one's twenties is rarely a suitable candidate for marriage . . . eh Giles?'

'What's that?'

Passing Giles a glass, William joined him by the fire. 'Women one marries and women one . . . Hell, you know what I'm saying!'

Giles looked uncomfortable. 'Well, as I met and married your sister while I was in my twenties,

William, I'm not entirely sure that I'm in a position to—'

'All right all right.' William smiled at him, off-puttingly conspiratorial; certain that Giles would say something quite different were Rachel not in earshot. 'But Honor . . . I mean, for a girl with a degree from Oxford, surely she can see she's not threatened – not for one moment – by some frippery ex-girlfriend of her husband's . . . and an Australian ex at that!'

Giles took a sip of champagne, for want of anything appropriate to say.

'So what if they're having problems on the baby front?'

'William,' said Rachel, glancing towards the door.

Lowering his voice a fraction, William leant closer to Giles and began filling him in on the details of Honor's condition. And Giles, who'd already guessed the salient points, could only smile uncomfortably. William might be making his life a misery here at Favenham but that was nothing – Giles realised – next to the effect that the man would doubtless be having on his daughter right now. It appalled Giles to think of the dire advice William would be giving the poor girl – and, worse, the impact of that advice on Honor's future happiness. He prayed that Honor wouldn't pay too much heed to her father. Prayed she'd have the strength of mind to break free from William's world, and the restricted life he expected her to live . . .

And in the church the following morning, Giles was on his knees – praying for pretty much the same strength of mind for himself.

Arriving late hadn't helped matters. The sudden drop in temperature had done something strange to

469

the inside of Giles's car and it had failed to start. So Rachel had gone ahead in William's civilised Range Rover with Evie, Ben and Nina squashed along the back. And while there was room for Giles in Charles's car – Jessica, who let nothing disturb little Flavia's routine, not even church at Christmas, was staying behind – it came at quite a price. Eleven o'clock had come and gone, and Giles was still hanging about on the drive, waiting for Charles to find his coat, and then his keys, and something for the collection . . . the pair of them had had to creep in behind the vicar and the choir. They were lucky to find anywhere to sit.

Up at the front – in the family pew – sat Rachel and William with the children on one side and Evie on the other, and the Beaumarises directly behind them. Honor's dark velvet beret and Edward's thin fair hair were easy to distinguish beside a heavily wrapped-up Lavinia. And Giles – lost in some side-aisle, with ivy tickling at his neck, sharing a carol sheet with a man in sandals – couldn't help thinking that it was all depressingly symbolic.

Here he was again, in the church where he and Rachel had been married, a church that had once reminded him of her at her most beautiful and him at his happiest . . . now representing the grimmer side of his vows. Rachel had insisted they'd only be staying on at Favenham for one more year, but Giles couldn't rid himself of the notion that it would now be for ever. The days when they'd spend a week at Favenham over Christmas, and then hurry back to London: those days, he felt, were over. He'd be here next year, and the year after – growing ever greyer and smaller and quieter; drifting ever further from Putney and sanity and everything, bar Rachel, that he loved. He imagined his

470

own coffin, up by the altar – and wondered for a second if she was worth it: sitting there beside her brother, seemingly oblivious to the sacrifices she was asking him to make.

And then he thought of life without her and knew that he had no choice. If Rachel was set on staying here with William – whether it was for another year, or twenty – then Giles, weakling that he was, would simply follow. He couldn't help himself. The alternative was so horrifying he could hardly contemplate it.

After the service, and in no mood for seasonal pleasantries at the back of the church, Giles decided to walk home. It was only twenty minutes across the fields – he'd done it once before with Rachel. And he certainly didn't fancy hanging round for Charles who, for some perverse Charles-like reason – he'd never before shown the slightest interest in God – was deep in conversation with the vicar. He even had a cup of coffee in his hands. William and Rachel were mingling with people Giles felt he should know better: that retired gardener with the bright blue eyes, a farmer from the other side of Allenham, the lady who used to run the village shop . . . Rachel knew them all by name.

Giles left the church. He walked out into cooler air – into the flinty smell of churchyard, and traces of smoke from the embers of an abandoned bonfire just beyond the wall. With the voices of the congregation fading, he followed a path around the side of the church and came to a sudden halt. For there just ahead of him was Evie, running towards Honor – who must have had the same idea as Giles and was standing at the far end of the footpath, lifting the latch on a narrow iron gate that led back into the village. It seemed a little stiff.

471

'You – you don't mind if I come too, do you?' he heard, in his daughter's breathless voice.

Extending his gaze to Honor, Giles saw her look round from the gate – saw the black brim of the beret cut across the side of the girl's forehead, her face winter-pale beneath. And then she smiled – properly – for the first time that Christmas.

Giles turned to go back to the others. As he left he heard the musical sigh of the iron gate closing, and the pair of them stepping through, out on to the tarmac of the road.

All night, Evie had been troubled by thoughts of Honor – by the brittle smiles, and by the fact that Honor and Edward had left shortly afterwards without even saying goodbye. She'd woken the following morning, determined to find a way of catching Honor alone that day – determined to find an opportunity to apologise to her before things got any worse.

Because of her place in the front pew of the church, Evie had heard the Beaumaris party arriving a good few minutes before she saw them: heard the creak of Lavinia's sticks coming up the aisle, and Honor's voice thanking someone. Evie turned to greet them, joining the rest of her family as they leant round the gothic wooden carvings of the pew, smiling and kissing, murmuring 'Happy Christmas' to the others . . . but that was the extent of their contact. For the rest of the service, Evie was forced to face forward, up towards the altar.

She could sense the three of them behind her. She heard the slight click as Honor unhooked a hassock and got to her knees to pray, and Edward fussing over his mother – was she comfortable? Warm enough?

'Give me your sticks, Mum. And . . . sorry Honor, you couldn't just . . . ?'

'Of course. Here, Lavinia. Let me . . .'

Later, she could hear Honor singing the same old carols that the two of them had sung together, year after year, for as long as Evie could remember; and the rustle of bank notes in Honor's purse as she opened it for the collection. It was even possible to see Honor's reflection – dark and narrow – in the well-polished brass of the lectern.

So to turn at the end of the service and see only Edward and his mother in the pew behind was – for Evie – quite a shock.

'Honor's walking back,' Edward explained, smiling as he pulled on his gloves and reached for Lavinia's sticks. 'Wanted to get a good start, I suppose – to be there in time for lunch.'

Evie glanced at her watch.

'I think she felt like the exercise,' he went on. 'And as I've got to take poor Mum home again . . .'

Evie looked down at Lavinia. She was sitting on Edward's left and seemed – in spite of all that fur and cashmere – desperately cold. Too cold even to look at Evie, far less smile at her. Just longing for Edward to get her out of there – back home to the comfort of her bedroom with its enveloping blankets, its eiderdowns, and its three electric fires.

'It's nothing serious. She's a bit tired, I think. It's been some time since her last treatment, and we just think it's best not to push it. I'm going to have to stay with her I'm afraid, but that's no reason – we thought – why Honor shouldn't be there with the rest of you for lunch.'

*

Thanking Edward, Evie hurried back up the aisle with as much decorum as she could muster. Wriggling, darting, squeezing . . . apologising her way through the departing congregation, she abandoned her carol sheet on the font, slipped out past the vicar and disappeared round the side of the church.

The day was windless and dry – hard-dry from the frost. And while the sky was cloudy, it had a settled frozen look that Honor recognised. The ground would be easy to walk on. No squelching mud. No damp grass. Just a thin white film of frost that sat against the cooler edges of the landscape: the twigs in the hedge, the dark chunks of plough, the distant fuzz of the Favenham woods.

Evie walked beside her, talking rather quickly – her breath visible in the cold air and a flickering frown on her face.

'It was a stupid thing to say, Honor. I mean, what do I know about relationships? Far less a proper marriage . . . It's not like I'm an authority!'

Honor smiled. 'Oh, I don't know,' she said, amused.

'And I suppose I always rather assumed that you – you and Edward . . . it was just so neat . . .'

Honor raised her eyebrows.

'So *suitable*,' Evie explained, hurriedly. 'Everyone so happy. Your families and everything. More like an arranged marriage than . . . than what it clearly is. I see that now, of course. With this whole baby thing . . . you have to love each other, to stay together. It *has* to be something special. And I'm just so sorry—'

'It doesn't matter.'

'But it does. And I— No, listen, Honor. Please. I want to say this.'

474

So Honor let her talk, walking on grimly as Evie apologised for never giving Edward a fair go; for underrating the love he and Honor shared; for taking so long to understand the tragedy of their childlessness. 'But I'm here now,' she said at last – taking Honor's arm and squeezing it lightly as the pair of them turned onto the path that led back up to the house.

But the path wasn't made for two people. It was densely lined with poplar trees that made it impossible to walk side by side, so they had to go single file, Evie first – hugging her coat a little closer and nestling her hands under her arms. Honor could see the tips of her bare fingers, poking round the sides of her back.

'And if there's anything I can do,' Evie went on, turning for a moment to meet Honor's eye and add some sincerity to what she was saying. 'Anything at all . . .?'

Honor smiled at her.

'I'm serious . . .'

'I know you are.' Honor's smile grew distant. 'But really, there isn't anything that anyone can do. It – it's just one of those things . . .' She couldn't quite finish the sentence. Couldn't bring herself to say that there was nothing Evie could do to make Edward love her the way he'd once loved Shelley Maclean. Couldn't bring herself to explain to Evie – not now – that her infertility was merely the tip of a drifting iceberg-marriage; that Evie had, in fact, been right all along: there was nothing so very special about her union with Edward; there was no overriding love to see them through this crisis; that it was – in many ways – an arranged marriage after all. Couldn't face the awkwardness of Evie realising that this wonderful sustaining love she'd

475

spoken of – this love that made even the most impressive career seem empty; this love that was somehow enough in itself, and didn't need a family to make it whole, was absent. Not when she herself had only just realised it.

'At least promise to come and stay with me next time,' said Evie, striding on, oblivious. 'Let me look after you properly, hmm? Instead of sneaking around like some school kid with a pack of cigarettes.'

Sinking on to the library sofa with a second slice of Christmas cake, Giles was just thinking how nice it was to have a moment's peace from the stress of lunch, of everyone pulling in different directions and nobody quite satisfied in spite of all that food and all those presents and Charles's daughter crying herself scarlet . . . when he noticed Honor walking past the window. It was almost dark outside and her face – blue-grey, distant, through the glass – had a disturbing absence of vitality, a sketchy weightlessness that reminded Giles of a figure scratched out from some large oil painting.

He pondered Honor's presence there at Favenham that day. Edward was coming to collect her after tea – he knew that – but why hadn't she simply gone back with him and Lavinia after church? Surely that would have been the normal thing to do. But then . . . Giles sighed. Things were far from normal in poor Honor's marriage. He understood that now.

It was warm and soft on the sofa. The cake was very good. The air was sleepy, and filled with the smell of smoking logs. Upstairs, he could hear the distant splashes and squeals of the baby having her bath – and Charles laughing. For a full minute Giles sat, eyelids closing . . . but it was no good. The thought of what it must have been like for Honor that day, with that beautiful noisy baby constantly around – constantly being talked about, constantly there as a reminder of what wasn't there for Honor – it must have been torture for her. And then, even more troubling, all those appalling things that William had said the night before . . . prodding at Giles's peace of mind like a bad tune.

'. . . *Ridiculous girl . . . You'd have thought she'd be* grateful *to Edward for wanting to stay married in spite of her rotten ovaries . . .'*

Putting the rest of his cake to one side, Giles got to his feet and quietly left the room.

It wasn't hard to find her. The darkness was not so far advanced as it had seemed from inside the library, and Honor's stationary figure – leaning against a kissing-gate that led into the park – was perfectly visible from the drive. For a moment, Giles hesitated. A thick mist was rising from the river. Something twittered in the reeds. The last thing she'd want was her uncle butting in.

But Giles, urged on by some inner imperative – some sense of limited opportunity – was unable to turn back. Coughing quietly, he approached.

'Hello.'

Honor turned, and it was clear that she'd been crying. The skin was rough and blotchy around her eyes and mouth, and the voice wasn't entirely balanced as, smiling awkwardly, she apologised for the way she looked.

'They always say that Christmas is stressful, don't they? I – I guess I—'

'Cigarette?'

Honor took one from the squashed packet he held out. Glancing at him, she held it up to the match he lit. Tentatively, she inhaled. And for a moment they smoked their cigarettes in silence: two dots of glowing orange, hovering at the gate. Then Giles shifted position. He turned around, resting his spine against the wooden fence so that he faced back towards the house – in the opposite direction from Honor, who continued to gaze at the darkening river.

'I hope you don't mind me joining you like this . . .'

'Not in the least.'

Honor exhaled some smoke into the night and turned, smiling. She liked her uncle; liked his unhurried manner, his way of letting life happen around him without feeling the need to control it all the time. He was the sort of person one could be with in silence, without any sense of a gap.

'It's just . . .' Giles wrinkled his nose. 'I'm sorry, Honor. Please say if you want me to bugger off. It's absolutely none of my business. In fact, I expect I'm the last person you'd want to confide in right now, but I – well – I just hope you won't think me intrusive – I mean, of course I *am* being intrusive, but it . . .' He glanced at her uneasily. 'What I'm trying to say is – is that—'

'You've been talking to Evie?'

'Christ, no!' said Giles, appalled. 'No, Honor! Absolutely not . . . She hasn't said a word. I promise you she hasn't. And – and as I wasn't entirely sure how much she knew, if anything, or how much you'd necessarily *want* her to know . . . I mean, of course Evie's your friend, but—'

'Dad, then.'

Giles was silent.

And Honor, sighing, continued, 'Can't blame him,

really. He's worried about me. Of course he'd want to speak to someone.' She dragged on her cigarette. 'I suppose he was saying I should count myself lucky and get on with my life . . .'

Again Giles was lost for words.

'And he's right,' she said, her certainty a little defensive. 'Of course I should. It's ridiculous to be like this. Ridiculous, to mind so much about – about something so . . .'

She was going to say 'petty', but the word stuck in her throat. The gift of fertility; the sincerity of a husband's love . . . who was she kidding? Such things weren't petty at all.

Giles looked up at a moonless sky, at traces of cloud and the occasional star. 'What matters, Honor, is what *you* think,' he said at last, carefully picking out his words as if treading through a stream. 'And I suppose what I want to say is that it's *your* marriage. *Your* future . . .'

Flicking cigarette ash into the long grass, he glanced at her. Honor wasn't looking at him, but he could tell from the absolute stillness – just a few involuntary flickers round her eyes – that she was listening deeply.

'And if you're miserable,' he went on, 'if, at heart, you're regretting something . . . If recent problems have made you think that your husband isn't the man you thought he was, if – if, for whatever reason, the idea of being with him for the rest of your life doesn't fill you with joy, then pretending otherwise, just to keep everyone else happy, might not be the answer.'

Honor remained motionless.

'Of course it's hard to admit that kind of mistake.' His voice was barely audible above the trickling of the river. 'Some people take years – decades, even. Some never get round to it . . .'

Honor listened to him speaking. She listened more to his tone than the words themselves, to the easy way he moved between differing attitudes: if this, if that . . . nothing rigid, nothing excluded. And suddenly all kinds of possibilities began presenting themselves to her. Yes, there were cracks in her marriage. But instead of the medieval wilderness she'd imagined on the other side, instead of something darkly vile and lonely – something to be shielded from at all costs – it was oddly light and airy out there beyond the shell. Tiny jagged lines of light were appearing all around the edges of her world.

'I think it takes a lot of courage to get up and walk in the opposite direction from the one that everybody else is expecting or hoping you'll take. I've always rather admired the – the humility, I suppose, of people who'll admit that they were wrong somewhere along the line, and then act to make things better. Even in the face of disapproval from people who can't or won't see the fuller picture . . .'

Honor drank it in, full of new respect for this uncle of hers, an uncle whom – to her sudden shame – she'd always regarded as something of a failure. Yes, she'd always liked him – but somehow that hadn't stopped her from going along with her parents' opinion that Giles Langton, while charming, had done nothing with his life. What kind of man could barely support his family? His murals and cabinets might be beautiful, his paintings quietly interesting, but could he live in the real world? Was he 'useful'? What sort of insignificant life had he offered poor old Rachel?

480

Yet Giles seemed to understand what it was like suddenly to find oneself on the outside of what was considered normal. And there, in the dark, Honor knew that whatever she said to him – it would be accepted. Whatever she wanted to do . . . that, too, would be okay. And with the daylight gone and the evening upon them – with cigarette upon cigarette vanishing from Giles's crumpled packet – she opened up completely, telling him not so much about her misery over the prospect of childlessness – for that, it seemed, was a given – as the things she'd discovered about Edward and Shelley Maclean.

'Not that Edward will admit it,' she finished, taking a final cigarette and leaning in to the match he'd lit. 'And who knows?' She sighed as she exhaled; sighed with a youthful veneer of carelessness that only served to confirm the opposite. 'Maybe I'm wrong. Maybe it was just a silly crush he had . . .'

Giles shook the match flame dead. 'I don't think so,' he said gently. 'From what you've just said, it's pretty obvious, even to me.'

'Obvious?'

'Isn't it?'

'Come on, Giles. If it was *obvious* that he adored her and didn't much care for me . . . If it was *obvious* that this marriage of ours was a mistake . . . that the only thing Edward liked about me was – was the "suit-ability" factor . . . you think I'd hang around?'

'You might if you loved him.'

Honor was silent.

'*Do* you love him?'

'I don't know . . .' she mumbled. 'I mean, it was easy when I thought he loved me. Easy to think I loved him back . . .'

481

'And now?'

'Now . . .' Tears filled her eyes. 'I so *want* to believe him, Giles. When he says I've got it all wrong, that he never loved her, and never wanted to marry her. When he says that it's me he wants . . . and when Dad says I'm so lucky . . . it seems so right to be thought of in that way: to be loved, and wanted, and lucky. When we're out and about, with everyone behaving as if everything's normal, it's not so difficult to fool even myself that we're just fine.'

'And then you come home again.'

Honor nodded. 'That's right,' she said, biting her lip. 'We come home. He disappears into his study. And – and all that's left is an empty nursery and Lavinia looking at me . . .'

She hadn't finished speaking when they heard a car pass over the cattle grid. It was too dark for them to see it, but for a moment they were caught in the converging beam of its headlights as it followed the curve of the drive and then swung on, round, up to the house. They both knew who it was behind the wheel.

Honor felt Giles waiting; felt the weight of the decision ahead. She could, if she chose, retreat ever further behind those pretty veils of smiles and manners and old-world rituals that would shield her from whatever difficulties life threw at her – from inconsequential differences with her friends to the shakier ground of her parents' separation and the ill-conceived marriage she'd embarked upon. She could live a life of belonging to the tribe, of pretending at love, and pretending at happiness, and pretending at being golden. And the people that were most fooled by it would no doubt be the people she'd end up spending her time with, because to be with anyone with more

482

perception would cause her too much pain. Or she could face the truth, with all that that entailed.

'I'd better go,' she said, tossing the cigarette out beyond the gate.

They walked up the path again, back towards the house. They passed the empty Audi parked discreetly to the side. They climbed the shallow flight of steps and went into the panelled hall where Edward was standing with William, turning the pages of a large Victorian photograph album.

'And here he is again. He . . . oh Honor, there you are. You must come and look. It's your great-grand-father's photographs, going right back to the 1890s . . . And my grandfather seems to be on every page! He . . . look, William. And *again*.'

'I think that might have been his brother. He did have a brother, didn't he?'

'He had two,' said Edward, peering a little closer. 'There was one that died in the Boer War – I expect this was him. Must have been just before the poor man left for Africa. And then there was a younger one, the pacifist who converted to Catholicism and married the Elliston girls' governess . . .'

'Oh yes . . .' Fascinated, William stood back from the book. 'Good Lord. I'd forgotten all about that. And those cousins of yours – the ones your mother *loathed*, appearing out of nowhere and asking to look round the garden . . .'

Neither of them noticed the door closing.

Giles remained in the hall, shaking off his gumboots. From time to time he glanced at Edward and William, lost in their old photographs, chattering on about their ancestors while Honor's footsteps faded out in the direction of the library. Putting his boots to one side,

Giles sat on a nearby chair. He bent right forward, rested his elbows on his knees, and – eyes closed – knew that in those oddly insignificant seconds Honor had made her choice.

And Honor, it seemed, wasn't the only person to reach a decision about her future that Christmas. For one bright morning – early the following week – five tatty suitcases stood expectantly in the hall, held together with careful knots in the green string that Giles was so fond of, and accompanied by a series of undignified plastic bags.

Persuading his niece to make the right decision – however awkward, however unpopular – had made Giles think again about Putney, about the plan to delay returning . . . and he knew now that he couldn't do it. He had to go home. The extra cash was exactly that: extra – and simply not worth another year of feeling like a refugee. Of course, he still had to convince Rachel to come with him, of course, but this time he would fight.

In the end, it wasn't nearly as difficult as he'd imagined. In fact it wasn't difficult at all. For Rachel, listening in silent admiration to Giles's account of his conversation with Honor . . . how he hoped he hadn't interfered too much; hoped it really was the right advice. He hadn't been prescriptive – hadn't told Honor to leave Edward – but nor had he encouraged her to stay . . . Rachel seemed to have acquired new faith in her husband.

'Not every marriage is worth saving,' she said, stopping to kiss his cheek – easily, almost absent-mindedly – as she passed him on the way to her dressing table. 'And the point is, Giles, she listened to

484

you. It was your advice, not William's, that meant something to her. You were the one who understood. You were the one that bothered to go out there and find her. Poor girl. I expect William was hopeless . . .'

Giles swallowed. It was just so long since he'd had any kind of praise, especially from Rachel. Unable to speak, he sat heavily on the edge of their bed.

'Darling?'

Giles shook his head.

'Oh darling, what's wrong?' She was up from the dressing table; up and round and next to him now, leaning to see his expression. 'I was only saying that you were right, that I'm proud of you, that—'

Giles swung round, clasping her close so she couldn't see his face. 'Come home,' he said, in a thick voice. 'Please, Rachel. Come back to Putney. I know it's not perfect. I know we'll always be needing more money – things will always be tight – there'll be no nest egg, and I won't be able to take you away on nice holidays every year, or buy you clothes from – from places like Harvey Nichols, or whatever it is that you . . .'

Rachel felt him clinging to her, and wondered what had prompted this sudden change of subject. What had Putney got to do with any of this? Why was he bringing it up now? It made no sense. And yet, with the warm body wrapped around her and the old heavy jumper with the great gaping holes in the elbows – holes she'd long stopped darning – there was something very certain, and very Giles, in the combination of shabbiness and passion and the heady smell of turpentine and oils . . . something that made Rachel forget her questions, cling back with equal vigour, and start to wonder why it was she'd ever listened to her brother.

485

'You'd have to make do with cheap bubble bath,' he went on, 'and we'd probably have the same old taped-up Volvo until the day we die . . .'

'I like the Volvo.'

Pulling back, he looked at her.

'I do,' she said deliberately. 'It's a hell of a lot more civilised than that noisy two-seater of William's. Can hardly hear what he's saying' – smiling now – 'but perhaps that's no bad thing. And I can certainly live without Xandra's Floris. And – and as for Harvey Nichols, why, only an idiot would shop there when you can get just the same stuff for under a tenner at Bicester Village . . .'

And the more Rachel thought about it, the more she laughed and joked with Giles about the sillier benefits of living on a shoestring – while happily discussing exactly when they'd leave for London, and how they'd break the news to William, and who they'd first invite for dinner in their lovely new kitchen . . . the more she realised that there were other more significant advantages to them moving back to Putney. It wasn't just her marriage that would benefit. There was William's to consider as well.

In the course of their year at Favenham, Rachel had developed a grudging respect for her sister-in-law. Knowing now what was involved, Rachel had to admit that Xandra had done rather well – both with William and with Favenham. Neither were easy to run. And for all the family complaining about her tendency to be grand, her spending habits, her flirting with the media . . . there was no getting away from the fact that Xandra Villiers had made William Montfort a good wife, and it was about time William realised this. Instead of taking scatter shots at his estranged wife's style and tastes, he needed to see what he was missing by not having her at his side. And for as long as Giles and Rachel were there to amuse him, and look after him, and spoil him, and skivvy around for him, how would that ever happen?

No, Giles had been right all along. They weren't doing William any favours, filling in the gap left by Xandra. The poor bear wouldn't be happy about them leaving, but it was surely better for him in the long run – she saw that now – to be left alone and uncomfortable, perhaps even a little depressed, so that he might appreciate everything his wife had done for him over the years.

Giles listened, smiling. But while – and not entirely to his credit – he was all for his brother-in-law spending a few months feeling 'alone and uncomfortable, perhaps even a little depressed', he didn't think Rachel should hold out much hope for Xandra returning any time soon. Not without a heavy dose of grovelling from William. And the sad truth of it was that there were plenty of women out there willing to fill those shoes without the man having to bend an inch.

Rachel wasn't so sure. It was well over a year – she pointed out – since the pair of them had separated, and neither had even tried to find someone else. William just needed to be sufficiently desperate, sufficiently contrite, sufficiently willing to beg. And as for Xandra . . . why, according to Nina, the poor woman had been in tears when they'd called on Christmas Day.

So on 4 January, with the Volvo loaded to bursting, with windows that didn't shut properly and a strange sound coming from the exhaust, Rachel and Giles departed. William tutted and shook his head. Turning back into the silent house, he headed for his office. His papers and accounts were perfectly in order, but he wanted to speak to Lillian about going to Tesco, and how to work the defrost on the microwave.

Chapter Twenty-Five

Honor and Matthew

William had no intention of letting Honor stay with him at Favenham. From his point of view, it was the only way she'd realise her mistake. With any luck she'd go crawling back to Beaumaris in a couple of months and the whole sorry business would be over. He even thought about calling Xandra to try to persuade her not to let Honor stay at Launceston Villas either, and probably would have done so had Xa not called him first.

'Oh thank God you're in, William. You . . . have you heard?'

'Hello, Xandra.'

'William, have you *heard*? About Honor, and—'

'Of course I have. I've known for weeks.'

Xandra choked on her coffee. '*Weeks*? Why didn't you say something? You . . . hell, William. Why haven't you done anything to stop it?'

'I don't think we've got much choice in the matter, my dear. She's pretty set on leaving him.'

'Is she now.'

'Plans to be out by the weekend.'

'Well she's not coming here, that's for sure. And if I hear that you're letting her back to live with you in Suffolk, I . . .' Xandra's voice was as low and as ominous as she could possibly make it, 'I swear you'll regret it, William. We need to make it as hard as possible for her . . .'

So Honor went to live at Morland Road. It wasn't glamorous or comfortable, but there were other things – like the particular sort of peace and security that Giles and Rachel *in loco parentis* would be able to offer her – that mattered more. Indeed, the arrangement suited all of them. Honor would get proper support and care; Giles and Rachel would have a small flow of rent money coming in – for Honor was insistent that she should pay her way; and Evie would have the satisfaction of it being her idea.

It was a little strange to begin with, Honor moving into the little room that Evie had once occupied, standing on the Langtons' doorstep with a small suitcase in her hand. Everything else (including the little bedside cabinet she'd been given all those years ago, the one Giles had decorated to match her mother's tasteful schemes for Honor's Oxford life) had either been consigned to storage, or thrown away, or sold – which, in truth, had more to do with Honor's preference for light baggage than because she was in any kind of financial trouble . . . much to her father's irritation.

William was convinced that a tiring job and a grotty flat would have had the desired effect. But Honor was now rich in her own right. Concern about excessive inheritance tax had prompted William to get his affairs in order well in advance of his death. And while that end had been achieved, it also meant that the substantial share portfolio that had been made over to Honor at the time of her marriage was hers and hers alone. William was only too aware of his daughter's resources, of her ability to meet the costs of infinitely larger and smarter accommodation than some poky old bedroom in Morland Road, and he couldn't work out why she hadn't, or why a right sense of independence and the company of people who understood her situation might have mattered more.

Certainly, he couldn't understand why she'd got herself such a very unimpressive, low-paid sort of job. Hard to understand why she was working at all. But if she had to do it, then – in William's view – Honor's job needed to be something smart and sharp, something that would raise the eyebrows. And for him to have to say at dinner parties that his educated and successful daughter was divorced, living in Putney, and simply the assistant to some unknown literary agent at the back end of beyond . . . it all rather stuck in the throat. Even bloody Edward wasn't playing ball – making no attempt to change her mind, or stall the divorce proceedings.

But Honor was relieved by Edward's refusal to fight. From time to time she noticed his signature on papers from their lawyers, but that was all. The marriage was over. Honor was free. A year or so later, on the death of his mother, she would write to him, and not be surprised to hear nothing back. Or learn shortly afterwards that Allenham was up for sale – a double spread in *Country Life*, with pictures of the great hall and the drawing rooms and a couple of the estate cottages – followed by a bit of local gossip, via Lillian, saying she wasn't certain but she had heard he was moving back to Australia . . .

It had to happen sooner or later, and Evie was prepared. Luckily it was a busy day. Thursdays often were – especially Thursdays in March – and this one was no exception.

Since getting back to the office after that turbulent Christmas at Favenham, Evie's workload had rapidly increased. Her rise in status had brought with it a rise in responsibility, which suddenly felt very real. And while it came as no surprise to her – while she was glad to be taking on more – the days of smoking and chatting in the cars outside the agency were most definitely at an end. By March, Evie was stretched to her limit.

With Marcus away skiing and Helen heavily pregnant in Clapham, her hands were full just running the place. Keeping an eye on Linda's hours, making sure that James wasn't doing anything too stupid (James might have been the most good-natured man in the business, might have worked at Chelsea Estates for over a decade, but he was still horribly capable of letting the simplest things slip through his fingers, and had absolutely no sense of 'territory' when it came to properties they shared with other agents) while also trying not to look too bossy or rub Nick's nose in the fact that she was now the one in charge . . . Evie barely had time for her own files.

It was the day that contracts were supposed to be exchanged – finally – on Mrs Brook's place in Earls Court. But Mrs Brook, who'd been on at them for months, was suddenly nowhere to be found. The purchaser's team were ready to go. The contract deposit was there. Evie had had calls that morning from Mr Patel's agent, his solicitor, even his fund manager had rung to ask what was happening. But radio silence from her client. More ominously, radio silence from the solicitor. Evie had left three messages for Samuel Parker of Heriot Parker – it sounded a pretty ropey place; she was certain it was Heriot taking the messages – and still no sign of a response.

'I'm sorry, Ms Langton. He was in earlier, but—'

'Does he have a mobile?'

'A what?'

'Oh for God's sake.' Evie stopped spinning and twirling on Marcus's chair – she'd moved to his desk for a bit of space, and the Brook papers were scattered in front of her. 'A *mobile*,' she repeated, slowly and loudly. 'A mobile telephone. You know – one of those modern, new-fangled devices that actually make it possible to speak to people while walking about?'

And then, looking up, she saw that Nick had come back in from a viewing. He was standing over the drawers of spare particulars, ostensibly searching for something while taking amused glances in Evie's direction. And Matthew was right behind him.

'I know what a mobile is,' the dreary voice intoned into her ear. 'You were just speaking rather indistinctly, and—'

'I was speaking perfectly clearly. Everyone here in the office got it. And – and my point, Mr Heriot, is that you need to locate your colleague, like . . .' Evie looked at her watch, 'like *now*. And your client, for that matter – who I know has a mobile telephone but seems incapable of using it. Because if someone doesn't get back to me in the next fifteen minutes or so, then this contract of hers will fall through. You understand that?'

Not waiting to hear if Mr Heriot understood or not,

493

Evie put down the telephone and busied herself pulling the Brook papers together to take back to her own chaotic desk.

'Everything all right?' said Nick.

'Everything's fine.'

Bending her head to the papers, Evie closed her eyes for a second. She'd always known that Matthew would come into the office again at some point – always knew she'd have to face him – and it was really very simple: all she had to do was be friendly. Friendly and straightforward. It would hold him at a distance far more effectively than any sort of complicated silence. And so, forcing the Brook contract from her mind, Evie came forward to the front of the office – smiling.

'Hi Matthew. How's it going?'

Matthew kissed her cheek. 'It's going very well,' he replied – his face impossible to read. 'In fact I've just put in an offer on that place you mentioned was coming up – the one in South Ken with the roof terrace and the good second bedroom—'

'We thought three-twenty would do it,' said Nick, anticipating the question.

Evie raised her eyebrows.

'Tried to persuade him to make it three-thirty – to be certain of it, but . . .'

'No harm in trying, eh?' said Matthew.

'And he does want to make some improvements.'

Evie nodded. 'Well, let's hope they accept it then,' she said, still holding the smile – and was all set to close the conversation and return to her desk when, out of nowhere, Matthew asked after Honor. He'd heard the news from Abe, and wanted to know if she was okay.

Evie's smile thinned a little. 'Oh, fine,' she said. 'Fine

494

as can be expected, I suppose, what with everything that's happened.'

Matthew nodded. 'And her parents?'

Evie looked at him. Her expression said it all.

'Christ.'

'I know. They won't even have her in the house, Matthew – either house. So she's had to move in with my parents in Putney until she finds a place of her own . . . and let's face it, that's hardly ideal for her right now.'

'I don't know.' Matthew smiled. 'I can think of worse people to turn to in a crisis.'

And Evie, smiling again – properly this time – was aware that she was losing the distinction between the desire to appear friendly, and the genuine warmth she couldn't help feeling towards Matthew. It was nice of him to say that.

'I – I suppose I just feel bad that I can't take her myself,' she went on. 'Honor could do with a few distractions right now, have a bit of fun, hang out with people her own age for a change. But I can't throw Abe out, and—'

'I could take her.'

Evie stopped.

'I'm serious,' said Matthew. 'I'm going to need a flatmate for that second bedroom – it's really not that bad – and to be honest, I can't think of anyone more perfect—'

'Great.' She was suddenly very brisk, marching back towards her desk, pushing aside a couple of files to get to her computer. 'You do that, Matthew. You . . . here – why don't I give you her mobile number? And Mum and Dad's number – you want that too? Okay. And I think there's even an email address if I can just . . .' – tapping, tapping, 'yeah – here it is. You got a pen?'

And then the office telephone rang.

'It's Mr Patel,' hissed Linda, her hand over the receiver. 'You want to take it?'

Evie nodded. Scribbling Honor's details down for Matthew on a card, she handed it over without a second glance and picked up her receiver.

'Hello?'

Mr Patel was calling to cancel his previous message. Contracts had, apparently, been exchanged over an hour or so ago, which of course meant that there was no need for Evie to call him or his lawyers back. He apologised for getting stressed. It hadn't been the easiest transaction . . .

Evie could sense Matthew hesitating at her desk.

'Well I'm certainly with you there,' she said, laughing – and turned her chair a little further round, inclining her head to the wall. 'But it's hardly your fault, Mr Patel . . .'

There was a rustle of paper as Honor's details were shoved into the back pocket of Matthew's jeans, and he moved away – back towards Nick, to pick up the spare set of particulars that Nick had now found for him . . . and then Evie heard him say something about his car, and not wanting to get a parking ticket.

'No of course not,' she went on, loudly and cheerfully. 'And that's wonderful about the contracts, Mr Patel. Thank you for letting me know. Although I have to say it's typical that I should be hearing about it from *you* when . . . Exactly! Or at the very least her solicitor should have done!'

She was laughing as the office door closed.

*

496

But there wasn't much to laugh about as the afternoon wore on. It was just one of those days, she told herself – suddenly noticing it was four o'clock and Linda wasn't there any more, and nor was Linda's pink handbag. James, meanwhile, who'd only just remembered he had a viewing that afternoon, was frantically searching the key cupboard for a set that clearly wasn't there.

'Didn't that girl from Wrights come for them earlier, James?'

James frowned.

'In fact, I'm sure she did. I saw Linda handing them over.'

'Fuck,' said James, slamming the cupboard door in a rare moment of rage. 'Fuck, fuck, fuck.'

'You could always show them Coulson Street, couldn't you?'

James sighed. Coulson Street was a dead duck. Everyone knew that.

'And what about Paradise Walk? I know it's under offer, and I know you don't like doing it James, but sometimes – just sometimes . . .'

James gave her a grateful smile. 'Thanks, Evie.' Turning back to the cupboard, he grabbed both sets of keys and made for the door. 'You're a star.'

Evie sat in a silent office. No one would be coming back now. Linda was gone. James was gone. And Nick – with Matthew's offer already under his belt that day, and an afternoon of viewings with a pretty girl whose rich absent father was looking to buy her a flat in Chelsea . . . Nick would no doubt have other plans when it came to five o'clock. She felt oddly close to tears. An afternoon of petty struggles had left her little time to think about Matthew and what had happened

497

earlier. It was only now, with the office empty and the day all but over . . .

Turning to the particulars of the flat he was hoping to buy, Evie tried to imagine Honor there. It wasn't difficult. The second bedroom was almost as good as the master; and then there was that fabulous roof terrace, made for sunset drinks *à deux*; and an intellectual-looking sitting room with rows and rows of bookcases that Honor and Matthew would have no trouble filling. What more could either of them want?

And she was still looking at it, still torturing herself, when the door opened and a glossy-looking woman with blonde hair and rectangular glasses breezed into the office. She seemed a little familiar.

'Hello,' she said, taking off the glasses.

Evie pushed back her chair and hurried forward, attempting a smile. 'I'm sorry. Miles away . . . What can I do to help?'

The woman didn't immediately reply. Nor did she smile back. Instead she looked Evie up and down in a vaguely disparaging way and said, 'You're not Evie Langton, are you?'

Evie fought off the playground urge to cross her arms and demand who wanted to know. Instead she said, in tones of acid politeness, 'Are you wanting to buy or let?' But her blood was rising. She hadn't felt this way since her waitressing days. 'We don't have much in the way of lettings at the moment, but if you're—'

'Neither.'

'I see. Then—'

'This isn't about property. I'm just looking for Evie Langton.'

'Well you've found her.'

Then the woman smiled unpleasantly. 'I thought as much,' she said. 'Although, for the life of me, I can't think what he sees in you.'

And then Evie knew exactly who she was. 'Well he can't have seen that much in you either,' she muttered, playground urges prevailing, 'or he wouldn't have dumped you, right? In fact, perhaps you should take some of that advice you seem so happy to dole out on a regular basis and just accept it when a man's no longer interested. Isn't that what you said in last week's *Mail*? Or was it Sally Jarvis? I always get the pair of you muddled up.'

'I am Sally Jarvis.'

'Yes of course you are. I'm so sorry,' said Evie, starting to enjoy herself. 'So what's the problem, Sally?'

'I want you to back off.'

Evie stared back, at first with surprise and then amusement as she realised Sally's mistake.

'And don't play the innocent with me, Evie. I know how much time you and he have been spending together recently.'

'I am his estate agent. It's not entirely surprising.'

'An estate agent he takes out to dinner?'

'Matthew's my friend, Sally. We do that sort of thing from time to time. But there's nothing more to it. I swear.'

'Then why won't you let me have him back?'

'Who said I won't?' said Evie, laughing. 'Go ahead! Help yourself! You might find it rather more difficult to prise him away from my cousin than from me, but don't let that stop you. I'm sure it's worth a punt.'

Sally frowned. 'Your cousin?'

'That's right. My cousin Honor. Honor Montfort . . .'

'Xandra Villiers's daughter?'

499

'Exactly. And I think that even you will have to agree that she's significantly more beautiful than either of us. Certainly more classy and intelligent.'

'But . . .' Sally seemed genuinely thrown. 'Hang on a second. I'm sorry, Evie. You – you're telling me that Matthew – Matthew Forrester – is in love with Honor Montfort?'

Evie nodded.

'Not you?'

Evie smiled. 'Come on, Sally. Which one of us would *you* want?'

'Fair enough. But Honor's married, isn't she? And—'

'Not any more.'

A flash of interest sparked in Sally's eye. 'Really?' she said, leaning against the edge of Linda's desk and taking out a packet of cigarettes. 'Christ. I'd no idea.'

'Not for much longer, at any rate. It's just a matter of paperwork.'

'I'm sorry to hear that.'

Both were silent for a moment. Both thinking of Honor and her divorce. Then Sally lit her cigarette and, grinning suddenly, went on, 'But I have to say it's hard to dredge up much sympathy for the woman when she's got a bloke like Matthew Forrester in the wings, don't you think?'

Evie grinned back. There wasn't much to like in Sally Jarvis but to Evie, just then – so lonely, so close to tears – there was something irresistible about the listening manner – the cigarettes, the smiles – and the sense of kindred spirit that Sally's words invoked.

'So go on, then. What's the ex like?'

'Dire. Don't go there.'

Both of them laughed.

*

By lunchtime the following day, Matthew's offer on the flat in South Kensington had been formally accepted. And after a few quick calls to his solicitors, his bank, and a surveyor Nick had recommended, Matthew took that scrap of paper from the back pocket of his jeans and dialled Honor's number.

It was hard for Honor not to feel flattered, but while she agreed to meet Matthew for lunch on Saturday and view the place, and talk terms . . . in truth, she wasn't sure. She could see it was the kind of move she ought to be making at this stage – certainly it would help to get her back into the swing of things; she couldn't hide in Putney for ever – but there was something very safe and calm about living with Giles and Rachel, something she felt oddly reluctant to leave

But arrangements were now in place. And reaching the end of a good morning's work, dragging herself away from a manuscript her boss had asked her to look at over the weekend, Honor got up from the little desk in Evie's room – the one overlooking the garden, the one that had seen so many hours of half-hearted revision – and headed out to meet him.

She had plenty of time. Passing the newsagent that Evie used to frequent, the same one that had sold her cigarettes at a time when she was clearly under age; the one she'd lingered in all those years ago when searching for Matthew's non-existent article about Diana Miller . . . Honor saw the news-stands and decided to go in. After three hours of dense intellectual manuscript, she could do with something light and mindless for the journey.

And so it was – with the Tube train creaking and straining over a shimmering wind-whipped river – that Honor idly turned another page of her tabloid

501

newspaper and came face to face with a picture of herself. It wasn't a bad picture, but as Honor read the accompanying text the colour drained from her face. Sally Jarvis hadn't minced her words. She'd been careful to say nothing defamatory, but there was no mistaking the implication. Xandra Villiers's daughter was getting divorced. Having been married to boy-next-door Beaumaris for less than four years, the ex-debutante was now spurning the safety of aristos and money, and – dear, oh dear, what would her now-so-establishment mother say? – didn't seem to have wasted much time on the romantic front. Not when rumour had it that she was shortly to be shacking up with ambitious young journalist, Matthew Forrester. For how long, Sally wondered, had this particular 'friendship' been going on? What was the real reason behind Honor's divorce? Had poor Beaumaris been taken for a ride?

Clutching the newspaper tightly in her hand, Honor walked from the station to Matthew's new address. He was standing – smiling, waiting – in the street. And Honor, saying nothing, merely handed him the paper and told him to look at page twenty-three.

Smile vanishing, Matthew did as he was told. He sat on a low wall that separated the off-street parking from the pavement, opened the paper and turned to the relevant page, reading and rereading Sally's piece. Then he stood up with the paper in his hands and, walking down the spiral staircase to the basement dustbins, angrily tossed it in. 'Bloody woman.'

Honor frowned. 'You know her?'

'Used to go out with her,' said Matthew, coming back up the stairs, shaking his head as he climbed.

And then Honor remembered. Of course. It was the

woman he'd spoken of that evening back in Soho, when Abe had treated them to dinner and Evie had looked so beautiful.

'Until I met Evie again. And,' sighing now, 'and I'm afraid that this is Sally's singularly unpleasant – and not untypical – way of getting back at me. Although why she had to involve you too . . .' He looked at Honor, sitting grey-faced on the wall. 'I'm so sorry.'

'It doesn't matter.'

'Don't say that. Of course it matters. It—'

'Really, Matthew. With everything that Edward and I have been through recently . . . it's nothing.' A trace of amusement lightened Honor's expression – a moment-ary break in the clouds. 'Might wind my parents up a bit, but that's no bad thing . . .'

Matthew smiled.

And then the shade returned. 'Just so long as you . . . I'm sorry, but I really do need to know this, Matthew. I need you to be honest with me . . .'

Matthew's eyes were shut. He held his hands with the palms facing forward, as if pushing at some imaginary aggressor, bending his head, blocking Honor's words . . .

'*Please*, Honor. If I had any interest for you in that way . . . truly, any interest at all . . . the last thing I'd be doing is asking you to be my flatmate. Can't think of anything worse than playing at friendship with someone you're in love with. In fact, it's precisely because I know there's nothing there – on either side – that I feel comfortable with the—'

'Of course,' she said, embarrassed. 'I'm sorry.'

'Not that you shouldn't ask me these things. There was a time . . . you're absolutely right. But . . .'

Honor waited.

'. . . but not any more.'

Their eyes met – Matthew's openly anxious, Honor's inscrutable.

'So what changed?' she said.

'Me.' Matthew looked away. 'I've changed. Maybe it takes a few rotten relationships – like the one I had with Sally – to realise what's important, what I've lost . . . I don't know. But the one thing I do know is that I threw away something special back then. I was wrong, Honor. I made a mistake.'

'So why aren't you asking Evie out? Why aren't you trying to win her back?'

'But – but I am!' he spluttered. 'I have been! Ever since Ian was out of the picture, I've . . . Jesus, Honor. You're her friend! Hasn't she said anything to you about this?'

Honor looked at her fingers. 'I have been a little distracted recently.'

'Sure. I'm sorry. I only—'

'But I did know you were taking her out to dinner, Matthew – that time just before Christmas. I knew she was looking forward to it.'

'She was?'

Honor nodded, smiling at him now. 'Wanted me to help her decide what to wear, that sort of thing. I think she was quite excited.'

'Then what the fuck's gone wrong?' said Matthew. 'What's happened? Why won't she have dinner with me again? Why's "Nick" suddenly in charge of finding me somewhere to live? It doesn't make sense . . .'

Honor was inclined to agree. Walking around the flat with him, she barely noticed whether the windows actually opened in the smart second bedroom or whether there was enough storage, as she puzzled the

504

question through. What *had* gone wrong? She knew that Evie had always loved Matthew – loved him deeply, even when she'd hated him. No one else had come close. And when she thought of Sally's article screwed up at the bottom of the dustbin . . . well, whatever Evie might have thought before, that was hardly going to help. No chance for Matthew now. No chance for either of them. It would be Evie's worst nightmare, there, in front of her, confirmed in print. In fact, the more Honor thought about it, the more it seemed—

'That article,' she said suddenly, towards the end of their lunch. 'That journalist – she hasn't met Evie ever, has she?'

Matthew shook his head. 'Knows who Evie is, I suppose,' he said, pouring sugar into his coffee. 'I had to give some sort of reason for dumping her like that, and it seemed so much more straightforward – kinder even – just to give poor old Sal the truth; say it had nothing to do with her, that it was really all about Evie . . . I remember I said how impressed I'd been by what Evie's done with her career, which was something I knew Sally would understand, and then—'

'So she knows where Evie works?'

Frowning, Matthew sipped his coffee. 'I might have mentioned it. Can't really remember. It certainly wasn't something we—'

But Honor's face, in contrast, was suddenly very clear – almost elated. It was enough to stop Matthew in his tracks. 'And you *told* Evie, didn't you!' she said, triumphantly. 'You *told* her that you wanted me to take your second room!'

'Of course I did. It was only because Evie mentioned that you were living with her parents that I thought of you at all. She was the one who gave me your number. But – but hang on, Honor. What are you—'

'I'm sorry.' Honor was on her feet, catching her bag on the side of her chair as she made for the door of the restaurant. And Matthew was up and after her – coffee abandoned, chair scraping as he rose.

'Honor?'

'So sorry,' she muttered, hurriedly searching through the coats at the door. 'I know it's rude . . .' He picked out her coat and handed it to her. 'I can't explain it now. But you – you'll understand when I . . .' The coat was on. 'I will call you later. I promise.'

Chapter Twenty-Six

Closing the Door

Giles sat in his smart new kitchen, looking out through elegant French windows at the early signs of spring. There were nice tight buds all over his wisteria, and promising shoots in his borders. The grass was a little patchy, with earthy sections at the far end where the tenants' children had put up a goalpost, but that wouldn't take long to grow back. No . . . settling more comfortably into the armchair and taking another sip of coffee – no, he thought happily, it was all looking pretty good.

Ever since they'd returned, he'd been like this. Nearly three months, and he still couldn't quite get used to it: to how wonderful it was to be back in his own home and to be so ridiculously proud of it. With its new layout, new lighting and added storage space, the kitchen now felt huge. And all the fancy equipment they'd been forced to buy by the letting agent to seduce potential tenants: the smart new dishwasher, the extraordinary coffee machine, the huge refrigerator with that swanky ice maker on the outside – all things Giles had cursed at the time . . .

'Well, do what you like,' the bossy girl had said, 'but I must say I think you'd be mad to ignore my advice. You'll get a better deal in quicker time if you get some smart appliances in here. They really will make a difference. With any luck, you'll make the money back in under a month, and it' – appealing now, to Rachel – 'it just seems such a pity to skimp at this stage, Mrs Langton, when everything else is looking so great.'

And damn her, she'd been right. What's more, it all belonged to them now. Giles loved taking guests down to the kitchen to get them precisely what they wanted to drink – clunking the ice out noisily and asking if that was enough.

But most importantly, he loved to see Rachel running her household the way she'd always wanted – 'God, this thing is wonderful, Giles. It even dries the sheets properly – no more hanging them off the banisters! And it took only twenty minutes to deal with all those socks . . .

Can't believe how much space there is in here. It . . . look darling . . . it's incredible. That's our entire load of shopping from Tesco, and we've still got three whole racks to go . . .

Never thought I'd actually enjoy unloading a dishwasher . . .'

But it was only now that everything worked so well; only now that it looked so good – with the smell of damp a distant horror, and all those cook books and homeless mixing bowls and random vegetables that had littered every available surface finally put away – only now could Giles see how awful it had been before. He'd always told himself he liked it that way, that tidiness was somehow aggressive. But now that the work was done, he had to admit to liking a bit more order around the place. Everything was still as comfortable as it had ever been – Rachel would never have a home like Xandra's; there'd always be some sort of clutter – but it was certainly fresher.

So there it was: a happy wife, a fresh kitchen, a wonderful view of the garden . . . it was all very fine from where Giles was sitting. He just wished they'd done it years ago, while Evie had still been around.

Not that they minded her living out. Now that they were used to it, Giles and Rachel were proud of their daughter's independence, proud that she'd found a place and a life of her own. If it meant they saw less of her – for weekdays were rarely an option, and week-ends often impossible – then that was a sacrifice worth making. But they still missed her and were delighted when Evie suggested – out of the blue that Saturday morning – that she might join them for lunch. Sadly, Honor wouldn't be there too. She'd been around all morning, deeply embedded in some erudite-looking manuscript from work, but had just that minute gone out. Rachel guessed she'd gone to look at that spare room of Matthew's. Certainly she'd heard them talking earlier.

'But – but anyway, darling, I'm afraid it's only the two of us. And we're not doing much. Just reading the papers.'

'It sounds great, Mum. I could do with a quiet afternoon.'

So she joined them for soup and cheese, and a perfect cappuccino made by Giles. She sat and listened while they told her their news: how Giles had got a nice commission from a hotel in Gloucestershire wanting hand-painted wardrobes for each of its eighteen bedrooms; how Rachel might have found part-time work with a friend who ran a fabric business; how nice it was to have Honor staying with them . . .

'Poor love. Although it does seem as if that place you found for her with Matthew might be just the trick. Which of course is sad for us, but good for her, I expect. She can't want to live for ever with a couple of old fogeys!'

Evie smiled.

'I hope he cheers her up,' Rachel went on. 'She seemed quite perky when she left – certainly perkier than yesterday, when Giles went with her to the lawyers. It was just some routine business – a signature, wasn't it?'

Giles nodded.

'But so depressing for her, so hard to know how to pick up the pieces when her wretched parents won't lift a finger to support her. I – I swear I could throttle them. More interested in their own selfish squabbles. I've had them *both* on the telephone, whinging into the night about how miserable they are, how lonely, how I just don't understand what a struggle life is on one's own . . .'

'You think they might get back together, then?'

Rachel sighed. 'You know what, darling? I'm not sure I care any more. If they do want to try again – and I actually think they might, he was certainly making noises in that direction last night – then they're going to have to do it on their own. Right now, it's Honor who needs looking after.'

Evie left them shortly afterwards. It was getting just too hard for her to remain cheerful, and with everyone else's problems so great, her own seemed suddenly pathetic – not to mention mean-spirited.

Why shouldn't poor, neglected Honor have Rachel's sympathy and Giles driving her to and from the lawyers, holding her hand, showing support? Why shouldn't she have had Evie's old bedroom these past few months? Just think of all the times Evie had slept in Honor's room, worn Honor's clothes, lived Honor's life. And why shouldn't she now move in with Matthew? It wasn't as if Evie could go there, not when she had her own proper house, and she could hardly complain when it was her idea in the first place.

And – wiping back the tears now as she drove across the river, drove east through Fulham into a glossier, trendier Chelsea that had somehow lost its magic now that she was living there – and why shouldn't they have lunch together? Or more, for that matter. Evie had no claim on him. No claim at all.

It was a simple case of jealousy. And Evie just couldn't bear it that – somehow, through suffering and a failed marriage, through the kind of things that should have made her weaker – Honor had moved right into the heart of Evie's territory, and was now pushing her out with all the innocent cruelty of a cuckoo chick. Couldn't bear it that the people she loved best seemed to have turned their heads so quickly towards her beautiful, fragile cousin. Most of all, couldn't bear it that she herself minded quite so violently. Not only was she less lovely than Honor, less intelligent, less alluring, less in need of sympathy and attention . . . she was also infinitely less pleasant, with her dog-in-the-manger attitude, her feelings of envy and impotence.

Abe was right to think that Evie might still be hurt by her cousin – more right than he could possibly know.

511

Pulling into a parking space at the end of her street, Evie got out of the car. With her mind full of jealous lists, self-hatred and wretchedness, she hardly noticed her surroundings: the afternoon sun on the pretty Chelsea houses; the old man stopping for his dog; and the slim dark girl with the tired face, standing at the far end of the street – wearing a beautiful navy coat – looking in Evie's direction.

'I was just about to give up!' she said, smiling, as Evie approached. 'I know you weren't expecting me, but I was only round the corner having lunch with Matthew and thought I'd call in on the off chance. You don't mind, do you?'

'Of course not.' Her expression blank, Evie found her set of keys and opened the door for her cousin. 'Come on in.'

They went inside. Honor first, followed by Evie – looking at the little boots that Honor was wearing and trying not to envy those, too.

'So how was your lunch?' she said at last, unable to stop herself.

'Oh fine,' said Honor, maddeningly casual. 'It was fine.'

'And you liked the room?'

'Sort of.' Honor began taking off her coat. 'Not that we talked much about all that in the end . . .'

Evie's heart sank. Of course they wouldn't have done. Matthew wasn't the sort of man to hang about. This time she didn't bother to stand aside for Honor to go first – but marched in ahead, throwing her coat over the stair rail and heading for the kitchen. 'You want a cup of coffee?'

Saying she'd love one, Honor went out on to the little terrace beyond the kitchen and looked at Evie's daffodils. She could hear Evie in the kitchen – the rush of tap water into the kettle, the opening and closing of lightweight cupboards, the clattering and clinking of cups and spoons – and decided to wait for the fussing about to finish; wait until Evie was quiet and calm in one of the kitchen armchairs, comfortably holding her coffee cup, before continuing.

'No,' she said, when the moment finally arrived, hoping that Evie wouldn't suddenly leap up again in search of sugar or chocolate. 'We hardly touched on the flat at all . . . because – oddly enough – it was you that he seemed to want to talk about.'

'Oh God.'

Honor leant forward a little. 'You don't still fancy him, do you?'

'Why? You want to have a crack?'

Honor didn't respond. For a moment, Evie wondered if she'd quite understood – or even if she'd heard. For Honor had put her coffee cup to one side and was bending down deep into her bag and pulling out a newspaper – a tabloid – flicking through it, searching for something . . .

'Well according to some,' she said, passing it over, 'it seems I already have.'

Frowning, Evie took the paper – folded back to page twenty-three – and for a brief moment there was silence. Just Evie's eyes flickering over Sally Jarvis's article and Honor looking on.

Then Evie put the paper to one side. 'I didn't say it like that,' she said. 'I promise you, I didn't. Yes, I told her she'd got it wrong: that it was you he fancied, not me – which is no more than the truth. But I never said that you'd—'

'Is it?'

513

'Of course it bloody is,' said Evie. 'Matthew's always fancied you. He . . . no, don't shake your head like that, Honor. I know he was in love with you. And yes, all right, I shouldn't have told that bitch about it. I'm sorry. But when she came in on Thursday, all guns blazing, demanding that I back off . . . I mean, *me*? *Back off*? And okay, so maybe I shouldn't have told her about you moving in with him either, but come on, Honor. You might not be thinking along those lines just yet, but it's got to be what Matthew's hoping for. I was only—'

'It didn't occur to you that Sally might have had a point?'

'Why should it?' Evie cried. 'He was quite happy to dump me for you, back at that dreadful Favenham weekend . . . Why should anything have changed?'

Honor was silent.

'And it's why you were so down on him to begin with, wasn't it? When you said he was careless, and seemed so lukewarm about it all . . . and I just thought you were being snobby about his job! And yes, I suppose it's why you could never totally discredit him when he finally did the decent thing and ended it with me – before I got hurt, I imagine you thought. Hurrah for good old Matthew! At least he didn't string poor Evie along.'

'That was years ago.'

'You think it makes a difference?'

'Of course it does.'

Evie shook her head. There were tears in her eyes. 'He was mad about you, Honor,' she said, her voice uneven. 'And I'm sorry, but I just don't think people get over that sort of feeling. Abe certainly hasn't. In fact, it was Abe that made me realise just how . . . I

514

don't think you have any idea quite how beautiful you are . . .'

'So are you.'

'No, I mean *really* beautiful. Something special. To be honest, I hadn't totally noticed it myself until Abe pointed it out, and—'

'Abe?'

'He's worried that I'll always be outshone by you. He's worried that it isn't good for me to spend so much time with someone who – who's always going to win, I suppose. He thinks it's about time I knew the truth, and I have to say I agree with him.'

'But it's *not* the truth!'

'Well of course you would say that.' Evie smiled. 'Because you're not only beautiful, but kind, and modest, and—'

'Come here,' said Honor, standing up.

'But—'

'I'm not listening to this rubbish any more. I . . . come *here*.' She pulled Evie from the chair and, still holding her arm, led her upstairs into the bathroom. 'Come, and look, and tell me what you see.'

Evie stopped in the bathroom doorway, with Honor right behind her – both looking at their reflections in the wall-sized mirror beyond the bath. Honor pushed her further in, and stood in silence, waiting.

'Oh I don't know, Honor. I see me, I guess.'

'And . . . ?'

'And you, of course.'

'And . . . ?'

Evie's eyes flicked back and forth. She saw Honor – with no makeup on her face, no hairspray, no great effort . . . but still poised, still with that innate physical serenity that even her disastrous marriage to Edward

Beaumaris had failed to destroy. And then she saw herself – slimmer, sure, and smarter. She had a different haircut – still shaggy, but shorter, more together – and a better wardrobe. She'd learnt how to make the best of herself, but—

'Oh come on, Evie. You really think you look worse than me?'

Silence.

'Right.' Honor came closer into the room. 'I see I'm going to have to do this feature by feature. So – what shall we start with? Hair, perhaps?'

'That's just a question of getting it cut, Honor. You could perk yours up in a matter of seconds—'

'Then you admit yours looks better than mine. Now height. There's not much in it, is there?'

'Not when I'm wearing heels . . .'

'And you think a man like Matthew wouldn't find heels more attractive than clumpy old boots like this?'

Evie said nothing.

'Okay. Now boobs: no competition. You have them. I don't.'

A small smile appeared.

'And your waist obviously looks better than mine because you've got the boobs—'

'And the hips,' said Evie, ruefully.

'But you admit you have the waist.'

Evie was laughing now. 'You can't do it like this, Honor! Beauty isn't so—'

'Easily defined?'

'Exactly.'

Honor stood back. 'Then why are you so sure that I have it, and you don't?'

Once more, Evie was lost for words.

516

'Why are you so certain that Matthew couldn't possibly fancy you?'

'Because he dumped me, Honor. He wanted you.'

Honor leant against the wall, sighing heavily. 'Matthew Forrester wanted me seven years ago, when I was very different . . . and so were you, Evie. And so, I'm sure, was he. People change.'

'Not always they don't,' Evie replied with feeling. 'Especially where falling in love is concerned.'

'Well that might be the case for you, Eves, but it certainly hasn't been for me. And – and anyway, do you think that Matthew would have spent the last two hours telling me how serious he is about you, how worried he is that he might have blown it, if *I* was the one he wanted?'

'He really did that?'

'Of course he did.'

'What, two whole hours?'

Honor smiled. 'Call him yourself if you don't believe me . . .'

Ten minutes later, she left the house. Matthew was coming over. He was coming now. And Evie, putting the telephone down with an expression that suggested she was still finding it hard to believe what was happening, was clearly incapable of sensible thought.

'You – you're not *leaving*?' she said, grabbing at the coat Honor was trying to put on.

Honor tugged it free. 'I certainly am.'

'But—'

'You think Matthew would want to find me here when he arrives?'

Evie hesitated. And Honor, smiling now, slipped the navy coat back on and reached for her bag. 'Good

517

luck,' she said, kissing Evie on the cheek. And then –
without looking up again – squeezed her cousin's arm
and left, closing the door behind her.

It was still bright in the open street. A little cooler,
maybe – the sun had slipped in the afternoon sky, and
another evening waited in the shadows – but Honor
was oblivious as she walked towards the Underground. Her thoughts were too full of what had just
happened – and would shortly be taking place –
behind her, in Evie's little house. Her eyes were down
and she was smiling. And it wasn't until she had to
cross the road – not until she needed to look up and
down to the end of the street to be sure that the way
was clear – that she saw Abe, striding towards her,
looking at the front page of a magazine. Even then, she
wasn't sure it was him. His figure had, for a brief
moment, indicated a different sort of man altogether
from the actor she'd once known. He was broader and
muscular, with shorter hair and a bunched-up sort of
energy that was only amplified by the sports kit he was
wearing and the fact that he'd clearly just been for a
run.

Pulled by her attention, Abe looked up from the
magazine.

'Honor!'

'Hello Abe.'

Smiling, Abe shifted the magazine under his arm so
that he could open a small paper bag that had been in
his other hand. Inside were five jam doughnuts. 'Don't
suppose I can persuade you to turn back again, can I?
Far too many for just me and Evie.'

Honor shook her head.

'You don't like doughnuts?'

She smiled back. 'No, no! I love doughnuts! I just

518

don't think I'd be very welcome back there, right now. And nor, I'm afraid, would you . . .'

Explaining to him why Evie needed the place to herself – why Matthew was coming over, and how they had little time to spare – Honor hurried Abe back the way he'd come. They stood in the shade at the end of the street while she continued to explain what had happened, telling Abe he'd got it all wrong, that Matthew really was serious about Evie this time, and that she – Honor – meant nothing to him.

'You're sure about that?' said Abe.

'Absolutely. He told me himself that it was Evie he wanted! You should have heard the way—'

'And you believed him?'

'Of course I did! Why shouldn't I?'

Abe looked at her, saying nothing. Honor looked back. And then – understanding suddenly what it was that he was saying in the silence, that it had nothing at all to do with Matthew, or Evie . . . she turned her head away.

'Honor, I—'

'Don't, Abe. Please.' She was examining her fingernails. 'Evie told me what you said to her. And of course I'm flattered—'

'I was only telling the truth.'

Honor turned even further away from him.

'Well it's the truth from where I'm standing,' he insisted.

Still she wouldn't meet his eye.

'Honor?'

'Oh, look!' she said suddenly. And Abe, looking, caught sight of a dark distant figure who had suddenly appeared at the other end of the street – a man's figure, hurrying round the corner and along the pavement in late low light . . . out of breath, stopping at Evie's door and rapping on it, ringing at the bell . . . 'Look, Abe! Isn't it great?'

Abe didn't reply. He knew what was really being said to him in those innocent exclamations. And as they stood together at the far end of the street – with Evie's door opening for a moment, and Matthew disappearing inside – Abe couldn't help but feel the contrast from the woman at his side. He understood now that no amount of rapping and ringing would open that particular door . . . and perhaps it was better that way. Some things – some wonderful things – were at their most beautiful when seen from a distance.

After Honor left – heading back to Putney, back to her manuscripts and a life she could call her own – Abe stood for a while in the street. He leant against a railing, and was just taking a doughnut from the paper bag when a girl he'd never seen before emerged from the house behind him. She stopped for a moment to lock the door behind her; and as she turned – putting the keys away and walking towards him – their eyes met.

They met with the peculiar intimacy of strangers, as if she and Abe could see right through each other . . . as if friendship and love and words spoken were really a sort of distancing; as if the closest two human beings could ever be to each other was what had just happened.

And then the girl moved on, adjusting the belt on her coat.